COLD
JUSTICE

Also by Katherine Howell

Frantic

The Darkest Hour

COLD JUSTICE

KATHERINE HOWELL

PAN BOOKS

First published 2010 by Macmillan, an imprint of
Pan Macmillan Australia Pty Limited, Sydney

First published in Great Britain 2011 by Pan Books
an imprint of Pan Macmillan, a division of Macmillan Publishers Limited
Pan Macmillan, 20 New Wharf Road, London N1 9RR
Basingstoke and Oxford
Associated companies throughout the world
www.panmacmillan.com

ISBN 978-0-330-52133-8

A CIP catalogue record for this book is available from
the British Library.

Printed in the UK by CPI Mackays, Chatham ME5 8TD

For Benette

ACKNOWLEDGEMENTS

This book came at a difficult time in my life, and for help, care and support beyond the call of duty I owe thanks to my agent Selwa Anthony; publisher Cate Paterson; editors Kylie Mason and Mary Verney; publicist Jane Novak; my friends from the job, Mel and Brian Johnson, Garry 'Syd' Francis, Steve and Jenni Flanagan, Justine Wilson, Col Benstead, Alan Smith, John Wood and Warren Leo; Simonne Michelle-Wells; Cynthia Currin, Libby Thompson and Kellie Gordon; Leah Giarratano; Karen Davis; the SF-sassy and Mphil groups, especially Michelle Dicinoski and Edwina Shaw; and my family – Guys, Crowes, Willises and Tenorios – with an extra thank you to my brother Phil for the title.

For technical advice, thanks to Adam Asplin, Esther McKay, Liz Dabbs, and Penny Sharpe, MLC.

Thanks to Sisters in Crime, and to Faye McCrow, winner of the Davitt award-night lucky door prize.

Special thanks to Benette, who read the manuscript along the way, held my hand through the toughest time when I feared I wouldn't make it, and never lost faith, even for a second. It's all for you.

ONE

'There's not much to it,' Station Officer Ken Butterworth said. 'Plant room, muster room, lounge through there, little kitchen off the side. Locker room and bathrooms along this way, and here's your locker key.'

Paramedic Georgie Riley folded her sweaty palm around it. 'Thanks.'

'So. Welcome to The Rocks.' Butterworth glanced at his watch. 'I don't know where she is.'

'You don't have to stay,' Georgie said.

'If a case comes in I'll go out with you.'

'I'll find my way around.'

'But what sort of a start to a first day is that?'

She smiled. 'How was your night?'

'Eighteen jobs, including a SIDS, a cardiac arrest on a bus, and a nightclub brawl with five stabbed.' He covered a yawn.

'Go home,' she said. 'Really, I'll be fine.'

'It's no problem.' He checked his watch again. 'I'm sure she won't be long.'

And in the meantime there's no way you're going to leave me alone. Georgie looked at the board where the keys hung. 'Which one will we be in?'

'Thirty-three,' Butterworth said.

She took the keys down. 'May as well begin checking.'

'Sure, sure,' he said. 'That's good.'

The traffic coming off the Harbour Bridge overhead filled the plant room with a continuous hum. Georgie unlocked the ambulance and shoved her bag between the front seats, then opened the side door into the back and climbed up. Through the tinted window she saw Butterworth frowning in the muster room doorway. Matt would tell her he was frowning because her partner was late, and that she was paranoid to be thinking what she was thinking, and would then remind her about the discussion they'd had about being reasonable – but Matt hadn't been bullied and shafted and betrayed.

She flopped into the seat beside the stretcher and yanked open one of the drug drawers. Cannulas lay rubber-banded together in size groupings, and syringes in their sealed plastic packets were jammed into two narrow compartments. She tidied the stack of alcohol swabs, straightened the boxes of adrenaline and dextrose and atropine, and checked the expiry dates of the six ampoules of local anaesthetic lined up against the side.

She was neither surprised nor startled when Butterworth popped his head through the door.

'Is it the same layout as you had?' he asked.

The ambulance service was one big network of who you'd trained with, who you'd worked with, who you knew. Butterworth looked a similar age to her Woolford boss, Ross Oakes.

'You've never been out there?' Georgie replied.

'I have.' He scratched at a boot scuff low down on the wall. 'But I've never looked closely in the drug drawers. Pass me an alky-wipe?'

She handed over a swab and watched him scrub at the black mark. She should ask him if he knew Ross. It was an innocent question, and, as they were talking about the region, it would be a natural one as well. She cleared her throat, but just then there was a flash of movement beyond the windscreen and the driver's door was yanked open.

'Sorry, Ken,' a woman said. 'Bloody trains.' A workbag sailed in and landed on Georgie's.

Georgie took a deep breath. *If she's a mate of Ross's, I'll never pass this assessment.*

Ken said, 'Freya, this is your new partner, Georgina Riley. Georgina, this is Freya Craig.'

The woman looked into the back and Georgie's heart skipped a beat. The hair was longer and darker, the face had filled out a little, but it was definitely her. In the same instant she saw surprise and dismay cross the woman's face.

Dismay?

'Hi,' Georgie said.

'George!' Freya squeezed between the front seats into the back of the ambulance and grabbed Georgie in a hug. 'How the hell have you been?'

Georgie resisted the urge to push her away. 'Good.' *Dismay?*

Freya pointed back and forth between them and said to Butterworth, 'Schoolfriends.' She crossed her first and second fingers. 'Like this.'

For a while, Georgie thought. *Until you disappeared without even saying goodbye and had me thinking you'd been murdered too.*

'Enjoy your reunion.' Butterworth stepped down from the truck.

Freya said, 'I didn't know you were in the job. How long?'

'Nine years.'

'Eleven for me.' She came in for a hug again but Georgie leaned back. She wanted to see her eyes. She wanted to be looking straight at her when she asked the question that had festered in her mind for nineteen years.

'Freya —'

Freya cut in. 'Talk about coincidences, hey?' She grinned, a wild look. 'All that time and here we are.'

The station phone rang and Butterworth answered.

'That'll be us.' Freya scrambled into the driver's seat.

After this job, Georgie thought. Another hour wouldn't kill

3

her. She closed the back and went to get the details from their boss.

'Person fallen into the harbour,' he said.

Georgie's skin prickled.

'Sure you'll be okay with it?'

He knows.

She took the scrap of paper from his hand. 'Of course.'

'The past haunts the present,' said Detective Sergeant Paul Galea.

Like I need reminding of that. Just sitting there in Galea's office, Detective Ella Marconi could feel the effects of her own recent past. She'd passed all the physical and psych tests and was fine, though she'd lost muscle mass and her shirt sat differently across her back. But once shot, she'd realised, you were never the same again, especially when you'd thought you were going to die. Things got clearer. You saw for certain what was important.

'Time passes,' Galea went on, arms resting on a closed file on his desk, a newspaper folded at his elbow, 'but the unsolved homicide never goes away. Unsolved, mind you, not cold. How can it be cold when the victim's family still lives it every day?'

Ella nodded.

'The good thing is that people with knowledge still live it too, and these people sometimes get religion, get divorced, get off drugs. They lose someone close and get an inkling of how it might feel. Their knowledge becomes a burden. Sometimes they tip us off; sometimes you knock on their door and they spill their guts.'

'I understand.'

'At the same time, however, the bad guys too have grown older. Their lives are settled; they have jobs, families – more to lose.' Galea's gaze became intense. 'Investigations into old cases open up old wounds, and sometimes people are driven to commit new crimes to protect what they now have.'

Just give me the file.

'In 1990, seventeen-year-old Tim Pieters was found dead in Pennant Hills.' Galea finally handed the file over. 'Pieters's cousin is in state parliament now, and had a bit of a chin-wag with the minister last week. There's this too.' He slid over the newspaper and Ella saw the article next to Pieters's photo above the fold – the cousin was opening a sports hall at Tim Pieters's old school that afternoon. 'Wander along there and see what strikes you. Just take it easy getting back onto the horse.'

Ella looked down at the photos in the file. Pieters, smiling in a high school photo. Then dead on the ground, leaves on his face.

I'll get back onto the horse all right.

Ella made a coffee and sat at a vacant desk in the empty Unsolved office. Everyone else was out on their own cases. The air was cool and still. Computers hummed, and Galea talked with someone down the corridor. She'd heard about his welcome speech: *The past haunts the present.* It was a wonder he didn't have it framed on the wall. Of course the past haunted the bloody present. Police work revolved around that fact. So did life itself.

She opened the file to Tim Pieters's school photo again. He'd had short brown hair, tanned skin and a wide smile. His grey school shirt was buttoned to the neck under a darker grey tie with gold diagonal stripes and the emblem of Macquarie Secondary College. They had a moment, looking into each other's eyes. *I've been to the brink,* she told him. *You went over and I can't help that, but I can find who is to blame. I know what's important, and it's you.*

She put her cup aside and got out an A4 pad. The first pages of the file were a bald summary of the facts. Early in the morning on Sunday, 21 October 1990, a girl walking her dog in the bush near Pennant Hills Park had stumbled across Tim Pieters's body. She'd run to the nearest house, five hundred metres away, and the occupant had called the ambulance. They'd arrived and requested police. General Duties attended first, then asked for detectives and Crime Scene.

A search of his clothing and the area produced no wallet or other identification, and he went into the system as 'unknown male'.

Just after eight o'clock Tamara Pieters looked into her son's room and found it empty. She and her husband John called Tim's friends, who admitted being out with him the night before but didn't know where he was now. The Pieters worried for an hour before calling the police. Officers went to their house and asked to see a photo, then broke the news. Formal identification was done at Westmead Morgue by both parents.

Tim was the middle of three children. His older sister, Haydee, had been in her second year at university and still living at home. His younger brother, Josh, was eleven. John Pieters worked as an architect with a city firm and Tamara Pieters did bookkeeping from an office at home. They described Tim as a good student, a social boy with a large circle of friends, keen to get his P plates and first car. They denied problems with alcohol or drugs. Tim had talked about going to uni when he finished school, though wavered between science and IT as course choices.

Ella turned to the scene photographs. The initial shots showed Tim Pieters lying face down in the undergrowth, dressed in blue jeans, grey sneakers and a white short-sleeved shirt. Various angles illustrated how far he was from the road and how well hidden the body was by the long grass and shrubbery. The girl who'd found him had stated that her dog had been off his leash and had run off into the bushes, and it was when she was trying to catch him that she'd found Pieters. Ella wondered what effect that moment had had on the girl's life.

A series of pictures showed Pieters being rolled onto his back, dead leaves stuck to his face. Ella wondered about the time his body had been dumped there, if it was after the dew had fallen, but reading on she found that the original detectives had noted the morning was dry but that there had been rain in the previous twenty-four hours and the undergrowth was still damp.

The autopsy reported the stomach contents were little more than the dark liquid of gastric juices mixed with alcohol, and stated that the dinner of meat and salad he was known to have eaten at the family barbecue at about six thirty that evening was probably vomited up due to his drinking. He'd been last seen by his friends in the pub at about eleven thirty, and the pathologist estimated time of death between midnight and 2 am.

Blood had pooled in parts of the front of the body not pressed against the ground. As livor mortis could begin within twenty minutes of death and was fixed in a couple of hours, it was believed that Tim had been killed somewhere else then dumped there. Tyre tracks were difficult to ascertain in the loose gravel, but photographs showed marks in the dusty edge between the gravel and the asphalt. One tyre was identified as a Bridgestone, another a Goodyear, both sold in the hundreds of thousands across the country. With neither tyre having distinctive damaged areas or wear patterns, they weren't much help as leads.

There were no injuries to Tim's body except petechial haemorrhages in his eyes; due to this and congestion in his lungs, the cause of death was determined to be suffocation. To kill a healthy young man in that manner with no signs of a struggle suggested incapacitation of some form, and she checked the toxicology screen. His blood alcohol reading was 0.09 per cent; a lot for anyone, but particularly an underage boy. The report estimated that such a level would have caused him to have moderate cognitive and motor-skill impairment, making him a vulnerable target, particularly if he'd passed out in the street. His friends had admitted using false IDs to buy beer and spirits at the Highway Hotel in Hornsby that night, as well as at other hotels on different dates.

It was also possible that Tim had known his killer and so had not put up a fight when taken. Ella read that his father, John, had been a suspect for a time, as he'd admitted going out alone to look for Tim late that Saturday night. He'd stated that he was unable to find him or any of his friends and had come home after an hour and a half of driving aimlessly about the area, so aimlessly that he found it hard to recall his exact route. The original detectives had noted that they'd been unable to determine where he'd gone or find any witnesses at all. Even his wife, Tamara, couldn't say for sure what time he'd come home. She'd gone to bed at eleven, before her husband went out, then had woken at three to find him snoring beside her.

Tim's uncle, Alistair McLennan, had also been out that night, caring for a dying cancer patient in Berowra. He'd said in his statement that he hadn't seen either Tim or John after the family barbecue earlier that evening; and the patient's husband had stated that Dr McLennan had arrived at their place at 11.20 pm and left at one, after his wife's peaceful death just after midnight. McLennan's wife Genevieve stated she'd woken up when he climbed into bed at one thirty.

Ella made notes. Reinterviewing all the family was a given, as was talking to Tim's friends. The boys might have been protecting each other then, but as men now in their thirties, possibly with sons of their own, they might have regrets and feel freer to talk.

Drops of blood had been found at the scene, dotted across leaf litter closer to the road. The leaves had been collected and the blood tested. It was not Tim's – he had no wounds, and a group test had shown the drops to be from somebody who was O positive, while Tim was AB negative. No skin was found under Tim's nails to indicate that he had scratched his attacker. Ella studied the photograph showing the drops' location and tried to imagine somebody suffering an injury while dumping him there. Getting scratched by a twig in the undergrowth wasn't going to cause that sort of flow. Maybe the killer had suffered the injury beforehand, perhaps in grabbing Tim off the street, or on something in the car.

DNA testing was a rare beast in 1990, and unheard of when there was no firm suspect to compare to a sample. There was, however, a note in the file saying that the sample had recently been taken for further analysis. Ella knew that there were officers going back over such cases looking for exactly this – physical evidence that hadn't been tested or samples that had been too small to use with the old procedures – because now, with the growing DNA database, they could enter a profile and sometimes get a match. She put the file aside and phoned the lab.

'Not done yet,' a male voice told her. 'System's so clogged.'

She sympathised, she really did, but she needed her result. 'When, then?'

'Call again in a week,' he said.

As soon as she put the phone down it rang.

'How's it going?' Detective Wayne Rhodes said, and her heart skipped at the sound of his voice.

'Great.' She told him about the case, then turned to the detectives' names on the front page of the summary. 'Do you know Will Tynan and Peter Constantine?'

'Constantine was a DS when I started at Penrith,' he said. 'He was a good guy. He might be retired now. I can't place Tynan though.'

'Thanks.' Ella scribbled a note about tracking Constantine down.

'Galea do his speech?'

'Yep. Seems a nice guy.'

'So . . . how are you feeling?'

'Fine,' she said. 'Perfect. No need to worry.'

He laughed.

'I know you,' she said.

'I know you do,' he said. 'You want to meet for lunch?'

'I'm going out.' She told him about the newspaper article. 'It'll be interesting to see who might be there.'

'I guess you'd be annoyed if I said be careful.'

'It's at a school in broad daylight.'

'I won't say it then,' he said. 'Have a good one, and I'll see you tonight.'

'Absolutely.'

She put the phone down with a smile, then focused on the pages before her.

Georgie was too nervous to reply as Freya bitched nonstop about the nightmare of driving to urgent jobs in the city while swerving the ambulance through the traffic to the Quay. She tried not to notice how the harbour glinted between the ferry terminals, or how she could smell the water in the air, and when Freya turned off the siren and stomped on the brake she made a big effort to keep her voice calm as she told Control they were on scene.

She and Freya piled the Oxy-Viva, cardiac monitor and drug box on the stretcher and followed an excited security guard onto the wharf. She kept her head down, trying to focus on the concrete under her boots, glancing only far enough ahead to see the huddle of people around a figure prone in a pool of water.

This is the city, she told herself, *and that was the country. This is a harbour, placid green water, while that was an angry brown river in flood. This woman* – she could see already it was a woman: long hair plastered across a narrow face, a beaded necklace brushing the concrete – *is out of the water. She is fine. You are fine.*

They reached the huddle and Georgie lifted the Viva from the stretcher. The watching crowd edged closer. She crouched in the pool of water beside the woman, who shivered in soaked black jeans and a white T-shirt. She lay on her stomach, propped on her elbows with her face in her hands.

Georgie put a hand on her shoulder. 'Are you okay?'

The woman flinched at her touch. 'I almost died.'

'Do you know what happened?' Georgie asked.

'She jumped off the wharf,' somebody said.

'I did not,' the woman snapped. 'Somebody pushed me.'

'Are you hurt?' Georgie asked. 'Can you tell me your name?'

The woman tried to sit up, grasping Georgie's arm for support. Her palm was clammy and cold. Her nails dug into Georgie's skin as she stared past her at the crowd.

'He pushed me.'

Georgie followed her finger to a shocked-looking man in his sixties, big fingers wrapped around the handles of a stroller from which a three year old in a Batman costume watched the goings-on with interest.

'Nobody pushed her,' a man said behind Georgie. 'I was standing right there, we were all waiting for the ferry to come in, and she just climbed the rail and jumped in.'

'I did not.'

'She sank like a fucking stone. Scuse the language. That guy there went in after her. Saved her life.'

Georgie saw a young man in a sodden suit and leaking shoes. His eyes were wide and he clutched the handle of a dry black briefcase with both hands. Freya went to make sure he was okay.

'That old guy pushed me!' the woman said again.

Here's another point of difference, Georgie thought: *this one's a psycho*. She took the blanket from the stretcher and wrapped it around the woman. 'Let's go up to the hospital and get you checked out, okay?'

'I want the police.'

'We'll have them see you at the hospital.'

'I want that man arrested. For murder.'

'Nobody died,' Georgie said.

'I could have.'

'Let me help you to your feet then onto the bed here.'

The woman glared at her. 'You don't believe me.'

'Look at you, you're shivering.' The young man had left, and Freya was back. Georgie nodded at her to bring the stretcher closer. 'Let's get you in the ambulance where it's nice and warm. What did you say your name was?'

'Don't you touch me.' The woman scrambled to her feet and pulled the blanket tight around herself, eyeing the watching crowd. 'You're all in on it together. You saw him push me in and none of you helped.' Somebody laughed and the woman bristled. 'I'll sue the lot of you and then we'll see who's laughing.'

Georgie said to Freya in a low voice, 'Blue ambulance.'

Freya pulled the portable radio from her hip and stepped away to call the cops. It was odd that they weren't already here, but at least there were more security staff making their way through the onlookers. Georgie saw the woman narrow her eyes at their approach and made her voice warm. 'Come on, let's get out of here, eh? Hop up on the stretcher and let's go to the hospital. We'll get you out of those wet clothes, find you a cup of coffee and something to eat.' The woman's index and second fingers were stained yellow. 'We'll scab a smoke from somebody too.'

'I'm not going anywhere.'

Freya came back and nodded at Georgie.

'What's that nod for?' the woman said. 'You telling secrets about me?'

'You want to know?' Georgie lowered her voice. 'The police are coming. If you don't want to deal with them, it's time to climb up on the stretcher and come to hospital.'

The woman spat at her boot. 'Pair of bitches.'

Georgie raised an eyebrow at Freya, caught her held-back grin and matched it with one of her own.

The woman stamped her bare foot in the puddle of water. 'Let them come. They can haul my dead, cold body out of the sea.'

'Let's not get stupid here,' Freya said. 'Nobody's dead and nobody's going to die.'

Georgie saw two security men sneaking along the side of the crowd. She took a step towards the woman to draw her attention. 'What's the point of all this bother? We go up to the hospital, we can get everything sorted out from there and let all these people get on with their day.'

The woman spotted the security guards. 'Don't you dare.'

'Come on now. What do you say?' Georgie put on her best wheedling tone while edging closer. 'Couldn't you go a cuppa? Life's too short to stand around here all wet and cold.'

She was almost within grabbing distance. Freya sidled nearer on the other side. The woman backed to the edge of the wharf and put her hands on the railing. Georgie heard the crowd draw its breath.

The woman raised a bare, skinny foot. 'Come closer and you'll get one.'

'Okay, fine.' Georgie held up her hands. 'Whatever you want.' They'd wait until the cops turned up and then she'd be their problem.

The crowd let out its breath. Freya put her hands on her hips and the guards looked mildly disappointed. Georgie listened for a siren over the ferry departure announcements and realised she'd forgotten all about her watery fears.

But then the woman stopped glaring at her, clambered over the railing and jumped in.

Georgie rushed to see the white blanket billow out in the green water as the woman sank, her head a dark blob in the centre. Freya stood still with her mouth open. The security guards began to strip off their radios and boots. Georgie swore under her breath and swung herself over the railing.

The water was cold. She struggled to keep her eyes open against the sting of the salt. The white of the blanket was a blur below her and she fought to swim deeper as her boots softened her kicks. A stream of bubbles rose up against her cheeks and she made out the vague shape of the woman's face turned up towards her.

She saw encrusted pylons from the corner of her eye and heard the deep throb of a huge engine somewhere close.

A current pulled her sideways.

She was running out of air. She wasn't going to make it.

Again.

But then the woman rose up, her face contorted, her hands reaching for Georgie. The blanket tangled round them. Her hand shot through it and scratched Georgie's face. Georgie tried to catch her wrist and haul the woman upwards. There was more movement beside her, a big dark shape, and she saw the glint of keys on a belt. The security guard grabbed the woman's upper arms from behind and yanked her away from Georgie. She saw his face for a split second, his cheeks bulging with air, his eyes asking a question that she answered by swimming upwards. He was faster, shooting past. She saw his feet in grey socks kicking hard.

The surface was silver from underneath then all golden light when she burst through. The railings were open and hands grabbed for her, pulled on her collar and tore it, seized and slipped off her wet forearms. She gasped and fumbled for a grip along the slimy underedge of the wharf. Beside her, the guard was shoving at the screaming, swearing woman, trying to heave her out of the water while she hit at the hands pulling her up.

Georgie's eyes burned and streamed from the salt water. Her mouth was full of the thin taste of diesel fuel. She took one hand off the wharf to rub her eyes and nose but her fingers were slick and green with algae.

'Holy shit,' Freya said.

Georgie squinted up at Freya's pale face. 'I'm okay.'

Freya reached down but Georgie didn't have the strength to pull herself up. 'Just give me a minute.'

'Grab hold anyway.'

Georgie grasped Freya's hand but kept hold of the wharf as well. The water below her felt bottomless. She looked down to see the blanket drifting in the current, an underwater ghost.

A strong hand grabbed her wrist. A police officer and one of the dry security guards hauled her upwards. She scrabbled at the wharf edge and kicked, losing a sodden boot, and was heaved onto the warm concrete of the wharf.

'You okay?' the cop said.

She nodded. 'There's a blanket down there still.'

'We'll get a diver before it buggers up somebody's propeller.'

Along the wharf, three more police and the other dry security guards dragged the howling woman from the water. They dumped her on her front and cuffed her wrists behind her. She turned her head from side to side, her hair across her eyes, swearing and spitting. The cops then heaved the guard, still treading water, out of the harbour. People in the crowd took photos with

their mobiles while a voice announced the impending departure of the Manly ferry on the next wharf over.

Freya took the sheet from the stretcher and wrapped it
around Georgie. 'Your face is scratched.'

Georgie touched the stinging spots on her chin and cheek
then looked at her fingers. 'Nothing major.'

'Still.' Freya pulled the portable from her belt. 'I'll get Control to send another crew for her then we can run up to the ED
ourselves.'

'I'm fine.'

'You're soaked and you've only got one boot. You're shivering as well. Come to the truck and I'll find you another blanket.'

Georgie said, 'Technically she's a near-drowning. I should
stay and look after her.'

'Technically she's a pain in the arse,' Freya said. 'Listen. I'll
stay and look after her till the others get here. You go to the
truck, get yourself all wrapped up in the back, have a little rest.
I'll be there as soon as I can.'

'Okay.'

Freya squeezed her arm. Her dark blue eyes were concerned.
'You're not short of breath yourself, are you? Didn't take any
water on board?'

'No.'

'I'm not going to get back to the truck in ten minutes and
find you overflowing with pulmonary oedema and making a
mess of my nice clean floor?'

'I'll call on the radio at the first sign of foam.'

Freya smiled. 'Good.'

Georgie pulled the sheet tighter around herself and started
off, head down, through the crowd. Somebody started to clap
and others joined in. A couple of people patted her on the back
and she heard someone say, 'Well done,' and then, 'Bloody psycho wasn't worth it'.

She reached the ambulance and climbed into the back. It
was empty and echoing without the stretcher. She took a blanket from the linen locker and sank soggily onto the vinyl seat.

See, it went fine. She's alive! There is no jinx, no taint.

The sun came in the window and she felt warmed, calmed a little.

It's like Matt said: we've left the past behind and it can't hurt us if we don't let it.

She looked out at the people pointing onto the wharf and talking, at the people walking past on the concourse. A little girl sat on her father's shoulders, his broad hands firm around her ankles, her hands flat on the top of his Wallabies bucket hat, a bigger version of her own. Georgie watched their passage, saw the man point at a ferry chugging slowly in and smiled as the little girl waved at it, then her gaze latched onto a man leaning on the railing behind them, staring straight at the ambulance, at the tinted window behind which Georgie sat.

Georgie shot out of her seat. She stumbled over the stretcher rails on the floor, her wet sock slipping on the lino, and kicked open the side door. She leapt down into a sea of red uniforms – a crowd of schoolchildren being herded past by their teachers. She tripped and almost fell onto one small boy, scrambled to her feet and out of the way, and backed up against the ambulance where she could look across the river of red hats.

The man was gone.

She stared right and left, but couldn't see him. She shakily picked up her blanket, retreated into the ambulance and locked the doors.

The past was not behind them at all. The past had followed her, right into the city.

TWO

Ella read that Tim had gone out that night with four friends: Gareth Wing and Damien Millerton who he'd known since kindergarten, and Steven Franklin and Christopher Patrick who he'd become friends with in Year Seven. Gareth Wing said in his statement that Tim had been quiet and had drunk more heavily than usual that night. Detective Will Tynan had asked why that was, but Wing hadn't known or even been able to guess. Damien Millerton, who'd said he was probably closest to Tim, had told Detective Peter Constantine that he thought something had been on Tim's mind for a while, a few months at least. He said that about three months before he died, when the two were walking home after a party, Tim had asked if he'd ever thought he was gay.

Ella's phone rang. She dragged herself back to the present. 'Unsolved, Marconi.'

'Hello, darling,' her mother said. 'How are you doing in there?'

'Fine,' Ella said. 'Busy.'

'You and your busy.'

In the background Ella heard her father say, 'How is she?'

'She's good,' Netta said to him.

17

'Is she coming for dinner?'

'I haven't asked her yet,' Netta said.

Ella said, 'I can't come tonight.'

'When then?'

'I'll let you know.'

'Because we want to hear about your first day back.'

'It's going really well.'

'No pain in your shoulder?'

'It's fine,' Ella said. 'I'm sorry but I have to go.'

'Ring when you get home?'

'Mum.'

'I know, I know, so kill me for worrying about you.'

'I'll talk to you later.'

'Bye,' Franco called.

'Your father says goodbye,' Netta said. 'Think about dinner for sometime soon, Ella, all right?'

'I will. Bye.'

Ella put the phone down and checked her watch, then picked up the interview transcript again. She wanted to be across as much of Tim's story as possible before she headed out.

'You or him?' Detective Constantine had asked Damien Millerton.

'Him,' Millerton said. 'If I thought that Tim was gay. Could I see it in him, that sort of thing.'

'Did that strike you as strange?'

'Shit yeah,' Millerton said. 'Anytime we talked about girls he used to go on the most, reckoned that when his family went on holidays to the south coast he always got heaps.'

'Did you believe him?'

'Not really, but he was my mate, so I wasn't going to call him on it, was I?'

'So what did you say that night?'

'I told him not to be a dickhead.'

'What did he say?'

'He went quiet for a bit, and we kept walking, and then he said if he told me something could I keep it secret. I said yes, and he said something had happened with a man, he didn't know what to do, he came and so he thought he must be gay. It was dark but I could hear he was almost crying. I tried to think of something to say, but I mean, shit, what do you say to that? Then this car came along, it was the brother of one of our mates from school, and he gave us a lift home.'

'Did you ever try to bring the subject up again?'

'No,' Millerton said. 'I figured if he wanted to talk about it he would. If he didn't then he wouldn't.'

'So on the night that he died,' Constantine said, 'did he give you any indication at all of what might be wrong? Was it related to that situation?'

'Nah. He said there'd been a birthday barbecue thing at his house for some of his family, and there'd been an argument.'

'Between who?'

'Him and his parents. He didn't say what it was about though.'

'Did you see him speak to anyone else in the pub that night, apart from your group of friends?'

'Like was he hitting on anyone, or getting hit on? No. Not that I saw, anyway.'

'Or just talking in general?'

'No.'

'Did you see him leave?'

'No,' Millerton said.

'When did you realise he was gone?'

'About midnight somebody asked where he was. I hadn't seen him for about half an hour or so, probably. We checked the dunnies and went outside in case he was spewing in the gutter but he wasn't there.'

'How far did you go, looking for him?'

'That was it,' Millerton said. 'We figured he got a taxi home. We went back inside and partied on. Shit, I hate myself for it now.'

The interview ended there. Ella put down the transcript and checked the autopsy report for any findings of semen or sexual assault, but there was nothing. Tynan and Constantine's summary described their fruitless efforts to learn more about Tim's possible relationship with a man: the rest of his friends denied being taken into his confidence, and his photo wasn't recognised at any of the local gay haunts. There had been a couple of gay bashings in the three months prior to Tim's death and the culprit, a man named Garry Thomas, was in custody at the time. Constantine had interviewed him and his known associates, but had written that Thomas's friends had solid alibis and the murder seemed like news to Thomas himself.

Ella frowned. Tim's friends might not have been telling the whole truth, and the same with anybody encountered at a gay hangout, especially if they thought it could lead to trouble or didn't want themselves identified.

She reached for her pen. *Ask his friends again.*

The next transcripts were of interviews with Tim's parents. Even on paper, Tamara Pieters's rage and grief was clear. John came across as shocked, stunned, almost paralysed with the loss. Ella learned that Tim was a good boy, a good student, had no enemies, nobody with a reason to kill or even harm him. But both Tamara and John admitted not knowing about Tim's drinking, nor that he and his friends were sneaking into pubs.

Constantine had told John what Damien Millerton had said. 'Did Tim ever raise this subject with you?' he asked.

'Never,' John said.

'Did you talk about sex with him at all?'

'I took him to an educational film one night when he was at primary school,' John said. 'I told him if he ever wanted to know anything, he only had to ask.'

'And did he?'

'No.'

'What was the argument about at the family barbecue that night?'

'Tim was misbehaving. I had to pull him into line.'

'Misbehaving how?'

'Not doing as he was asked, answering back.'

'What did "pulling him into line" involve?'

'We argued about what was appropriate behaviour, and then I told him he couldn't go out with his friends.'

'That was all?'

'How do you mean?'

'Did it become physical?'

'You're asking if I hit my son? No, I did not.'

'You didn't need to restrain him, anything like that?'

'No, I didn't.'

'Your wife said that you went out later that night.'

'We realised about nine that Tim was gone,' John said. 'Tamara and I argued about what we should do and how we would punish him when he got home.'

'You had different thoughts on that?'

'I told her this was serious and that we should take away his bike and his Walkman and refuse him driving lessons for three months. She said we could ground him for two weeks and that would be enough.'

'That must have been aggravating, especially when you were already angry with Tim.'

'I know what you're saying.'

'What am I saying?'

'I read crime novels, I watch the shows. I know you always look at the family first, and I know how it sounds when I say that, yes, I was already angry with Tim and then I was angry with Tamara too. None of it means I killed my son.'

'I haven't said that you did.'

'And now even saying this . . . Can we just finish? Yes, I was angry at Tamara. Is that what you want to know? We argued on and off over the next couple of hours and then she stormed off to bed. I stayed up, and after a while I couldn't stand it and went out in the car looking for him. I don't know how I thought I'd be able to find him because the chances that he would be walking down any street as I drove down it were small.'

'But you still went looking.'

'Yes.'

'Where exactly did you go?'

'I went out onto Pennant Hills Road and went south first. I drove past the Millertons' on Boundary Road, then I headed north. I know I went past Steve's and Gareth's and Chris's houses in Thornleigh but I'm not sure in which order.'

'What time did you leave the house?'

'After Tamara went to bed, which was about eleven, I think.'

'Care to guess how long afterwards?'

'I really can't say. If I'd known I would be attacked about it I would've made a note.'

'Nobody's attacking you.'

'I lost my son.'

'And we're trying to find out who killed him,' Constantine said. 'Sit down, please, Mr Pieters.'

'I *lost* my *son*.'

The transcript said that John Pieters broke down sobbing and the interview had been ended for that day.

Ella checked her watch. She had five minutes before she had to leave. She flipped forward in the transcripts, past interviews with Tim's sister, Haydee, pausing at the one with his brother, Josh: a brief half-page with the explanatory header that the interviewee had Down's syndrome and was accompanied by his mother. Ella felt for the boy as he cried all the way through the session, repeatedly telling the detective that Tim was gone and the bad man had done it.

She had just found the next interview with John and checked her watch again – one minute – when a familiar voice said, 'I heard you were back.'

She looked around to see Detective Murray Shakespeare loitering in the doorway. 'Here I am,' she said.

He came over. 'What have they got you doing?'

'This and that.' She watched his gaze move over the pages and felt possessive. 'Much going on in the squad?'

He picked up the photo of Pieters in his school uniform. 'You got new evidence, new DNA results?' She could hear the interest in his voice.

'A relative is a politician and throwing his weight around,

wanting it reviewed, that's all.' She tried to sound casual as she stuffed the transcripts and scene photos into her bag. 'I doubt there's much in it really.'

He looked at her notepad. 'Ask his friends what?'

'Just checking details.' She shuffled the rest of the papers together and closed the file. 'Anyway, I have to go out.'

'Where to?'

'Long story.' She slung her bag over her shoulder. 'Catch you later.'

'Is it to do with the case? Should you be going alone? I could ask if –'

'Bye, Murray.'

In the car she checked the street directory, then opened the transcript on the passenger seat. She didn't have time to read it now but planned to grab it up at every red light between here and there, so that by the time she met John Pieters, as she was sure she was about to do, she would know whether he'd again protested his innocence too much.

Freya hesitated, then knocked on the locker room door. 'Ready?'

Georgie came out in a dry uniform, the wet one dripping in her hands. 'I didn't hear the phone.'

'Control hasn't called,' Freya said. 'I know it's busy, that's all.'

The sooner we're flat out, the sooner you'll have no time to ask me questions I don't want to answer, she thought.

'I'll just hang these up.' Georgie started into the plant room then looked back. 'Could you grab my boot? It's on the floor in there.'

Freya went into the locker room. It was steamy from Georgie's shower. She picked up the wet boot and the damp towel it was sitting on and avoided herself in the mirror.

In the plant room, Georgie was arranging her uniform on the clothesline screwed to the wall. She took the towel from Freya and added it. 'Chuck that in the bin,' she said, nodding at the boot.

Freya dropped it in, a hollow thud that matched how she felt.

'I'd better call Control,' she said.

'Don't want a cuppa first?'

Freya shook her head and started towards the ambulance.

'Hang on,' Georgie said. 'I want to ask you something.'

Oh crap.

'I'd better call.' Freya reached across the driver's seat and picked up the microphone. There was always a heap of work waiting so they should get a job immediately and Georgie's question would hopefully be forgotten. 'Thirty-three to Control.'

'Stand by, please, Thirty-three.'

Georgie leaned in the passenger door, her arms folded on the seat. 'Hey –'

Freya interrupted before she could say anything more. 'The cops want to put you up for a bravery award.'

'They should give it to that guy who went in the first time,' Georgie said. 'Anyway, I wasn't really thinking. It was more stupid than brave.'

'While I just froze.'

'You had the portable.'

'It would've taken me two seconds to get it off.'

'It doesn't matter,' Georgie said. 'The woman's okay.'

'I'm supposed to be your assessor. I'm supposed to be, like, the senior person.' The one who led the way. Freya felt small and inconsequential.

'This doesn't change anything,' Georgie said.

Freya raised the mike. 'Thirty-three.'

'Thirty-three, as I said, stand by.'

He sounded cranky. She shouldn't call again. She shot Georgie a glance, saw the question building on her face, and started speaking again. 'I saw you leap out of the truck before, at the Quay. You frightened the hell out of me. I was coming back from the wharf and I saw you fly out and I thought, oh crap, she *does* have pulmonary oedema. She *is* putting foam on my nice clean ambulance floor.'

'I thought I saw someone I knew,' Georgie said. 'Freya, why –'

'Like a friend, you mean?'

'Freya, listen.'

'Who was it?' Freya started to sweat, knowing what was coming.

'Freya,' Georgie said, 'why did you leave school without saying goodbye?'

Don't panic, stay calm, just give her the answer you've practised.

'I didn't mean to.'

'Just slipped your mind, did it?'

'It's not like it seems.'

'I thought you'd been murdered.'

Freya couldn't stop the laugh.

'What's so funny?' Georgie's face was red. 'What did you think I would think? One day you're there and the next you're not. I called your house and for the first two days the phone rang out, then it was disconnected. I went round there every day after school and banged on your door and got no answer, and finally one of your neighbours saw me trying to look in your side window and told me she'd seen removalists there days before and that the real estate agent had started bringing possible new tenants through. Nobody could tell me where you'd gone and I cried myself to sleep for *weeks*.'

'I laughed because the murder was the reason that we went,' Freya said. *Stay calm. Hold her gaze. She can't tell how much of this is a lie.* 'Mum and Dad lost it completely. Overnight they decided we were going – they found a house in Orange, got me into Oaktree College with my cousin. I woke up one morning and they were packing around me. They wouldn't let me out of their sight even to come and say goodbye.'

'You never even wrote.'

'It was too hard! I knew what you'd be feeling because I felt it too. Plus you know I was never good at English composition. I just couldn't find the words. In the end it was easier not to try.'

'Except for that birthday card,' Georgie said. 'To Georgie, happy birthday, from Freya. That's real communication, that is.'

'I was young and stupid and I thought something was better than nothing.'

'It wasn't.'

'I figured that out after I sent it,' Freya said. 'I'm sorry.'

Georgie blinked back tears. 'You hurt me.'

'I know,' Freya said. 'I'm so sorry.'

Georgie looked down at the seat.

'I've been wanting to find you for a while,' Freya lied. 'I looked for you on Facebook and MySpace and Friends Reunited. I had an email drafted up to explain it all. I didn't know if I'd ever find you and I felt bad that maybe I'd never get to clear it up.'

'I don't use any of that stuff.'

'And how lucky that we meet up now.' Freya wondered if Georgie was buying any of this. 'Actually, not lucky. It's more like we were meant to find each other and sort this out.'

'You think?'

'Thirty-three,' Control called.

'I do think,' Freya said. *Look me in the eye, show me you believe me!* 'Don't you?'

Georgie climbed into her seat and clipped in her seatbelt. 'Better answer him.'

'Thirty-three, are you on the air or not?'

'Thirty-three,' Freya answered.

'At last. Go to Macquarie Street, please, for a woman ill on the steps of the State Library.'

'Thirty-three on way.'

Freya rehooked the mike and got behind the wheel. She pulled out of the station, pressed the button to close the roller door, and flicked on the lights and siren.

'Know the city much?' she asked.

Georgie shook her head.

'It's a rats' nest.' She was still sweating and could feel herself wanting to babble. Georgie was silent in her corner. Silent and disbelieving? She tried not to think about it too much. 'So anyway, I meant to say earlier that Ken suggested I drive, for the start of things at least.'

'It'd be good for me to learn sometime.'

'It's what Ken suggested.'

Georgie shrugged.

Freya felt antsy and blasted the horn at a man who bolted across the street in front of them. 'Suicidal moron.'

When she screeched to a stop outside the library, a woman lying on the steps smiled and raised a hand.

'Hilary,' Freya said. 'Frequent flyer. There's nothing wrong with her. Nothing detox wouldn't fix, anyway.'

Georgie got out without speaking. Freya turned the engine off and worried about whether Georgie believed her and what it might mean if she didn't.

Georgie walked to the library steps, still considering Freya's story of why she'd disappeared from school. 'You rang?' she said to the woman.

'I'm sick, love,' the woman croaked. She looked to be in her fifties, her skin tanned and leathery, her blue jeans more brown with grime. Her feet were bare and swollen, the skin around her nails chapped and inflamed. She coughed and spat a plug of yellow phlegm on the footpath. 'I'm so sick.'

'Sick in what way?' Georgie asked.

The woman reached out. 'Help me up, love.'

Georgie saw the filth under the fingernails and caked in the lines of her palms.

Freya stood beside Georgie, hands on her hips. 'Don't let her touch you. When the cops pick her up, she wipes her shit all over the inside of the paddy wagon.'

'Coppers.' The woman snorted. 'Say anything.'

Georgie said, 'Do you need to go to hospital?'

'No, she doesn't,' Freya said.

Hilary slumped back down on the steps. 'I am sooo sick.'

'Sick how?' Georgie said again.

'Just sick! Look at me! I'm probably dying.'

'She's pissed and she's a pain in the arse,' Freya said. 'She does this all the time. When we do take her in, the nurses throw her in the waiting room and she walks out three seconds later.'

'Sooo sick,' Hilary moaned.

Freya nudged Georgie and started back to the ambulance. 'Come on.'

Georgie looked at Hilary. She did stink of wine. Back at home, Georgie knew the equivalent locals well enough to know when they were just bunging it on. But she was on assessment here. Then again, Freya was her assessor and pissing her off was not a good idea.

'I have a pain in me chest,' Hilary said.

'Don't try that one,' Freya said.

'I do, I really do. Ooh, it's right here.' She clapped a hand to the centre of her chest.

'For Christ's sake.'

Georgie rubbed her forehead. 'What's it feel like?'

'Like an elephant standin' there.'

'What a crock,' Freya said.

'Does it hurt when you breathe?'

'No, it just feels kinda tight.'

Georgie looked at Freya. You couldn't listen to a patient say that, even a pissed frequent flyer, and not treat and transport. She went to the ambulance and got the Oxy-Viva.

Freya said, 'It's bullshit.'

'She's got the symptoms.' Georgie fitted an oxygen mask to Hilary's face.

'The fake symptoms.' Freya stood in front of Hilary. 'After a meal, are you? A shower? Think we're going to waste our time and effort and the taxpayer's money going through all the rig-marole of a chest pain when you just want a lift to lunch? Jesus, you smell.'

'So sick,' Hilary said through the mask.

Georgie crouched and wrapped the blood–pressure cuff around Hilary's arm. Her body odour made her eyes water. 'Mind bringing the monitor?'

'It's bullshit.' Freya folded her arms.

Georgie looked up at her. 'I would like the monitor, please.'

Hilary laid her cold, filthy fingers on Georgie's arm. 'You're such a dear.'

'She's faking.'

'I'm still going to treat her.'

Freya didn't move. Anger swelled Georgie's throat. Protocol dictated that the treating officer of the shift was boss and the driving officer fetched whatever equipment they wanted. This was like being at Woolford again, the night she'd asked Ross to bring in the stretcher for a patient and twenty minutes later went out to find him having a smoke. 'Idiot doesn't need the stretcher,' he'd grunted, and got into the driver's seat.

It was impossible to work like that, and in an instant she saw the assessment ending that afternoon, the rubberstamp hearing tomorrow, the devastation of being unemployed the day after. Was this Freya's aim? She'd said they were meant to work together to clear up the mess of their past, but maybe it was to continue Georgie's shafting in the present.

But then Freya turned on her heel and went to the ambulance and Georgie heard the clunks of her pulling the stretcher out. Not what she'd asked for, but something nevertheless.

She smiled at Hilary. 'Once I get you in the ambulance I'll do a tracing of your heart, and give you some medication, and we'll see if we can't get that pain to go away.'

'You are a sweetie. Let me give you a kiss.'

'That's fine.'

'No, no, come here.' The cold fingers tightened on her arm.

'Really. It's okay. You don't need to.'

Georgie struggled to see the dial on the sphygmo while keeping out of Hilary's reach, but her hairy chin loomed and Georgie caught a faceful of her breath and almost gagged.

'I want to, darl.' Hilary tried to pull her close, her grip surprisingly strong. 'It's like a little present.'

Georgie resisted. 'We're not allowed to accept gifts.'

'Just a little kissy-kiss.'

Hilary yanked her arm. Georgie pulled away and lost her balance and sat backwards on the footpath.

'You don't want to kiss me?'

'I have a husband,' Georgie said.

'Fuck husbands.' Hilary hawked and spat on the footpath by Georgie's boot. 'And fuck you too if you don't want to kiss me. Bitch.' She tried to slap her.

Georgie dodged her hand. 'Calm down.'

Hilary leapt to her feet. 'Bitch!'

'Hey –' Georgie said, but Hilary took off. The sphygmo was torn from Georgie's hands and the oxygen tubing stretched out to its full length and the Oxy-Viva tipped over, then the mask snapped from Hilary's face. The tubing tangled around her bare feet for a second then she was clear and running down the footpath.

Georgie was on her feet. 'Jesus.'

'Told you she's nuts,' Freya said.

'She's still got the cuff on.'

Freya folded her arms. 'She can't be very fast; she's just a poor old thing with chest pain.'

Georgie started to run. Hilary's small headstart seemed to grow larger with each new pedestrian who looked their way; and when people started to laugh, anger and hurt fuelled Georgie's legs.

What did I ever do to you? I was nice, I was looking after you. And then you go and do this.

She got Hilary before she reached the road, grabbing her arm in a grip so hard she shocked herself.

'Ow.'

Georgie tore the cuff from her arm. 'If you still want to go to hospital I'll call the police to take you.'

'Fuck off.'

'Gladly.'

She walked back to the ambulance, her face hot, aware of Hilary's stink on the cuff. Freya had put the stretcher away and was collecting up the Oxy-Viva.

'This needs a wash,' Georgie said.

'I bet.'

Freya took the clean cuff from inside the ambulance and put it in the Viva. Georgie threw the soiled cuff on the passenger side floor, stripped off her gloves and washed her hands with Hexol, then got in and did up her seatbelt.

Freya slid behind the wheel but didn't start the engine. 'I didn't know she was going to try to hit you.'

Georgie kicked the sphygmo cuff out from under her boots.

'And I do get it,' Freya said. 'You're on assessment, you want to do everything right.'

'I believed her,' Georgie said.

'I know you did.' Freya glanced in the side mirror. 'Here she comes again.'

Georgie looked out to see Hilary reseat herself on the steps and flip them the bird with one filthy finger. 'Nice.'

'Isn't it.' Freya fired up the engine. 'What a job. We train all these years, study till our eyes practically fall out, practise intubating and cannulating and all sorts of stuff so we can save people's lives, and then we get people like her and the crazy at the wharf.'

'Shield of protection, that's us.' Georgie picked up the radio. 'Thirty-three's clear at the scene. Ambulance not required.'

'Thanks, Thirty-three,' Control said. 'Head for Mascot. Got an air ambulance transfer from there to the North Shore, elderly male for rehab.'

'Copy,' Georgie said.

'Bloody hell,' Freya said. 'How can I assess you if we do crap all the time?'

Georgie looked at her. She sounded almost genuine.

Freya met her gaze. 'You know, I meant that about being sorry. About leaving so suddenly.'

Something in Georgie softened. Whatever else was going on, she felt Freya was telling the truth about that. 'I know.'

'I'm glad that we met so I could tell you that,' Freya said. 'You know how it is when things from your past hang over your head.'

Did she ever.

'Thirty-three, cancel that,' Control said. 'Got a code two for you in First Fleet Park, near Alfred Street, CPR in progress.'

'Three's on the case.'

'More like it.' Freya flipped on the lights and siren and accelerated through an orange light.

Georgie said, 'Need me to look it up?'

'Nope, it's right at the Quay.'

Georgie's stomach slid downwards. No. It was ridiculous to think that. Wasn't it?

'A good assessment job,' Freya said. 'Finally.'

Georgie nodded. *He will not be there.* She braced an arm against the door as Freya stamped on the brakes behind a clueless driver, and tried the deep breathing that the counsellor had taught her.

Everything will be fine, everything will be fine.

Yeah, right.

Callum McLennan paused for breath. At the urging of Anna, his staffer, he had mentally rehearsed this glance out across the crowd and the crescendo that he put into his voice. It felt melodramatic, but the mass of students and parents before him was motionless and there was no sound from behind him where his aunt and uncle, Tamara and John Pieters, sat beside the college principal, Dion Entemann. Anna nodded at him from the floor. The journalists next to her were writing madly. She'd been pleased to see how many had turned up, and had whispered, 'This will really help your profile.' Callum had been pleased too, because every one meant another article about Tim, another printing of his photo, and someone somewhere would surely remember something.

'These students and all the others like them across the country are our future.'

Bit of a cliché, he'd said to Anna when she'd run him through it. Clichés are the backbone of the politician's speech, she'd replied. *Anyway, they won't notice when they hear what you're going to say next.*

'It is the life in these young people that we must value.' He was embarrassed to feel a lump in his throat. 'Every single life is precious, and so it is my privilege to be able to announce that there is to be a new investigation into the homicide of my cousin, Tim Pieters, in whose name I declare this centre open.'

With an emotional tremble in his hand that he hoped nobody noticed, he raised the scissors and cut through the ribbon strung between portable basketball hoops beside him. The electronic scoreboards above the proper hoops on the courts winked on, the bright red letters flashing TIM TIM TIM.

The crowd clapped. Dion Entemann stood up to give Callum the kind of double-grip prolonged handshake he was becoming used to in this new career. In the hospitals, people were too busy for more than a quick grasp, if that.

'Thank you,' Entemann said. 'We're honoured to have you here.'

'The honour's all mine.'

Callum felt Anna's hand at his back, angling him better for the photo op. He smiled into the lenses with Entemann still shaking his hand. As soon as the flashes went off Callum freed himself and went to his aunt and uncle.

'Great news,' John said. 'When will they be out to interview us?'

'The minister said it would take a little while for the detectives to get up to speed on the case,' Callum said.

'Days, weeks?' Tamara said. 'Months, God forbid?'

'Tar,' John said.

'I don't see why we had to get a member of the family into parliament to have anything happen.'

'It's not like that,' Callum said. 'The Minister for Police told me these cases are never closed, that detectives review all of them from time to time to see what new evidence might have come up.'

His promise to 'assist as required' – meaning anything from

supporting the minister in an undefined number of ballots to quietly backgrounding journalists against colleagues he wanted targeted – had certainly helped. Callum didn't care. Whatever it took. Being up there and seeing all the kids in the Macquarie uniform had hardened his resolve. He would suck up, work the system, kick heads wherever he had to, until the bastard who murdered Tim was caught.

'Nobody's been to see us in six years,' his aunt said.

John put his arm around Tamara's shoulders but she shook him off. He said, 'This is supposed to be a cheerful event.'

'There's no such thing.'

'I'm sorry,' John said to Callum.

'Don't apologise for me,' Tamara said.

'He's helping us.'

'I know that.'

'Then . . .' John gestured around them.

'What? Have a nice time? Chat and smile? Pretend I'm happy?' She glared at him then walked away.

'Don't worry about her.' John gripped Callum's arm. 'What you're doing is good.' He followed Tamara off the stage.

'He's right,' Anna said behind Callum.

'So is she,' he said. 'It shouldn't happen just because I have access to the minister's ear.'

Anna shrugged. 'Whatcha going to do?'

'Things like this shouldn't be political.'

'Everything's political,' she said. 'By the way, nice work up there.'

'Your speech.'

'Like I said.' She grinned. 'Now follow me to the people's level and start networking.'

She'd told him earlier what to do: begin talking with the clos-est person while she searched out the people he really needed to speak to. The nearest person was a dark-haired woman. She stood alone looking at the framed photo of Tim in his school uniform, currently on a white cloth-draped table but soon to hang on the wall.

'My cousin,' Callum said.

She turned to look at him. 'So you said.'

'Callum McLennan, MP.' He put out his hand.

She shook it briefly. 'Detective Ella Marconi.'

Anna came back. 'Callum, may I speak to you for a moment?'

'In a second,' he said.

'That's fine,' Ella said. 'I'll be here.'

Callum had to let himself be herded across the sprung floor to meet various local somebodies and grey-haired old boys. He chatted briefly then as soon as he could, he muttered to Anna, 'I need to go back.' She frowned but excused them from the group.

'She's a detective,' he said.

'On your cousin's case?'

'Why else would she be here?'

'Maybe she's an old girl.'

'Why did she identify herself as a detective then?'

Callum's heart pounded. He took a deep breath. He was impressed with Ella's cool attitude and her strength and he wanted to impress her in the same way.

'I'm back,' he told her.

'So I see.'

'Are you investigating my cousin's case?'

'I am.'

Callum held back a shiver. This woman was going to solve the case, he could feel it. 'Anna, would you get my aunt and uncle, please?' He looked at Ella. 'I mean, if you don't mind? They'll be delighted to meet you.'

'Not at all. I'm keen to meet them too.'

John and Tamara followed Anna over and Callum introduced them. 'Detective Marconi is on Tim's case.'

John shook her hand. 'Thank you for coming.'

Tamara said, 'Where's your partner?'

'I'm working alone.'

'How can that be?'

'The main thing is that it's being investigated,' Callum said.

The detective had no doubt heard worse tones of voice but he didn't want her to be annoyed with them.

Ella acted like she hadn't heard it at all. 'Are any of Tim's schoolmates here?' she asked John.

'Not that we're aware,' he said. 'I mean, none of them have come up to speak to us, and I don't know that we'd recognise them nowadays.'

'Seeing as it's been nineteen years,' Tamara said. 'Were you taken off another case to work on this?'

'No.'

'What were you doing?'

'I was recovering after being shot.'

'You're injured too?' Tamara said.

Callum thought Ella might justify herself, point out that she was working so she'd obviously been cleared for duty, but she didn't.

'I'm going to do everything in my power to bring your son's killer to justice,' she said instead.

'Yes, but your power isn't much, is it,' Tamara said.

'Tar, come on,' John said, but Tamara shot a cold glance Callum's way.

'I expect you to tackle the minister about this,' she said. 'Saying the case is being investigated again, but only putting one officer on it and an injured one at that. How many of these cold cases have you done?' she barked at Ella.

'Your son is my first.'

Red spots appeared high on Tamara's cheeks. 'This is an insult. Callum, for all your grand words about the youth being so precious, Tim clearly doesn't rate at all.' She stalked away.

John sighed. 'Sorry.'

'It's okay,' Ella said. 'She can't rage at the killer, so she rages at those around her. We see it often.'

'I can imagine,' John said.

'I hope you don't mind me saying,' she told him, 'but you've done well to stay together. Many marriages don't survive something like this.'

'It's not been easy,' John said. 'She's been on medication but is still unstable at times.'

'Really,' Ella said. 'I'm sorry to hear that.'

Callum felt anxious to get on with it. 'How can we help you with this?'

'At some point I'll need to speak to everyone in the family –'

'When?'

'I'm not sure yet,' Ella said. 'It takes a little while to become properly familiar with the case.'

John was nodding. 'We understand. But anything we can do, you let us know.'

'I will,' she said.

Callum put out his hand again. 'Thank you.'

She shook her head. 'Thank me when I solve it.'

Georgie saw a man run out into the street as they approached the Quay. He gestured for Freya to drive into a space that was much too narrow, and when she drove past, heading further along the street to a spot where she could climb the gutter and enter the park, he shouted and punched the side of the ambulance.

Freya shook her head as she looped the ambulance across the grass to the people clustered there. 'We're everyone's punching bag today.'

Georgie was out the door the second Freya stopped. 'Quickly!' someone shouted from the cluster. She yanked open the side door to grab the Oxy-Viva and stepped back into the waver from the street.

'You should've told me,' he panted.

She went to go around him but he followed close by her side. 'You should've told me you'd seen me but were going further along. Then I wouldn't have hit the ambulance.' He held up his hand. 'I think I hurt myself.'

Georgie heard Freya snort behind her. She ignored the man and fixed her gaze on the huddle. Feet in brown leather shoes stuck out of one end, and she could see the up-and-down movement of someone doing compressions. She scanned the group standing around. *Focus, now. He isn't here.*

'Can you please look at my hand?'

Georgie pushed her way into the knot of people. The victim was a big man, flat on his back, his face congested and purple and his eyes half-open. The woman doing CPR was good at it and when she looked up Georgie recognised in her eyes that she was in the job.

'Story?'

'Collapsed six minutes ago. I saw him go down. Wife says no complaints beforehand.' She nodded and Georgie looked over to see a woman in her sixties sitting weeping on the grass. 'Agonal resps for about five minutes. History of bypass three years ago, hypertension, CAD. Hi, Freya.'

'Hey, Penny. This is Georgie. You okay to stay for a bit?'

'No worries.'

Georgie opened the intubation kit and prepared a tube. Freya attached the monitor and Georgie saw he was in asystole. Not good.

She yanked on gloves and opened the man's mouth. The first glance always told you so much – was this going to be easy or hard? The man was big with a bullish neck, but at least there was no vomit.

Freya strapped a tourniquet around the man's arm.

The waver crouched behind her. 'I think I really did some damage.'

Georgie opened the laryngoscope and slid it into the man's pharynx. No view of the cords whatsoever. *Crap.*

She came out, fitted the Laerdal mask to his face and did some serious bagging.

'You okay?' she asked the woman doing compressions. 'Need a break?'

A bead of sweat fell from Penny's cheek. 'Sfine.'

'I'm in.' Freya released the tourniquet and taped and bunged the cannula.

'Excuse me,' the waver said.

'Excuse *me*,' Freya said. 'We're a little busy.'

He muttered something and sat back on his haunches.

Having pinked the patient up a little, Georgie slid onto her stomach with her elbows by his ears. She tilted his head back, searching with the laryngoscope once more.

Shit.

Freya was watching her with a question in her eyes. Georgie started bagging again and checked the monitor. It wasn't the end of the world if she couldn't get the tube in. Yes, it'd be good for the appraisal, but she could still run the arrest well. She looked at Freya. 'Ten of adrenaline.'

Then movement in the watching people caught her eye. *Oh no.* The man was there. Watching her.

Georgie tried to concentrate as she attempted the tube again. 'Cricoid,' she said to Freya, hoping the extra pressure on the patient's larynx would bring the vocal cords into sight. Her field of vision was split in two: the half in the man's throat was dark and purplish, the half in the outside world was bright with sunlight. Freya pushed her fingers against the man's neck, but it was no good: there was no flash of white cords.

She came out and bagged him again, keeping her eyes on the mask in her hands and away from the watching crowd. She could feel Freya waiting for her decision. She frowned and tried to focus.

'I'll try once blind,' she said.

Freya still waited.

'Oh, and atropine, please.'

She flushed at forgetting such basics. It was that man in the crowd. She turned her head just a fraction and saw him from the corner of her eye. He was behind a heavy-set woman so she couldn't fully see his face. His arms were folded and his eyes were hidden behind reflective sunglasses. She felt under such close and fury-filled scrutiny that her skin crawled.

A police officer crouched beside them. 'How's he doing?'

'Touch and go,' Georgie lied.

'The wife was asking if she could come over.'

Georgie looked at the man under her hands, his body shift-ing slightly with each compression by the off-duty paramedic. He looked like crap. He looked like the corpse he practically was.

'She's sure?' Georgie said.

The cop nodded. 'I'll stay with her.'

'Okay, thanks. Just give us a minute.'

'Atropine in,' Freya said. 'Still asystole.'

Georgie bent over the patient's head and took a deep breath. Going in blind was hard. You had to put your mind on the end of the tube and hope to somehow mentally guide it into place between the cords. You couldn't just poke around because that could send the cords into spasm, which would make them close against you for what felt like forever, and might damage them so that even if the guy came back from the brink his voice could be buggered. It was better to be alive with a shitty voice than dead, no doubt about that, but best of all was, naturally, alive with the same old voice. She picked up the tube and tried to block out the thoughts, block out the man in the crowd, the copper who hadn't waited like she'd asked but was helping the wife over just in time for her to watch Georgie muck about in her husband's throat.

Okay. She tilted the man's head back and went in again. *Smooth and fast. Let's do this. Come on, universe, help me out for once!*

She felt the tube slide into the pharynx but from there it could've been anywhere. A thought popped into her head, a memory of being a trainee and asking her mentor what you felt when the tube went between the cords, how was it different from the times that it didn't. All you feel is pissed off, he'd said, because you have no clue, you have to attach the bag and inflate the lungs and listen to the chest with the stethoscope, and only then do you find that it's not in and you have to come out and try again.

The tube slid somewhere. *Oh please . . .* She connected the bag and squeezed.

Freya pushed the earpieces of her stethoscope into place

and listened hard, in both of the patient's armpits, then over his stomach, and shook her head.

Dammit.

Georgie pulled out the tube and fitted the mask into place again.

'Will he be okay?' The wife sank to her knees beside him and put her hand on his trousered shin.

'We're doing everything we can for him,' Freya said. 'He got excellent CPR immediately and that counts for a heck of a lot, and we're doing all the treatment now that the hospital would give him.'

Georgie blushed with shame. It wasn't the end of the world to miss a tube, it happened to everyone, but this felt bad. She glanced up at the off-duty paramedic who didn't meet her eye. She would know what a shambles this was turning into and that it wasn't just the tube. Georgie was disorganised and distracted. She was meant to be in control of the entire event and look at her – she was forgetting drugs and she couldn't stop herself from glancing up at the man in the crowd.

He was still there, as motionless as ever. Georgie shivered.

'Do you want to load and go?' Freya said in a low voice. 'Georgie?'

'Yes.'

That too. It was her decision when they would move and she should've made it long minutes ago. It would be nice to explain why she was so unfocused, but to admit what she was fearing was just . . . crazy.

THREE

Ella stood on Britannia Street with her back to the passing cars. The sunlight warmed her shoulders and the breeze brought the sound and smell of grass being mown in Pennant Hills Park as she stared into the shadowed undergrowth. She held the crime scene photos in her hand but didn't need to look at them again to remind herself where Tim Pieters had lain. It had been a lot of years but the place hadn't changed so much: the trees were still back from the road, and shrubby bushes and long grass still covered the ground between them and the gravelled border of the roadway. Tim had been dropped into the far edge of the bushes, at the base of a grey-barked tree. She thought of that night: somebody bringing him here, dead or dying, in their vehicle and carrying him into the grass. Had the killer dropped him? Flung him? Laid him down carefully? She knew he'd felt none of it but she didn't like to think of him falling even the short distance from someone's arms.

She stepped through the long grass and touched the tree's rough bark. There was nothing at its base; no flowers, no old ribbons that had once tied flowers on, no sign of what had happened there. It was just a tree.

A car slowed on the street. She looked around. It kept going and she watched it drive out of sight. This was a residential street that led only to more of the same. The busiest days would be the weekends, when hordes of parents and kids would flood in and out of the sports fields and playgrounds. Back in 1990 there'd been fewer houses in the area, and Tim's body had been dumped here either late on Saturday night or very early Sunday, so it was possible that the car stopped on the edge of the road had been seen by nobody at all.

At least, nobody who'd come forward.

Ella looked at the positions of the streetlights then compared them to the photos. Nothing had changed. She stared further up the street at the first house next to the park, the house the girl had run to after she'd found Tim. When the case had last been looked into six years ago, the same man was still living there. Once she'd checked out his statements, she'd be back out here on that door-step, fingers crossed that he was a) still alive and b) still there.

She opened the car door and put the photos back with John Pieters's second interview transcript. It had been much the same as the first – John still angry and defensive, and Detective Constantine continuing to ask about where he'd gone the night Tim was killed. John had insisted that he couldn't remember. She had read that his car had been examined and he'd been interviewed twice more, the final time with a lawyer present, and though it was clear that the detectives had their suspicions, there was nothing to charge him over.

At the school he'd struck her as friendly and keen to help, though it was interesting that he'd volunteered the information about Tamara being unstable. Knowing that they were both going to be questioned, a canny person might do such a thing to suggest the other is unreliable. The Pieterses might still be together but Ella got the sense, even before John spoke, that it wasn't all sunshine and flowers; and, as Galea had pointed out, when relationships changed so did what people said to police.

Callum McLennan was even keener to help. She'd known he was watching her as she talked to John, obviously aware that his uncle had been a suspect even though he himself must have only been a child at the time. She would read his statement when she got back to the office. Kids often picked up stuff that went unnoticed by others. He seemed a decent man and, judging by the emotion she'd seen during his speech, one deeply affected by what had happened.

Ella got back into the car. For now she had more reading to do, but she'd decided during Callum's speech that she would be out this way again tomorrow for a surprise visit to John and Tamara. It took no brilliance on John's part to work out that a detective would've turned up today, and maybe he would equally prepare himself for a knock on the door tomorrow, but she was still looking forward to watching him in his home environment, and talking to him – and Tamara – at length.

Georgie rested the case-sheet folder on Thirty-three's bonnet and sighed. St Vincent's Hospital's ambulance bay was quiet, which pleased her because the last thing she wanted to do was joke around with other paras. She felt shrivelled after that job, sad for the man who lay under a sheet in the resus room. It wasn't down to the tube, she knew that in her head, but she couldn't help but feel in her heart that if she'd been able to get it things might have gone differently. If she'd been able to do that, maybe she would've maintained her focus, maybe she would've run the thing better.

Freya came out of the Emergency Department with a patient ID label on her finger. Georgie stuck it on the case sheet.

'I'm sorry about that one.'

'Probably a massive MI,' Freya said. 'Nothing anyone could've done.'

'Still.'

'What?'

'I didn't do as well as I should've.'

'Happens to all of us.'

Georgie smoothed down the sticker's edges. The man had been sixty-one and lived in Earlwood. *On a nice day out with his wife,* she thought. *Enjoying the weather and the harbour.* 'I stuffed up that tube.'

'Bullnecks can be impossible,' Freya said. 'Don't sweat it.'

Georgie shook her head.

'I'm serious,' Freya said.

'So am I. I stuffed up.'

'With what? So you were a bit slow off the mark with the drugs. We got them all in, we got going soon enough. We did what was required.'

Georgie frowned at the sticker. 'I was all over the shop.'

'So you'll do better next time. It was probably the after-effects of the last job. Your brain was addled by eau de Hilary.'

Her smile made Georgie feel like opening up and explaining the true reason why she'd been so haphazard. And why not? Maybe it would be good to talk about it.

She took a deep breath. 'It's because of this guy.'

Freya raised her eyebrows. 'Other than your husband?'

'Not like that,' Georgie said. 'This guy who was at the scene.'

'The one who punched the truck?'

Georgie shook her head. 'He was in the crowd, he was wearing those mirrored sunnies. You must've seen him.'

Freya gave her a quizzical look then glanced past, and Georgie looked around to see a young woman with a tear-streaked face stumble down the driveway.

'Hold that thought,' Freya said.

She went towards the woman and said a few words, and when the woman half-collapsed against her she put her arm around her shoulders and helped her towards the ED doors. From Freya's glance over the woman's head, Georgie guessed this was a family member of the man she'd failed to save. By her age she had to be a daughter, and Georgie didn't want to think about her going into the ED, falling into her distraught mother's arms, the two of them sobbing over the cooling body. Instead she looked up the driveway to the street.

A flash of sunlight off mirrored sunglasses by the wall caught her eye.

It was him.

She started running.

He took off. She reached the top of the driveway and followed him, boots pounding the footpath. He dodged the bus shelter and ran straight into an old woman who fell into the gutter with a squawk. He ran fast, elbows tucked in, and Georgie saw the distance between them growing. By the time she reached the corner she knew she had no hope. She put a hand on the wall and looked breathlessly into the next street but he was gone in the crowd of pedestrians.

She hurried back to the woman in the gutter. 'Did you know that man?'

The woman put out a filthy hand. 'Hello, lovey.'

Oh crap. Georgie took a step back. 'Hilary, did you see that man? Would you recognise him again?'

'What man was this?'

'The man who knocked you over.'

Nobody else had been walking on the street at the time. No people going past in cars had stopped. Hilary was her only witness.

Hilary frowned. 'Didn't you do it?'

Georgie took another step back. 'It was a man.'

'Are you sure?'

Georgie looked up at the light poles and the walls. CCTV cameras. Thank God. They would've captured everything.

'Where are you hurt?' she asked Hilary.

'I'm fine, sweet. Just help me up and I'll be on my way.'

'You should get checked out properly.'

'Don't need to go back in there, just had lunch.'

'You really should at least have someone look at you. Listen, I'll bring a wheelchair out, you won't even have to walk.'

'Thank you, my lovely, but I'm all right.' Hilary clambered to her feet.

'But this needs to go on your records, so they know what happened.'

Hilary was already tottering off, and she waved one hand behind her head and kept going.

Georgie watched her for a moment then went back into the ambulance bay.

Freya was crouched by the ambulance, collecting the case sheets that had fallen out of the folder. 'What happened to you? I come out and you're gone and this is on the ground and blowing all over.'

'That guy in the mirrored sunnies was here. Did you see him? He must've been right behind the patient's daughter.'

'Maybe he's a rello too.'

Georgie shook her head. 'He ran away when I tried to approach him.'

'Why'd you approach him? Oh, look at this.' Freya held up a case sheet smeared with brake dust.

'I'll explain later.'

Georgie went into the ED, past the family room with its closed door that failed to muffle the sounds of sobbing, and up to the nurses' desk. 'I just witnessed an assault on the street outside and I think you need to call the police.'

The hassled nurse barely glanced up. 'Injuries?'

'Patient, ah, didn't stay.'

He frowned. 'So there's no complainant.'

'It was Hilary,' she said.

He snorted. 'Say no more.'

'But the police can still look into it, can't they? They could at least look at the CCTV and see who it was.'

'Cameras are busted,' he said.

'You're kidding me.'

He shrugged. 'We don't have enough money to pay for the nursing staff we need. Electricians are way down the list.'

Georgie walked away, past the family room, and hesitated. Maybe the daughter had seen the man in the mirrored sunglasses. But so what if she had – what did that prove?

Maybe just enough.

But there was no way in the world she could knock on that door. Just no way.

She'd have to find out some other way.

★

Anna drove them back into the city. 'That went well.'

'Thanks for your help,' Callum said.

'My job,' she said. 'Now listen, that man you were speaking to at the end there, Benson Smith, you need to call him tomorrow and ask him to lunch. I think Thursday next week is free.' She thumbed through her Blackberry, one eye on the screen and one on the road. 'Hmm. Friday might be better.'

'I think I'm going to call that detective.'

'To go to lunch?'

'To say thanks. See if she wants to talk to me.'

'That's good,' Anna said. 'Now, Benson Smith used to be the mayor and is –'

'I think she really could do it,' Callum said. 'I got that feeling from her. She's really focused.'

'It's her job.'

'Didn't you feel it? The energy coming off her?'

She glanced at him.

'It's not like that,' he said.

'Did I say anything?'

He sat back in his seat and looked out the window at the pink afternoon clouds. Ella could really do it. He felt a thrumming low down in his spine. He'd become a doctor to *do* things, to have an effect, to change the course of events. He'd become an MP because he'd been told he could do the same on a bigger scale. So far it hadn't worked out that way – there were meetings, and meetings about meetings, and great scads of paper to wade through, and still the emails and letters and phone calls flooded in from his old colleagues: 'We're counting on you to help us'; 'We need help or this ward/theatre/department will close'; 'We are close to breaking point, we cannot go on'. But his requests for meetings with the Minister for Health were absorbed into the minister's office and never heard of again. He hadn't realised the difference in scope either. It seemed so obvious now, but in the hospital it was him and one child with respiratory difficulties at a time, and never mind how many people were waiting – he could be in the moment and change that course.

Whereas now, there was so much to do, so many people asking for his help, and all of it urgent but none actually a here-and-now life-threatening emergency, so it was useless to try to think like a doctor and triage the onslaught.

Tim's case was something to cling to. He had done this one thing, helped get it reopened, and now this detective, Ella, was on it, and he felt the thrumming increase at the thought that she could really do it, and his family would get to face the culprit, and their courses might be steered just a little back to where they should have been.

1990

He sat on the wall beside the barbecue, kicking his heels against the brickwork and watching Aunty Tamara pour herself another glass of champagne. There was something about his family that made their birthdays all fall within the same two months. It was the genes, his dad said. 'I'm a doctor, so I'd know, right?' Callum was never entirely sure whether he was joking, but all it really meant was that every year they came to Aunty Tamara and Uncle John's house for a barbecue tea and a cake massive enough to fit the names Tamara, Olive, Genevieve and Callum on it. And then it was only a few hours' sleep till his birthday started for real, and this year he was getting the red BMX and they were going to the track at Castle Hill for the whole afternoon. He kicked harder at the wall, seeing himself on the BMX, doing a wheelie further than he'd ever done before. Scott said BMXs were special, they were made special so you could do more stuff better. Callum had told Tim that, and Tim had said it was bullcrap, Scott only said it because he had a BMX himself and Callum didn't (yet) and so he was big-noting his bike. But Tim wasn't into BMXs anyway, so what would he know?

Tim stabbed the sausages so hard that Callum heard the fork tines hitting the barbecue plate. Tim was seventeen, six years and a whole world older than him. Callum watched him frown at the cooking meat, saw the muscles move under the skin of his forearms. They'd learnt all about puberty at school; he knew about the hormones and crap that ran around in your blood and made you change 'from a boy into a man' as that film they showed was so fond of saying. He could see the faintest moustache on Tim's upper lip and the changed planes of his face. He wondered what it was like. Did you feel it when the hair started to grow? When it started in other places too, did you just wake up one morning and look down and there it was?

Tim rapped the fork on the top of Callum's head. 'What are you staring at, fuck-knuckle?'

Callum blushed. Tim sniggered. Callum felt so young and hairless. 'You're not supposed to swear.'

'Fuck that, and fuck you too.'

Uncle John loomed but didn't seem to have heard the swear-ing. He yanked the fork away from Tim. 'You're supposed to be cooking.'

'I am!'

Uncle John jabbed at the steak and sausages. 'One task, that's all we give you, and you still end up skylarking.'

Callum watched Tim glare at his father then turn his stare on him, and he dropped his gaze and kicked the wall.

In the Unsolved office, Ella reread John Pieters's statements then looked up Peter Constantine on the police intranet. He was still in the job and worked in the Area Command office in Lismore.

She picked up the phone.

'You bet I remember that one,' he said. 'I'm glad to hear somebody's onto it again.'

'What do you recall about John Pieters?'

'Ah, the father.' Constantine paused to let loose a hacking smoker's cough. 'Scuse me. The father had no alibi, and he struck me and Will as a little off.'

'Anything specific?'

'He was really angry,' Constantine said. 'Going on about how it shouldn't have happened, he'd told Tim not to go out, that sort of thing. Have you spoken to him?'

'Just a quick chat today, but I'm going there again tomorrow. He seemed very friendly and helpful. As you can imagine.'

'Hmm,' he said. 'Nothing came of it when we tried, but it'll be interesting to see if time has changed anything. We also took a run at a local perv, what was his name –'

'Garry Thomas.'

'Yeah, nothing there either. And then there was that Wade Tavris – his car was seen skulking nearby, then it was in that robbery and found burnt out later. His girlfriend was his alibi, and I heard when they looked at the case a few years ago they were still together, but you never know your luck. We found no actual evidence though, so whether the car really was stolen as he claimed – well, who knows? Oh, what about DNA? You get anything on those blood drops?'

'Being processed,' she said.

'I hope that shows something. We poked sticks under every rock in the area, shook up the dirtbags and scumsuckers for miles around, talked to hundreds of kids at his school, teachers, tuckshop ladies, maintenance men – shit, we even dressed a dummy in his clothes and stood it on the side of the highway outside the pub in Hornsby – and we got nothing that led anywhere. And believe me, Tynan and I checked it all.'

'Is Tynan still in the job?'

'Dead ten years. The big C.' Constantine coughed again. 'It's getting me too, unfortunately. But anyway. Good luck, and let me know how you go, all right?'

'Thanks,' she said. 'Bye.'

Among the people they'd interviewed at the time were seven locals with records of assaults against young men. Ella propped the file by the monitor and entered their names. One was dead, two were in jail, one hadn't appeared on the system since that time, and three had further records of assaults, drink driving, drug convictions and fraud. One of these, the Wade

Tavris that Constantine had mentioned, had been released from jail late last year. Ella read that he'd been convicted on a manslaughter charge after an unprovoked attack on a young man outside a pub in St Ives five years ago. There'd been nothing further on his record and his parole was going okay. His alibi for the night of Tim's death was his girlfriend, Jane Lincoln, who said he'd spent the night at her flat, though nobody else could corroborate it. He lived in Pendle Hill now, and Ella put Lincoln into the database, crossing her fingers that she didn't appear at the same address.

Searching . . . searching . . .

It must be peak hour on the network. Too many requests frying up the synapses. Ella got up for a coffee.

In the small kitchen a note was taped to the hot water system with 'do not use' scrawled across it. Ella looked in the cupboards for the back-up kettle but found only a dead cockroach and a couple of sugar sachets. She went back to her computer to find it still searching, then ducked downstairs to the café next door.

When she got back to her desk, the long black single shot with one sugar burning her hand through the corrugated cardboard cup, she found the search was done. Jane Lincoln now lived in Concord, a considerable distance from Wade Tavris. Ella smiled into her coffee and hoped that the distance was more than just physical.

It was already late in the afternoon; Lincoln would have to wait for her surprise visit. Instead Ella turned to Callum's statement, taken on the Monday after Tim died.

'My name is Callum McLennan and I'm eleven years old.'

He'd been accompanied by his father, Dr Alistair McLennan. Callum was asked about the birthday barbecue held at the Pieters's house.

'There was an argument,' he'd said.

'Between who?' Constantine had asked.

'Tim and Uncle John and Aunty Tar.'

'Do you know how it started?'

'Tim called me a rude name and Uncle John came over and

said he wasn't cooking the food right. Tim was angry but he just walked away. Later, after tea was over but before they brought the cake out, I heard Tim and Uncle John arguing near the pool. I don't know if it was still about the cooking or not.'

'Was it about swearing at you?'

'I don't think Uncle John heard that.'

'What did Tim call you?'

'I can't say it.'

'It's okay,' his father said.

'We need to know,' Constantine said.

'Well.' He paused. 'It was the f word, with knuckle on the end.'

Ella smiled.

'Thanks,' Constantine said. 'Did you see anyone else arguing, or just your uncle and Tim?'

'I saw Aunty Tar and Dad talk to Tim too. Not for very long though. Both times Tim kind of stamped away.'

'Did Tim ever tell you if he had any enemies? If he'd been in a fight with anyone?'

'No,' Callum said. 'I don't think Tim liked me much. He didn't talk to me like that. Mostly it was swearing, or he'd give me a dead leg or a Chinese burn when nobody was looking, or hit me on the head like he did with the fork at the barbecue.'

Ella guessed he'd started crying then because his father had asked for the interview to end. Poor kid. She saw his date of birth and realised he'd turned eleven the day that Tim's body had been found. Talk about special birthday memories.

It was well after six when Freya pulled up to the station after a busy afternoon. The doors were down, nightshift already out working, and James was leaning on the bonnet of the Commodore talking to a man in his thirties while Robbie jumped along the low wall beside the footpath.

'That's my husband, Matt,' Georgie said as the man waved.

'That's mine, James,' Freya said. 'And our son, Robbie. And

I'm betting that hunched over her iPod somewhere in the car is our daughter, Ainsley.'

She pressed the remote to raise the roller door and backed the ambulance in.

Robbie dashed to the front grille. 'Turn the siren on! Turn the siren on!'

'Not tonight.' Freya had the start of a ferocious headache and the thought of the extra noise made her want to hit someone. 'Did you get your braces?'

He came to the window and bared his teeth.

'Lookin' good,' Freya said.

'Very smart,' Georgie said.

'They hurt,' Robbie said. 'Dad said I could have a McFlurry for tea.'

'Did he,' Freya said. 'What's wrong with vegetable soup?'

Robbie made a gagging sound and ran away.

'Kids,' Freya said. 'You got any?'

'Not even planning.'

'Smart.'

Georgie laughed, picked up her bag and the wad of case sheets and got out. Her husband was all smiley-smiles as he came up the driveway, then looked concerned at the scratches on her face. Freya watched them and saw James was watching them too. *How long since we hugged like that?* She could remember it, how she'd felt moulded to him, her head fitting against his chest, curves against curves, but now something else was there. Or was absent – she hadn't worked out which. Her arms always felt strange around him, and generally he was already moving back when she dropped them away.

This was not how she'd wanted to be as a woman.

She got out of the ambulance and slammed the door.

Up close Georgie's husband, Matt, was gorgeous. He smiled and shook her hand as Georgie introduced them. 'Nice to meet you,' he said.

'You too.'

James came up at a trot. Freya introduced them.

'Down from the sticks, I hear,' James said to Georgie, then faked a jab and cross at her head and laughed: haw haw haw. 'Testing your reflexes. You gotta be ready for anything now you're in the big smoke.' He nodded at the scratches on her face. 'I can see it's already taking it out of you.'

Jesus. Freya wanted to close her eyes and be somewhere else. She wanted not to see the awkward smile on Matt's face and the embarrassed glance Georgie gave her, and the way her husband still had his guard up, ducking and weaving.

She grabbed the case sheets from Georgie's hand. 'We'll be a few minutes with paperwork.'

'Okay,' Matt said.

Haw haw, from James.

In the muster room she turned to Georgie. 'I'm so sorry about that.'

'It's fine.'

'He has trouble when he meets people. He's shy and he tries to cover it up and it comes out as crap like that.'

'It's fine, truly,' Georgie said. 'It's nothing.'

They started filing the case sheets and Freya wondered what her life looked like to Georgie: a husband who acted like a dickhead, a cheeky son, a daughter who never even showed her face.

'You're really lucky that Matt was able to move down with you,' she said.

'His work was happy for him to come,' Georgie said. 'He's doing a training program while he's here. He gets to walk across the bridge twice a day to work: he loves it.'

'Where are you living?'

'My brother's a stockbroker and owns a flat in Milsons Point. He's in London for a couple of months so we're staying there.' Georgie closed the file. 'How about you? Are you nearby?'

'I wish,' Freya said. 'We're in Homebush. Not too far, so I can't really complain. It doesn't compare to Milsons Point though. You got water views?'

'Yeah, it's beautiful.' Georgie looked around. 'We done?'

Freya nodded. She felt she wanted to say something else, but what was there to say?

'Thanks for a good day,' Georgie said.

Freya smiled. 'You too.'

They locked the place up and went out. Matt and James were talking and James hurriedly wound up the conversation as they drew near. Freya didn't want to think about what he'd been saying. She wished he could calm down a little. He used to be so confident, like Matt was now, standing there all relaxed and smiling at her. James looked like he didn't know what to do with his hands. Seven years at the school at Cronulla where he didn't get on with the principal or his fellow teachers, where he'd intimated to her that he sometimes felt bullied but wouldn't talk about it further, had ground away at him. He grabbed Robbie in a headlock. Robbie yowled as he knuckled his skull. Freya's headache worsened.

'See you tomorrow,' Georgie said to her.

'See you.'

She got in the car as James heaved Robbie into the back. Ainsley sat hunched against her door, earbuds in deep.

'Turn it down,' Freya said automatically.

Ainsley scowled.

'Buckle up, buddy,' James said to Robbie. 'You too, chicken.'

'Don't call me that,' Ainsley said.

Freya watched Matt and Georgie walk up the footpath hand in hand.

James got behind the wheel and followed her gaze. 'He's a good-looking guy.'

He used to be secure too.

'Thanks for picking me up,' she said.

'Robbie's appointment ran late so we thought we'd hang around.' He squeezed between taxis onto George Street. 'Matt works in finance, knows about the markets and all that. He's going to give me some advice on getting an investment up and running.'

'With what money?'

'Look in the glovebox.'

She took out an envelope addressed to James with the emblem of Macquarie Secondary College in the corner. 'Oh my God, you got it?'

'I got it.' His grin was miles wide. 'I'm giving my notice at Cronulla tomorrow. Eleven more days and I am done with that place.'

'Fantastic. Well done, honey.'

She unfolded the letter and started to read. *Dear James Craig, we are pleased to be welcoming you as a science teacher at Macquarie,* blah blah, *start in three weeks,* so on and so on. She skimmed the rest and was about to look up and smile at him when the name at the bottom caught her eye.

She put a trembling finger on the page.

James looked. 'Dion Entemann. He's the principal. Really nice guy.'

Freya saw her past explode into life before her eyes. *Dion's hands all over me . . .*

'He's got a couple of daughters at the school himself,' James went on. 'One doing the HSC, one in Ainsley's year.'

Dion up the front of the drama group, telling us to act like we're in love, me trying not to catch his eye, and Georgie beside me, giggling and elbowing me, as oblivious as anyone ever can be, and me acting my heart out, trying to pretend I really am just an innocent sixteen year old.

'Freya?'

'Huh?' Her head was spinning. *Oh my God.*

'I spoke to him this afternoon. The school musical is on tomorrow night and he wants us and the kids to go along. Put in an appearance, meet a few people. You're not working, right?'

First Georgie, now Dion. What is happening to my life?

'Freya?'

'I'm not working,' she said weakly. *Oh my God.*

'I'm not going,' Ainsley said.

'Yes, you are.' James looked at her in the rear-view mirror.

'I'm going to the movies with Celia and Pareese and Donatella.'

James glanced at Freya. 'We've been meaning to talk to you about them,' he told Ainsley.

Freya struggled to pull herself together. 'Not here.'

'Oooh, busted,' Robbie said.

'Shut up, metalmouth.'

'James, please,' Freya said.

'She's got to know sometime.' He looked in the mirror. 'When I start at Macquarie, so do you.'

'*What?*'

'It's long past time we got you away from that school and those goth friends of yours −'

'We're not goths!'

Freya heard the tears in her daughter's voice and put her hand on James's leg. 'Let's save this for home.'

Ainsley kicked the driver's seat. 'This is bullshit.'

Robbie gasped. 'Um-ah!'

'Enough.' James glared at them both.

'You can't do this. You can't just make me change schools.'

'You'll have no friends,' chanted Robbie.

Ainsley punched him. Robbie screamed and burst into tears.

'Enough!' shouted James. 'Both of you stop it right now. When we get home you're going straight to your rooms and I don't want to hear a peep out of you for the rest of the night!'

'What about my McFlurry?' Robbie howled.

Freya pressed her fists to her ears and tried to think.

'It's not fair!' Ainsley raged. 'I hate you all!'

Freya closed her eyes, trying to concentrate, trying to block out her daughter's pain for just a minute.

It'll be okay. He probably won't even recognise you − and even if he does, he'll be every bit as keen to hide the past as you are.

Keener.

'Well, I'm just glad you're okay.' Matt swung Georgie's hand as they crossed the bridge.

'I'm fine.'

'Even though –'

'Yes,' she said. 'Even though.'

They moved to one side of the path to let a jogger go by.

'And is Freya part of the cabal?' he asked.

'Stop laughing.'

'Did you hear a single haw-haw pass my lips?'

She elbowed him. 'I don't know if she is or not. It's weird, though. I knew her in high school, and you should've seen her expression when she first saw me this morning. Hundred per cent dismay.'

'There you go then,' Matt said. 'She can't be part of it. If she was, she'd have known ahead of time it was you and would've been all prepared.'

'Not necessarily. She might've known she was getting some-body for assessment, somebody she had to fail, and that the person's name was Georgina Riley. She only knew me as Geor-gie Daniels, and if I didn't know she'd got married, why would she know that I had?'

'You've really thought this through.'

'I'm serious.'

'Maybe the look on her face was surprise,' he said. 'Ever think of that? And what expression did you have?'

'I don't know. Probably surprise as well.'

'You can't immediately judge her whole moral system by a fleeting expression,' he said. 'How well did you know her at school?'

'We met in Year Seven,' she said. 'She was two years older than me but had missed a lot of school when she'd lived overseas with her parents. We were best friends within a few months and I still thought we were when she suddenly left. There was no phone call, no goodbye or anything. I freaked out, didn't know what had happened – I thought they'd all been kidnapped or murdered or something. Finally I heard she'd gone out west to boarding school. Once I got the address I wrote to her every week for a whole term. I wrote notes in class like we'd done for years, numbered them in order and posted them to her. She wrote back once, a birthday card sent three weeks late.'

'Maybe she was busy,' Matt said. 'Boarding school – she was probably trying to keep afloat, make new friends. Maybe she was so homesick it hurt to write to you.'

Georgie saw herself at fourteen: awkward, gangly, lurching through puberty, her friendship with Freya a lifebuoy she clung to in the storm of her furtive, pathetic life.

'She hurt me.'

Matt put his arm across her shoulders. 'That's probably the reason for her expression,' he said gently. 'She remembers all that and she feels bad.'

'She said that when I asked her.'

'There you go then.'

'But even as she was saying how she's sorry and how she'd wanted to find me to tell me that, I could see there's something else going on in her head.'

'And that's why you think she still might be part of the cabal?'

'I just don't trust her yet.'

Matt pulled her close as they started down the stairs into Milsons Point. 'You're beautiful when you're paranoid.'

She wouldn't tell him about the man she'd seen at the Quay and St Vincent's then. That'd make her so damn beautiful she'd explode.

After dinner, they went out onto the balcony. If disasters could ever have good timing, Georgie had to admit this one did, what with rents in Sydney being so awful. Similarly, the lease on the flat Matt's copper brother, Adam, had been renting in Woolford had run out and now he was able to live at their place and look after things. Still, the unjustness of it all ate away at her.

'This is awright, innit?' Matt said. The lights were coming on in the CBD and the sky was pink and blue over the darkening land.

'I miss home,' she said. 'I miss the grass and the animals and the house.'

'I do too,' he said. 'But this isn't bad.'

She could hear TVs playing in nearby flats, and cars crossing the bridge, and a siren somewhere distant. At home, eleven kilometres from town, there was the sound of birds in trees, and rain sometimes, and the only time you heard a car was if one was coming up the two-hundred-metre driveway, before it was drowned out by Harry's barking.

Matt finished his coffee. 'I'm going in for a shower.'

Georgie waited until she heard the water running then got the phone. Adam answered on the third ring.

'It's me,' she said.

'Hang on.'

She pictured him walking through their house, heard the screen door slam, the squeak of the hinges on the aviary door.

'I'm in,' he said.

'I can't hear them.'

'They're half-asleep, all just looking at me from their perches.'

'Where's Harry?'

'Sitting outside the wire.' Adam moved the phone away from his mouth. 'Speak! Harry, speak!'

The bark echoed down the line and brought tears to Georgie's eyes. The sound died away and was replaced by the peeps of Matt's finches.

'They're all flying around me now,' Adam said.

'How is everything?'

'Pretty good. Except there was a big storm last night and those young double-barreds died.'

'Oh no.'

'I came out partway through to check them and they all seemed okay, but this morning they were dead on the ground,' he said. 'I'm really sorry.'

'It's not your fault.' She felt for Matt. He loved all his birds and loved the young ones more than anything. She heard the shower stop and spoke quickly. 'Any trouble with the McCrows lately?'

'Not that I've heard,' he said. 'Why?'

'Oh, just curious.' She turned her back to the bathroom. 'I bet they all walk the streets real happy they got rid of me.'

'Haven't seen them really.'

She didn't know how else she could ask if Barnaby McCrow was around without being too obvious. If Adam knew she thought she'd seen him – or someone – watching her, he was certain to tell Matt, and Matt would think she was losing it. She would bide her time, see what happened. Ask again next time perhaps.

'Tell you who I did see,' he said. 'Friendly. We got called to this big prang, into the big tree at the bend near the Stratton place. Guy's pissed as a newt, trapped in the wreck, swearing his tits off, takes a special dislike to Friendly and keeps trying to swipe at him while we're cutting the door off. Friendly asked how you are, said he misses you. Said they all do.'

'Not all of them,' Georgie said darkly.

'You know what I mean,' he said. 'Everyone who matters.'

Georgie felt the bite of homesickness. 'Is Harry still there?'

'Speak!'

Harry spoke. The birds cheeped and peeped. Georgie imagined the view from the aviary, the lavender and rosemary gardens leading up to the house, the spread of land to the south, the trees in the distance over which they'd watch storms come up, the purple and black of the clouds making a contrast with the olive green and browns of the leaves that hit her in the heart.

'I want to go home.'

'I know, George,' he said. 'Hang in there.'

Matt was behind her. She turned to face him. 'I want to go home,' she said again.

She held out the phone and he took it and she went out onto the balcony. The tiles were cool underfoot, the headlights streamed across the bridge, and a sudden breeze brought the salt smell of the water. Yes, this was nice, but it wasn't their white house with the gardens they'd dug in themselves, and the chook run they'd built that hot weekend, and the dam down the hill.

She heard Matt say, 'I'll call you back,' and hang up, then he squeezed her shoulder. 'Okay?'

'I'm going to beat this assessment if it kills me,' she said. 'I'll show them all, and go back out there, and Ross will have to eat his words and quit, and Kaspar will get the S/O's job, and we'll be back home with all the animals and everyone will be happy.'

'Okay,' Matt said. He lightly touched the scratches on her face.

'I mean it.'

'I believe you.' He kissed her.

'The babies died.'

'Even if we were there, it could still have happened,' he said. 'We'll breed more.'

They stood with their arms around each other. She could hear the easy movement of air in and out of his lungs, the deep beat of his heart.

'I'm fine, you know,' she said.

He pulled back to look at her. 'Where did that come from?'

'Just so you know.'

'Okay,' he said. 'Good.'

Ella put the chair into position by her bedroom door and looped the rubber exercise band around the handle. She fitted the other end around her wrist and pulled. After fifteen reps the pain burned into her shoulder and chest, and she touched the trembling muscles with the fingers of her other hand. *You can do it! Pain is good!* Mental shouting was good too.

She closed her eyes and counted with one-half of her mind while the other focused on Wayne prodding a stirfry in the kitchen, a towel around his waist, his hair still wet from the shower they'd shared.

He came into the room, spatula in his hand. 'Mind if I put the news on?'

'Go ahead.'

Nineteen, twenty! Wayne's bare legs below that towel!

The newsreader's voice blared into the room: '– *Pieters, mother of Tim, found murdered in Pennant Hills in 1990, chained herself to the fence of Parliament House in protest over the police response to her son's case.*'

Ella let go of the rubber band as the screen filled with the image of Tamara Pieters in the same blue dress she'd been wearing at the school, her wrist chained to a metal fence and security guards and police conferring behind her.

'Shit,' Ella said.

'Tim lived for fewer years than it's taken the police to solve his case,' Tamara called to the camera. 'And even though the government's saying it wants to clean up the state's messy past, that it's putting money into investigating past crimes so the families can have so-called closure, they give us one detective who's brand new to this type of case, injured and working alone, and today when we met she couldn't explain a single step of what she proposes to do.'

'She never asked me that,' Ella said.

Wayne put his hands on his hips.

The news cut to the Minister for Police looking harassed on the steps of Parliament House. 'Mrs Pieters is mistaken,' he said. 'There are two detectives working on her son's case and between them they have considerable experience in the field. The case was only recently taken up by these officers, and it is against policy to discuss the steps of an investigation with anyone.'

'Two?' Ella said.

Wayne looked at her. 'Who's he talking about?'

'Oh God.' Ella sagged in her seat. 'What if it's Murray?'

The newsreader was on again, describing the details of the case, Tim's face from his high school picture smiling over her shoulder. She finished by asking for anybody with any information to contact the Unsolved unit.

'That'll bring all the nutters out of the woodwork,' Wayne said, and went back into the kitchen.

Ella put her wrist back through the band but she'd lost heart for it now. What if she went in tomorrow and found Murray perched on her desk? She thought back – he'd stayed on the floor when she'd left. Oh no. He could have spoken to Galea. They might know each other. Oh crap – his father. That would be it. Frank Shakespeare was sprinkling shit into her life once more. He'd made it his mission to trip her up ever since that time on her first homicide case when she'd barked at him to get the fuck out of the crime scene before she had him arrested. It wasn't her fault: he'd been wearing civvies and it'd been *really* dark, and she dared anyone to recognise the Assistant Commissioner under those circumstances. He'd been retired a few years now but the blue network didn't stop at pension age.

She yanked the band off the door and shot it across the room at the TV.

FOUR

Ella straight-armed the door of the Unsolved unit and walked in tall. She and Wayne had talked during the night and before they'd gone their separate ways from her house that morning, and she was resolute. The chances were slim that her new partner would be Murray, but if it was, well, she hadn't taken crap from him before and she wouldn't do it now. She had a plan for how to work the case and knew where she would begin. Let him read the file and try to catch up.

Her good mate Detective Dennis Orchard – working with him would be a different story. He'd get a laugh out of her problem, no doubt about it, but he was on long-service leave, trekking in Nepal with his wife, Donna, and wouldn't be back for weeks.

She knocked on Galea's closed door but there was no answer. She went into the office. Jackie Fitzhugh was there with Simon Casey, both drinking from steaming takeaway cups. 'Morning,' they said.

Ella put her bag down. 'Anyone else here?'

'Just us,' Jackie said. 'Who're you expecting?'

'Nobody special.'

Ella sat at her desk and opened the file. This morning she

was going to approach John and Tamara Pieters on their own turf, and in order to be across the entire family's versions of what had happened that evening when Tim and John had fought, she needed to finish reading the statements.

Tim's sister, Haydee, had said she'd heard their father telling Tim off for being rude to their Uncle Alistair and Aunt Genevieve. 'Then when Dad said Tim couldn't go out that night, Tim lost it. He started shouting at them, saying they never listened, they didn't let him talk, just told him to shut up and get on with whatever they told him to do, all they ever did was boss him around.'

'Then what happened?' Detective Tynan had asked.

'I was in the kitchen and he came rushing through and almost knocked me over,' she'd said. 'I said something like, watch it, idiot, and he told me to fuck off. I said he was being a little shit and what exactly was his problem and he should pull his head in. He said I was a complete bitch and stomped upstairs. I heard his bedroom door slam and his radio go on. That was the last time we spoke, because an hour or so later Dad went up to talk to him and found the radio still on but Tim gone. He must've sneaked out when we were all outside. Dad was furious. He was storming about, and Mum was telling him to calm down, it would do no good to go after him, he could be anywhere. I only found out the next morning that Dad did go out looking but couldn't find him.'

Ella felt sorry for her. She read to the end, learned that Haydee knew of nobody who might want to harm Tim, then turned to the statements of Tim's aunt and uncle, Genevieve and Alistair McLennan.

Genevieve had said that she'd asked Tim to cut her a slice of the birthday cake and he'd muttered something like 'Get it yourself' and walked away. 'I asked him to come back and repeat himself but he refused,' she'd said. 'Alistair heard this and asked what was the matter. Tim just stood there not saying a word. Alistair tried to make him apologise to me but he wouldn't. Alistair tried to reason with him, saying there was no need for attitude, we were all family, there to care for each other, all he needed to say was sorry and that would be the end of it, but Tim turned and walked away.'

Ella flipped forward to see what Alistair had said about that.

'Teenagers,' he'd said. 'Their brains are different, they have all these hormones rushing through their systems, they don't consider consequences or other people's perspectives or feelings. I wasn't the least bit surprised when Tim walked off.'

'What happened then?' Constantine had asked.

'As I got Genevieve her piece of cake, I heard Tim and John start to argue. I heard John say that they hadn't raised him to act that way towards his family, and Tim said that family wasn't worth shit. Olive – that's Tamara's and Genevieve's mother, she lives with us, and it was her birthday the day before – heard that and gasped, and John really hit the roof. He told Tim to go to his room and stay there, that he was grounded until further notice. Tim started shouting how that wasn't fair, nobody took any notice of what he wanted or needed, they just told him what to do. John told him to go, and Tim rushed into the house.'

Ella leaned back in the chair and stretched her shoulder. Across the room Jackie and Simon were collecting their stuff to go out.

'Any idea when Galea will be back?' Ella asked.

'Sorry.'

That was fine. She could wait to find out who she was going to be teamed up with, and in the meantime work a little faster.

Olive's statement added nothing new. Ella scanned her page of notes one final time and decided she was ready.

The Pieterses still lived in the same house. Ella wondered about that as she raised the brass knocker and let it fall to strike the wood, a hollow sound.

Tamara Pieters opened the door, John coming down the stairs behind her.

'Good morning, Mrs Pieters, Mr Pieters. May we talk?'

Tamara frowned. 'Where's your partner?'

'Busy with other inquiries.'

It wasn't a lie; whoever he, or she, was, they were doing something somewhere.

'Come in, please, Detective,' John said.

Tamara Pieters moved just far enough for Ella to step in. 'I'm not apologising for yesterday.'

'There's no need to,' Ella said. *You can chain yourself to whatever you want.*

'I'll do whatever it takes, you know,' Tamara went on. 'I'll kick up as much stink as I have to to get this case looked into properly.'

'I completely understand.'

Ella smiled at her but Tamara kept her eyes on the door, which she pushed shut with a bang the instant Ella was clear. Ella followed John down the hall, trying to imagine Tamara's feelings: your young son is killed, the police come up with nothing, you struggle on somehow, maybe sometimes you forget it for a while, and now, almost twenty years later, you have to rehash every painful detail once more. *But then*, she thought, taking a seat on the lounge John indicated, *wouldn't you be keen to catch the killer, no matter what? Wouldn't the pain of raking over old graves* – she held back a shudder at her use of the old cliché – *be worth it, if we manage to solve it this time?*

Of course, that was the problem, right there. *If.* Tamara, standing now in the doorway, her eyes straying from Ella across the room to the framed pictures of Tim and his siblings that filled the opposite wall, probably didn't believe the case would be solved. *The older the case, the colder the trail.*

'Coffee? Tea?' John Pieters asked.

Ella blinked. 'Black coffee with one, thank you.'

John clinked about in the kitchen. Tamara stayed in the doorway, one white-knuckled hand gripping the jamb. Ella looked at her, then at the photos. 'May I?'

Tamara shrugged.

Ella crossed the beige carpet. The wall was a chronological

record of the family's life, starting with a couple of early pictures of John and Tamara, young and laughing on a seawall somewhere, then waving from a white Mini, then smiling in a formal portrait at their wedding. The next picture was of a hugely pregnant Tamara, followed by her and John, grins from ear to ear, a swaddled sleeping baby held between them. That would be Haydee. There she was again, aged about three, planting a kiss on the head of a baby Ella guessed was Tim. Then there was Tim as a toddler and Haydee in school uniform with baby Josh. His Down's wasn't so evident there, but in the next picture, taken when he was about two, the condition was obvious.

The photos progressed through Christmases and birthdays, new bikes, plaster casts on Tim's arm at one point, Haydee's leg at another. There was Haydee at the end of high school, her uniform covered in signatures, carnations behind both ears; and there was Tim holding his School Certificate – and then Tim was gone. A picture of the family without him, around Haydee in a gown and mortarboard, everyone's smiles except for Josh's appearing forced.

'It tore the heart out of our family,' Tamara said, right at Ella's shoulder.

'I can understand that.'

Tamara studied her. 'Can you.'

Ella held her gaze. 'I can't imagine it, but I can understand it.'

Tamara turned away and sat down as John came back with a tray of coffee cups and a heavy-set young man.

'This is our son Josh,' he said.

Josh put out his hand and Ella took it in hers. 'Nice to meet you.'

'You're going to catch the bad man who hurt Tim?'

'That's the plan.'

He smiled at her. She smelled chocolate on his breath.

'I'm going to my room, Dad,' he said, and headed upstairs.

Ella sat down opposite John. Tamara was in a chair to one side, her body angled away from Ella, her chin in her hand and her eyes on the ceiling.

Ella said, 'I know this is upsetting to have to go over again, and I'm sorry about that.'

John held up a hand. 'May I show you something first?'

'Of course.'

He took a box from under his chair and set it in his lap, and Tamara muttered something. It looked to Ella like a plain cardboard shoebox, decorated long ago with paint in blue swirls. He held the corners like it might fly away if released.

'Tim made this when he was in fifth class for his Matchbox collection.'

Ella nodded.

John lifted off the lid and took out a thick spiral notebook, two hundred pages Ella guessed, made even thicker by the clippings he'd glued in. 'I've been making some notes.' He handed it over.

The first page was blank, as if to give the reader an extra second to reconsider their actions and close the book again. The second page held a glued-on, folded-up sheet of newspaper, and as Ella carefully unfolded it she realised it was the original report of Tim's murder from the local paper. The paper was yellowed and soft with age. She stared down at the page and heard Tamara Pieters get up and leave.

'If you turn to the back,' John said, leaning towards her, 'you'll see.'

Ella refolded the newspaper clipping and closed the cover, then turned the notebook over and opened the back.

MILAT. The word was black and stark, underlined and boxed in with heavy strokes of a biro, as if the lines could contain the word and what it meant.

James Gibson, missing in 1989 – his body found in Belanglo in 1993 – his backpack and camera found in GALSTON GORGE in Feb 1991.

'It's possible, don't you think?' John said. 'Milat was all over the place, working on the roads. Galston's not far north, and if you come down the Old Pacific Highway from there you go straight past the pub where Tim was that night.'

Ella looked up at him then back at the page.

'I told the police about it six years ago. They said they'd take it into account but I never heard any more. I just wanted to let you see. I wanted to show you. I mean, it's possible, that's really all I'm saying. It's not impossible.'

'No,' Ella said. 'It doesn't fit Milat's known actions, though.'

John shifted in his chair. Ella felt for him.

'I will look into it,' she said gently. 'Thank you.'

John stared at the notebook. 'I was supposed to protect him. That's my job as his dad. But I didn't know he'd gone. And even if I knew he was going, what could I do? Should I have grabbed him, locked him inside? Is that even right?' He looked despairing. 'But why worry about that, when anything would have been better than what happened?

'I went out looking, I searched and searched. And to know that at the same time, somebody had him, somebody was hurting him and he was dying, makes me feel . . .' His hands shook. 'It just about kills me.'

Ella nodded.

'I think about it,' he said. 'I wonder if I drove past in the car. I wonder if Tim saw me and cried out for me to help him.' Tears poured down his face. 'He was my son, and I let him down.'

Ella saw a box of tissues across the room and brought it over. It was good that he let it out, that he get comfortable with her. She put her hand on his shoulder.

'I'm sorry,' he said after a couple of minutes, wiping his eyes. 'This isn't helping you.'

She handed him his cup of tea. 'Where did Tamara go just now?'

'Out the back.' He sipped. 'She spends a lot of her time in the granny flat there. She has problems, as you probably saw on the news last night. She likes to spend time alone. She doesn't sleep well and her restlessness affected my sleep too.'

'So she moved out there?'

'It was the best thing,' John said.

Interesting.

'You'll have to forgive her for being a little hostile,' he said. 'She put all her hope into Tynan and Constantine, got close to them, I guess, but then over time the case went nowhere. Eventually the detectives were changed – which I understand, it happens, people move on to different jobs – but one night she said to me with this awful realisation spreading across her face that this is just a job for them.'

'While to her it's her whole life,' Ella said.

'Exactly.' He put his cup on the table. 'There's no doubt that it's changed the whole family, but she in particular has found it extremely hard. She said to me once that she sees the world differently now, that the fact that Tim could be killed changed her relationship to everyone. She said she still walks through shopping centres looking at people, thinking, is it you? Is it you? It haunts her that the person is out there but will probably never be identified.'

'I still have some hope, though she tells me I'm a fool,' he said. 'I know what she's saying, everyone knows that the longer a case goes unsolved the less chance there is of solving it, but I can't help it. I have to hope for justice for Tim, and also, I guess, I hope that if the killer is found then some part of my heart might be repaired. Just a little.'

Ella nodded. 'It makes sense to me.'

Her mobile buzzed in her pocket. 'Excuse me.' She checked the screen. Her parents' number. She let it go to voicemail.

'You can take that if you need to,' he said.

'It's fine.' She hesitated before going on. 'John, I need to ask you some questions.'

'I know. Ask away.'

'I've been reading about the argument you and Tim had at the barbecue. Tim seemed angry about something before it all started, but none of the statements say what it was.'

He nodded. 'We've all asked ourselves the same thing. I remember he was in a bad mood that evening and didn't want to be there, but it's a family tradition and I told him he had to. Also, I guess maybe my pulling him up about getting on with the job of manning the barbecue, which he usually enjoyed but that night was terrible at, put him in a worse one.'

'Had something happened in his life?'

'Again, I don't know,' he said. 'He was going through an uncommunicative stage and it was almost impossible to get more than a grunt out of him. I talked to his friends after it happened and they said he'd been moody that night, they presumed about the argument, but he hadn't confided in them. He never really did.'

'Except Damien Millerton.'

'You're talking about the gay thing.'

'Yes.'

'I don't know,' John said. 'I didn't know about it then, and I've thought and thought about it since, and I never saw any indication that he might have been that way, or that the experience Damien thought Tim was talking about had actually happened.'

'Do you think one or both of them was lying?'

'No, no,' he said. 'I think Damien might have either misunderstood him or . . . I don't know. I just can't see it.'

It wouldn't be the first time parents had no idea what their kids were doing. They'd already said in their statements at the time they hadn't known about his drinking, and sexuality was something that kids kept even closer to their chests.

'Do you know if Tim had a girlfriend?'

'Not that I knew about,' John said. 'There was nothing to indicate anything was going on: no phone calls or letters that I knew of, and he wasn't sneaking out at night or anything like that.'

Ella nodded. In 1990 there'd been no email, no IMing, no mobile phones to ask about. 'Have you kept in contact with his friends?'

'Damien and Gareth stayed around for a while; they'd drop in and see us every month or so at first, then, on Tim's birthday, and then when they finished high school,' he said. 'Tamara couldn't stand to see how they were growing, that they were young men by the end of high school and Tim hadn't got that far. It was hard for them too, I've got no doubt about that, and I always told them how grateful I was that they took the time to come around.'

'When was the last time you had contact?'

'About five years ago we got a card from Damien saying he was getting married. Haven't heard from Gareth for probably eight, maybe ten, years.'

'They haven't been in touch now that the case is in the news again?'

He shook his head.

'Did Tim have a family doctor?'

'His uncle, Tar's brother-in-law,' John said. 'Alistair McLennan.'

'Was he aware of what Damien had said?'

'I don't know. I never talked about it with him. I'm not sure if he ever brought it up with Tar; if he did, she never told me.'

'Does he live locally? I'd like to speak to him sometime.'

John crossed to a hutch and took out a business card. 'That's his surgery address and phone number.'

Ella saw it was in West Pennant Hills, just five minutes away. But first a quiet word with Tamara. 'Thank you.'

'Anything to help.' John's eyes were wet with tears. 'Anything.'

Georgie glanced at Freya, who was hunched, frowning, behind the wheel. 'You okay?'

'What?'

'Are you all right?'

Freya made a face. 'Stuff on my mind. Domestic stuff, you know.'

Georgie almost made a crack about James and his haw-haw laugh but caught herself. 'I know the feeling.'

Freya overtook a bus. 'Would you mind if I asked you something?'

Georgie put her elbow on the sill. They were on the highway, heading west to pick up a patient at Nepean Hospital for transfer to Royal Prince Alfred. The morning sun shone through the rear windows, lighting the inside of the ambulance. The sky was burnished blue and Georgie felt good, even though she knew what Freya was going to ask. 'It's about the accident, right?'

'Huh?'

Georgie glanced across at her. 'The accident that got me sent here. The one where I hit the guy lying on the road.'

'I heard about that,' Freya said.

Usually people wanted all the details so they could imagine themselves in her place and think how they wouldn't have done what she did, how they would've stayed calmer and not got into the same situation.

'That's not your question?' she said.

Freya shook her head and something lifted inside Georgie.

'I wanted to ask how long you've been married.'

'Eight months,' Georgie said. 'You?'

'Fourteen years,' she said. 'Ainsley's fifteen going on twenty-one, and Robbie's ten, and sometimes I wonder who the hell's life I've stepped into. My mother once said to me that my turn would come, that I'd realise when I had kids of my own what I put her through, and wouldn't you know it, she's right.'

'I remember your mum,' Georgie said. 'How's she doing? And your dad?'

'They're okay. Yours?'

'Same.'

Freya pulled out to overtake a truck heaped with tyres. 'So.'

Here it comes. 'The accident.'

'Well, yeah. D'you mind?'

'Not so much any more,' Georgie said. 'It was three weeks before our wedding. I was on call, and I'd been out and done a chest pain with my mate Kaspar. The job was past his place so I'd picked him up on the way to save him driving his ambulance, you know? Afterwards I'd dropped him back at his house and was driving home in my ambulance about midnight. It was dark, I mean really dark: no moon or anything. Our house is eleven kays out of town so I was on small country roads, no lights, no traffic around, nothing. I almost hit a roo and was swearing about it – we had ambulances in the workshop all the time because of roos – when I rounded a bend and hit something lying on the road.'

Freya was silent.

'I thought I'd run over another roo, one that somebody else had hit,' Georgie said. 'I pulled over to check for damage to the ambulance. As I got out I looked back along the roadway but it was too dark to see anything. At the front of the ambulance I bent to see the grille and bonnet.' She'd said these words so often, in her statements to police, to management, to her union rep. It never got easier. 'There was a bit of green cloth caught in the edge of the numberplate. A bit of T-shirt.'

'Shit.'

Georgie left out the shakes, the stumbling run back to the driver's door, the screeching U-turn. 'I hit the high beams when I turned and saw him lying on the road.'

'Oh shit, Georgie.'

'He was unconscious, hypoventilating. He had head and abdo injuries. I screamed on the radio for help.' They'd played that back to her and she'd hardly recognised her voice, words running into one another, *dilatedpupilsfacialfracturesavulsedjaw*. 'There were tyre marks on his skin. I couldn't get the tube in so had to bag him. I got the monitor on and his rate was slowing. I couldn't stop bagging to cannulate. I screamed into the portable for the back-up to hurry.' *Getmesomefuckinghelp!* 'An ambulance finally pulled up but nobody got out.'

'What?'

'Kaspar was driving, he had his door open a little bit so the cabin light was on. I could see that the S/O, Ross Oakes, was in the passenger seat. He had hold of Kaspar's arm so he couldn't get out.'

'What? Why?'

'Ross said later that he was concerned about where I'd parked my ambulance and whether they should move theirs to protect the scene more,' Georgie said. 'Kaspar said that was right, Ross was indeed going on about that, while he – Kaspar – was yelling that they needed to help me and worry about the vehicles later. But Ross wouldn't let him go.'

'Holy crap.'

'I guess it wasn't long, one or two minutes maybe, but it was long enough for me to see absolutely red,' Georgie said. 'I ran over to the ambulance and screamed at Ross to get out and help. He did, but later that night he reported me for leaving the patient, said I'd panicked and I wasn't fit to do the job. The man died and the area super came out and I was suspended. Ross claimed that I could've stopped the ambulance before running over him, I was probably looking at myself in the mirror or something and not watching the road, and I should be charged. The police investigated and found it truly was an accident and didn't charge me, but the dead man's family, who are related to Ross through some distant cousin, believed him and between them all they started this campaign to get me sacked.'

'What the hell was his problem?'

'He's one of those old-school guys who reckon girls shouldn't be in the job,' Georgie said. 'When I got engaged, he bitched about how first I'd take maternity leave and then would be wanting to go part-time and expect special treatment like not having to work overtime because I had a baby at home. He reckons girls get priority treatment from the bosses and get promoted faster, and cause problems on the station because nobody can relax and be themselves while there's a girl around. Two previous female officers had left after making a heap of complaints about him and finding that management just didn't want to know. It was easier for the bosses to sweep it under the carpet than try to deal with it, especially when you tried to explain the things that were happening – like that he was pissing on the toilet seat in the ladies and, yes, I could be certain of that because it was only him and me on the shift and it wasn't there before and I sure hadn't done it; or that he'd use a distinctly different tone of voice with me than with the others. The bosses told me I was being silly. Or else it came down to his word against mine. Especially when he'd done such outrageous things that they found it hard to believe me. Like that email I supposedly sent to every officer in the state: that was him.' She shook her head. 'I'll never keep my password in my locker again. I should've guessed he'd have a master key.'

'I remember that email,' Freya said. 'We all just figured it couldn't be real.'

'I wish management had felt the same way.'

'How on earth could they have thought you wrote it? Who would say they fantasised about stabbing their patients and colleagues?'

'They said because I was just out of the psych ward I could have sent it and "not remembered".'

'Oh, I didn't – I mean, we honestly thought the whole thing was a hoax.'

'No, I really was in a psych ward,' Georgie said. 'Because of a job I did where this girl died. You know how it is. Sometimes one gets through your defences.'

Freya nodded. 'Sorry again.'

'It's okay,' Georgie said. 'But as I said, that was nothing in comparison to some of his other stunts. A few months after the accident, we collected an old lady from a nursing home and took her to hospital for treatment for a UTI. She had pretty bad dementia, so she didn't speak or interact, just lay there in her own little world. Ross was driving –'

'Jesus, you had to work with him even after that?'

'He rostered us like that,' Georgie said. 'I think he thought he'd get under my skin quicker that way. Anyway, this poor old lady was a concentration camp survivor and she had a number tattooed on her arm. In the hospital, we were about to slide her across to the Emergency Department bed when Ross catches sight of it. He grabs hold of her arm and starts rubbing his thumb across the tattoo, and he says, "Imagine, a Nazi put this on her. A Nazi held her arm while she screamed and writhed, just like I'm holding her now", and he tightened his grip until she started to wince.'

'No way.'

'I got stuck into him, told him to let her go and leave her alone,' Georgie said. 'But then he looks across the bed at me with this glint in his eye, looks around to check nobody's nearby, then bends down close to the lady and hisses "Heil Hitler!" in her ear.'

'Oh my God.'

'I rushed round to his side of the bed and yanked him away. "What the hell is wrong with you?" I said. He said, "She can't hear, she can't understand, so what's the big deal?" I was so angry I couldn't even speak. We moved the lady onto the bed then Ross took the stretcher out. I bent down to her and said I was so sorry, I even hugged her as best I could, her just lying there, but she didn't move or speak or respond. I hope she didn't understand him, but who could tell?

'I found the nurse and asked if she'd heard it, but she hadn't. Nobody had. So when I put in my complaint to the area super, Ross denied it all, said it was a horrible thing to accuse him of, he would never, ever do such a thing.' She shook her head. 'They believed him, and there was another black mark against my name.'

'But what a thing to invent!' Freya said. 'Who on earth would make that up?'

'That's what I argued,' Georgie said. 'It didn't matter. Ross was orchestrating this whole thing against me, and in the end the pile got so big, and what with the dead man's family complaining to the media, management decided to act and sent me here.'

'Oh man, he really hates you.'

'It's because I stood up to him from my very first day,' Georgie said. 'He made a crack about my lunch looking like dog food and started barking. I told him to stop it. He said, "Ooh, this one's a lively bitch," and came right up to me and air-humped my leg, if you can picture that. I told him to back off or I'd call the area super. He laughed and did it more so I got on the phone.'

'And let me guess,' Freya said. 'Nobody else was on station to back up your version of events.'

Georgie nodded. 'Ross put on this big act, whining about how all the girls who come to Woolford cause such trouble and this is why they shouldn't be allowed in the job. The super hemmed and hawed and said we should just try to get along.'

'Good old management.'

Georgie nodded. 'I'm curious: why did they tell you I was coming?'

'They said you were here for a six-week review and assessment. At the end of the period, if you were judged non-competent there'd be a hearing at which you'd be asked why you should keep your position.'

'The famous rubber-stamp hearing,' Georgie said. 'In other words I'd be sacked.'

'I have to say that was the impression I got.'

'Was it Butterworth who told you?'

Freya shook her head. 'Our area super came to the station, and Ken called me into his office to talk to her. She said there'd been some trouble at your home station and it was thought best to assess you somewhere else.'

'They didn't elaborate about the trouble?'

'I asked,' Freya said. 'They didn't tell me.'

'What's the super's name? Where's she from?'

'She's never worked out that way, far as I know,' Freya said. 'Lilian Stronach. She's been in the job about seventeen years, mostly as S/O on the northern beaches then back into the CBD the last few years. Been the super here for about a year now. Seems okay. She listens, at least.'

'That only really counts if she acts on what she hears,' Georgie said.

Even if Stronach hadn't worked out west, it was possible that she'd met Ross some other way, or that somebody higher up was pulling her string, and that the planned outcome was indeed to have Georgie face that so-called hearing. Although the fact that she hadn't told Freya the details of the situation hinted at the possibility of an astute mind.

It didn't really matter. It was best to trust no one.

'Mate, you'll be fine. And dinosaurs like Ross can't go on forever.' Freya drove into the hospital. 'His meteor is coming.'

Georgie said, 'But what worries me is what kind of shit-storm he'll try to pull off before he dies.'

Callum sat at his desk with Ella's card in one hand and the phone in the other.

'Feel like some reading?' Anna said.

He looked up at her. She held a collection of meeting minutes and committee reports half a ream thick. 'More?'

'This is only some of it.'

He sighed. 'Just leave it there.'

She put it down in front of him then went back to her desk. Callum swivelled his chair away from the pile and pressed Ella's number into the phone.

'This is Detective Marconi of the Unsolved unit. Please leave your message and I'll call you back when I can.'

He thought for a split second about hanging up. 'Hi, it's Callum McLennan. We met yesterday at the school, at the sports-centre opening for my cousin. Tim Pieters.' He shut his eyes. 'I just wanted to apologise for my aunt. That is, I take it you saw the news last night? I had no idea she would do something like that, and I hope it hasn't caused you any problems. Also, uh, I wondered if you wanted to interview me. Just let me know.' He recited his mobile number. 'Thanks very much.'

He pressed the button, the line clicked in his ear and it was over. He put the phone down gently. She was probably terribly busy, she could be on the edge of some breakthrough; anything could be going on in there.

He stared out the window at the green spire of St Stephen's across Macquarie Street.

1990

The day of the funeral was hot. Callum's new birthday jeans were too big. His mum cupped the back of his neck with her hand, then threaded a belt through the loops and pulled it tight.

'How's that?' she said.

'Good.'

Going downstairs behind her, he slid his thumb under the bunched-up denim pressing into his stomach.

In the garage, he stood by his bike against the back wall while his mum helped Nanna Olive into the front seat. His dad put his hand on the handlebars then rubbed Callum's shoulder. 'How you doing?'

'Fine.'

The drive to the crematorium was long and bright. Callum stared out the window at the people doing normal things on this normal Wednesday, a mother and child arguing in the car next to them at the lights. He thought of Scott and Andrew and the others at school, burning more lines on their plywood squares in Art, while he was in a car next to his mother, who kept raising her sunglasses to dab her eyes and look across at him.

'You all right?' she said.

'Yep.'

His dad glanced around. His eyes were red. Directly in front of Callum, Nanna Olive sighed and sighed.

There were TV crews set up outside the chapel. Inside it was gloomy at first, then Callum saw the coffin on a silver stand at the front, piled high with white flowers. His mother took his hand as they walked up the aisle. Her palm was sweaty and he felt the muscles moving as her fingers tightened and loosened against his. They sat in the second row from the front, and Josh turned and smiled at them and held up a red toy bulldozer.

'Nice,' Callum said.

Uncle John had his arm around Aunt Tamara's shoulders. Haydee was crying against Nanna Olive's chest. Beyond them was the coffin. Callum tried not to look at it, but then music started playing, a song he didn't know but which made his mother cry and tighten her grip and his father take her other hand, and all that time the coffin just stood there and he couldn't help but imagine Tim inside it, Tim's long legs under that bit of the flowers there, his face up the other end, all of him lying still under the lid.

'You okay?' his mother whispered.

He lifted her arm over him and pressed into her side, sliding down on the chair so his head was in her armpit. He listened to the beat of her heart instead of the talking going on up the front. He closed his eyes so he didn't have to watch Uncle John stand by the coffin with one hand clutching the shiny wood and the other dropping pages, and Aunt Tamara gather Haydee and Josh to her like a hen pulling chickens in under her feathers.

He concentrated hard on the sounds of his mother's heart-beat and breathing, the air going in and out, the movement of her ribs against his face, the feel of her arm down his back and her hand on his hip. When music played again and people cried louder, he squeezed his eyes closed and went further into that warm place. When she placed her other hand on his face and tilted it up to her, kissed his forehead and whispered that it was over, he came back.

There were sandwiches and cake and cups of tea on the verandah. He stood with Josh, who put a slice of cake in the bull-dozer's scoop and knelt in the dirt and ferried it around among the rose bushes. He butted the dozer into Callum's school shoe and the cake fell out. 'Tim's dead,' he said. 'The bad man did it.'

The bad man. Callum thought about him being out there somewhere and wondered if he felt anything about what he'd done. He saw the detective he'd talked to, holding a cup of tea and listening to somebody but with his eyes everywhere. Callum looked around as well. Schoolboys in uniform pushed their socks down in the heat, a woman in a hat patted Aunt Tamara's arm, a man brought Nanna Olive a glass of water. Uncle John and a man in a blue suit stood together talking, the man hold-ing two cups of tea as Uncle John used both hands to wipe a paper serviette across his forehead then across his eyes and keep it there.

The detective watched Uncle John steadily. Callum had overheard his parents talking late last night and knew that the police thought maybe Uncle John had done it. He didn't think it was right for them to think that. Uncle John was as gentle as his dad. In fact, if he'd had to pick anyone in his family as most likely to kill someone, it would've been Tim himself.

The man put his arms around Uncle John, the teacups still in his hands high behind his back. The detective ate a slice of cake. Josh ran the dozer over Callum's shoe and the sun beat down on them all and Callum wondered if something so broken could ever get fixed.

Ella walked out the back of the Pieterses' house to the granny flat. Sunlight glinted off the in-ground pool and leaves dotted the top of the brick barbecue. Ella pictured the family here that last night, the smell of the meat cooking, the birthday cake on a plastic tablecloth, the argument rising up into the air.

The door of the granny flat was closed. Ella knocked.

Tamara opened it and looked out.

'May we talk for a moment?' Ella said.

Tamara came out and sat on the low wall by the barbecue. Ella stayed on her feet.

'John said you spend most of your time out here now.'

Tamara shrugged.

'May I ask why?'

'He snores,' she said. 'I can't sleep through it any more, so I put the light on to read then he wakes up and complains.'

'The other bedrooms weren't far enough?'

'I could still hear him. If I don't get any sleep I feel even worse than I do normally.'

Ella nodded. 'John and I were just talking about the argument at the barbecue on the night that Tim died.'

Tamara shrugged again.

Going to be like that, is it?

'I'd like to know what you remember of that evening.'

'Everything,' she said.

'About the argument specifically.'

'Tim was cranky that evening, and he wasn't happy about cooking, and then he was rude to my sister and her husband, and then John had words with him, and then he left.' Tamara slapped the leaves from the barbecue plate. 'It's all in my statement.'

'So I read,' Ella said. 'Your thoughts haven't changed?'

'Into what?'

'Let me try this another way,' Ella said. 'Who do you think did it?'

Tamara stood up. 'That's surely a question for me to ask you.'

'That isn't an answer, Mrs Pieters.'

Tamara went into the granny flat and shut the door. Ella knocked.

'Mrs Pieters, open the door, please.'

She heard the lock turn. Her mobile rang. While knocking again, she looked at the screen. Galea.

'Where are you?' he said. 'There's a letter here about your case.'

She stepped away from the door. 'From who?'

'Anonymous.'

Ella started running across the yard.

FIVE

Ella burst into Galea's office. 'What's it say?'

He held out an evidence bag containing a sheet of blue paper. She took it and read the single line: *You need to talk to the girl who found the body.*

The handwriting was stiff and blocky. Deliberately disguised. She turned the bag over. The back of the page was blank.

'Prints?' she asked.

'A couple of smeared partials, nothing good enough to use.'

'Envelope?'

'No usable prints there either.' He held out another evidence bag. 'Posted last night in the city, probably at a postbox in the southern end of the CBD. Self-adhesive stamp and back, so no saliva for DNA.'

Ella reread the front. *The girl who found the body.*

'I guess it's a response to Tamara's performance on the news last night,' Galea said. 'Someone's got significant guilt to act so quickly.'

It was a good sign.

At her desk Ella checked her phone messages with one hand while pulling up the case file with the other. Her mother had called, and she remembered the voicemail beep earlier. Well, that would have to wait. Callum had called too, and while thumbing

87

through the sheaf of statements she scribbled a note to herself to call him back.

The statement by the girl who'd found the body was three pages long. Georgina Elisabeth Daniels had been fourteen and living with her parents in Hampden Road, not far from the Pieters family's house. She'd been walking her dog early that Sunday morning and when the dog hadn't come out of the long grass by the road she'd gone in to get him. She'd run to the closest house for help, then returned to the body to 'kind of stand guard'. She'd said, 'I was worried that somebody else might find him, you know, a little kid or something, and freak out.'

Ella thought it was lucky she hadn't freaked out herself. At fourteen she was hardly a mature adult.

The ambulance came, then the local police, and she'd given her details, then this official statement had been made later that day, by which time Tim had been identified. Turned out they'd gone to the same school. Tim had been two years ahead of her and she'd said she didn't really know him.

She'd signed her name at the bottom of each page, a girlish and self-conscious signature with an elaborate loop in the 'G' and a circle over the 'i'.

Ella studied the letter again. What could she know that she hadn't already told them? Had something happened in the intervening years? Often information came from disgruntled ex-partners, but it wasn't as if Georgina had had one at the time of Tim's death. Unless she'd known more than she'd let on and had told somebody since?

Ella read the interview with Ronald Gordon, the occupant of the house where Georgina had gone for help. Nothing that he said stood out as odd either, though there were more documents detailing a second death in the street that day. Eighty-two-year-old Lucille Oldham had lived five doors up from Gordon and was found in her house by police officers during the canvass of the street. The front door was wide open and she lay just inside, wearing a nightie and dressing gown. She had no signs of injury and the post-mortem found she'd died of a heart attack during that night. Constantine speculated that she may have seen or heard something, gone to her door to investigate, and somehow come into contact with or been threatened by the killer, but none of the other neighbours had noticed anything odd, none had heard a sound, there was no evidence of a break-in to follow up, there was in fact no evidence at all, and the investigation into her death had gone nowhere.

Ella turned to her computer and typed in Georgina's name and date of birth. It came back with a match to a Georgina Elisabeth Riley living out in the west of the state. She picked up the phone and dialled her number.

'Hello?'

Ella explained who she was. 'Is Georgina Riley there, please?'

'She's in Sydney. She's a paramedic stationed in The Rocks,' the male voice said. 'I'm her brother-in-law, Adam. I'm a senior constable here in Woolford. Is everything okay?'

'I need to speak to her about a statement. Do you have a number where I can contact her, please?'

'Got a pen?'

Ella wrote down the mobile number he recited and thanked him.

'No worries,' he said.

Ella dialled Georgina's number.

In RPA's ambulance bay, Freya tucked the clean sheet over the stretcher mattress and put the folded blanket on the end. She was sick to death of the thoughts going round and round in her head: worries about Dion, about tonight when she'd see him, whether he'd recognise her, and what would happen then. Nothing, she tried to tell herself, *nothing*, but it seemed impossible to believe. She sat on the ambulance's back step and sighed.

Georgie stuffed the plastic-wrapped pillow into the pillow-case and plumped it down on the bed, then eyed the café across the road. 'Coffee?'

'Not for me,' Freya said. 'Feel like crap.'

'Domestic stuff can do that to you,' Georgie said. Her mobile started ringing and she took a few steps away to answer.

Domestic, whatever, Freya thought. Tonight would take just a few hours and then it'd be over, and who knew, maybe she'd never have to see him again. Maybe he really wouldn't recognise her. Maybe she was getting all knotted up for nothing. She pulled herself to her feet and loaded the stretcher into the ambulance. Maybe . . . Oh, bullshit. It was going to be bad.

'Hey.' Georgie had her hand over the phone, a funny look on her face. 'Do you remember Tim Pieters?'

Past and present collided and the earth shook under Freya's feet.

'You okay?' Georgie grabbed her arm. 'Here, sit down. You look like you're going to pass out.'

'It's . . .' Freya struggled to think. 'Abdo pain.' She put a hand on her right lower quadrant for effect. *Oh no. No, no, no.*

'Do you remember him?'

'Rings a little bell,' Freya lied. 'Guy from school who was killed?'

Georgie nodded. 'This is a detective wanting to talk to me about how I found his body. They've reopened the case.'

The world spun.

'She says it's urgent. Reckon it's okay if I say to meet me here? Reckon Control will give me a little time?'

Freya shut her eyes and tried to breathe.

'Man, you look terrible,' Georgie said. 'You should go in and see a doctor.'

An idea fell into Freya's burning brain. 'I think I will. Tell Control we're off the road for a bit and you can meet the detective while I'm getting seen.'

'Great! You want a hand to get in there?'

'It's okay.' Freya got up, hand pressed to her side. As she walked slowly away she heard Georgie say into the phone, 'Can you come to RPA?'

When the Emergency doors slid shut behind her, she sagged against the wall, trying to clear her mind, trying to *think*.

Okay. Even if she had to lie to a doctor, she would stay inside for as long as it took for Georgie's little tête-à-tête to be over, because if she was to run into that detective, and Georgie mentioned that she'd gone to Tim's school too, oh, and she'd left pretty much right after he died – well, that was curious wasn't it? There was sure to be digging. And while she and Dion had been lucky before, she was terrified that their luck might have run out.

The single good thing was that through Georgie she might be able to find out what exactly was going on, and just how much they knew.

This had to be it. Late model dark blue Falcon, unobtrusive aerial on the back. Georgie watched the car pull into the Police Only spot in RPA's ambulance bay. The woman who got out was a little on the short side, her dark hair blowing everywhere in the breeze, her sense of purpose obvious.

'I'm Detective Ella Marconi,' she said. They shook hands. 'So what do you remember about finding Tim Pieters's body?'

'I was walking our dog at about six,' Georgie said. 'He was a pain, he had this internal clock and woke up that early every day. The other days of the week Mum or Dad took him for a walk, but Sundays I had to do it, and get the paper while I was out. I didn't mind really. It was kind of nice being out and about early, before anyone else.' She felt like she was clogging up the story with useless information but the detective didn't appear bothered. 'We headed down towards the park because he liked to have a run there on the oval. We were going along the side of the road and I'd let him off his leash already.'

She remembered the crunch of the gravel under her feet, the smell of the bush, the conversation of a family of magpies as they pecked their way across the oval. Wally's tags jingled on his collar as he trotted along then veered off into the grass.

'I kept walking and called him. When he didn't come I jangled the chain on his lead but he still wouldn't come out.'

She saw herself standing there in the sunshine, one hand on her hip, thinking he'd found something disgusting to roll in, and when she got home she'd have to postpone flipping through the paper in the sun and give him a bath instead. 'I went back and called him again. I could hear his tags clinking. I told him he was a little shit.' Big words for the fourteen year old she'd been. She remembered them falling into the sunlit morning like stones. 'Then he whimpered.' The sound had chilled her. 'I thought he must be hurt, or maybe trapped in some way. I went into the grass and saw something but I didn't really have time to think about what it was because the next thing I was right on him.'

She remembered the utter stillness of the body. She'd told kids at school who asked, with their eyes full of a curiosity and desire that she now saw every day when people brought up her job, that he'd looked asleep, but he hadn't. He'd looked dead.

'Go on,' Ella said.

Georgie blinked. 'Wally was snuffling round near his face. I shouted at him, and when he came back I grabbed him and started running to that house.'

'You were frightened?'

'A little, I guess,' Georgie said. 'Mostly I just knew I had to tell somebody. And he was . . . I don't know, I could recognise from his back that he was young, and it felt so wrong that he was lying there, and nobody knew where he was. His family, I mean. They would've been worried.'

Ella nodded. 'And then what?'

'I banged on the door until the man opened it,' Georgie said. 'He had the shits until he saw my face. I told him what I'd seen and he called triple 0. I felt like I had to go back there, and was on my way, the guy following me, when the ambulance turned up. I showed them where he was.'

She remembered the sky-blue of their uniform shirts, and how they'd moved into the grass so calmly, with no fuss; they knew what they were doing and they weren't afraid and it showed. She remembered thinking, *I want to be like them.*

'When they came out they said they were very sorry but he'd passed away.' She remembered that phrase. She used it herself now. 'The taller one asked if I was okay, did I know him, was I feeling faint or anything. I said I couldn't tell if I knew him until I saw his face, and that so far I felt okay. They thought the guy from the house was my dad for a minute, then once they realised he wasn't, they offered to get their controller to call Mum and Dad. I said yes, and suddenly felt a bit shaky at the thought of them coming there – I think for some reason I wanted to protect my mum, like if possible I didn't want her to even know that this had happened, could happen to somebody around there. Especially someone who might've been as young as me.'

'When did you realise who he was?'

'I would've known if I'd seen his face, but they never asked me to look,' Georgie said. 'I was kind of shooed away, much to Mum's relief. I found out that afternoon when I had to go to the station and give a proper statement.'

'How well had you known Tim?'

'Only to see around the school,' she said. 'He was two years ahead of me. I don't think we'd ever actually spoken.'

'Were there rumours about what might have happened?'

'There were a few,' Georgie said. 'One was that he was gay and he'd gone with somebody willingly but then got killed for whatever reason.'

'Did you hear how that started?'

She shook her head. 'Rumours go around schools like wildfire and sometimes there is no reason. There wasn't one for that, as far as I heard.'

'Okay.'

'But another was that it was some kind of drug thing.'

'Was he a user?'

'I don't know,' Georgie said. 'He didn't really hang out with that crowd, but otherwise I couldn't say.'

'Did people talk to you about him? Other kids at the school?'

Georgie nodded. 'It was all questions, though. They asked

what he'd looked like, could I smell him, were there flies, was he shot or stabbed, was there blood and guts. The counsellor pulled me out of class and asked how I was doing too.'

Georgie remembered the woman's long hand over her forearm like a damp and tepid towel. She hadn't wanted to talk to her, with her brown beads and slow nods and prepared facial expressions. Especially when under it all Georgie'd seen the same eager desire to pry that the kids had.

'I just kept telling people he looked like he was asleep. They had nowhere to go with that.'

Ella nodded. 'Is there anything new in your thinking about the case?'

'No, why?'

'Nothing's changed? You haven't remembered something?'

'No.'

'Do you talk about it much?'

'Hardly ever.'

'When would you talk about it?'

'If I got teamed with someone new on the road and we got talking about murders and stuff we'd been to, maybe.'

'Ever outside the job?'

Georgie shook her head. 'Why?'

'What would you say if I told you that somebody sent us a letter implying that you know more about this case than you're letting on?'

Georgie was stunned. 'What?'

'So you're surprised.'

'Of course! I just told you everything I know.'

Ella's gaze was steady.

'I mean, you must have read my statement from then. Did I just leave anything out? Or add anything new?'

'No.'

'What did the letter say I'm supposed to know?'

'It wasn't clear on that.'

'Who sent it?'

'Anonymous.'

'Well –' A thought struck Georgie. 'Wait. I know who it's from.'

'Who?'

'I was bullied at Woolford, where I used to work. The ambulance boss there is in cahoots with some local people and I'd say it's one or all of them doing this to hassle me even more.'

Ella narrowed her eyes.

'Some people knew about it out there,' Georgie said. 'All they'd have to do is search the web for details about the case and they'd have enough information to sound convincing.'

'But to what end?'

'Like I said, just to hassle me. They want me to quit.'

'Why would they want that?'

Georgie screwed up her face. 'It's a long and complicated story.'

'Try me.'

Georgie told her about the accident. As she spoke she wondered if she should mention the man she thought she'd been seeing, but decided against it. Ella was already looking at her a little oddly.

'Can you give me these people's names?'

'With pleasure.' Georgie recited the list she knew by heart. Sometimes she was annoyed that she couldn't get them out of her head; other times the memory showed its worth. 'Is this, like, perjury?' Maybe they'd go to jail.

Ella wrote in her notebook. 'Proving who sent it could be tricky.'

'What about fingerprints?'

'Also tricky.'

Georgie got the feeling she didn't believe it was them. 'But who else would do it? And why?'

'It's one of the avenues we'll explore,' Ella said.

Georgie's phone rang. It was Control. 'Are you guys available?'

'I don't know. What is it?'

'Urgent call from a medical centre in Bondi,' Control said. 'Ten-year-old girl with cyanosed legs. Doctor's stating it's meningococcal and I've got no one else.'

Georgie looked at Ella. 'I have to go.'

'That's fine,' Ella said. 'I might be in touch again later. Thanks.' She went back to her car.

'Yes or no?' Control was shouting down the phone.

'I'll find Freya.'

Georgie hurried into the Emergency Department and found Freya slumped in a chair in the corridor. 'You been seen yet?'

Freya shook her head.

'Control's got a cyanosed meningococcal in Bondi and wants to know if we can go.'

'Where's the detective?'

'She just left.'

'Tell him we're on it.' Freya pushed herself to her feet.

They hurried from the ED, Freya slowing a little at the door, Georgie repeating the medical centre's address before hanging up.

'You sure you're okay to go?' she asked Freya as they got into the ambulance.

'Must've just been cramps,' she said. 'Buckle up.'

'You don't need me to drive?'

'Make sure it's tight.' Freya gunned the engine.

They tore from the driveway with lights flashing and siren screaming. Georgie braced herself against the door and glanced over at Freya. She did look better. Thank goodness. Cyanosed legs with meningococcal was bad. If the girl didn't get IV anti-biotics soon she could very well lose those legs, if not die. She might die anyway.

She felt the ambulance lurch under acceleration and knew Freya was thinking the same thing as her: Bondi was really too far away.

The path to Ronald Gordon's house was terracotta pavers edged with lavender bushes. Ella climbed the four timber stairs to the door thinking about Georgie. She seemed genuine, and Ella had to admit feeling disappointed that the letter could be a hoax. Still, one step at a time.

She drew a breath and knocked.

A balding and grey-haired man opened the door a crack, said 'No, thank you,' and closed it.

She knocked again, and when he looked out frowning she held up her badge. 'Detective Ella Marconi. Are you Ronald Gordon?'

'Oh. Sorry.' He opened the door fully. 'Sorry. Yes, I am.'

She smiled. 'Were you living here twenty years ago?'

His eyes widened. 'You're here about the Pieters boy. I was the one Georgina came to. I called the ambulance and waited with her until they came.'

He looked down the sunlit street towards the place where Tim was found. Ella looked as well. There were trees blocking the view but she wondered how many had been there back then.

'Please come in. Can I offer you coffee?'

He showed her to a cream velvet lounge in a spotless lounge room and went into the kitchen. A ginger cat lay Sphinx-style on the carpet and stared out the French doors at a starling on the lawn.

Ronald brought in a tray and put it on the coffee table. 'Milk?'

'Black with one, thanks.'

He handed her the cup. 'Can I ask you, how is Georgina? Do you know?'

'She's well. She's actually a paramedic.'

'Oh, good for her.' Ronald rested his cup and saucer on his knee. 'What about the boy's family?'

'As you'd expect.'

'It's so sad. And to think it was never solved. But now you're looking into it again?'

Ella nodded. 'I wanted to ask you what you remember about that morning.'

'Well, first of all I was woken up by the banging on the door. I thought it was kids – kids mucking around, I mean – and went down to give them a piece of my mind, and threw the door open and there she was.'

He had a distant look, as if seeing it all again.

'She was just about crying, but trying to be brave,' he said. 'She was holding her little dog and first I thought he might have been hit by a car. I said, "Is he okay?" And she said, "There's a boy down there." The tone of her voice . . . it chills me now to think of it. I was confused, I didn't understand. I said, "What boy? Is somebody bothering you?" She said, "I think he's dead."'

His hands shook. Ella took his cup and put it on the table next to her own.

'Thank you,' he said. 'I asked where, and she pointed down the road, and for some reason I thought maybe *he'd* been hit by a car and I told her to come inside and I rang the ambulance and found a blanket, because all I could remember of first aid was to keep them warm. I got dressed very quickly, and she had already gone back out when I came back downstairs. I followed her down the street. She was still carrying her dog, holding him tight, up to her face. I had the blanket. I couldn't see anybody on the roadway, which seemed strange, then the ambulance came along. She pointed to where the boy was, in the long grass as it turned out, and the ambulance went down there and the officers got out and went to see him. We went close, but not too close, and stayed near the back of the ambulance. She was still holding her dog. I wanted to say something to her – as the adult in a distressing situation, I felt that was the right thing to do – but she seemed very contained, and in the end I couldn't think of anything. So we just waited, and then the officers came back. They thought I was her father and spoke to me first. I said I hadn't seen him, that she was the one. They looked after her really well, they said the kind of things that I had wanted to say.'

Ella nodded.

'They called her parents, and when they turned up they thanked me. Her mother was trembling. I felt it when she shook my hand.' He looked out at the lawn. 'She sent me a card that Christmas, thanking me again. Though I did nothing.'

'You helped her daughter when she needed it.'

'Anybody else would have done the same.'

'But you were the one who did. No wonder her mother wrote to you. It meant a lot.'

He dashed his knuckles across his eyes.

'Mr Gordon,' she said gently, 'no doubt the detectives asked you this at the time, but did you see anything or anyone odd that morning? Or can you recall hearing anything strange the night before?'

'Not a thing,' he said. 'I wish I did. I wish I could help.'

'How thick were the trees out there at that time? Could you see the location?'

'There were more shrubs, so you could see even less than you can now, actually. If a car was there at night you'd see some of the headlights, I suppose, but certainly that night I noticed nothing.'

'None of the neighbours either? You didn't hear anything on the neighbourhood grapevine later?'

'No. They talked about it all the time though. It really shook people up. Such a young boy, and being murdered. This is a quiet street. Things like that happen in other places. People wondered what the world was coming to. And then with Mrs Oldham too, it was just terrible.'

'That must have been upsetting.'

'She lived just up the way,' he said. 'Lovely old stick. Busy-body, but give you the shirt off her back. Terrible to think that somebody could creep into our community and wreak such havoc and not one single person sees or hears a thing.'

Not one person that we know about, you mean.

She smiled at him. 'Thank you for your time.'

The traffic was thick and slow. Freya twisted the wheel, revved up and over median strips, roared down the wrong side of the road while flashing the headlights at oncoming cars just in case they couldn't see the two-tonne vehicle hurtling towards them, and swore the whole time.

'Oh, look at this moron. Oh crap, what's he – oh shit.' The driver in front hit the brakes. 'Idiot!'

Freya locked it up behind him but managed to yank the ambulance to the side. There was a bang as she hit a street sign, which slammed the mirror back against the body. 'Still alive over there?'

Georgie dropped the window and pushed the mirror back into place. 'So far.' She gripped the seat as another dithering driver ahead of them propped then accelerated then tried to climb onto the median. 'How much further?'

'Too far.' Freya hit the horn to change the siren from wail to yelp, then pressed on it hard as another driver started to nose out of a parking space. 'What are we, invisible? Silent? Jeezus.'

Georgie snugged up her seatbelt and thought about the case ahead. The doctor should have the girl on oxygen, should have alerted the Children's Hospital at Randwick that she was coming in, might have even cannulated and taken bloods. This was not a case where they would muck around on scene; it'd be in with the stretcher and out again asap, load and go. Put the monitor on in the back, do whatever else her symptoms required, but the main thing was to get her to hospital quick smart. Meningococcal was a bastard and could kill you as soon as look at you.

They approached a red light and Freya braked. At the last second it turned green and she accelerated to go through, then a little yellow car shot out of the side street and into their path.

'Oh fuck.'

Georgie cringed in her seat, expecting the bang and crunch of metal on metal, seeing how they'd hit the back corner of the yellow car and spin it across the street, how they'd be spun as well and end up wrapped around a light pole, and they'd be trapped in the wreck, and they'd never get to their ten year old with meningococcal, but the yellow car squeaked past just in time.

Freya's knuckles were white on the wheel. 'Did that just happen?'

'Maybe we should slow down.'

'Ten years old and cyanosed. Plus he ran the red.' Freya screeched around a corner. 'We're nearly there.'

'You just said it was too far.'

'Well, whatever.'

'Then how about slowing down? It's my life in this cabin too.'

'Chrissake,' Freya said. 'We're not about to die.'

'We might be.'

'Stop with the fatalism, okay? I'm trying to concentrate.'

'Thirty-three, what's your ETA?' Control asked.

'Three to five,' Freya said, and Georgie repeated it into the mike.

'Thanks, Thirty-three, doctor is enquiring.'

'Any update on patient's condition?' Georgie asked.

'Patient is conscious and cyanosed. Doctor has asked if you would hurry.'

'Thirty-three copy.' Georgie hung up the mike.

Freya barked laughter. 'Yeah, cos we're only cruising now, aren't we.' She blasted the horn at a slow driver.

Georgie rubbed her forehead and thought about the patient. She'd seen a couple of bad meningococcals before, one a four-year-old boy who was drowsy with the typical rash on his chest, the other a girl of nine with severe photophobia and headache who developed the rash on the way to hospital. The boy had lived, though he'd lost three fingers and five toes. The girl had died. How bad were you if you were cyanosed already?

Freya tramped on the brake outside a low brick building where a dumpy woman waved frantically from the doorway. Georgie called on scene to Control, then jumped out and grabbed the Oxy-Viva.

'Quickly!' the woman called, then rushed inside, letting the door slam before Georgie reached it.

She yanked it open and went in. The waiting room was full of people but there was no sign of the woman. One of the waiting patients pointed down a corridor to the left.

'Thanks,' Georgie said.

She found them in the third room on the right. The young girl lay on the bed looking frightened, while a grim-faced doctor, complete with dangling stethoscope, dictated a letter to the woman who'd waved them down out the front and was now attacking a computer keyboard at the desk. 'In conclusion –'

Georgie went to the patient. 'Hi, I'm Georgie. How are you?'

'Okay.'

'She's not okay, she's cyanosed,' the doctor snapped.

The girl was covered from the waist down by a blanket. There was no oxygen mask, and no cannula in her arm. She didn't look sick. Georgie put her hand on her forehead, then rested her fingers on her wrist to take her pulse.

'What's your name?' she asked.

'Kim.'

'Can you please get going? The mother's already left and she'll be wondering where you are.'

Georgie heard Freya wrestling with the stretcher in the narrow corridor. 'It'll just be a minute till we're ready.'

'No, now,' the doctor said.

'I really can't until the stretcher's in.'

The doctor huffed and went out into the corridor, followed by the woman. Georgie heard Freya say, 'Please don't yank it.'

She smiled at Kim. 'What happened?'

'I told Mum I had a headache, and we didn't have any Panadol so she brought me here. Then the doctor went all funny about my legs.'

'What's up with them?'

Kim kicked the blanket off and Georgie saw that her skin was blue in patches. It didn't look like cyanosis though.

'It comes off, look.' Kim licked her thumb and rubbed her leg. 'I told him but he didn't listen. And Mum panicked and wouldn't listen either.'

Georgie wet a paper towel at the sink and wiped it across Kim's leg. She smelled sunscreen as the blue came off.

'What have you been up to today?' she asked.

'We went to the beach,' Kim said. 'We're staying in a motel and the bedspread is that colour. I think it rubbed off on me when I was playing.'

Georgie got another paper towel and cleaned off the rest of the dye. She heard the doctor bark at Freya in the corridor and Freya's voice grow tight. She opened the Oxy-Viva and got out the sphygmomanometer and took Kim's blood pressure.

'How's your headache now?'

'Gone.'

'Feel sick at all?'

'Nope. I feel good.'

Georgie squeezed her arm. 'Hang on there a sec.'

She went to the doorway. Freya was stormy-faced at the far end of the stretcher as the doctor and his assistant tried to pull the near end into the room.

'I'm telling you, it won't make the turn,' Freya said.

'We don't need it,' Georgie said. 'It's not cyanosis.'

'That girl is critically ill and needs urgent transport immedi-ately,' the doctor said.

'It's dye,' Georgie said.

Freya let go and the stretcher hit the wall and dented the plaster. The woman muttered something and ran her fingers over the spot while the doctor fixed Georgie with a cold stare. 'I have requested –'

Georgie held up the blue-stained paper towels. 'She had sunscreen on her legs and it's leached colour from the motel bed-spread. She's fine. She doesn't even have a headache any more.'

The doctor didn't look at the towels. 'I've requested urgent transport and that's what I want.'

Georgie exchanged a glance with Freya. 'If we could call Kim's mother and tell her the situation, I'm sure –'

The doctor took a step closer. 'I insist that the girl be taken to hospital right away.'

There was a slight tremble in his voice. Georgie knew she was pushing it to hold out any further. Even this was risking a complaint – precisely what she didn't need. 'Okay.' She tilted her head at Freya who nodded and started backing out with the stretcher.

The doctor grabbed at it. 'We need that.'

'She's fine to walk,' Georgie said.

Inside the room, she smiled at Kim. 'How about we run you up to hospital and meet your mum?'

Kim slid off the bed with a smile. 'I've never been in an ambulance before.'

Georgie zipped up the Oxy-Viva and took her hand. 'Let's go then.'

She looked at the woman as they walked past. 'Could you bring that letter out when it's done, please?'

Ella drove slowly past the scene. Still just a tree among other trees, long tangled grass, short shrubby bushes and not much else. She didn't know what she was looking for, but she felt that every time she was in the area she should drive past, so she did.

She turned at the roundabout and headed back to Pennant Hills Road, Tim's uncle her next target. Her mobile rang and she saw her parents' number on the screen. Answer or voice-mail? Voicemail. She was busy.

Alistair McLennan's surgery was a plain brick structure on the fringe of the shopping village in West Pennant Hills. She had to park way down the street, and walked back past an enormous purple bougainvillea whose dropped flowers covered the foot-path. A path of grey railway sleepers led to the surgery steps and a bell tinkled when she pushed open the door.

A woman with dark eyes and grey hair cut short and sharp smiled up from behind the desk, and smiled even wider when Ella held out her badge and introduced herself.

'You're working on Tim's case?'

Ella nodded. 'Is Dr McLennan in?'

'He should be back from his house call any moment,' she said. 'I'm his wife, Genevieve. Tim's aunt. It's nice to meet you.'

They shook hands.

'I thought doctors didn't do house calls any more.'

'Not many do, that's for sure.' Genevieve looked past Ella to the street. 'Here he comes.'

Dr Alistair McLennan was so tall his almost-white hair brushed the top of the doorway. He wore grey trousers and a light blue shirt and around his neck hung a thick black stethoscope with his name engraved on the stainless-steel bell. His hand was warm and freckled across the back, his grip firm. *A good doctor's hand*, Ella thought, *one built to reassure*.

'Good to meet you,' he said.

In his office, he gestured for her to sit down and moved a plastic model of the human spine off to one side.

'I hear you were Tim's GP.'

He nodded.

'Just out of curiosity,' she said, 'is there some kind of regulation that says a doctor can't treat family members?'

'Not at all,' he said. 'For emotional reasons, in some circumstances it makes good sense not to, and as a GP I wouldn't treat my wife or son. But Tamara and John were happy for me to take care of their kids and I was happy to do it.'

'I guess there's no problem with getting appointments that way.'

He grinned. 'Or bulk billing.'

'How often did you see Tim?'

'Not often. They were fit, healthy kids. Josh had some problems, of course – he's got a heart murmur I keep an eye on – but Tim and Haydee I only saw for the regular childhood illnesses. Chickenpox, mumps. Tim had a greenstick fracture of his left radius once. Tar and John called me and I took him to the hospital.'

'Can you remember the last time you saw him as a patient?'

'I can check.' He moved the computer mouse. 'I know it was within a few months of his death. Let me see . . . yes, it was on 7 September 1990.'

Six weeks before he died. 'What was that for?'

'Acne,' he said. 'Tim was concerned about his break-outs and Tar asked me to talk to him.'

Ella didn't remember Tim's skin being bad in the photos she'd seen. 'What did you tell him?'

'The usual stuff. It's not your fault, it's hormones, but you can help by keeping it clean and going slow on the junk food. I offered him antibiotics too, but he didn't want them.'

'Did he confide in you?'

'Never,' McLennan said. 'You're asking because of the gay rumour?'

'About what Damien Millerton said in his statement, yes,' she said. 'You don't believe it?'

'I don't think it was true at all, and unfortunately Tim isn't here to tell what was really said that night.'

'You believe Millerton was lying?'

'I didn't know him so I couldn't say, but I knew Tim and I never got any indication that he might have been like that.'

'What kind of indication?'

He looked uncomfortable. 'I had a young man once as a patient and with him I knew. I just knew. Tim wasn't like that. He was just an ordinary boy.'

Ella made a note and wondered why boys who were gay couldn't be 'just ordinary' too. 'He never talked to you about sex?'

He shook his head. 'Boys tend to get their information from their friends. Asking an adult is the height of embarrassment.'

'Let me ask you this,' she said. 'What would have happened in the family if Tim had said he was gay?'

He tugged the ends of the stethoscope. 'It would have been fine.'

'Really?'

'Of course. He was Tar and John's son, he was my nephew. He was a great kid and we loved him.'

'Did he know that?'

He looked at her. 'Tim was murdered. He didn't kill himself because he was gay and struggling with coming out.'

'I'm fully aware of that,' Ella said. 'I'm just curious about the family dynamic. Millerton said Tim was upset over an argument that had happened that evening at the family birthday barbecue. Do you remember that night?'

'Again, allow me to point out that he didn't kill himself over an argument.'

'I'm aware of that too.'

'It was merely a case of a moody teenage boy being annoyed with his family and wanting to be somewhere else, and those wishes coming up against the will of his parents.'

'He was rude to your wife.'

'He was rude to all of us,' Alistair said. 'Do you know many teenage boys, Detective?'

She smiled at him. Rude didn't even begin to cover the attitudes of the boys that cops usually met.

He didn't smile back. 'Tim was taken by somebody and murdered. The argument had nothing to do with that, and I'm concerned about your apparent focus on it.'

'We look into every angle,' she said. 'Even those that might not seem important or necessary to you.'

'You're right that it doesn't seem important to me.' He adjusted the position of the plastic spine. 'Tamara told me about your aggressive attitude and, quite frankly, I am unimpressed. She is a grieving and unstable woman. If the fact that you've reopened the case isn't difficult enough for her, you then treat her with so little respect.'

Ella said, 'She wants the case reopened.'

'She wants the case reopened with all the state's detectives on it, you mean. She can't have that and so this paltry effort just causes her more stress. Let me ask you straight out, Detective: what are the odds that you'll solve this?'

'It's impossible to say.'

'But I know you have a ballpark in mind,' he said. 'I won't embarrass you by asking again, but we both know that the likelihood of identifying the culprit, let alone charging him, let alone gaining a conviction, is so small as to be laughable.'

Ella's hackles rose. 'We don't investigate on the basis of likelihoods.'

'Look at it through Tamara's eyes,' he said. 'She put her hope in the detectives before and they failed. She's managed to go on. Now it's all being brought up again. What will happen when you fail too?'

'I understand your concern for your sister-in-law,' Ella said, 'but it's my job to find her son's killer.'

Alistair's clear blue eyes rested on her. 'I hope for her sake that you do.'

At the Children's Hospital Emergency Department, Freya let Georgie and Kim go in without her.

She paced the ambulance bay. She examined the truck's side mirror. She looked at her watch and the way that time was rushing her so quickly towards tonight. She got back into the ambulance and tried to work out what an innocent person would say about the detective's visit and how they would say it.

Georgie came out smiling. 'Nice kid.'

'Idiot doctor.' Freya made herself loosen her grip on the wheel so her knuckles regained colour. 'We almost got killed because of his incompetence.'

'What can you do? At least the kid's okay. Her mum practically jumped out of her skin to see her walk in.' Georgie reached for the microphone. 'Thirty-three is clear.'

'Stand by, Three.'

Freya forced herself to rest a casual elbow on the wheel. 'So what did the copper want?'

'She asked what I remembered about that morning.'

'Must be hard, so many years later.'

Georgie shook her head. 'It's like it was yesterday. I told her everything, though it was already all in my statement, and then she said somebody had sent her a letter about me.'

'What?'

'Thirty-three,' Control said.

'Thirty-three,' Georgie answered.

'Head to Randwick Nursing Home and I'll get back to you shortly.'

'Copy.' Georgie hung up the mike.

Freya couldn't think straight. 'What kind of letter?'

'It said she should talk to the girl who found the body.' Georgie opened the street directory.

Freya's throat was dry. 'Was that all?' she croaked.

Georgie ran her finger down the index of nursing homes. 'That's what she said. She seemed to think I knew more about Tim than I was letting on. I said I had no clue, and that the letter was probably written by Ross and the other idiots at Woolford.'

Of course, of course. Freya tried to slow her racing heart. *It must be that, because nobody knows anything.*

'Aha. Bond Street,' Georgie said. 'Know where that is?'

Freya grasped the key with a trembling hand. Nobody knew anything except her and Dion, and she hadn't breathed a word, and there was no reason for him to either.

It had to be Ross Oakes. Had to.

SIX

Callum stood by the pool in Tamara and John's backyard. It was hot in the late afternoon sun and he knew he'd be sweatier than ever for the speech to the Chamber of Commerce tonight, but Josh was swinging his feet in the water and smiling up at him. He wasn't going anywhere.

'Mum was on the telly.'

'I know.'

Callum didn't know where Tamara was; she hadn't answered his knock on the granny-flat door, but that didn't necessarily mean she was sleeping off a tranquilliser haze. She might be busy upstairs in the house. She could be out shopping, or having coffee, talking and laughing with people. Or she might be watching him through the motionless granny-flat curtains.

A beetle paddled in circles in the water and he got the leaf scoop from its hook on the fence and rescued the thing, knocking the side of the scoop against the pebblecrete so the beetle toppled out. Josh laughed as it puttered off to the lawn. Callum replaced the scoop and thought about how much time he'd spent here over the years, how he'd probably been here more frequently after Tim died than before, for a few years at least. The end had come one day when he was seventeen. He'd climbed out of the water and stood on the pool deck, so aware of himself, the water trickling off his skin, the sun on his shoulders and back, just so conscious of being alive, when he'd heard a noise and turned to see Tar running from the back door towards him. Remembering the look on her face made him shiver still; he'd seen in her eyes first the belief that he was Tim and then the recognition, the awful, awful recognition, that he wasn't. She'd tripped and fallen to her hands and knees and stayed there sobbing, and in an instant he'd gone from feeling godlike in his youth to knowing he was just a nervous boy in black Speedos, too nervous even to pat her shoulder, instead running past for help.

He'd realised then that he'd been co-opted by his father into a kind of replacement for Tim. As he'd grown older, he'd looked more and more like him – their build and their hair exactly the same. But even before that Alistair had sent him over to hang out, to fool around with Josh, and he remembered the time they'd been playing Star Wars: he'd been Vader in the black bedsheet and stifling mask, Josh in Tim's old karate gear being Skywalker and fighting him on the landing, shouting at him to do the breathing, do the breathing, and Callum had felt strong arms wrap around him from behind. The mask had come off and he'd found himself in John's tearful embrace. It had been uncomfortable, and after a moment John had let him go and walked away without a word, and Callum had known then, like he knew later by the pool, that for a moment it had seemed Tim was back home. It made him feel strange that when they looked at him they saw not their nephew but the space that Tim had left. He saw it in their eyes as he got his HSC, turned eighteen, then twenty-one, graduated from uni – all those milestones they should have had with their boy who looked so much like him.

He'd spoken to his dad about it once, asked him why he'd sent him over there so often.

'Why do you think?' Alistair had said.

'Because you feel bad for them?'

'Tamara's your mother's sister, of course I feel bad,' he'd said.

'But the reason is that there's a silence in their house now, and if you can help ease suffering then you should.'

After the pool day, though, Callum had started to make excuses. He needed to practise the trumpet more; his HSC was coming up, he really should study harder; he had to research different unis and course options and carefully, painstakingly, fill out applications. Alistair had given him looks but said nothing, and over time he wasn't going there a few times a week any more, or even once a week, but slowly dwindling to once a month and then less. Josh missed him, and used to call him up and ask when he was coming back, saying that Skywalker's force was getting stronger and he'd now be able to beat Vader with his eyes almost completely closed. Callum had felt bad, but the memory of Tamara's face by the pool kept him away.

'Nice evening,' John said, startling him. 'Sorry, I was tied up on the phone.'

'Callum saved a bug,' Josh said. 'It's over there now.'

'I just wanted to ask if you'd talked with that detective,' Callum said.

John nodded. 'She was here earlier.'

'Dad rang me to say she'd been out to see him. He's concerned it's digging up the past too much. That it's not good for Aunty Tar.'

'He rang to say the same to me, but Tar will be fine,' he said. 'You've talked with the detective too?'

'Not yet.'

John nodded, and seemed to read something in his eyes. 'Tar really will be fine.' He squeezed Callum's shoulder, and Callum saw his gaze focus on his hair.

'The detective seems smart,' he said, resisting the urge to move his hand up to his head.

John nodded. 'I think she gets it. Thank you for doing this for us.'

'I'm sorry it wasn't done before now.'

John pulled him into an awkward hug then released him.

Josh patted his shoe with a wet hand. 'Love you, Cal.'

'Love you too, mate. I'll see you later.'
In the car, Anna was reading the paper. 'Done?'
'I need to get a haircut,' he said.

Back in the office, as the late afternoon sun slanted in the windows, Ella read the six-year-old notes in the Pieters's file about Ivan Milat. John had indeed brought it up with the detectives then, and they'd checked it out thoroughly but found no links.

She turned back to the anonymous letter. She believed Georgie when she said she knew nothing more than what was in her statement. Ella had heard thousands of people tell thousands of stories, a goodly proportion of them complete crap, and she liked to think she had enough nous to at least pick when somebody was genuine. The way Georgie spoke about that day was totally convincing.

She put her notebook by the computer and typed in the name of Georgie's road-accident victim. *Ivor McCrow*. Up he popped, a shining beacon of decency in society if ever there was one. Good old Ivor was born in 1980 and had a juvenile record dating from his fourteenth birthday, moving smoothly into the adult record on his eighteenth. Driving unregistered, stolen vehicle, stolen parts, drunk and disorderly, resist arrest – then the list ended on 21 September 2008. *Deceased*. Ella clicked through to the case listed by the date and read the details of the sketchy outline Georgie had told her.

Crap.

How awful to go through that, to do your best to save someone when your boss wouldn't help you, to know they'd died because you happened to be driving on that bit of road at that time even though their stupid drunk-ass self shouldn't have been lying there in the first place.

Ella entered the next name. *Barnaby McCrow*. He was two years younger than Ivor but had worked hard to make up for it, starting his juvenile record at twelve, doing everything Ivor did plus a spot of assault, a little welfare fraud, even a bit of drug dealing. Ella wondered how much the McCrows had really done, considering police could never catch everyone at everything.

There were two older brothers, Hamish and Francis, and a sister, Martita. They all had records for similar offences, Martita a few more with the drugs and less on the cars, and then Ella found their mother. Faye McCrow had been jailed for a year in the seventies after siphoning money from a bank where she'd been a teller, and had convictions after then for drug offences and welfare fraud. She looked like she'd been clean for the last five years, but perhaps she sat at home and taught the kids the ways of her world, an evil matriarch living off the proceeds of her teachings.

It wouldn't surprise Ella to know that these people were indeed behind the letter, unconcerned about it misleading the case and not caring about wasting police time. To people like this, police were the enemy.

She typed in the name of Georgie's old boss from Woolford: *Ross Oakes*. Like so many paramedics he was listed as having been a witness in a number of cases, but also appeared as a victim. She clicked through and read that he'd been punched by one of his own officers, who'd been convicted and given a bond. *And no doubt sacked*, she thought. In her experience paramedics tended not to beat each other up, and she wondered what was behind it, how much provocation there might have been. Maybe not much, if Georgie's depiction of Oakes was accurate. She'd said that Oakes was some distant cousin of the McCrows, and that was one reason why he'd joined in the harassment of her, the other being that he was simply a bastard.

She sat back and stretched her shoulder. It was almost time to go. Wayne was bringing dinner over to her house, Thai from that takeaway place she liked, and the DVD of *The Wire* that was going around his office. It was one hell of a show but she was tired and needed coffee now to keep her going until then.

In the little kitchen, a silver-haired man in grey trousers and a grey shirt was looking at the hot water system. Ella remembered it was out of order.

'Reckon you can fit it? Or should we hassle them for a new one?'

He turned to her with a frown and her world imploded.

Frank Shakespeare. Oh my God.

She reversed quickly, out of the little kitchen and back into the office. *Oh God.* If it wasn't bad enough that she'd shouted at him that time years ago to get out of her homicide scene because she'd thought he was a nosy passer-by, she'd now mistaken him for a maintenance man. Ex-assistant commissioners didn't appreciate such things. Couldn't see the humour in it. She tried to smile at herself but she couldn't see the humour in it either.

She sank into her chair, feeling sick.

What was he doing here? Once retired, that should be it: you went and you didn't come back.

But perhaps more to the point was what was he doing here in the Unsolved office, where she still hadn't learnt who her new partner was to be and where Murray had eyed her case like a thieving bloody seagull?

Georgie climbed the steps onto the Harbour Bridge and started north with her head down. Her scalp was tight and her shoulders sore. She still felt awkward around Freya, and not just because she'd been all over the place today, first interested when Georgie had told her about the accident, then moody and distant during most of their other jobs. Georgie wished she could believe Freya's story about why she'd left school and forget that look of dismay, not let any of it bother her, but she'd never been that hard-shelled person and didn't know how to become her now.

At least the shift was over. Now they had two days off and she could talk it all through with Matt tonight, clear out her head, and see things freshly on Monday.

The sun was going down but it was still warm. Her boots struck the concrete footpath evenly and it was a pleasure to be moving faster than the peak-hour traffic. Overhead the metal superstructure was dark grey against the blue evening sky, and her shadow stepped steadily along from one fence panel to the next. The Opera House shone in the sunset and tourists gathered at the fence and fired off their cameras as if the sails would be gone tomorrow. She smiled at one couple, who then said something to her in Japanese and held out their digital camera, pointing at themselves and at the Opera House and harbour behind them.

'I'd love to,' she said.

She stood with her back against the fence to the highway and snapped off a few shots, wide at first then zooming in. The couple said what she guessed was thank you and shook her hand. It was during this that she glanced south and saw him.

He leaned against the pylon, watching her.

She only realised she'd tightened her grip on the Japanese man's hand when he said something and tried to pull away.

'Another one,' she said and reached for the camera.

They let her arrange them facing north. In the first shot, the man by the pylon was obscured behind the Japanese woman's head. For the second one she stepped to the side and looked over the camera past the couple. The man's face was impassive below his reflective sunglasses and he raised one hand in a lazy mock-salute.

She took the picture, and another, and another. The Japanese man said something.

'Sorry,' she said, but didn't give the camera back, instead pressing the button to see the photos she'd taken. 'If I give you my email —'

The Japanese man put out his hand.

'Just a sec.'

She scrolled back and forth. The couple were there, the pylon behind them, the other tourists, but no man. She moved to shield the screen from the sun and checked again and frowned. She looked up. The pylon stood alone.

The Japanese man put his hand on the camera. 'Thenk you.'

She let it go. The breeze picked up and whipped the smell

of exhaust across from the traffic. She gripped the fence behind her and stared at the path to the south. It wasn't possible. Was it?

A group of tourists came past, talking about how great the bridge was, and she realised the man could have stepped in behind them when he saw her aim the camera. And then he could have ducked in behind another group before this lot came too close. Just because she couldn't see him now didn't mean he wasn't still there.

She set off north. She held her head high but the back of her neck prickled and the path home was long. She walked faster and felt in her bag for her phone.

'Hi, this is Matt. Thanks for calling. Please leave your message and I'll call you back.'

'It's me,' she said. 'I'm on my way across the bridge. If you're home, can you come and meet me, please? It's such a beautiful evening, the water looks fantastic.' She didn't want to hang up. 'Hope you get this, hope to see you soon.'

She kept the phone in her hand and glanced over her shoulder. A bunch of people were spread out across the path and keeping pace with her, fifteen metres back. She couldn't see past them. She stepped out a little quicker.

The flags streamed in the wind high above her. Her breath came hard in her chest. A ferry foamed white water on the harbour and the footpath stretched out before her and she felt the urge to run. She looked back. The tourists had clumped tighter, forming a wall she couldn't see through.

The breeze gusted and her skin went cold. The noise of buses braking and laughter from the tourists filled her ears when she so badly wanted silence to listen for running feet. She tried to get a grip, tried to be rational and think through what could actually happen, what were the odds. If it was Barnaby, what was he going to do here in broad daylight, with tourists and traffic passing by? If it wasn't Barnaby, if it was . . . that other . . . then she had nothing to worry about. He couldn't hurt her. She believed in physics and chemistry, after all, in the logic of the body, that when the heart stopped consciousness left and that was it. She'd seen countless people go and some come back, and it was like turning a light switch off and on: the circuit was either there or it wasn't; there wasn't some echo of the light left to float about and follow others.

Or so she'd once thought.

She wanted to run.

She was past halfway. She lengthened her stride. She tucked her bag against her side as if reducing wind resistance. The corners of her phone dug against her palm.

'Hi, this is Matt. Thanks for calling. Please leave your message and I'll call you back.'

'It's me again. Are you on your way? See you soon, I hope.'

She was on the downhill slope, she told herself. She was getting faster. He would have to get around the tourists and then catch up. She had run from things before, people, situations; the best self-defence tool a paramedic had was their feet. She could be fast, and the adrenaline she felt would make her faster.

She wouldn't think about it not being Barnaby. She didn't believe. She refused to.

She was nearing the northern pylon. She could see the end of their street down below. Pedestrians wandered, none of them identifiable as Matt. She dialled him again and this time didn't leave a message.

She looked back. The tourists were still there, though they had dropped off her pace. She looked ahead to the stairs that led down to Ennis Road. The shops there would still be open. She could rush down the stairs and into a shop and pretend to be buying something for dinner. She could ring Matt again and wait for him in there.

She focused on the top of the stairs. Her back tingled with the feeling of being watched. She glanced back but still couldn't see him.

'Hey.'

She stopped dead.

Matt came up the last few stairs and took her arm. 'You okay?'

Her heart started again. 'You frightened the crap out of me.'

'Sorry. I got your messages and thought I'd surprise you.' He kissed her. 'How come you're all clammy?'

'There was this guy.' She pointed south. 'Behind the tourists.'

'Can't see anyone.'

'Wait till they come past.'

Even as she said it, Georgie knew he wouldn't be there. He'd have turned and gone back the other way when she wasn't looking. The tourists came by laughing and talking and the path behind them was empty for a hundred metres.

'What was he doing?'

'Just walking.'

'Following you?'

'It felt like that.'

'Call the cops?'

She made a face. 'I just wanted to get to you.'

'But you were worried.'

'I guess so,' she said. 'I didn't . . . I mean, I thought it was . . .'

'Who?'

'Barnaby McCrow.'

He rubbed his chin. 'Maybe we should call the cops.'

'Nothing really happened.'

'But this is the second time,' he said. 'You thought you saw him – or one of them – yesterday too. Otherwise you wouldn't have wanted to know if they'd been seen around town.'

Thanks very much, Adam.

'I don't know for sure if it was him.'

'If we report it, the cops can look into it,' Matt said. 'This could be serious. He's got motive.'

'What if we ring Adam and ask him to go and check for us?'

Matt was silent for a moment. 'Okay,' he said. 'But if Barnaby's not around, we make it official.'

'Okay.'

He took her hand. 'Not so clammy any more.'

Only because she'd been wiping it on her trousers, but she nodded anyway.

★

James smiled at Freya in the mirror. 'You look incredible.'

She was putting on lipliner and couldn't smile back. She winked instead and he seemed happy enough with that and went back into the bedroom. Freya capped the liner and put it down, then did her lipstick, focusing on that, avoiding her eyes. James might not see the worry and doubt in them but she sure as hell could.

She dropped the lipstick into her bag and turned away from herself. 'Kids ready?'

'Rob?' James called, doing up his tie. 'Ready, mate?'

'Yeeees.'

'Ains?'

There was no answer. James sighed.

Freya sat on the bed and slipped on her shoes. 'I'll go.'

Ainsley's room was at the end of the hall. She'd wanted to paint the door black, and when James refused she'd painted A4 sheets of paper instead and Blu-Tacked them on. It had been a month and the hall still stank of paint. One sheet was coming loose and Freya pressed the corner down, then knocked.

'What?'

'You ready?'

Mutter, mutter.

'Sorry?'

'I'm not going.'

'Yes, you are,' Freya said. *If I have to, you have to.*

Ainsley opened the door. 'It's not fair.'

'It's just a few hours.'

'I'm talking about the whole thing.' Ainsley lifted her chin and Freya saw the child she'd been at three. 'It's not right that you can make me change schools.'

'Your dad and I talked about it for a long time and decided this was best.'

Ainsley shook her head. Her black bob swung around her ears. 'It's not right.'

'I'm not going to argue with you. It's been decided. Now get your boots on and let's go.'

Ainsley sat on the floor to do so and again Freya saw the child she'd been, this time at eight, struggling to lace rollerskates.

'I love you,' she said.

Ainsley scowled at the floor.

In the car, Robbie chattered away about what Barney said to Philip at recess and how much longer Lucas would have his cast on for and who got put on the wall for playing brandings.

'Who gives a toss,' Ainsley said.

'Hey.' James looked at her sharply in the rear-view.

She rolled her eyes.

'Why do you wear those stupid boots?' Robbie said.

She punched him in the arm and Robbie howled.

'Enough!' James barked.

Freya looked out the windscreen. It was twenty minutes to Macquarie and she had to prepare herself to see Dion again. He was forty-two now. He might be losing his hair, wear his trousers belted high over his paunch, have liver spots on his hands. She wondered if he was still married to Andrea. Chelsea would be twenty now. It was strange to think about it all again, when for so many years she'd kept it safely tucked away in a place in her head where she never, ever went. Add to all that the news of the letter somebody had sent the police and it was no wonder she felt sick.

'You okay?' James said.

'Huh?'

'You were frowning.'

'A bit tired, that's all.'

He squeezed her knee. 'Thanks for coming.'

She smiled at him.

In the back Robbie whined about his arm and Ainsley sighed like Freya remembered sighing so often at her age, feeling suffocated by all this domesticity and everydayness. She turned to look at her daughter, who looked pointedly out the window at the night. Freya thought of what she'd been up to at her age. Despite James's opinion of Ainsley's behaviour, she wasn't doing too badly at all.

The closer they got to Macquarie, the tighter her gut clenched. She tried to tell herself that he wouldn't remember her; nineteen years was a long time and people changed a lot between the ages of sixteen and thirty-five. Her surname was different too. She tried to see herself being introduced by James, shaking Dion's hand, smiling politely, and walking away with him none the wiser. Tried, and failed.

James squeezed into a spot on the street and they crossed the lawn towards the hall in a motley group, Robbie running ahead, James and Freya in the middle, Ainsley dragging behind as far as possible. James frowned back at her but Freya kept going.

'She'll catch up,' she told him.

Light streamed from the doorway and Robbie jumped inside. Freya took a deep breath and followed.

The hall was crowded, the student orchestra warming up, people talking and laughing and finding their seats. Kids ran everywhere.

James took her hand. 'I'll introduce you to the principal.'

Freya could feel herself breathing fast as she was led through the mass, bracing herself. *He won't know you. He won't.*

Suddenly there he was. He was neither balding nor paunchy. He was tall and fit and looked thirty-five. He smiled at them and came striding over, his legs long and strong in dark khaki trousers. 'James, how are you?' They shook hands.

'This is my wife, Freya.'

'Nice to meet you.'

Dion put out his hand and Freya took it, unsure what to expect from touching him. His palm was firm and warm and his fingers were strong around hers. She looked into his eyes. Either he was extremely adept at hiding his thoughts or he didn't recognise her.

'Nice to meet you too,' she said, and let his hand go.

'This is our son, Robert, and our daughter, Ainsley,' James said.

Dion shook hands with both of them. 'I hear you're starting with us here soon,' he said to Ainsley.

She looked at the floor and shrugged.

'Say yes, Ains,' James said. 'She is.'

Dion smiled. 'You're in Year Nine?'

Ainsley muttered, 'Yes.'

'So's my daughter Alice,' Dion said. 'She's by the door there. Would you like me to introduce you?'

Ainsley glanced at the bored-looking girl in the black jeans and T-shirt and sloped off towards her without another word.

'Thank you,' James said. 'Is your wife here?'

'She is.' Dion waved across the hall and a sturdy blonde made her way over.

Freya recognised her immediately, though she'd only seen her a few times at the drama group many years ago. Some people didn't change that much at all, she realised. But she herself had. *Right?*

'My wife, Andrea,' Dion said. 'This is James and Freya Craig.'

They shook hands. Freya glanced at Dion. He wasn't looking at her.

'Let's take a seat, shall we?' he said. 'It's about to start.'

He shepherded them towards the third row and Freya sank weakly into her chair as Dion and Andrea headed off to their seats.

'Nice people,' James said as the lights went down. 'Might have some new friends there.'

Freya felt sick.

There was lots of singing and dancing, illustrating some story that Freya couldn't concentrate on, then an intermission. 'I have to get some air,' she said to James, and pushed her way outside. Students served tea, coffee and cordial from trestle tables in the quadrangle, and she went up to the nearest. 'Any chance of a cup of ice?'

He frowned. 'I'll go and find out.'

Freya pressed her back against a stone column. People milled about, all happy and cheerful, none of them with any problems at all.

'Is yours an emo too?' Dion said beside her. 'Your daughter?'

Freya held herself together. It was still possible that he hadn't recognised her. 'Actually, she rejects all labels imposed by our patriarchal society.'

'Fair enough.' Dion surveyed the crowd. 'Decent turnout.'

She nodded.

He lowered his voice. 'It's good to see you again.'

'Don't.' Goose bumps rose on her neck.

'I just needed to say that.'

'Don't.' She shook her head. 'It's not . . . The police have reopened the case.'

'I saw it on the news.' He raised his coffee cup to hide his mouth. 'They can't know anything.'

'They got a letter about the girl who found the body.'

He stared at her.

'Your cup of ice,' the student said behind her.

'Thank you,' Freya managed.

'Dion! Don't just stand there gawping, come and talk.'

A heavily made-up woman laid her blood-red nails upon his jacket sleeve and dragged him off. He looked back at Freya once and she suddenly felt like she didn't know how to arrange her face, what secrets she was giving away to everyone there.

James came up. 'Feeling better?'

'Not really.'

Freya gripped the plastic cup so tightly its sides started to split. She tipped it up and chewed a mouthful of ice, needing the freeze to calm her blood more than ever, needing the surge of cold water down her throat to stop the tightening grip that fear had on her neck. She wanted to be at home, well away from here, away from Dion and the past he represented, away from thoughts of dogged police detectives and the truths they might uncover.

The morning sun warm on her shoulders, Ella stood up and stretched her back. Wayne was right into this, on his hands and knees in the grass, humming as he uprooted things with the new fork.

'This is onion weed,' he said. 'It's got no place in a decent garden. You have to dig down and get the little bulb. If you just rip off the top the bulb sends out more shoots and it goes everywhere.'

Ella nodded though he wasn't looking at her to see it. Which was good, otherwise he might have seen in her eyes that she didn't really care. The onion weed flowers were kinda nice, and so long as there was something green growing in the garden beds she didn't mind what it was. And wasn't the difference between a weed and a proper plant a mere technicality?

She'd thought she would like this new domesticity. That morning they'd gone to Bunnings and Wayne had spent a happy hour wandering through the Saturday morning crowds, filling a plastic basket with things they apparently needed. Ella had trailed behind, thinking about Tim. And Murray.

'This one on your fence is another weed. Japanese honeysuckle. Again you have to be careful because if it gets away from you it just runs wild.'

'Okay.' She liked that one too.

'This is good soil,' Wayne said. 'We could really do something here.'

She should get back down there with him but she hated the feel of the dry dirt on her skin.

'How's your case?' she asked.

'It's the weekend, sweetheart,' he said.

'We didn't get time last night to talk about it.'

'It will still exist on Monday.'

She noodled with the new rake in the grass. 'Speaking of Monday, I wonder if Murray will be there when I walk in.'

He looked up at her. 'Honey.'

She guessed he wouldn't be overjoyed if she wanted to talk about the letter again either.

'Do you like roses?' he said. 'We could plant some along here. They'd look really good.'

'Aren't they a lot of work?'

'Not really. A little bit of regular maintenance and you're laughing.'

Ella twisted the rake in the grass. 'I don't like thorns.'

'You can get them without thorns now.'

'I prefer things like palms.'

'Palms would grow well here too.'

She didn't want to think about it. If they decided on plant types he would want to go to the nursery. She should get down there next to him. She looked back at the house, thinking of the case notes in her bag.

'Want a glass of water?' she asked.

'I'm fine. Here, let me show you something.'

Her mobile rang in her pocket.

'Didn't you turn that off?'

She couldn't place the number on the screen.

'If it's not somebody you know, you shouldn't answer.'

'It might be important.'

'It's your day off.'

The phone rang and rang. Wayne went to take it out of her hands and she pulled away.

'Ella,' he said. 'It's the weekend.'

'The job doesn't end because of that.'

'You need your own time.'

The ringing stopped. After a moment the voicemail alert sounded.

'You didn't want water, right?' she said.

'Leave the phone here.'

She almost laughed.

'I mean it,' he said. 'Give me the phone. I'll turn it off.'

'No way.'

The sun shone down on them standing there. The rake handle was hard in her hands. *This is our first fight*, she thought.

'The job is just that. It isn't life,' he said. 'And you know I'm only trying to help you.'

'Do me a favour and don't.'

He knelt and rammed the fork into the earth.

Inside the house she put the phone on the bench and got herself a glass of water. She drank looking out the window at the back of Wayne's head. He didn't glance around. *Don't try to control me*, she thought at him. *I don't do it to you.*

She called voicemail.

'It's Callum McLennan here. I'm sorry to ring you on the weekend, but if you have time, I mean if you're working today and you have time, could you call me back, please? Thanks.'

She remembered his message of yesterday. She should've called him back. She owed him, really. She went into missed calls and dialled his number.

'The mobile you have called is turned off or not answering. Please try again later.'

Murphy's bloody law. Not even voicemail. She put the phone down and got another drink of water.

'Enough for me in the tap?' Wayne said behind her.

She got a clean glass and filled it for him.

He smiled. 'Thanks.'

She watched him drink.

'Call them back?'

'No answer,' she said.

'That's the universe pointing out it's your day off.'

She raised her eyebrows.

'I'm joking,' he said. 'I know how important it is to you, but working every day isn't good.'

'The case has just started. I want to build some momentum.'

'It's been stalled for nineteen years,' he said gently.

'Even more reason.'

He put his glass in the sink. He was standing close to her and she could smell the dirt and grass and sweat on him. He placed one hand against the side of her neck. 'You're so warm.'

She looked into his eyes. 'You shouldn't try to control me.'

'I don't want to control you.'

He leaned forward and kissed her. She felt his stubble against her chin and his hand slid further round the back of her neck.

'So now you're sucking up,' she said when they came up for air.

'You think so?'

She locked her hands behind his back and pulled him in tight. 'I do.'

'And is it working?'

'I'll have to think about it.'

He held her face in his hands and kissed her again.

She felt his breath warm against her cheek. One of his fingers stroked her earlobe. Close up she saw the flecks of light in his brown eyes and his pulse in his throat.

'You're pretty warm yourself,' she said, and slid her hands under his shirt. 'I think that if you took this off you'd be cooler.'

'Possibly,' he said. 'And possibly the same with you.'

There was grass in his chest hair. She kissed it out. He stroked her bare shoulders and slid her bra straps down. She felt his erection pressing against her stomach and pushed her hands into the back pockets of his jeans and pulled him closer. He trailed his fingers around her sides and unclipped her bra in one smooth and easy movement.

'You've done that before,' she said.

'This morning.' He smiled. 'You've forgotten already?'

'I have a vague recollection.' She kissed him. 'I don't think it happened in the kitchen though.'

'Unlike this time, you're saying.' He draped her bra over the taps.

'Yes.'

She pressed him back against the benchtop and drew her nails lightly over his ribs then slid her hands down across his stomach to his belt buckle. He bent and kissed her breasts as she popped open the button on his jeans.

A mower started up next door, right over the fence from the window where they stood. Wayne started to laugh. 'I guess it would drown out any noise we might make.'

Ella took his hand and led him to the bedroom. She pushed him onto the bed and straddled him, squeezed his shoulders and kissed him. She felt his hands all over her and broke out in goose bumps. She fumbled beneath herself at his jeans and in a moment he was kicking them off while tugging at hers.

They rolled over. He flung her jeans over his shoulder onto the dresser. She grabbed him and pulled him close and then her mobile rang.

He pressed his head into her neck. 'Don't.'

'I'm not,' she said into his hair.

'I felt you start.'

'It was fright.'

It wasn't, and she knew he knew it. The phone rang on. She bet it was Callum and wondered what he wanted to talk about. Maybe he would leave another voicemail and actually say something this time.

'It's the weekend.'

'You said that already.'

The phone stopped ringing. Wayne nuzzled deeper into her neck and she brushed his hair off her ear so she could listen for the voicemail alert.

When she heard the chime she kissed Wayne's neck, but he lay still.

'You going to go check it?'

'Does it feel like I am?' She ran her hand down his back.

'I can feel you thinking about it.'

Lucky guess. 'But I'm still here,' she said.

He rolled off. She let her hands flop to her sides. The back of her hand came to rest against his hip and she stroked his skin with her little finger but after a moment he got up.

'You're going?'

'Garden's not weeding itself.' He pulled on his jeans and walked out.

Ella lay there for a moment and stared at the empty doorway. She listened to him put his shirt on, then open and close the door as he went outside. She got up and went to the kitchen herself and saw he'd folded her bra and shirt and left them in a neat pile on the table. She pulled them on, watching him out the window. The mower was loud next door and it was hard to think.

Wayne's shirt lifted up when he bent over and the skin was pale and vulnerable underneath it.

She picked up the phone, hesitated, then dialled voicemail.

Freya's head was killing her. She'd hardly slept, then had to face the Saturday morning shopping scrum to get groceries. Damn family, never stopped eating.

Robbie changed the radio station again.

'Robbie, please.'

'But I don't like this song.'

Freya turned the thing off.

'Aww.'

She looked at him and he sat back in his seat. She had to give him credit: he knew when to stop. Unlike Ainsley. Though that wasn't true: Ainsley knew when to stop, she just chose not to. After not wanting to go last night, she'd then spat it when James had said it was time to leave. Freya had walked away, and by the time they came to the car where she'd been seatbelted in for twenty minutes with her mind a total mess, nobody was speaking.

Robbie brushed sugar from his lap onto the floor. She'd bribed him with doughnuts to come along, but then he'd steered the trolley into the shelves and broken a huge jar of coffee, and when she took the trolley off him he'd dragged along behind her whining.

She braced the wheel with her knee and rubbed her eyes.

'You'll crash,' Robbie said.

'And then we'll all be dead.'

He frowned.

She didn't know what was wrong with her. 'Sorry, mate.'

'What do dead people look like?'

'Like they're sleeping.'

His frown got worse. 'So when I'm asleep I look like I'm dead?'

'Actually, it's more like they're asleep but also different.'

'Different how?'

'Like something very important is missing.'

'Where do they go?'

'Nobody knows.'

She'd looked into the eyes of the dead and silently asked them that very question. She'd looked into the eyes of the revived and done the same out loud. Some didn't believe they'd been dead, thinking instead they'd simply passed out for a moment, even when she showed them the ECG strip and said, 'Here's where your heart stopped and here's where it started again.' Some believed her and still said it was like passing out. A few wouldn't talk about it. One woman wept at being back, crying out to her dead daughter who she said was smiling at her from the end of her bed. A man pulled her close and whispered in her ear that there was chewing gum on the sole of her boot, and that she wasn't to worry, that everything would be okay in her life, everything would turn out for the best. Out at the ambulance she'd sat with her socked foot on her knee and her boot in her hands, staring at the gum caught in the tread, and thought about kneeling by the man and doing compressions, how her soles had faced up, and how he'd been unconscious the entire time she'd looked after him.

She shivered.

'Want me to put the heater on?' Robbie reached for the switch.

'I'm fine.' She looked over and he smiled at her. She smoothed the back of his head where the hair always stood up. 'Thanks, buddy.'

Maybe everything would be okay.

She turned into their street with a lifting heart then saw a strange car in the driveway. A dark blue sedan. The detective. She gripped the wheel hard. Thoughts flooded her head – *drive straight past, just keep going, you and Robbie can find somewhere to stay, you have food to last you a week* – but she knew there was no option. She braked with a trembling leg and turned into the drive.

'Who is it?' Robbie said.

'I don't know.'

He reached over her arm and pressed the horn with three fingers. She turned off the ignition and sat with her hands on the wheel, trying to take a deep breath. The front door opened and Dion came out. Freya's vision blurred. This wasn't the detective but it still wasn't good.

'Ainsley just took a message from somebody named Philip for you,' Dion said to Robbie through the driver's window.

Robbie was out of the car and running up the path in an instant.

'Sorry,' Dion said. 'I just brought Alice over to see Ainsley. I didn't know James would be out.'

Freya opened the door and got out. She felt nervous having him there, as though it would be obvious to anyone who looked what had gone on between them.

At the boot, Dion stepped closer. 'I couldn't find you after the show last night.'

'We had to go.' Freya glanced up at the house.

'Tell me about the letter.'

'It just said to talk to the girl who found the body. The detective came to talk to Georgie at work. It's probably a prank by some people who are hassling her.'

'Who's Georgie?'

'Her surname use to be Daniels. She was in the drama class, when we . . . Anyway, she's a paramedic now and we're working together.'

He rubbed his face. 'So the police think the letter is fake?'

'That's what Georgie told them.'

'It has to be that then. Who could know anything?'

'I don't know.'

She looked into his face for a second. He shot a look at the house. 'Nobody could,' he said.

'Exactly.'

He sniffed, and brushed at his nose with the back of his fingers. In that gesture and in his eyes she could see the young man he'd been. She had an urge to put her hand on his waist but didn't.

He said, 'It'll be okay.'

'Of course it will.'

But neither of them moved, and the unspoken hung in the air: *what if it wasn't?*

SEVEN

Georgie stared at the photo of Tim Pieters in the weekend newspaper. 'This is the guy I was telling you about.'

Matt came onto the balcony. The breeze off the harbour flapped the pages and he moved the coffee cups to hold the corners down. 'Does it feel weird to see him?'

'Sort of.'

The article talked about unsolved cases and the fascination that society had with them. The journalist said that the police refused to discuss Tim's case because of the new investigation, but quoted family members and past detectives from other cases. One said, 'Justice needs to be served, even if it's cold.' The statement gave Georgie the shivers.

Matt sat down to read. She tried to focus on reading too, but couldn't. She shifted about in her chair, then pulled his arm towards her to see his watch.

'It's only been forty minutes,' he said.

'All he had to do was get on the phone.'

'Maybe he went to talk to people.'

'Maybe.'

Georgie couldn't sit still. She put her feet up on a chair then back down. She got Chris's binoculars and inspected the ships

134

on the harbour. She tapped her nails on the glass-topped table until Matt looked up at her.

'Too loud?' she said.

'Just call him.'

The home phone rang out and his mobile went to voice-mail. 'It's me,' she said. 'You know where we are.'

She put the phone down.

'And so we wait again,' Matt said, still bent over the paper.

She took the phone inside and dialled another number. 'Hey, Friendly, it's George.'

'Mate! How's it going?'

'Good. Sort of.'

She told Kaspar about the cardiac arrest and Freya's on-again, off-again attitude.

'She in with Ross?'

'Not as far as I can tell,' Georgie said. 'You heard anything there?'

'Just his usual spouting off about how you won't be back, if you did he'd quit, blah blah. You better pass. We all want him gone. Oh, and you back, of course.'

She could hear his smile. 'It's all I think about,' she said. 'Listen, you seen much of the McCrows?'

'Took Rose across to Broken Hill for her morph pump refill on Thursday. That was fun.'

'See any of the boys when you picked her up?'

'Only Hamish, who stood about frowning,' he said. 'Martita had a bit of a mutter. Faye was there too, of course, lording it about: don't pick her up like that, what are you, an idiot, be gentle she's just an old lady! The usual.'

'No sign of Francis or Barnaby?'

'Nope. Saw Francis earlier in the week in town though. Gave me the finger.'

'Lovely.'

'You know it. And Liam said he caught Barnaby trying the doors of the ambulance when he came out of a job at a funeral on Wednesday.'

'Wednesday,' Georgie said. 'Definitely Wednesday?'

'Yep, outside the Anglican Church.'

People were always fainting in the Anglican Church. 'They so need aircon.'

He laughed. In the background, the job phone rang, its tones so familiar to Georgie they made her heart skip a beat.

'Got to go,' he said. 'Talk to you later, okay?'

'Have fun.'

She took the phone back to the balcony and sat facing the harbour. So Barnaby had been in town on Wednesday. She'd first seen him – or someone – on Thursday. He could've flown down, or caught the train or bus, or driven overnight.

She didn't know what to think of any of it.

She would have to wait to hear what Adam said.

The downstairs intercom beeped and Matt jumped up and went to buzz James in. 'You want me to make some space out here?' she called.

'Nah, we'll stay in, I think.'

He went to put the kettle on and a minute later there was a knock at the door. Georgie heard him answer and heard James's haw-haw laugh coming through the flat ahead of him.

'Oh wow, look at your view of the bridge!' He came out to lean on the railing. 'Hi, Georgie, how are you? Isn't this something?'

No fake punches today – that was good. She smiled at him, but then he came in close.

'Your husband's going to show me how to become a rich man like him.' He waved a hand at the apartment.

'This isn't ours,' Georgie said, but he was already looking back out at the water.

'I thought we'd work inside,' Matt said in the doorway. 'Stop the papers flying off in the wind.'

'And miss this view?' James turned to the table. 'More coffee cups and we're laughing.'

Please, Georgie thought, *no more laughing*.

James saw the article and pressed his finger on the photo of

Tim Pieters. 'Now there's a school uniform I know. Freya went there, and I start teaching there in a couple of weeks.'

'Georgie went there too,' Matt said.

'Oh – yeah, of course she did. You and Freya were mates.' James smiled at her then looked back at the newspaper. 'This kid was murdered, was he?'

'Georgie found his body,' Matt said.

'Wow, really? I didn't know that. Is that why you joined the ambos? Can't get enough of them dead bodies?' Haw haw.

Georgie smiled tightly. 'I think I heard the kettle.'

'Was this Freya's Tim?' James said.

Georgie stopped in the doorway, thinking she'd heard wrong. 'Sorry?'

'That sort-of boyfriend she had. The one who was her first and everything. She told me he'd died but didn't say it was murder.'

Georgie couldn't think straight. 'Freya was going out with a boy named Tim from our school who died?'

'Weren't they just sleeping together? She was pretty vague about it, then when I asked what he died of she got all self-conscious and clammed up. Though by then, of course, I'd already told her every detail of my first time, embarrassing fumbles and all.' He suddenly seemed to really look at Georgie. 'You didn't know?'

'I had no idea.'

'Oh God,' James said. 'Don't tell her, she'll kill me.'

Georgie gripped the doorframe, trying to get this new fact into her mind.

'You okay?' Matt said softly.

'I don't know.'

She went inside and sat down. What had been going on with Freya that she'd not only kept the relationship to herself but then didn't mention it after Tim died? Georgie thought of the Monday after his death, when she'd met Freya in rollcall. The whole school had heard by then, and kids whispered as she passed them in the corridors. Freya had hugged her and asked if she was okay. She hadn't pried, hadn't wanted to know what he'd looked like, had just sat with her and been her friend. She was calm and contained and, unlike a lot of girls in their year, some of whom, Georgie thought, would've been hard-pressed to pick Tim out of a crowd, she hadn't shed a tear. And even now, after Georgie had talked about him and the case and the detective yesterday – not a word.

What did it mean?

'You can come if you want,' Ella said.

Wayne wiped sweat from his cheek. He hadn't said a word since she'd made contact with Callum and agreed to meet him. Now she was showered and dressed and standing by the pile of weeds with her car keys in her hand and her bag over her shoulder. She wished he would at least look at her.

'You know that you don't have to keep on with it,' she said. 'It's your weekend too. Do nothing for a while.'

Wayne dug with ferocity. She heard the blade cut into the soil. She didn't know what to say. Would he be happy if she cancelled the meeting and got back into her gardening clothes and scrabbled there in the dirt with him? Probably. Would she? No way.

'I have to go,' she said.

He flung a weed onto the pile. Dirt spattered her shoe.

'I'll see you later.'

He didn't glance around. She waited a moment longer, she wasn't sure for what, then walked out to her car.

Callum was already there. He looked different from the last time she'd seen him, smart and straight in his suit at the school sports-centre opening. Now he wore jeans and a blue shirt, along with a somewhat nervous expression. He jumped to his feet when he saw her walk in.

'Thanks so much for coming. What can I get you?'

The café smelled of expensive coffee and Ella sank into the chair breathing in deeply. 'Long black,' she said. 'Double shot.'

Callum paid and brought the coffees over. He sat opposite her and fiddled with a sugar sachet before pouring it in.

Ella took a sip and the coffee hit her stomach like a bomb going off. *Perfect.*

'I'm sorry I didn't call you back sooner,' she said.

'It's fine,' he said. 'I know you're busy. I hope I haven't called you away from something important today.'

'Nothing that can't wait.' She put her cup down. 'I read your statement. It's awful that it happened, but even more so that it happened on your birthday.'

He nodded.

1990

His new bike shone red in the sun, and when Callum smoothed the damp cloth across the paintwork it got even redder. Looking at it, putting his hands on the nubby grips, getting on and resting his weight on the seat, made him feel like his heart was too big for his chest and something was wrong with his knees.

A bike like this needed a name. Such a thing would require thought, however. Careful consideration, as his dad liked to say. Callum felt that after the first real test this afternoon at the track he would know the bike's ways and its soul, and then would be able to choose the perfect private name.

He looked at the watch Nanna Olive had given him. It wasn't a bad one – a Casio digital thing – but he would've preferred the chunky sporty type with the extra dials. It was 10:37. Dad had said they would go at one. 'Too bloody far away,' Callum said softly, trying out the swear.

He could ride around the yard, or he could go out onto the street. But there was something about just sitting next to it, getting on and off it, picking at the string-like tags of extra rubber on the tyres and polishing off the non-existent dust, that made him thrill. Maybe he would just sit there for a while, then it would be lunchtime, and soon after that they would go. Dad already had the bike rack on the car. Callum decided to get another rag from the bag in the laundry to wrap around the bar to make sure the lovely red paint didn't get scratched.

His mum screamed.

He dropped the bike.

'Gen?' his dad shouted from somewhere in the house.

Callum was on his feet and shaking as his mum screamed again.

His dad ran past the sliding doors towards the kitchen and Callum followed.

His mum was clutching the bench beside the microwave with both hands, her fingers white on the edge, the phone swinging free on its cord from the wall. Her face was so wet Callum thought she must have spilt water.

'What is it? What is it?' his dad was saying.

'Tim's dead.'

Callum felt the world shift under his feet. His dad stared at his mum in disbelief. The toilet flushed down the hall and Nanna came into the room.

'What was that noise?' she asked.

'Tim is dead. Killed.' His mother sobbed. 'Murdered.'

'Oh God, no.' Nanna stumbled and his dad caught her and helped her to a chair.

His mum leaned across the bench and wept into her hands. Callum didn't know what to do or where to look. He went back outside to where the bike lay on its side, the handlebar dug into the grass. He didn't know anyone who'd died. He couldn't see how it was possible that Tim wasn't here any more. He picked the bike up and brushed the dirt from the end of the grip and remembered how Tim had called him fuck-knuckle and hit him on the head with the fork, then something burst in his heart and he dropped the bike again and cried.

His dad packed his mum and Nanna into the car. Callum

wheeled the bike into the garage and propped it against the wall. His dad felt his back jeans pocket and frowned.

'It's on the bench,' Callum said. It felt strange to be talking about normal things like wallets when everything was different.

His dad started back into the house. As he passed the back of the car, his shoulder knocked into the bike rack. 'Fuck. Fuck!' His dad bunched his fist and hit the stem of the rack so hard his knuckles split and the car rocked on its tyres. 'Fuck!' He covered his face with his hands. Blood ran down his wrist and dropped from his elbow in fat red beads which burst on the concrete, and Callum suddenly saw Tim in his head, dead like a cat he'd seen on the road once, and fell to the floor stone-cold unconscious.

He blinked. Ella was across the table, listening. His coffee was going cold. He took a gulp and added another sugar. 'I guess I'm rambling.'

'It's fine,' she said. 'What happened then?'

He stirred the coffee, round and round. 'We drove to their house. The adults were in the living room and we kids stood about not knowing what to say, what to do. To see your parents like that is . . . I mean, we were grief-stricken too, but it felt like our grief was something we could cope with seeing and sharing. Theirs was something else altogether.'

Ella nodded.

'We kind of gravitated outside and sat together on the patio. Haydee was sobbing in waves. She'd stare off into space for a while then lose it, calm down a bit, stare off then lose it. Josh was all over the place. Sometimes it was like he didn't get it, like everything was completely normal, and then he'd say something like, "Did the bad man get Tim, did the bad man do it?" He kept asking and asking, and finally we said, "Yes, the bad man did it." But even then, you know, every so often he'd ask us again.'

Ella listened.

'I had this image in my head of Tim like a dead animal on a road,' Callum said. 'But I'd never seen a dead person and just couldn't comprehend that he was gone. I'm sitting there thinking that, and looking at Haydee and Josh, and I didn't know what to say. The words "I'm sorry" just don't cut it. You know?'

'I know.'

He glanced up, then back at his cup. 'I can't tell you what it means to me that you're looking after Tim now.'

She shifted a little on her chair. 'How do you get on with your aunt and uncle these days?'

'Pretty well,' he said. 'I mean, we always have done.'

'How do they get on with each other? How long has she lived in that granny flat?'

'Maybe four months. Sometimes I think they might split up, except for Josh. He doesn't do well with change.'

'Tamara doesn't seem to agree with John's ideas about Tim's death and the investigation,' Ella said.

'I think maybe she blames him for Tim's death,' Callum said, then immediately regretted it when he saw Ella's eyebrows go up. 'I once heard her saying to Mum that he was too strict and Tim had needed a bit more gentleness.'

'You think there's resentment there.' She wasn't asking.

'I don't think anyone can tell what's really going on inside a marriage,' he said. 'Even the people involved can't always be sure, because they each have their own point of view on everything and who's to say which is right?' He flushed. 'At least, that's how I felt when my own broke down four years ago.'

'But,' she prompted.

'But yes,' he said, 'I think Aunt Tamara holds a lot of anger and resentment towards Uncle John.'

When Ella got home, Wayne was mulching a row of five rose bushes. 'I know you don't like thorns but I'll deal with them for you,' he said.

She wrapped her arms around him.

'I'm filthy,' he said.

'I don't care.'

She felt his hands slide down her body.

Georgie was lying on the bed staring at the ceiling when the phone finally rang. Matt brought it in.

'Sorry,' Adam said.

'Sfine.' She looked at the clock radio: 4:50 pm. James had gone home hours ago, after asking her again not to mention Tim to Freya. She'd lain there stewing ever since, wondering how she could *not* say something. And there was a legal question involved now too, because the detective would surely want to know.

Matt sat by her feet and rubbed her leg.

'I talked to the sergeant,' Adam said. 'I mean, he overheard me asking about the McCrows and wanted to talk to me.'

Georgie sat up.

'He'd had a call from that Detective Marconi about the letter, asking whether he thought they might've written it.'

'What'd he tell her?'

'That they could've done it in a heartbeat,' he said. 'I told him what might be going on with you and we went for a drive around their usual haunts. Took us a while but we eventually spotted every last one of them.'

'Oh.'

'I hope that helps.'

'It's good,' she said. 'Thanks.'

'Anytime.'

She put the phone down and lay back on the pillow. 'He saw him today.'

'So that's good,' Matt said. 'Between him and Kaspar, we know it wasn't Barnaby you saw.'

Georgie shook her head. 'Unless somebody is certain they saw him out there on the same day and at the same time that I thought I saw him here, we don't know anything.'

Matt sighed.

'I know it sounds stupid.' She felt frustrated and angry. Besieged.

'It's all these things happening at once, that's all.' He squeezed her foot. 'You're stressed. You saw somebody who looked a little bit like him and it got in your head.'

'I'm not having a relapse.'

'I didn't say that.'

She looked at him.

'I said you're stressed, that's all.'

She pulled her foot from under his hand. 'I think I'm going to have a sleep.'

He sat there for a moment, then kissed her forehead and got up. She rolled away from him.

I am not losing it.

EIGHT

On Monday morning, Ella stopped at the café next door to the police building and bought a coffee in case the heater upstairs was still broken. It made her scalp tighten to think of her encounter with Frank Shakespeare and she hoped she wasn't destined to always put her foot in her mouth around him. No, she thought, what she really hoped was that she would never see him again.

She took the lift up, walked into the Unsolved office and stopped dead.

'Hi.' Murray smiled from the previously vacant desk.

You have to be kidding.

'Guess what I've got?' he said.

Herpes? she wanted to say. *The plague? Early-onset familial Alzheimer's, which might mean both you and your dad will be out of my life soon?*

She put down her bag and her coffee. 'Are you here because of what I said to your father?'

'Last week, or the first time?'

She put her hands on her hips. 'Last week.'

'Nah,' he said. 'I was already assigned.'

So it was just an ordinary case of nepotism rather than

revenge. It was good to know where she stood.

'You haven't guessed.' He waved a lumpy manila envelope.

'What if instead I bring you up to speed, as per normal procedure?'

'No.'

No? This was going to make for some interesting teamwork.

He pulled a tape from the envelope and held it up. 'Follow me and listen.'

He played it in one of the interview rooms. Ella stood with her teeth gritted.

The triple 0 operator came on the line. 'Police, fire or ambulance?'

A woman said, 'Ask the police why they haven't talked to the girl.'

'You want the police?'

'They need to talk to the girl who found that boy's body in Pennant Hills. I sent them a letter.'

'I'll put you through to the police now.'

'It should've been on the news,' the woman said. 'They didn't get my letter. You tell them.'

There was a click and another voice said, 'Police,' but the line was already dead.

Murray pressed stop.

'I already talked to the girl who found the body,' Ella said.

'Maybe we need to talk to her again,' Murray said. 'In a more official capacity.'

'They get a trace on the call?'

'Public phone in a shopping centre in Miranda.' He took the tape from the player. 'Where did you say this girl works?'

Ella drove them to The Rocks ambulance station and gave him the bones of the case on the way. She felt annoyed and second-guessed after having been satisfied that Georgie truly knew nothing more than she'd said. When she mentioned that for the second time, Murray stroked his lip with his thumb and fore-finger and said, 'Let's just see, shall we?'

The station roller doors were up and a buzzer sounded when they walked in.

Georgie came out of the office. 'Hi.'

'Georgina Riley?' Murray strode up and put out his hand. 'Detective Shakespeare. I understand you've already met Detective Marconi.'

Georgie nodded. 'Is it about the guys?'

'What guys?' Murray said.

'The ones who wrote the letter.'

'Not exactly,' Ella said. 'Can we sit and talk somewhere?'

The station office was small and had only two chairs. Georgie motioned for them to sit down. 'Freya?' she called out.

'What?' a woman's voice replied.

'Could you bring in another chair, please?'

There was a pause. Ella looked at Georgie and wondered why she didn't just grab one herself.

'Okay,' came the reply. A moment later a chair appeared in the doorway and Ella got a glimpse of a woman in a paramedic uniform moving away.

'Thanks,' Georgie said. She seemed disappointed for some reason that Ella couldn't work out.

Murray opened his notebook on his knee. 'Can you run through what happened that morning when you found the body of Tim Pieters, please?'

'Again?'

Murray shot her a look. 'Is there some reason you don't want to talk about it?'

'Not at all,' Georgie said with a glance at Ella.

Ella wanted to shrug, or roll her eyes a little, to show Georgie she knew how this was and she was sorry but what could she do? But she didn't, and with just the hint of a sigh Georgie began to tell the same story she'd told last week.

Ella could hear Murray's pen scratching as Georgie spoke. She watched for any sign of fabrication but Georgie recounted the story without difficulty. *See?* she wanted to say to Murray. *We talked already. All is cool.*

147

When Georgie finished, Murray frowned at what he'd written. Ella watched Georgie watching him. She seemed about to speak, then held back, crossing her legs the other way and staring at him. *Good for you*, Ella thought. *Don't fall for that 'give them a silence and they'll fill it with words' trick.*

'What is it you're not telling us?' Murray said.

'What?'

'The letter.'

'It's bullshit,' Georgie said. 'I know the sergeant out at Woolford told you that those guys probably wrote it.'

'Detective Marconi tells me he said it was possible, not probable.'

'Well, whatever,' Georgie said. 'Who else would've sent it?'

'We've had a phone call too,' Murray said. 'The caller was a woman.'

'They have a sister.'

'The phone call was made last night from Miranda.'

'Maybe she drove down yesterday,' Georgie said. 'They no doubt have friends who'd be happy to help out too. Because again, who else would do this? And why?'

'You tell us.' Murray folded his arms.

'There's nothing to tell.'

There was an edge to Georgie's voice now. Ella wanted to kick Murray. There was being a tough cop and then there was being stupid. Georgie was far from a suspect.

'Why are they telling us that there is?'

'I just told you,' Georgie said. 'What do you want me to say?'

'I want the truth.'

Georgie threw up her hands.

The phone rang. Ella heard the other paramedic answer it in the next room, speak briefly then hang up.

'Job,' she called.

'I have to go.' Georgie stood up.

Ella followed her out to the ambulance, hoping to get a moment to smooth things over a little, but Murray was right on her heels. Georgie's colleague got in the driver's seat and started the engine. Ella glanced over at her, then saw Georgie watching her with a hopeful expression.

'I'll follow up about the letter,' Ella said.

Georgie nodded.

'Thanks for your time.'

She and Murray went outside. The ambulance accelerated past them and onto the street and the roller door came down with a clunk.

'Strange woman,' Murray said. 'If I say I want to hear the story again, I mean I want to hear it. Did she think I was kidding?'

'I guess she feels she's telling it over and over.'

'So what? It costs her to do that?' Murray opened the car door. 'I'm the detective and it's my job to ask questions. She's the witness and it's hers to answer. What could be simpler?'

Ella got into the driver's seat. 'Maybe she didn't like your attitude.'

'I have no attitude.' He gestured at the road. 'Let's go.'

Ella rolled her eyes, started the car and pulled out.

Freya roared towards the Cross as if it was trying to get away from her.

'So what is it?' Georgie asked.

'Siege.'

Freya looked everywhere at once going through an intersection. She had the green but that yellow car had spooked her. She trusted nobody.

'Fun,' Georgie said.

Freya was just glad to be out of the station and away from those cops. She'd stood nervously in the lounge room, unable to settle, praying and praying for a job. Though it could've been one where she didn't have to sit in the ambulance with Georgie for who knew how long.

'Thirty-three,' Control called.

'Thirty-three,' Georgie answered.

'Police advise you are to stand off two blocks from that

location,' Control said. 'An officer will meet you.'

'Thirty-three copy.' Georgie rehooked the mike. 'Wonder how long this'll take.'

Freya clenched her jaw tighter and glared at the traffic. She'd spent shifts with paramedics who rubbed her so far the wrong way she could hardly bring herself to speak with them, shifts with idiots who talked nonstop about total shite, who drove through red lights on non-urgent cases because they were talking so much, who didn't sit with the patient in the back but came up to the resus seat and yakked at the back of her head from there. This, though – this could be a whole new class of torture, because Georgie knew about Tim.

On Saturday night, James had been rabbiting on about the investment strategies Matt had shown him, and she'd been half-listening while she made dinner, thinking mostly about Dion and the letter, and the next thing James was almost in tears, saying he'd let her secret out, he was so sorry, he'd had no idea Georgie didn't know.

She'd turned with the saucepan still in her hand and he'd actually flinched.

'Tell me,' she'd said, slowly, evenly. 'How does that even come up in conversation?'

A newspaper article, blah blah.

'And Georgie was shocked, was she?'

He'd nodded.

Freya had thought fast. 'Not surprised. I made it up.'

James had furrowed his brow. 'Why?'

'I thought it sounded better than the truth,' she'd lied, putting the pan back on the hotplate.

'Which is?'

'That I was drunk at a party and I didn't know who the hell it was.' She'd stirred the bolognaise sauce with a tense hand.

James had looked unconvinced. 'But why say it was him specifically?'

'I thought I'd be more believable if it was someone real, and he was the first boy to come to mind.'

'But –'

'Does it really matter?' She'd banged the spoon hard against the pan rim. 'I lied, and I'm sorry about that. But you still shouldn't have told what was shared in confidence.'

He'd looked bewildered, but had the good sense not to bring it up again and she hoped he never would.

The irony was that while he thought he'd let her secret out, he had no idea what her secret really was.

Nobody did. Except Dion.

'I think that's the corner,' Georgie said now.

Freya hit the switches to turn off the lights and siren, and braked by the cop who walked out into the street with his hand up.

He smiled in Georgie's window. 'Nice day for it.'

Freya nodded. 'Where do you want us?'

'Lob in there.' He pointed to a small park. 'Could be a while.'

'What's the story?' Georgie asked.

'Some twit with a handgun and a grudge against his bosses. He's got five hostages.'

'Crap,' Georgie said.

The cop nodded. 'We'll call if we need you.'

Freya parked where he'd said and turned off the engine.

Georgie rested her elbow on the sill. 'This place gets more and more like the States every day.'

Freya put her folded arms on the wheel and didn't answer. Down the street, cops were busily doing cop stuff. The sun was warm already and she put down her window. Georgie was in the shade and settling back in her seat. Freya pushed her sunglasses firmer on her face but the glare still hurt her eyes and her head. She felt in her bag for Panadol, then realised she had nothing to wash them down with. She stuck her head out the window. There was one tap in the pissy little park but the council had taken the top off. There were no shops visible in either direction.

She swallowed her pride. 'Don't suppose you've got any water?'

'Sorry.'

Dammit.

At the bottom of her bag she found a piece of chewing gum with the wrapper stuck to it. She peeled it off as best she could, then started chewing. Once a bit of saliva had collected she put the two Panadols in her mouth and swallowed. The taste made her eyes water. She swallowed and swallowed but they stuck halfway. She coughed. She felt Georgie looking at her.

Don't you dare ask me if I'm okay.

'You okay?'

The voice was male and came in her open window. Freya peered from watering eyes to see a man standing there looking in. She couldn't see much detail but could smell his body odour and the beer on his breath.

'She's fine,' Georgie said brusquely.

Freya swallowed hard and got the tablets down. She blinked away her tears and found the man leaning against the door, his forearm along the sill like they were old mates living in the country who'd stopped on a dirt road for a chat. She glanced at Georgie and saw she was frowning at the man's arm, and felt slightly better to know that people draping themselves all over the ambulance annoyed her too.

She looked at the man. 'Can we help you?'

He stopped chewing his yellowed moustache. 'What kinda baby you got under the bonnet in this thing?'

'We don't build them,' Freya said, 'nor do we maintain them. We drive them and look after patients.'

'Yeah, but don't they teach you even that?'

'To what end?' Georgie said.

'Huh?'

'Why would we need to know?' Freya said.

The man scraped a brown fingernail across a sore on his chin in a thoughtful way. 'How about you let me look in the handbook?'

'Confidential,' Georgie said.

'It's just a handbook.'

Freya shrugged. 'We don't make the rules.'

The man looked down the street towards the cops. 'What's going on down there?'

'Police stuff.'

'How come you're here too?'

'Paramedic stuff.' Freya wished he would piss off.

He frowned, then grinned. 'Hey, which one does the mouth-to-mouth?'

'Neither of us,' Georgie said.

'Then how?'

'We have equipment,' Freya said.

'That's no fun.' He smirked.

'That's life,' Georgie said, reaching for the microphone. 'Would you excuse us, please?'

The man looked confused. 'What?'

'Mind your arm,' Freya said, and pressed the button to raise the window.

He stepped back and stayed watching as Georgie raised the microphone to her mouth.

'He stinks,' she said.

'He's even worse closer up,' Freya said.

'Do I look believable?'

'Frown a bit. Listen and nod and frown a bit.'

Georgie listened and nodded, then said, 'How's that?'

'Perfect.' Freya listened and nodded and frowned too. 'How long do you think we have to do this for?'

Georgie turned her head towards the man. 'I'm guessing a while.'

'We can do that.'

Georgie listened and nodded. Freya frowned.

'I can't stand it when they lean all over the truck,' Georgie said. 'I mean, if they wouldn't do it to a cop car, they shouldn't do it to us.'

'My thoughts exactly,' Freya said. 'What's he doing now?'

'Watching,' Georgie said. 'Nothing better to do, I guess.'

'What a life.' Freya leaned on the wheel and nodded.

They were silent for a moment. Georgie sighed. 'Those detectives wanted the same story again.'

'Uh-huh,' Freya said. *I am cool and uninterested, so you might as well change the subject.*

'I asked them why and they – actually the guy did all the talking really – he said he just wanted to hear it. He had the shits too, like I shouldn't have asked.'

Freya was aware that Georgie was watching her and she leaned casually back in the seat and fake-yawned.

'He brought up that letter again, and said that now somebody had rung in and said the same thing,' Georgie said. 'I told him those guys out at Woolford were probably behind both things, but he had this attitude as if now that there were two things I *must* be lying. Then this job came in.' She hung up the mike. 'He's starting to wander away.'

'Thank God,' Freya said. It was getting hot in the cabin. Once the man was well on his way down the street she'd start the engine and run the aircon. If she did it too soon, he might think something exciting was happening and come back to see.

'But it makes me wonder,' Georgie said.

Freya stared out the windscreen before realising that no response was itself a form of response. 'Mm.' *So very cool, so extremely uninterested.*

'I wonder about what's really going on, and who knows stuff about the past that they've kept to themselves.'

Freya could feel Georgie's eyes boring into her face. 'I guess that's what the police are trying to find out.'

'I guess they are.'

Georgie's voice held something that Freya didn't like at all. She leaned forward and started the engine and turned up the aircon, and down the road the idiot bloke turned back with a look of clear interest.

'Oh crap,' Georgie said.

Hooray.

★

They found the phone in the shopping centre easily. It was attached to a column between a discount store and a supermarket, and an elderly woman in a bright pink headscarf was absentmindedly running her finger around the phone's buttons as she talked into it.

'Trying for prints would be a waste of time,' Murray said.

Ella looked up and around at the ceiling and saw a CCTV bubble down the mall and a sign to centre management just past it.

The receptionist in the management office smiled when they walked in. 'How may I help you?'

Ella showed her badge. 'I'd like to speak to your security officer, please.'

'Certainly.' The girl called somebody on the phone and the next minute a young woman came into the room.

'Becka Lawrence, security.' She shook Ella's hand then Murray's.

He smiled at her. 'How lovely to meet you.'

Ella shot him a look but Becka just nodded. 'We can talk in my office.'

The office was a tiny space with two chairs. Becka pushed one towards Ella but Ella shook her head. 'I'm fine.'

Murray sat. 'Thanks.'

Becka stayed on her feet as well. 'How long have you guys been cops?'

'Sixteen years, give or take,' Ella said.

'Ten,' Murray said.

Becka nodded. 'I'm applying next year. Working on my fitness now.'

This was great. A would-be cop would do everything in her power to help. Ella smiled at her. 'You'll get in no worries, I'm sure.'

'Absolutely,' Murray said. 'You look fit enough to apply now.'

Becka glanced his way then back at Ella. 'So what can I do for you?'

Ella told her what they needed and Becka turned to her

computer. 'This place is good with their camera system.' The screen showed real-time shots from various cameras throughout the centre. 'It's all digital so it's stored right here for months.'

'It's the camera looking onto the public phone near that discount shop,' Ella said. 'A triple 0 call was made there on Sunday night at eight forty-one.'

Becka's fingers flew on the keyboard.

'Typing's a good skill for a cop to have,' Murray said.

Becka nodded briefly. 'Here it is.'

They watched it in silence. Ella saw a woman walk into view, dressed in a white short-sleeved top and jeans. She had short, dark hair and a dark handbag over her left shoulder. She looked around, first into the supermarket, which was open, then towards the front of the closed discount store. A couple walked past holding hands and she turned her back a little, then stood by the phone a moment without doing anything.

'Making up her mind,' Ella said softly.

The woman put her hand on the phone, hesitated again, then lifted the handset and dialled. The timer on the screen clicked over to eight forty-one. Ella felt goose bumps steal up the back of her neck.

She couldn't see the woman speak, only the way her head moved, how she looked sideways once when somebody crossed the edge of the frame. When she'd hung up, she walked quickly away.

'Wow,' Becka said. 'What did she call about?'

'The big H,' Murray said. 'Homicide.'

Becka's eyes went wide. 'She knows who did it?'

'She knows something,' Ella said, still watching the screen. 'Are there cameras in the car park? We need to see if she got into a car.' Movement at the corner of the frame caught her eye. 'Was that her again?'

'Where?'

'Go back a second.'

Becka did so. Ella stared at the screen. The woman came back across the lower edge and went into the supermarket.

'Oh my. God,' Becka said. 'They have cameras everywhere in there.'

'Let's go.'

The supermarket security officer was a short and heavy-set man. 'Dougal,' he said gruffly, before sinking back into his chair and tugging his woollen vest down over his stomach.

'We're after footage of a woman who came in here at eighty forty-five on Sunday night,' Ella said.

'She knows something about a homicide,' Becka added.

Dougal put his fat fingers on his keyboard. 'Lessee then.' He clicked through a menu and selected a view of the entrance, running it on fast forward until he neared the time. People straggled in under the camera. 'Quiet night,' he said. 'What's she wearing?'

Murray described her. Dougal slowed the film further. Ella watched the timer in the corner then focused on the screen.

'Come on, darlin',' Dougal said.

And there she was. Ella felt the goose bumps again. *Her face is visible.* She wasn't looking straight at the camera but you could see enough.

'Bewdy,' Murray said.

Dougal hit a button and froze the screen. He peered closely.

'One of your regulars?' Becka asked.

Dougal frowned. 'Don't recognise her. You?'

'Nope.'

No, it couldn't be as easy at that, Ella thought. *Of course not.*

Dougal skimmed through views from different cameras. They saw her pick up a loaf of bread then go to the eight items or less register.

'What's she paying with?' Ella said.

Please, please, please, EFTPOS, please . . .

Murray squinted. 'Cash.'

Dammit.

The woman picked up her bread and walked out of shot. Dougal stopped the tape, plugged a USB stick into the computer, clicked and dragged the frames, then handed the stick to Ella. 'Locked and loaded.'

'Thanks,' she said.

Back in the security office, Becka pulled her chair up close to the computer. 'We have a number of cameras around the car park. I'll try to find her as she left, probably via the eastern doors because that's closest to the phone there.'

She hummed as she typed and scanned the screen. Ella held the USB stick loosely in her hand, rubbing her thumb along its edges, as if it was a diamond she would take back to the office and show off.

'This is her, right?'

Murray leaned close. 'Yep.'

They watched the woman cross the car park to the driver's side of a light-coloured sedan, something like a Commodore, then get in and drive away.

'Can hardly see the plate,' Becka said.

'Technical can clean it up,' Murray said. 'We might get enough to track her down.'

'That's so cool.'

'It is, isn't it?'

Murray was practically preening. Ella turned away.

Between the car and the woman's photo, which they could plaster all over the shopping centre and put in the media as well, they would surely find her. Ella wondered if she was indeed part of this alleged gang of conspirators dedicated to getting Georgie Riley in the shit, or if she really knew something about Tim and when he was found.

In the ambulance cabin the air was cool but the silence was stifling. Georgie had caught Freya casting wary glances her way and now she shot one back at her. 'What?' she demanded.

'What?' Freya said.

'You looked like you were about to tell me something.'

Freya shook her head. 'Don't think so.'

Georgie narrowed her eyes. Freya was so obviously on edge, constantly shifting in her seat, turning her wedding ring round and round her finger, frowning out the windscreen and squeezing the steering wheel so hard the muscles stood out on her forearms. Maybe James had told her what he'd said. *If he did, there's no need for me to stay silent.*

'How was your weekend?' she asked.

Freya snorted. 'Crap.'

'Yeah?'

'I'm either working here or working at home,' Freya said. 'Washing, cooking, cleaning, running around. Never stops.'

'James help much?'

Freya snorted again.

'Seems a nice guy,' Georgie said. 'When he came over for that investment info we had a bit of a chat. Did he tell you?'

'He may have mentioned it.' Freya shrugged. 'I was cooking dinner and wrangling kids and putting a load of laundry through so I'm not really certain.'

'I know what you mean.'

Freya muttered.

'Sorry?'

'I said, you have no kids.' Freya pressed her thumb and forefinger to her eyes. 'There's no comparison.'

Georgie bristled. *If she thinks that flinging barbs will make me shut up and back off, she'd better think again, and quick.* 'I know,' she said.

'Good.'

'No. I mean, I *know*.'

'Know what?'

'About you and Tim.'

Down the street a smiling police officer started their way.

'Tim who?'

'James told us.'

Freya kept rubbing her eyes. 'James is an idiot.'

'How did you and Tim get together?'

Freya said nothing.

'You may as well tell me,' Georgie said.

'Tell you what?'

Oh, the advanced stalling techniques! 'Or you could just tell the detectives.'

'It's not true.'

'Bullshit.'

The police officer was at Freya's window. She lowered it.

'All over,' he said. 'Peaceful surrender, nobody injured. Fly free, my fellow emergency service personnel.'

Georgie smiled. 'Have a good one.'

He walked away and Freya raised her window again. 'You can believe what you want but it isn't true.'

'Bullshit again.' Georgie picked up the mike. 'Thirty-three is clear at this scene, no longer required.'

'Perfect timing,' Control said. 'I have a pedestrian hit-and-run on Oxford Street in Paddo.'

'Three's on the case.' Georgie slammed the mike onto its hook. 'The detectives should be told.'

'It isn't true.' Freya lurched the ambulance down the gutter and onto the street.

'I don't believe you.'

'Fine,' Freya said. 'See if I care.'

'Then you won't care if I call up that detective and let her know.'

Freya hit the switches for the lights and siren. 'That's slander.'

'It's only slander if it —'

'Hearsay then. Whatever.'

'I'll say it's a rumour I heard. I told her on Friday about the rumours that went around the school and she listened, so I'm sure she'll be interested in another one.'

Freya tore onto Victoria Street. 'I can't see why she would.'

'What you can see doesn't matter,' Georgie said. 'She needs to know.'

'You a cop now, are you?' Freya hit the brakes to avoid a panicking red Mini then ripped around it on the wrong side of the road. 'I think you're in the wrong uniform then.'

Georgie held on as Freya took the corner into Oxford Street, siren screaming, lights flashing off shopfronts and signs.

No more – for now. It was time to focus. The traffic was chock-ers. Georgie could see the accident site ahead and snugged up her latex gloves as Freya roared down the wrong side of the road. Pedestrian versus car usually resulted in trauma to the legs, probably the head too. She was good with trauma.

Usually.

She pushed away the snide voice and the argument and the whole thing with Tim, and put her hand on her seatbelt, ready to get out.

Four police huddled around the woman lying on the road-way. One was on his knees doing something, and another turned away and retched. Georgie could hear someone wailing, even though the window was up. She reached for the microphone. 'Thirty-three's on scene.'

'Thanks, Thirty-three.'

Freya braked to a stop. Georgie jumped out and opened the back sliding door to grab the Oxy-Viva. The wailing turned into shrieks and she hurried across the asphalt.

The relief in the cops' eyes at her arrival was clear and Georgie could see why. The woman's left cheek was torn open, and though the cop's gloved and shaking hands tried to hold a blood-soaked dressing over the wound, the woman's struggles made it gape, revealing the white of bone and teeth underneath. Her right arm was fractured halfway down the humerus, and each time she thrashed, her shoulder moved and then the arm followed floppily a second later. Her left knee was avulsed and one broken end of her left femur bulged against her skin below her denim shorts, and her arms were covered in abrasions full of road gravel. She was screaming for her mother.

'She won't lie still,' the young copper said, his voice cracking.

Georgie knelt beside him. 'You did good. Do you know her name?'

'ID says it's Lucy.' Another copper held the woman's open wallet and her blood-spattered handbag. 'She's twenty-three.'

Georgie pressed a clean dressing to Lucy's cheek and leaned close. 'Lucy, look at me. Can you tell me what happened?'

Lucy wailed. 'Muuuum!'

'Lucy!'

'Muuuuuuuuuuum!'

Georgie looked around. Freya was there now, setting up the oxygen mask and monitor. It would be good if they could play nicely, for Lucy's sake.

Of the cops standing about she picked the one who looked the most calm and least pale. 'Kneel here,' she said. 'Hold her head until we can get a collar on to protect her neck.'

He did so. Georgie slipped the oxygen mask over Lucy's head, using the strap to keep the dressing on her cheek for now. Freya handed her a collar and she strapped it around Lucy's neck. 'Keep supporting her,' she said to the cop. 'You're doing good.'

'Sinus tach of one thirty,' Freya said brusquely, one eye on the monitor, the other on the sphygmo dial as she inflated the cuff and fitted the earpieces of her stethoscope into place at the same time. 'Ninety on fifty.'

Georgie shone her torch into Lucy's eyes. 'Equal and reacting.'

'Muuuuuuuuuuum!' The shriek was deafening.

'It's okay, Lucy, it's all going to be okay.'

Georgie started a quick nose-to-toes examination while Freya clipped a tourniquet around Lucy's arm and palpated for a vein. Head was good except for the face; neck appeared uninjured, but better safe than sorry, hence the collar; left arm intact except for the abrasions, and now splinted to protect the cannula Freya was inserting; right needing splinting for the fracture; chest had equal movement and felt undamaged; abdo soft, though it was hard to know about tenderness when all Lucy did was scream whether Georgie was touching her or not; pelvis was firm; left leg bad, but right was kicking well.

'I'm in,' Freya said.

'Hartmann's and five of morph, please,' Georgie said.

Once that was on board she would organise a log roll to check Lucy's back. For now she got splints from the truck and put one on the fractured femur. Lucy's screams started to diminish.

'Five in,' Freya said. 'Hartmann's running wide open.'

Next, Georgie splinted the right arm and Lucy started to breathe rather than wail.

'Lucy, can you hear me?' Georgie said.

'What happened?' she sobbed.

'You were hit by a car,' Georgie said. 'You don't remember?'

'What happened?'

It was the persistent concussion-caused question that Georgie had heard so often over the years. 'You were hit by a car. Everything's going to be okay. Just try to keep as still as you can.'

'What happened?'

Freya went to get the stretcher and Georgie moistened a clean dressing and applied it more carefully to Lucy's cheek, gently closing the wound as best she could then taping and bandaging the dressing in place.

'Hurts.'

'I know, Lucy, I'm sorry.'

'What happened?'

'You were hit by a car,' Georgie said. 'Hold still there, Lucy, we're just going to roll you onto your side so I can check your back.'

She organised the police to help, and felt along Lucy's ribs and spine before bringing her down again onto the spineboard so they could lift her onto the stretcher.

Once in the ambulance, she rechecked Lucy's pupils, blood pressure, oxygen saturation and ECG. Her left foot had a strong pulse, which meant the femur fracture was well-aligned. She felt her right wrist. The pulse wasn't so strong there but the skin was warm and pink.

'Looking good, Lucy. How are you feeling?'

'What happened?'

'You were hit by a car,' Georgie said. 'You're in an ambulance. Everything's going to be okay.'

For the first time Lucy seemed to focus. She blinked at Georgie and tried to look around.

'Don't move your neck,' Georgie said. 'There's a collar on it to protect it. I know it's not all that comfortable.'

Lucy lay flat on her back staring at the ambulance roof. Tears flooded her eyes and Georgie paused in adjusting the flow of Hartmann's to wipe them away for her. 'It's all going to be okay,' she said again.

'It hurts.'

'I know,' Georgie said. 'Do you know what day it is today? Do you know where you are?'

Lucy was vague on the details at first, but her level of consciousness improved as Freya drove them smoothly to the hospital. Georgie gave her another five of morph and set up another bag of Hartmann's for maintenance. When she asked Lucy to squeeze her fingers with her right hand, testing sensation and power below the fracture site, Lucy did so, then kept hold. Georgie felt her trembling and tightened her own grip. Sometimes holding hands counted more than anything else.

She looked up at the rear-view and met Freya's eyes. Freya didn't smile, but neither did she frown.

At the hospital, Georgie gave the nurse a detailed handover then helped to transfer Lucy onto the Emergency Department bed.

She put her hand on Lucy's shoulder. 'They're great people here, they'll look after you really well.'

Lucy welled up. 'Thank you for everything.'

Georgie smiled at her. 'You're most welcome.'

Outside, she settled into the ambulance's passenger seat to write her case sheet. So what if she and Freya had argued? She was happy, strong, good at her job. This was exactly what she'd needed, a decent trauma that reinforced to her why she was in the service and provided a bloody good case for the assessment. She nodded approval to herself. *Job well done.*

Freya rattled about in the back of the ambulance. Georgie listened with half an ear as she wrote, hearing the noise of zips and lockers opening and closing as Freya restocked the Oxy-Viva, the clanks and bangs as she loaded the freshly wiped and made-up stretcher back in, the whir of the monitor printing out the ECG strip. The air was full of the alcohol from the environmental wipes she wielded. It was the smell of Georgie's life.

Freya dropped the ECG strip over her shoulder. 'Here you go.'

'Thanks.'

Georgie tore it into six-second sections and stapled them to the case sheet. The back was silent and she realised Freya was still there, sitting in the resus seat at the head of the stretcher and looking out the windscreen. Georgie followed her gaze. It had started to rain. She bent to her paperwork again, but Freya didn't move.

Twenty-three-year-old female pedestrian struck by a car. The scratching of her pen was loud in the quiet. Georgie felt Freya's eyes on her, felt her silence grow, taking up the cabin, pushing her back into her seat.

'A good job,' she finally said.

'Kind of,' Freya replied.

Georgie wrote the next line and told herself not to be drawn in. It was a good job. She ticked the treatment boxes and filled in the drug and fluid doses and drew on the printed figure to indicate Lucy's injuries, and tensed her shoulders against Freya's gaze, and fought hard, but finally couldn't help but look up. Freya was watching her.

'You know I have this report to fill in about you at the end of each week,' she said.

'I've seen it done,' Georgie said. 'It's a pain. I'm sorry.'

Freya shrugged. 'It's not that. I'm just not sure what to write.'

Georgie felt the air leave her lungs. 'I guess it's never easy.'

'You got that straight.' Freya yanked stuffing from a hole in the driver's seat upholstery. 'I mean, that job there, for example.'

'Yep?' Georgie pressed her fingers hard against the corners of the case-sheet folder.

'Well.' Freya left it hanging.

When feeling returned to her fingertips, Georgie filled in their surnames, employee numbers, the date and location of the accident with obsessive neatness. *I will not speak first.* It was like high school all over again. She'd always spoken first back then, unable to bear the swelling silence, the aching desire in her throat to say something to heal the petty disagreement. Now she gritted her teeth and held it back. She could see from the corner of her eye that Freya was playing with the bit of stuffing, twirling it around her finger while she gazed out the windscreen. Georgie didn't know how she did it, how she'd always done it. She herself could never act so unconcerned.

'It's so hard, sometimes, when you *think* you've done a good job.' Freya sighed and rammed the stuffing back in the hole. 'It'd be such a pity if you failed.'

Her eyes on the floormat, Georgie saw it all.

'Wouldn't it?' Freya said. 'I mean, think of everything you'd lose. Your job, maybe your house if you couldn't pay your mortgage, and I guess it'd be tough to get another job once they knew you got sacked from this one, plus stupid Ross what's-his-name would win –'

'I get it,' Georgie said.

'Get what?'

'What you're saying.'

Freya shrugged. 'All I'm saying is what a pity it would be if you failed.'

Georgie felt sick and angry and hurt. She'd thought the assessment might be at risk because of the tentacles of Ross Oakes, never because of something like this.

'Such a *terrible* pity,' Freya said.

NINE

They dropped the USB stick into Technical on their way through the city. Ella's mobile rang as she was about to get back into the car. She saw her parents' number and sighed.

'Do you know how many messages I've left?' Netta said.

'I'm sorry,' Ella said. 'I should've called you back.'

Murray put his hand out for the keys.

'I called this number, your home phone, and at the office.'

'I'm sorry.'

'I even called your old number in Homicide and asked if they knew where you were.'

Ella closed her eyes.

'Didn't they tell you?' Netta said.

Murray waggled his fingers.

'I've been out.' Ella reluctantly handed the keys over and got in the passenger side. 'I've been busy.'

'Too busy to let your poor mother know that you're still alive.'

'Of course I'm still alive.'

'How am I to know that?'

'Don't give her a hard time,' she heard her father say in the background.

167

Netta shushed him.

'I mean it,' he said. 'She won't want to come for dinner tonight.'

'Of course she'll want to come for dinner tonight,' Netta said. 'After making us worry like this, she'll absolutely want to come for dinner tonight.'

'I was going to have dinner with Wayne,' Ella said.

'Bring him! Stella from down at the club gave me some lovely fresh eggplant and I'm making those rolls you like. I'll make extra. It's time we met him anyway.'

Ella could hear the joy in her mother's voice. 'Okay.'

'Half six? Or seven? Whenever you like.'

'Okay. Bye.'

She rang Wayne. 'I've just received a summons. Mum wants us there for dinner tonight.'

'Great,' he said. 'Meet at your place when?'

'Six thirty'd be good.'

'See you then.'

She put the phone away. It was overdue, she had to admit. It was the thought of the sizing up that would go on, the glances between her parents, the scrutiny that poor Wayne would be under, that had made her less than willing. But there was no getting around it. She would just have to remember to tell him that whatever else he said he had to praise the cooking.

Murray turned off the Great Western Highway into Concord.

'Pendle Hill and Wade Tavris are that way,' Ella said.

'We should drop in on his ex first.'

'Little consultation might've been nice.'

'You were sorting out your social life.'

'For all of five minutes.'

He shrugged. 'We're almost there now.'

She looked out the window at the sun on the leaves and tried to count to ten.

'Listen,' he said. 'I read your reports. I think Tavris is the one to focus on.'

'Really.'

'That family-barbecue-argument angle – I can't see it. Whereas Tavris had the car that was a) seen near the pub where Tim and his friends were, and b) later found burnt out.'

'The car he claimed had been stolen, and that was used in a robbery that night.'

'Claimed being the operative word.' Murray turned off Concord Road. 'And he couldn't have done the robbery himself?'

'So he grabs Tim off the street, kills him, does the robbery, dumps the body, burns the car? Busy boy.'

'Kinda handy that it was "stolen" that very night,' Murray said. 'The robbery is a nice extra touch. Makes it almost convincing.'

'Did you read the reports? Constantine and Tynan got stuck into him good. Plus there was no evidence found –'

'Because it was destroyed in the fire.'

'– none on Tim to link them together, and Jane Lincoln was a solid alibi even six years ago when they spoke to her again.'

'But now they've broken up,' he said. 'Which is why we're going to see her first.'

Ella folded her arms. 'If we see Tavris first we can pressure him with the knowledge that we're going to talk to Lincoln later.'

'If we see Lincoln first, we can pressure Tavris with the knowledge that we've just talked to her and he doesn't know what the hell she's said.'

Ella shut her eyes, the better to count to twenty.

Jane Lincoln lived in a unit on the second floor of a tired brick building overlooking a service station. Ella followed Murray up the stairs. *She might be at work*, she thought. *We might have to talk to Tavris first after all.*

Murray knocked on the locked screen.

The door opened and a woman in a pink dressing gown looked out. 'Oh.'

Ella held up her badge. 'Jane Lincoln?'

She was already unlocking the screen. 'Yes.'

The living room was small, the brown carpet thin and worn. The TV was muted. A rumpled blanket and pillow lay on the lounge and a box of tissues and bottle of cough syrup stood on the coffee table. Jane Lincoln wiped her red nose then pushed the tissues into her pockets. Sue didn't invite them to sit down.

'I saw the news,' she said. 'I know this is about Wade.'

'Are you still in contact with him?' Murray asked.

'Nope,' she said. 'I left him five years ago and that was that.'

'Why did you break up?'

'Because he's a bastard.'

'Meaning what?' Ella said.

'Meaning he's a bastard,' Jane said. 'Things hadn't been good for a while, then one day he came home pissed and hit me. I took the next day off sick and moved out while he was at work. Stayed with my sister for a while then found this place.'

'Did he try to get in touch?'

'He called up work for a while. They used to put him on hold and never pick up again. He gave up after a month or so.'

Ella said, 'What did you think when he was questioned about Tim Pieters's death?'

'That he didn't do it.'

'You still think that?' Murray said.

'I know it. He was with me all night. I'll swear that on a stack of Bibles.'

'You were awake and watching him?'

Jane gave him a look. 'Is that what you do when you have somebody stay over?'

'I'm just asking how you can be sure that he didn't sneak out.'

'I sleep light,' she said. 'I would've woken up.'

'How can you be certain?'

'I just am.'

'What about his ute?' Ella said. 'Where was it parked?'

'Like I told the detectives back then, it was on the street. My unit was at the back of the block. We couldn't have seen or heard anything even if we'd been expecting it to get stolen. First thing we knew about it was when Wade went down to go out and came back up swearing.'

'Did you know that Wade's been in jail?' Murray said. 'He just got out.'

'I didn't know he was out yet, but yes.'

'Killed a man,' Murray said.

'I know.'

Ella started to speak but Murray cut across her. 'If you want to change your statement now's the time to speak up.'

'I told the truth.'

'Think for a moment,' Murray said. 'While reflecting on Wade's true nature.'

'I stand by what I said.' She folded her arms. 'He might've killed somebody since, but the night that boy died he was home with me.'

Murray jangled the keys irritably on the way back to the car. Ella crossed behind him and yanked them from his hand. 'Disappointed?'

'She must still have feelings for him.'

'After five years?'

'She was with him for, what, fifteen? And then she leaves just like that?' Murray said. 'There's no closure there.'

'Sounded like she had plenty to me.' Ella started the car.

'As for that sleeping lightly thing – you can't tell me she can be one hundred per cent sure.'

'There's no evidence.'

'Wade's ute wasn't broken into.'

'Those old things can be opened with practically any key,' she said. 'No need to smash a window when you can do that. Plus, it was hot-wired.'

'Another extra touch.'

Ella turned west into spits of rain. 'Don't forget that the killing was accidental.'

'That's only what the court decided,' he said. 'May I remind you that the truth does not always out.'

Freya hid in the tiny run-down kitchen of the dead man's house, sick with shame.

They'd finished at the hospital in silence, then responded on a call to this man, collapsed, and found him dead in his lounge room. Freya had asked Control to send the police, while Georgie had comforted his friends and explained this was normal procedure in all sudden deaths. Now the old couple had gone back next door, and Freya and Georgie were alone in a silent house with a cold, stiff body and the world's biggest elephant.

Freya peered around the doorjamb. Georgie sat on the lounge by the body, her elbows on her knees and her head down. Freya's stomach cramped with guilt and regret. When she'd first seen Georgie in the ambulance she'd felt alarm, yes, but also joy. Before everything changed that year in high school, they'd been great friends. Best friends. Although, she thought now, best friends probably shared more than she'd felt able to.

She turned away. On the wall by the whirring fridge a calendar said it was still 2005. The ceiling was covered in greasy dust, the air smelled of chops and the small window that looked out onto the back lawn was painted shut. A frypan, white with grease, sat on the grimy stove and a cockroach skittered into the drain in the sink. Freya kept her arms close to her sides and looked out at the rain-damp, overgrown lawn and thought about Tim.

It had started after a soccer match against Pennant Hills High. She'd been in Year Eight. Both the boys' and girls' teams had played, the girls first, and she'd come off the field exhilarated at their win, the blood pumping hard in her veins. She was supposed to go back to school, but had stayed sitting on the low fence, seeing the clods of dirt fly from the boys' boots and the sunlight flash on their golden shirts. Afterwards she'd gone into the change room for a drink of water and Tim had been there. They'd started talking. She'd sat down on the bench. The room smelled of stale sweat and damp concrete but she could smell him too, his deodorant, his energy. He had reached over her to get his bag from the shelf and brushed up against her. She'd put her hand out, curious. She'd heard him breathe in. There was nobody else around. He'd slid his hand along her shoulder and the touch of his fingers on the bare skin of her neck was electric. Her hair had come loose from its ribbon and fallen down over his hand. The golden cloth of his shorts made ridges between her fingers and underneath it he was hard and trembling. She'd moved her hand and watched his face, curious, and as he came he clutched her shoulder and she'd felt power like nothing before.

The next time was at the movies. They'd bumped into each other at the shops. Fifteen minutes later they were sitting in the dark. She remembered his hands on her skin, the movement of his fingers, how she'd pressed her face against his shoulder, and the feeling of even more power.

Later, outside, he'd asked her to be his girlfriend.

'No.'

He'd looked shocked.

'Let's just stick with this.'

It seemed easier, better. She'd seen girls with boyfriends, how they went everywhere together, the neediness on both sides. She didn't want to be that way.

She glanced into the lounge room again. Georgie hadn't moved. On the wall next to her hung a sepia photo of the dead man in his air force uniform. Freya had looked at it while Georgie checked the body when they'd first arrived. He'd been handsome in his younger days. She couldn't tell what he looked like now because he was upside down over the side of the lounge, his skinny white legs pointing out of tartan boxers at the ceiling, his yellow soles motionless in the air. The five bottles of Anginine and three Nitrospray squirters dotted about the coffee table and the one fallen from his hand showed his poor health as well as his likely cause of death. She imagined him sitting on the lounge and looking at that photo of himself and wondering where the hell that young man had gone.

She made her foot scuff on the filthy linoleum but Georgie didn't look up. Her heart hurt. When she'd been asked to do this assessment she'd known there was something odd going on – between that email, which nobody in their right mind could imagine that Georgie had sent herself, and Stronach's mention of trouble at her home station, how could she not? She'd been determined to do a solid job, to judge the person only on her work, and to be fair even when other people in the service couldn't, or wouldn't. But now look. She was as bad as the rest.

But what could she do? If she admitted to the cops that she'd been with Tim, they would ask when and why it had ended. There was no way she could tell them that. Then they'd ask what she knew about his death, and she couldn't tell them that either.

She had no other option.

She turned away from the unmoving Georgie and looked back out the window.

About a month after that movie, a month during which they'd met up in dark bus shelters, different cinemas, behind isolated classrooms and in bushland near the school, she and Tim had wagged afternoon classes and gone to his house. Everyone was out. He'd been sweating and nervous. He'd kept pulling back, asking, 'Is that okay? Is that okay?' She'd drawn him nearer and held him tight and felt his muscles tense against her. Again, more power.

And again he'd asked her to be his girlfriend. He'd been hurt by her refusal and threatened to not see her again. She'd shrugged and kept getting dressed. He'd relented, holding her hand, wanting to cuddle. She'd said she had to go.

Two weeks later she'd joined the after-school drama group with Georgie. That first afternoon the teacher, Dion Entemann, had gone around the circle of students introducing himself and shaking hands with each one. He was twenty-three, a man with strong hands and a sweet smile and knowledge in his eyes.

With Georgie giggling beside her, Freya had smiled back, and squeezed his hand, and knew, just *knew,* that things were going to change.

There was a knock at the door. 'Police.'

Freya was already at the doorway. Georgie jumped up from the sofa, and the legs wobbled but the body didn't fall. They didn't look at each other as they went to the front door.

The cops were burly, their belts heavy on their hips, a blue clipboard under the younger one's arm. Georgie gave them the story, told them their names and contact details for The Rocks station, and said goodbye.

Freya walked outside, smiled at the neighbours, and got in the ambulance. Georgie followed, slamming her door and ramming in her seatbelt.

Freya pushed down her guilt. She had to be strong. She had no choice.

She just had to hope that Georgie didn't decide that her threat meant Freya had something to hide and therefore she *must* call the detective, no matter what.

The rain had stopped by the time they reached Pendle Hill where Wade Tavris lived in what had once been a motel. Ella parked on the street and walked up the wet concrete driveway with Murray striding out ahead of her. At the driveway's far end a graffitied wall and two dead eucalypts failed to block noise from the Great Western Highway. The front office door was painted and padlocked shut and a warped blind hung on the inside of the dusty glass behind a Bankcard sticker so faded it was almost white.

Tavris lived in unit five. Ella saw a number on the door to unit two and empty screw holes suggesting numbers on the rest. She stood to the side of five's door while Murray knocked.

The door opened and a short, skinny woman looked out at them. Ella felt sized up and recognised in an instant.

'He's not here,' the woman said.

'And your name is?' Murray said.

The woman considered either the question or her answer. 'Sharon Fielding.' Behind her a child started to cry. She looked over her shoulder and the crying stopped.

'How long have you and Wade been together?' Murray asked.

'Four months.'

'Mind if we have a word?'

'Aren't we already?'

'I mean, can we come in,' he said.

'I know what you mean.'

Sharon didn't move from the doorway. She turned her head to look inside the room again, her dyed red and blonde hair swinging stringily over her shoulder. She muttered something about coppers and stepped back.

The room was small and made even smaller by the chunky furniture squeezed into it. The air was damp. Toddlers' clothes were draped along the back of a worn red velvet lounge while the toddler in question sat sucking his thumb and feeling a balding spot on the cushion. Sharon sat next to him and folded her arms.

'He reported yesterday.'

'We're not here about his parole,' Murray said.

Ella glanced about. The chairs by the table were piled high with papers, plastic bags, flattened beer cartons and clothes. The table itself was covered in car engine parts.

Sharon looked at the child and he looked up at her. His legs stuck straight out on the lounge and he smiled at her around his thumb and clapped his feet together as if in excitement. Ella couldn't recognise anything remotely exciting.

'How long have you lived here?' Murray asked.

'Couple of months.'

Ella saw a school tunic on a coathanger hooked on the handle of the broken pantry door. 'How many of you?'

'Four,' Sharon said. 'My older kids are with my parents in Doonside.'

'One bedroom?'

Sharon tossed her hair back over her shoulder. 'DOCS knows.'

The tunic was ironed, Ella saw; the iron sitting on a folded towel on the kitchen bench. 'Is Wade working?'

'Bits and pieces.'

'It's hard,' Ella said.

Sharon looked at her as if that was the most stupid thing she'd ever heard. Of course it was hard. Ella wondered what it cost to live here and how it must feel to have no other option. The tunic was for a girl aged about ten and Ella pitied her, imagined trying to do homework here and how strong you would have to be to break free of this life. She looked at Sharon and realised too late that all this was showing in her eyes as Sharon straightened her spine and glared.

'I'm sure you know the name Tim Pieters,' Murray said.

'That boy in Pennant Hills,' Sharon said. 'Wade dint have nothing to do with it. He's not like that.'

Murray laughed.

'Hey,' she said, 'that arsehole at the pub was pissed and came at Wade with a broken bottle.'

'We read the witness statements,' Ella said.

Sharon rolled her eyes. 'They were all friends. Wade wasn't even s'posed to be there. He told me all about it. He was working with a removalist over there and they went there for one beer, and he went outside for a smoke and –'

'Okay,' Murray said.

'It was only one punch,' Sharon said. 'He didn't want to kill him.'

'He did though,' Murray said. 'And we need to talk to him. Here's my card. Have him call when he gets in.'

'You see a phone?'

'Or we can just come back at random times.'

She grunted. 'He'll use next door's.'

Murray grunted back and walked outside.

Sharon let the card drop on the lounge. The child tilted his head against her arm and she encircled his leg with her fingers.

177

Ella nodded at him. 'What's his name?'

'Devorn.'

'Nice.'

Sharon shrugged like she knew what Ella really thought and didn't care.

'Bye,' Ella said to the child, and he smiled at her.

Murray was already halfway down the drive, hands deep in his pockets. She was hurrying to catch up when a ute coated in grey primer turned into the driveway. The man behind the wheel looked at them, and she saw both that he picked them as cops and wasn't surprised they were there.

'Here we go.' Murray turned around.

They followed the ute back up the drive. The man parked and got out with his hands on his hips. 'What now?'

'Wade Tavris?'

'Yes.'

'You know the name Tim Pieters?'

He sighed. 'I saw that on telly and I knew you'd be back.'

'I told them,' Sharon said from the doorway.

'I didn't do it.'

'Tell us again about that night.'

Wade smelled of sweat and dust. Up close he looked tired. 'Read the statement I made back then. Read the notes they made when they came to talk to me again six years back.'

'We have,' Ella said. 'We want you to tell us.'

Sharon stamped inside and slammed the door.

'I was working as a brickie's assistant at a site in Castle Hill,' Wade said. 'We worked that Saturday morning then went to the pub. In the evening I went to Jane's flat in Hornsby. We had Chinese from this place down the road. We went to bed. The next morning I found my car was missing and I reported it. The day after that the cops turned up at the site. I did nothing wrong but I lost that job. Enough?'

'You should know that we've just had a chat with Jane Lincoln,' Murray said.

'So what?'

'She's still got some issues with you.'

'I don't care what she's got,' he said. 'I didn't do it.'

Ella said, 'You know what's interesting about old cases? We can now get DNA results from samples we couldn't test before.'

'And it's funny,' Murray added, 'how often it's somebody we looked at way back then who proves to be the culprit.'

Wade shrugged.

Murray stepped closer. 'We're telling you this because we like our suspects to be fully informed.'

Wade dug his hands into his pockets and stared at the ground. Ella and Murray let the silence stretch out. Wade didn't look up.

'Let's give the man some thinking time,' Murray said to Ella. 'We'll be back, Wade.'

Murray turned away. Wade lifted a small cement-spattered Esky from the tray of the ute, stamped across the concrete and flung open the door to unit five, and as Ella followed Murray she could hear the sound of arguing from inside the unit, even over the rush of the highway traffic.

Callum sat on Tim's bed and watched Josh going through his cupboard.

'Lots of things in here,' Josh said.

It wasn't really Tim's bed because it was a spare room, but anytime guests came they stayed in one of the other spares. Only when space got really tight did anybody sleep in here.

Josh backed out of the cupboard and held up Tim's Macquarie College soccer shirt. 'Tim played soccer.'

'That's right, he did,' Callum said.

He had half an hour before his meeting with local hospital staff. Anna had suggested using the time to talk to people before the meeting, let them get to know him, but he'd told her to drive here instead. He wanted to talk to John. As soon as he'd knocked on the door, however, Josh had latched onto him and dragged him upstairs, John following to stage-whisper that Josh was focused on Tim again, probably because of what was going on, people talking about him, that sort of thing. 'Just listen,' he'd said. 'That's all you can do.'

'Tim was my brother,' Josh said now.

'That's right.'

'The bad man got him.'

Callum felt uncomfortable nodding, but it was true. Some bad man had got him.

'Have they got the bad man yet?'

'They're looking.'

'That lady's going to find him.'

'She is,' Callum said. 'That's what she's doing right now.'

Josh went back into the cupboard. 'Will the bad man get me?'

'No, you're perfectly safe.'

His voice was muffled. 'Tim said he would always protect me. But Tim's not here.'

'But I am,' Callum said. 'I'll make sure that bad man doesn't get you.'

Josh came out with soccer boots on his hands. 'Tim saved me.'

'He was good like that.'

'I love him.'

'So do I.'

Callum was surprised to feel tears prick his eyes. It'd been almost twenty years – but he knew that didn't mean much. The loss was still the loss. And looking at Josh standing there fitting the studded soles of the boots together, Callum felt the echo of the grief, the high-water mark of the tsunami that had torn through the family. He wiped away his tears with the back of his hand.

Josh came to sit next to him. 'You want a hug?'

'I'd love a hug.'

Josh put his arms around him, the boots still on his hands. Callum hugged him back and felt the warmth and life in his body. God forbid anything should ever happen to him.

'Love you, mate.'

'I love you, Cal.'

After a moment Josh handed him the boots and crawled back into the cupboard, pushing boxes and plastic bags of clothes out behind him as he dug into the back. He came out smoothing a narrow golden ribbon over his arm like a maitre d' with his white towel. 'Can I play with this?'

'Sure.'

'It's shiny.'

Callum nodded, the boots balanced on his thighs. 'It's pretty.' He checked his watch. If he was going to talk to John he needed to do it soon. First, though, he had to work out what to say.

Josh draped the ribbon over his hair and smiled.

'Nice.'

It felt like prying, and they'd never been a family who got into each other's business. It also felt like being less than supportive. Callum wanted to ask the question – since Ella had asked it of him he couldn't get it out of his head – but worried that it was the wrong thing to do. And what did his desire to know actually mean?

He was helping Ella, that was all. He didn't suspect John. He just needed to know. It was his family too.

He made up his mind and stood. Josh was still playing with the ribbon. Callum leaned into the cupboard and put the boots into Tim's old sports bag on top of the shirt.

'I have to talk to your dad,' he said.

Josh nodded, pulling the ribbon between his outstretched fingers. 'Bye.'

'Bye, mate.'

Downstairs, John was eating a pear over the kitchen sink. Callum leaned against the bench. Out the window he could see that the door to the granny flat was shut but the window was open, the curtain moving in the breeze.

'How's she going?' he asked.

John shook his head. 'She hasn't spoken to me all day.'

'Is she angry?'

'About what?'

Callum coloured. 'The investigation?'

'I don't think it's that.'

'Ella?'

'Partly.'

'She's just doing her job,' Callum said. 'Like the detectives did before, when they thought that you might have been, um, involved.'

John dropped the core into the bin and didn't answer.

Callum soldiered on. 'It's weird, talking to the detective, thinking about it all again. It makes me question some of the stuff I remember. Or think I remember.'

'Coffee?'

'No, thanks.'

John filled the kettle and switched it on.

'For instance,' Callum said, 'the barbecue that night. I remember you and Tim arguing, but I remember that he was angry even before that.'

'He didn't want to be there.'

'I saw him trying to talk to you.'

'Yes, about how he wanted to leave.'

'He was almost crying.'

John frowned. 'Was he? I don't remember.'

'He was behind you. You were lighting the barbecue. He looked really upset.'

'Like I said, he didn't want to be there.'

'Why?'

'He just didn't,' John said. 'But there was no question of him missing it and I told him so.' The kettle clicked off. He poured the water into the cup and spooned in coffee and sugar. 'Sure you don't want one?'

Callum shook his head. 'Uncle John, does Aunt Tamara blame you for Tim's death?'

John dropped the spoon in the sink. 'I blame me for his death.'

'What?'

'If I'd been able to find him that night he'd still be here.'

'But . . .' Callum began, then hesitated.

'But what? Isn't that what you meant?'

Callum wasn't sure what he'd meant, but he was ashamed of what he'd thought when John gave his answer. 'I'm sorry,' he said.

'For what?'

He shook his head again. 'I have to go.'

When they got back to the office, Murray went straight to his desk to call the lab about the DNA results while Ella updated Galea.

He held out the photos that Technical had sent over. 'You have a partial plate.'

The photos showed the woman getting into the light-coloured sedan and then the car driving away from the camera. The tech guys had done a great job with their computers: while part of the plate was obscured by parked cars, Ella could make out the three letters PQW. The car was definitely a Holden Commodore.

'This is great.'

'Look at the next ones.'

She flipped forward to the enhanced shots of the woman's face from the supermarket tape. The pixels were gone and the image was much sharper and clearer. Ella felt she'd only have to glance at the real-life woman to be able to match her to this.

'These are excellent,' she said. 'We'll get them out to the papers for tomorrow.'

Murray was still on the phone when she reached her desk. 'They're checking,' he told her.

Ella entered the partial plate into the database and got eleven Commodores back. Four were in country areas – Laurieton, Kiama, Lismore and Coffs Harbour – so she scratched those for now. Four were dotted about the greater Sydney area: one in Hornsby, one in Campbelltown, one in Bankstown and the last all the way out at Blackheath. The other three were in the south and south-eastern suburbs, likely locations for regular shoppers to Miranda, and these she highlighted yellow as her first ports of call.

'Thanks anyway.' Murray hung up. 'Not done yet.'

'Still?'

'When it is, they'll compare it straightaway with Tavris's sample taken in prison,' he said. 'I have a strong feeling about him.'

'I know you do,' Ella said.

'And I know you don't.' Murray cracked his knuckles. 'We'll just have to see, won't we.'

'We sure will.' She showed him the photos and the list of cars. 'Let's get something written up to send to the papers with the woman's picture, then start on these addresses.'

The closest address to the shopping centre was in Caringbah. It took them the best part of an hour to get there through eye-squintingly bad traffic. Ella drove slowly past the house and Murray said, 'There it is.'

The pale yellow VN Commodore was on the lawn. Ella parked one house up and took another look at the woman's photo before getting out.

They walked up the driveway, looking at the car. It had a shabby paint job and there was a P plate jammed in next to the numberplate. They stepped up on the timber patio to the screen door. The door behind it was open and Ella saw a hallway with a small table and an old-style telephone. She smelled meat cooking. Murray knocked.

A woman came up from the back, wiping her hands on a tea towel. 'Yes?'

Ella showed her badge. The woman came closer to see. She wasn't the woman from the tape.

'Are you Francesca Ritter?' Ella asked.

'Yes.'

'You're the registered owner of the Commodore there?'

'Yes, but my son Will drives it.' Francesca glanced past her at it. 'Has he done something silly?'

'Can you tell us where it was last night?' Murray said.

She put her hands on her hips. 'If he's done something silly I'll wring his bloody neck.' She turned her head. 'Will!'

Ella heard grumbling from the back of the house, then a lanky teenaged boy appeared at the end of the hall. 'What?'

'Come up here,' Francesca said. 'Police want to know about your car.'

Will slouched forward and Francesca jabbed him between the shoulders. 'Stand up straight.'

Will's eyes took in Ella and Murray then went to the car as if to make sure it wasn't being towed.

Ella said, 'Were you driving that car last night?'

'I was at my cousins' place.'

'Tell the truth,' Francesca said.

'Ask Aunty Laura. We had pizza and watched DVDs.'

Ella pulled out her notebook. 'What address was this?'

'Fifty Sunrise Avenue, Maroubra,' Francesca said. 'See, she's going to check that,' she said to Will. 'You'd better be telling the truth.'

'I am!'

'Did anybody else drive the car last night?' Murray said.

'Better not have,' Francesca said darkly. 'If you let your cousins behind the wheel you know what –'

'I know,' Will said. 'You'll take it off me. Nobody drives it but me.'

Ella believed him. The look in his eyes when he glanced past her again at the car showed how much it meant to him. But still. 'The keys were on you the entire time?' she asked.

'Yes,' he said.

Francesca pinched his shoulder. 'Are you sure?'

'Yes!'

'If anything –'

'Muum.'

Ella held back a smile. 'Thanks for your time.'

'Do you need to inspect it?' Francesca said. 'Is there damage to something?'

'That's fine,' Ella said. 'Thanks again.'

She went down the steps hearing Francesca saying, 'If you've been silly, if I find out that you've been silly,' even as she crossed the footpath behind Murray to her car.

'Want to talk to that aunt?' he said.

'Let's check out the other local ones first.' She started the car. 'You never know who might open the door.'

Georgie flipped angrily through the standing orders then slammed the folder closed. There was no help in these pages. She had to decide for herself whether to confront Freya, tell Butterworth, or call the detective.

If she told Butterworth she wanted to change assessors, he would want to know why. If she said because Freya had threatened to fail her, he'd ask Freya if that was true and she'd deny it. If Georgie told him it was a personality clash, he might tell her to suck it up and get on with the job. If she said their past history made things awkward – well, that wouldn't work, because Freya had already told him they'd been best buddies at school. And even if he did assign her another assessor, there was a chance that *they* might be in the cabal. At the very least they were going to be a workmate and friend of Freya's, and once she got in their ear, Georgie was in more or less the same boat as now.

She glared out of the office window into the plant room where Freya was fiddling around in the back of Thirty-three. If she confronted her, she couldn't imagine what Freya would say or where it would get her. She tried to picture them having a conversation but all she could see was Freya's stony face.

She shoved the folder into its spot on the S/O's shelves and slumped back on the chair.

If she called the detective, would Freya really fail her? If Freya was indeed lying about Tim then she should have nothing to hide, so there should be no problem. Freya could tell the detective she'd made it up and that would be that.

So why the threat?

Georgie flung the plant room door open and almost ran into Freya who was coming the other way.

'Sorry, mate,' Freya said. 'Got a minute?'

You bet I do. Georgie followed her into the lounge room.

Freya perched on the edge of a recliner. Georgie stayed on her feet and folded her arms. 'This isn't right.'

'I know,' Freya said. 'That's why I want to talk to you. To say I'm sorry. Things have been tough at home lately, and I know people say you should leave all that behind when you come into work but I just can't. I've been cranky and irritable and, as you say, it's not right.' She smiled up at Georgie.

Georgie stared at her. 'Is that all?'

'I'm sorry?'

'You apologised for being cranky but not for threatening me.'

Freya's eyes widened. 'What are you talking about?'

'At the end of that pedestrian job you were saying what a pity it'd be if I failed.'

'Yeah, and?'

'You went on and on about it, about how you had to write that report and how hard it is to know what to say.'

'It is hard,' Freya said.

'You said . . .' Georgie faltered. What had she said, really?

'I said it's hard when you think you've done a good job.'

Georgie felt like stamping her foot. 'What was wrong with it?'

'You should've checked her back earlier.'

'That's a judgement call.'

'I disagree,' Freya said. 'And your nose-to-toes examination was rushed. You could have missed serious abdominal injuries.'

Georgie shook her head. 'The job went well.'

'Hey, I'm just saying.' Freya sat back in the chair. 'This is my role while we're working together and we both have to get used to it. I like you, Georgie, and when I said it'd be a pity if you failed I meant it.'

Georgie was shaking. If you took her on her words alone, yes, that was what Freya meant, but there'd been a subtext as well. Georgie hadn't imagined it. Freya had been telling her that if she told the detectives what James had said about her and Tim, she'd be failed. She was certain.

Freya smiled up at her again. 'So . . . friends?'

'I don't believe you.'

'You think I don't want to be your friend?'

'I think you're lying,' Georgie said. 'About the threat and about Tim.'

'Sit down,' Freya said calmly.

'No.'

'I just want to talk to you.'

'So talk.'

'You've been through a lot,' Freya said. 'That stuff you told me about Ross the other day is enough to send anyone off the deep end. Plus you had the accident, and there was that girl you mentioned who you couldn't save, and you've been in hospital too. I can understand why you feel victimised and why it would seem that anything anyone says to you contains a threat of some kind.'

'I didn't imagine it.'

'I know you didn't,' she said. 'It's not your imagination at work here. It's another part of your brain that's misinterpreting what's going on.'

Georgie felt her hackles rise. 'I'm not crazy.'

'Again. Misinterpreting. Your mind is on high alert all the time and picking up signals that aren't really there. Like when you're threatened by a patient and for a while afterwards you expect it from everyone. It's not real, there is no threat, but your brain sets you on edge for it anyway.'

Georgie frowned. She couldn't think straight. She'd wanted to confront Freya and clear things up, not finish in this muddy pool.

'Everything is okay,' Freya said. 'We can improve your work. You don't have to fail. We'll stick together and I'll help you and you'll get through it with no worries.'

Georgie looked at her. *Even that sounds funny to me.*

'And you have to turn down that part of your brain that's telling you lies,' Freya said. 'Everything really is going to be fine.'

The job phone rang and she got up, gave Georgie's shoulder a squeeze then went to answer it. Georgie stood there, feeling the imprint of her fingers and wondering what the hell had just happened.

TEN

The second address on the list was in Ramsgate. Ella cruised along the beachfront, her window down, breathing in the salt air. Murray had brought a wad of statements and reports and was reading.

'You been in touch with Tim's schoolfriends yet?' he asked.

'How many days have I had this case?'

'Just asking.'

The house was in a tiny backstreet. A white Commodore stood in the front yard on blocks, its wheel arches pitted with rust and a hole in the back window. The parcel shelf was split and water-stained. A ripped piece of tarp lay on the ground next to the back wheel. There were no plates.

The two concrete steps to the front door of the house were cracked and the top one wobbled under Ella's feet. When Murray knocked, the wood sounded damp, the noise not carrying at all.

The knob turned but the door didn't move. 'Push it,' a feeble voice said.

Ella put her hand flat on the wood and pressed, wary of the door popping open and knocking the person down. The paint felt soggy against her skin.

'Harder.'

Murray put his shoulder to it and shoved. It budged just a fraction. The base squeaked against the floorboards and jammed.

An old man's bleary blue eye and white-stubbled chin appeared in the gap. 'Harder.'

'Move back a couple of steps, please,' Ella said.

He shuffled away. 'Okay.'

She turned to put her good shoulder alongside Murray's and they counted down then heaved. The door scraped back half a metre.

'That'll do,' the man said, coming back to the opening.

She got out her badge. 'Are you Peter Petropolous?'

'Senior,' he said. 'There's also Peter Junior, my son. He's at work. He's an engineer with the council.'

'Is that his car?'

'He's got two.' He turned his head away to cough. 'He's got a red Mazda as well.'

'Do you have the numberplates for this car?' Murray said.

He frowned. 'I guess so. Somewhere. I'll go look.'

From this side the car was in even worse condition, the back passenger door missing its handle, the bottom of the front door eaten away by rust. The grass underneath was dead and rotting. 'I think we're pretty safe here,' Ella said in a low voice to Murray.

'Here y'go.' The old man thrust the plates at her. PQW 296. They were dusty and stuck back to back with old and peeling sticky tape.

'Thanks.' She handed them back. 'Much appreciated.'

'Pull the door shut again? Ta.'

Murray dragged it back into its frame.

'Ta,' the man said again, through the wood.

In the car she crossed the Commodore off the list. 'So much for that.'

'Where's the next one?'

'Kingsgrove. The rest are out west and north, then there are some in the bush too.'

Murray tapped the pages. 'What do you say after Kingsgrove we go back to the office and look up these schoolmates?'

Ella rolled her eyes. 'How about we see what we learn there first?'

The house in Kingsgrove had holes in its fibro walls. A beat-up green and primer-coated Corolla was parked crookedly in the carport. A screen frame with no screen hung from one hinge at the front door, held out of the way by a dead pot plant, and inside the house somebody was playing the drums badly. Ella knocked on the door and stood to one side. Murray waited on the dead lawn with his arms folded.

'Yerp?'

The female voice came from the window beside her. She held out her badge to the shadowy shape. 'Rosanna Desmond?'

'Yep.'

'Open the door, please.'

The shape disappeared. 'Shut up for one minute!' The drums stopped. The door opened. The woman who stood there had short, dark hair and a passing resemblance to the woman in the CCTV from the shopping centre. 'Can I see that badge again?'

Ella let her look. 'You own a beige Commodore, registration PQW 990?'

'What's happened to it?'

'Is it here?'

Rosanna shook her head. 'I lent it to a friend a week ago after her car shat itself. It was this old beat-up Datsun? They reckon it's the motor, but she's got no money, and she's got these little kids, they're like two and four? And she has to get them to childcare and herself to work.'

Ella narrowed her eyes. That was a lot of information to just volunteer. 'Where were you last night?'

'Here,' she said. 'Why?'

'Alone?'

'My brother was here too.' She turned. 'Basil! Get up here.'

The boy was tall and heavily built. His black crewcut had white stripes dyed into it.

'Where was I last night?' she asked him.

'Here.' He twirled the drumsticks.

'What did we do?'

'Watched DVDs. *Cloverfield*. *Gone Baby Gone*.' He fumbled a drumstick.

'Nobody else can vouch for that?' Ella said.

'Just me and him.'

Ella opened her notebook. 'What's your friend's name, the one who has your car?'

'Why?'

'Because I need to know.'

'She's scared of cops. She got pulled over once by this motor-bike cop? And he was like really mean.'

'We're not highway patrol,' Murray said.

Ella said to Rosanna, 'We need her name.'

'Okay, okay,' she said. 'It's Heather Preston-Hayes. What's the big deal about the car anyway?'

'Address?'

'Flat Six, Seventy-three Railway Parade, Campsie.' She folded her arms. Basil played the sticks against the doorframe. She lashed out, trying to grab them, and he stamped off. 'Idiot,' she said.

'You are,' came the muffled reply.

Ella said, 'Is she at work now?'

'You're not going there.'

'The address.'

Rosanna sighed. 'She works in a clothes shop in Burwood. In the Plaza. It's called Highest Fashions, something like that.'

Ella closed her notebook with a snap.

'She didn't do anything,' Rosanna said. 'Neither did I.'

'Thanks for your time,' Murray said.

'But what's the deal with the car?' she called after them.

Ella drove off, then got stopped at the next lights. She looked at Murray. 'Feel anything promising?'

'Not really.'

Well, she did. One of these cars had to pan out and Rosanna's story was just off enough to make her antennae twitch.

The Plaza was busy. They found the shop, Higher Fashions, on one of those 'you are here' boards. The shop itself was small and squeezed into a corner. Inside, a young woman with red hair tied up in a black scrunchie was folding T-shirts at a table. There were no other staff to be seen.

She smiled at Ella. 'Help you?'

'Heather Preston-Hayes?'

The smile faded. 'Yes.'

Ella showed her badge. 'You are currently in possession of a beige Commodore, registration PQW 990?'

She nodded. 'It's not my car though.'

'Where is it now?' Murray said.

'In the car park, I hope. On the roof. Staff parking.'

'Where were you last night?' Ella said.

'Home with the rugrats. Why?'

'Was anyone else there?'

'Just me and them.'

'You had the car?'

She nodded. 'I've had it for almost two weeks.'

'Has anyone borrowed it in that time?' Murray said.

'No.'

'Rosanna hasn't had the need to use it at all?' Ella asked.

'No,' she said. 'Her brother has a car too and she uses that, or he drives her around.'

Ella nodded. 'We need you to show us the car.'

'But I can't leave the shop,' she said. 'I'm the only one who works here. If the boss finds that I've gone out, even for a minute, I'll lose my job.'

'Can't somebody from next door cover you?'

'Not allowed. Not even to go to the loo. I have to wait till the boss comes in.'

'That sounds –'

'I know,' she said. 'I need the job and he knows it.'

Ella nodded. 'Where's the car parked?'

Heather drew a scratch map on a bit of paper for them, and they walked back through the centre and took the lift up to the roof. Outside, the afternoon was bright, a hot wind blowing. The white concrete was blinding. Ella squinted at the map in the shade of her hand.

'There it is.' Murray pointed to a far corner.

The Commodore was parked nose to the wall. A reflective sunshade made the inside of the car dim, and Ella went close on the passenger side, shielding her face with her hand to look inside. Two child seats were in the back, and a Dora the Explorer doll lay on the floor.

'Not our vehicle,' Murray said. 'Look.'

She went to the driver's side and stopped short at the sight of the dark grey front-quarter panel. Murray crouched and ran his fingers across it. There were a couple of dings and a deep scratch across the wheel arch, and the exposed metal underneath was starting to rust. They'd been able to see this part of the car clearly on the CCTV. This wasn't it.

She sighed. 'So much for that.'

Murray grinned. 'Schoolmates, here we come.'

The building was tall and old and shabby, with a yellow bulb on in the foyer even at mid-afternoon. Nobody was there to meet them.

Freya pressed the lift button. Georgie stood nearby. She hadn't said a word since they'd left the station. Freya got the feeling she was trying to decide whether to believe her. Either that or she was planning to call the cops regardless.

She hit the lift button again. 'What's with this thing?'

Georgie looked back out the grimy glass doors at the street and didn't answer.

Freya tried to think what the chances were that Georgie would leave of her own accord. She felt ashamed of each new thing she did, and annoyed at being put in the position where she had to lie and bully and try to make Georgie feel like it was all in her head. It was a cheap and nasty shot but, as she pointed out to herself again, she had no option.

The lift doors wheezed open and they stepped in. It smelled of disinfectant poured over urine. Freya watched Georgie frowning at the brown lino floor and fought back a frown herself. The stress of the situation had made her face tight, and she caught herself wondering where they went from here.

The door opened on the fifth-floor landing. The green carpet was worn down to the backing in a path between the lift and the four apartment doors. Freya let Georgie go first, and stayed a step behind as she knocked on the door of 503. 'Ambulance.'

Locks were released and the door opened the width of a security chain. A wizened old man peered out. 'Is that the ambulance?'

Georgie showed him the patch on her sleeve. 'That's me.'

The man closed the door and slid the chain off. 'She's in the toilet.'

Freya followed Georgie and the man down a narrow hallway made narrower by the enormous gilt-framed paintings hung on both walls. The light was too poor to make out most of the pictures, though Freya got a fleeting glimpse of some tragic bowl of misshapen fruit as she went along sideways to avoid hitting anything with the equipment.

The man stopped at the end and pointed to a closed door. 'In there.'

Freya put down the monitor and drug box. Georgie knocked. 'Can you hear me?' she asked.

'Yes, dearie.' The voice was little and old and female. It came from low down.

Freya watched Georgie try the handle. It turned. She pushed against the door and it opened a crack then the old lady yelped. 'Fingers.'

'Sorry.' Georgie pulled it shut again. 'Can you get up, or move back from the door so I can open it?'

'No.'

'We've tried that already,' the man said.

'Are you hurt?'

'No, just stuck.'

'You can move all your arms and legs?'

'Yes.'

'How did you end up on the floor?'

'She slipped off the toilet,' the old man said. 'She's done it before. She knows she's not supposed to close the door but today she did.' He raised his voice at the wood. 'And now look what's happened.'

'It's okay.' Georgie started feeling the hinges in the gloom.

Freya's eyes had adjusted now and she could make out the closest painting. It was a big boxy pig, staring out at the viewer with the knowledge of the abattoir in its eyes. She shivered.

Her phone rang. Georgie shot her a look. Freya walked back to the front door and answered.

'It's me,' Dion said. 'I'm sorry. I got your number from the next of kin form in James's new staff paperwork.'

'I'm at work.' Freya turned her back to Georgie. 'I've only got a minute.'

'Freya,' Georgie called.

'Hang on a second,' Freya said to Dion.

'Freya!'

'What!'

Georgie pointed at the portable on Freya's belt. 'You need to call police rescue.'

Freya stalked down the hall, twisted the radio out of its socket and thrust it at her. She heard Georgie mutter something as she walked away but ignored it.

Dion said, 'Have you heard anything more about the letter?'

'There's been a phone call as well,' she said in a low voice. 'She told them again that it was the people who hate her but she doesn't think they believe her.'

'Who else can it be coming from?'

'I can't think of anyone,' Freya whispered. 'It has to be them.'

Silence. Then Dion said, 'That old lady.'

'She died.'

'I know that,' he hissed, 'but maybe –'

'Freya,' Georgie called.

'Hang on,' she said to Dion, and turned around. 'What?'

'I need your help. If you're not too completely flat-out busy.'

That was one snarky tone. Freya said to Dion, 'I have to go.'

'You don't think –'

'No, I don't,' she said. 'Look, it'll blow over soon and we'll be fine.'

She hung up and walked down the hall, trying to be calm. They wouldn't find out. Nobody knew except her and Dion.

She reached Georgie. 'What do you need me to do so urgently?'

'Wander downstairs in about ten minutes and meet rescue.'

Freya looked at her.

'Problem?' Georgie said.

Freya bit back her reply. They both knew they weren't supposed to use their phones while on a case. Georgie had her fair and square. 'No problem,' she said. 'Anything I can do in the meantime?'

'I don't think so.'

The old man had brought a chair to sit on and watched as Georgie tapped on the door. 'People are coming to help us get the door off, then we can get you out of there,' she told the woman.

'Okay,' came the quavery reply.

Freya gazed into the eyes of the sorrowful pig and felt like she too was awaiting her fate.

When Ella and Murray got back to the Unsolved office they opened the file to Tim's schoolfriends' names and took two each to enter into the database.

'Finished,' Ella said a moment later.

'Your computer's newer,' he said.

'Suck it up,' she said. 'Whatcha got?'

'Steven Franklin did six months for drug offences in the late nineties, apparently clean since, now lives in Stanmore. Christopher Patrick is just coming up now . . . he has no criminal record and lives right here in Parramatta. You?'

'Damien Millerton – he's the guy who reckoned he was closest to Tim and who mentioned the gay thing that nobody else said they'd heard of – lives in Cherrybrook and has no criminal record. Gareth Wing died in a car accident three years ago.'

Murray looked at his watch.

'There's no way I'm working late,' she said.

'Your mum'd kill you, I know. I was thinking we could call them and see where they work then plan to hit them up tomorrow.'

Ella was already dialling Millerton's home number. A machine picked up after six rings. 'Thanks for calling the Millertons. We can't take your call here and now but why not try our mobiles?' She scribbled the number given as Damien's.

Murray put his hand over his phone. 'I'm onto Franklin's stoner flatmate. He's gone to see if he's in.'

'Hope he remembers to come back.' Ella dialled Millerton's mobile.

'Hello?'

'Damien Millerton?'

'Yes.'

'This is Detective Marconi of the New South Wales Police,' she said. 'We'd like to speak to you about Tim Pieters.'

'Oh.'

She waited a moment. 'Tomorrow morning suits us best.'

'Is this necessary?'

'Yes, it is.' She pulled a face at Murray.

'It's just that I'm really busy.'

'We'll try not to take too long.'

He was quiet.

'Is there a problem?' Ella said.

He sighed. 'It's okay. Do you need me to come in?'

'We can come to you, save you time. Where do you work?'

'From home.' He rattled off his Cherrybrook address. 'Early would be good.'

Ella glanced at Murray, who sat with his eyes closed and the phone clamped to his ear, looking about as far from making an appointment as it was possible to be. 'Let's say nine. See you then.'

When she hung up Murray opened one eye. 'Not happy?' he said.

'He's reluctant for some reason. You still waiting?'

'I can hear him singing. Can't make out the song though.'

She looked at her watch.

'You go,' he said. 'I'll give this guy two more minutes then call the other one.'

'Sure?'

He nodded. 'See you tomorrow.'

Ella was almost home when her mobile rang. She pulled over to answer.

'Is this a bad time?' Callum said.

'Not at all. How are you?'

'Up and down,' he said. 'I talked to Uncle John today.'

Ella wound up her window to hear better. 'What about?'

'I told him that I remembered something else from the barbecue, that Tim was angry before any of the arguing started.'

'Angry about what?'

'I don't know, and John said he hadn't noticed,' Callum said. 'Then I, uh, asked him if Tamara blames him for Tim's death.'

Whoah! 'What did he say to that?'

'He said he actually blames himself, and I feel terrible because my immediate thought was that he did something to him,' Callum said. 'But why would I think that?'

Because you suspect he really did?

'I'm not sure,' Ella said. 'You sound like you've thought about it a lot since then, though.'

'I can't stop. I think maybe it's because I knew he was something of a suspect at the time. Then I'd thought about you asking if Tamara was angry at him, and why she might be. And when he said he blamed himself, I just . . . I don't know. The thought was suddenly there.'

'Did you say anything?'

'No, I had to go, and I was glad to get away,' he said. 'I was ashamed. I felt like it was written all over my face.'

'Hmm,' Ella said.

'What?'

'You said you remembered that Tim was angry before the arguments.' Ella hesitated. She didn't want to put ideas into his head, but if there was a clue there she wanted him to winkle it out. 'I wonder if you noticed something else at the time? Something that you haven't quite remembered yet but which is on your mind all the same?'

Callum was quiet for a moment. 'I suppose it's possible.'

Her phone beeped with another call.

'After all, I did remember that he was angry first,' he said. 'I could even see him trying to talk to Uncle John, and Uncle John wasn't listening.'

'There you go,' she said. The phone kept beeping. 'Don't force it, and see what bubbles up. Listen, I'm really sorry but I have to go. Let me know if anything surfaces, okay?'

'I will. Thanks.'

She looked at the screen. 'Hi, Mum.'

'Just checking you're still coming over,' Netta said. 'We're so excited about meeting Wayne at last!'

'Me too,' Ella said. 'And I'm not just saying that.'

'See you in an hour!' Netta sang.

Wayne accepted the plate. 'Thank you so much, Mrs Marconi.'

'Please, call me Netta.' Her mother patted his shoulder. 'There's plenty more if you're still hungry after.'

He looked at the mound of food. 'I'll see how I go. Thanks.'

He smiled across the table at Ella, and she smiled back until she saw his gaze drift past her to the framed photo of her at eleven that her parents had brought out of the spare bedroom just for the occasion. She looked at them. *Are you trying to embarrass me?*

Franco put his hand on hers. 'It's so nice to have you both here.'

Netta handed the rest of the plates around and sat down. 'It is. Just lovely.' She picked up her knife and fork and nodded at Wayne. 'Eat up. Big strong man like you, you must be hungry after working hard all day.'

'He spent the day in the office,' Ella said. 'I was out and about though.'

Netta nodded. 'Both so busy. Lucky you have me to cook for you.'

Ella eyed her mother. *Do not go there.*

'Thank you again for planting the roses,' Netta said. 'It's so nice that you've got something growing in Ella's garden now.'

Wayne nodded, his mouth full.

'There always was stuff growing there,' Ella said.

'I mean proper plants,' Netta said. 'Not just grass and weeds.'

Ella's phone rang. She put her hand on her pocket. Wayne looked at her.

'Is that your other boyfriend?' Franco said with a grin. 'Didn't you tell him you were busy tonight?'

Netta slapped his arm playfully. 'Leave them alone.'

The phone kept ringing. Ella dropped her gaze from Wayne's and brought the phone out under the table. It was Callum. She put her thumb on the answer button but didn't press it. She felt Wayne's eyes on her still. She put the phone away, and it stopped ringing then a moment later the voicemail alert beeped. Wayne laid down his knife and fork and sat with his elbows on the table and his fingers interlocked at his chin. She couldn't escape his eyes.

She pointed behind herself. 'See that photo? I was an elf in the Christmas pageant.'

'She wanted to be an angel,' Franco said. 'Never seen anyone cry so much.'

'Sobbed and sobbed,' Netta said.

Wayne still hadn't picked up his cutlery.

'Interesting pageant actually,' Ella said. 'For a sort-of Catholic school, I mean. That we had Santa and so on there.' She felt herself blathering and reddening.

He didn't say anything.

'You're not hungry?' Netta said. 'It'll get cold if you leave it too long.'

He raised his eyebrows at Ella.

She tilted her head back. Then she took the phone out, ignored the little envelope on the screen, and turned the thing off. *Happy now?*

He picked up his fork. 'This is delicious, Mrs Marconi.'

Netta smiled back, her head on one side. 'You think so?'

'Absolutely.'

Ella pressed her fingers to her eyes.

She drove away from her parents' house with Wayne waving out the window. The instant he wound it up she said, 'I didn't appreciate that.'

'I guessed as much.'

'It's my phone and it's my life.'

'But are you really living it when your total focus is work? When you can't even turn the thing off when you go to your parents' place for dinner?'

She rested her wrists on the wheel. 'It's just because of this case.'

'But there's always another one, then another one. The job will consume your life if you let it.'

That didn't sound so bad.

'It'll consume you as well.'

He really had no idea. She was the one in control. She hadn't turned the phone back on, even when she went to the loo. She knew there was a message from Callum and she wasn't checking it. Were they the actions of somebody being consumed? *I don't think so.*

At her place he stood on the step.

'Are you coming in?' she said.

'Do you want me to?'

'Do you want to?'

'You answer first.'

She put her hands on her hips. Her bag swung against her leg. She felt the corner of her phone bump her knee.

'I want to,' he said.

'Good. Me too.' She held the door open for him.

Inside, she put her bag down and poured them each a glass of red. He plumped up the cushions on the lounge. 'Next bit of *The Wire*?'

'Sounds good.'

She put the glasses on the coffee table and sat down. He fired up the DVD player and sat beside her.

'Listen,' he said. 'I'm sorry if you thought I was being controlling.'

'You're sorry if I *thought* that?'

He picked up the remote. 'I'm sorry if I was being controlling.'

'You were.' She took it off him and pressed play.

'Is my apology accepted?'

'I'll think about it.' She settled back into the lounge. He took her hand and started to massage her palm. 'Sucking up won't help.'

'So you say.' He kissed the tip of her index finger.

She stared at the TV. From the corner of her eye she could see his head bent over her hand. Beyond him, her bag beckoned from the kitchen table, and possible reasons for Callum's call ran through her head.

'I'm just concerned about you,' he said. 'I've seen people get eaten up by the job. It's not pretty.'

'I know,' she said.

'The way you are makes you a great copper but also puts

you at risk. You get so into it, you let the case take you over. You haven't even been doing your physio exercises.'

'Sometimes I do them at work,' she lied. The little message envelope glowed yellow in her mind. 'Let's just watch, okay?' *And think . . .*

He lay back with her hand against his chest. Ella kept her eyes on the TV but imagined Callum out there waiting for her to call him back.

He squeezed her hand. 'Hear that?'

'What?'

'What Lester just said to McNulty.'

She focused on the screen. 'Yeah.'

'No, you didn't.' He took the remote and skipped back a scene.

Lester said, 'The job will not save you.'

'I don't know,' McNulty said. 'A good case —'

'Ends. The handcuffs go click and it's over. And the next morning it's just you in your room with yourself.'

Wayne pressed stop and looked at her.

She squeezed his leg playfully. 'But sometimes you're in my room too.'

He raised his eyebrows.

'Oh, come on,' she said. 'You're bringing down the mood.'

'You should think about that conversation.'

'I've decided I don't do "should".' She grabbed for the remote. 'Can we just watch?'

He released her hand. 'Maybe I'd better go.'

'Wayne.'

'What?'

'I don't know.' She turned off the TV. 'I guess you need to do whatever you think is right.'

He got to his feet and looked down at her. 'Take some time and think about it. I'll call you tomorrow.'

She stared at the blank TV. She was tired and over it. 'I hate games.'

'I'm just trying to help you.'

'By pulling away whenever I do something you disagree with? By trying to control me with your behaviour?'

'It's not like that.'

'It's exactly like that, and if you can't see it then we have a problem.'

He rubbed the back of his neck. 'I'll call you tomorrow.'

She shrugged. He stood there a moment longer then kissed the top of her head and left.

His car started up and drove away. She let her chin sag briefly to her chest, then jumped up and got her phone.

Half an hour later she pulled up outside the café. It was small, warm and brightly lit. Again, Callum was waiting. Ella sat opposite him and smiled.

'I'm sorry to keep calling,' he said.

'Don't be. I'm always pleased to talk.'

He fiddled with the salt shaker. 'I guess detective work is a little like doctor's work. Time is elastic, so-called normal working hours are irrelevant, and you go where you're needed when you're needed there.'

Ella felt like grabbing his hand in gratitude. How come he got it when Wayne didn't? 'It's about commitment,' she said.

'Exactly.' He smiled. 'If you're going to do a job, you should do it properly. You should give yourself over to it completely.'

Oh, this man!

'I could tell from the moment I met you that this is what drives you,' he said. 'I'm so pleased you have Tim's case, because I know that drive means you won't stop.'

She couldn't help herself now, she had to seize his hand.

His fingers curled around hers. 'You are going to find the killer.'

I am.

They ordered coffee. She felt like she was with an old friend. It was comfortable and there was no pressure, and it made her realise how often Wayne put her on edge.

'I actually called because I remembered something else.' Callum put down his cup. 'At least, I think it's a memory.'

'Tell me,' she said.

'I know you said not to force it but I couldn't stop imagining that night at the barbecue. Tim was trying to talk to John and was angry, at least partly because he was being ignored. I tried to remember back to when we first arrived, and I'm certain that John and Tim were already at it even then. I have this vague idea that I overheard Tim say to John, almost begging really, that it wasn't about going out, he just wanted him to come upstairs so he could talk.'

'Okay.'

'And again, I don't know if this is a proper memory or not, but I have a recollection of John saying something about how he knew Tim's tricks, he wasn't going to be softened up like that, he'd told him he couldn't go out and that was that.'

Ella considered this.

'Now that I've said it out loud it sounds like nothing.' Callum turned red along his hairline. 'How can I remember anything from nineteen years ago? How come I didn't tell the police back then?'

'You were eleven,' Ella said. 'Your brain absorbed things you couldn't possibly know the meaning of at the time but which help you make sense of things now. And being interviewed by detectives at that age, when your cousin had just been murdered and your family was awash with grief, wouldn't have made for good recall. You knew there'd been arguing and that was all you could say.'

'I suppose.' Callum turned his cup around and around. 'So what do you think this means? If it really is a memory?'

'I don't know.'

She did know: John Pieters was becoming ever more clear as a strict father whose rules were deliberately broken by his son after a slow build-up of arguing over that very subject. A father who would kill? That was yet to be determined.

★

It was after eleven when she pulled back into her driveway, still musing on the subject. The sensor light over her front door went on, startling her. She saw movement in the doorway and hit the lock button with her elbow, then recognised Wayne coming towards her.

'Where have you been?' he said.

'Bloody hell, you scared me.'

'Then we're even.' He tried to open her car door. 'Where have you been?'

'Give me two seconds to get out, will you?'

He stepped back.

'How long have you been sitting there?' She looked back out to the dark street. 'I didn't even notice your car.'

'It's there,' he said.

'Lucky somebody didn't see you lurking and call uniform.'

He didn't smile. 'Where have you been?'

'Don't worry, I'm not cheating on you.' She walked to the front door.

'You were working.'

'So what if I was?'

'After everything we talked about,' he said sadly.

'You talked about it.' She rammed the key into the lock. 'You told me what you think and feel, and I think and feel differently. What's so hard to understand about that?'

He stood on the step, looking up at her. 'I love you.'

'I . . . what?'

'I love you.'

She raised her eyebrows. 'Are you sure?'

'Yes.' He was looking at her with a question in his eyes.

She pressed her lips together. She couldn't say it back to him, and she couldn't shake the thought that love was another way to control a person.

What was wrong with her?

The silence between them lengthened, then he pushed his hands into the back pockets of his jeans and looked down the driveway. 'I guess I'd better go.'

'Wait,' she said. Maybe it would just take time. Maybe he really meant it. Maybe this was a new page. 'Want a cup of tea?'

He smiled. 'That'd be nice.'

ELEVEN

Ella walked into the office early the next morning, thinking more about Callum than what Wayne had said.

'Have you seen them?' Murray said.

'What?'

'The newspapers, with the CCTV image of the woman who called. They came up really well.'

'Give us a look.'

He passed them over. They did look good: the picture was clear, the article short and to the point.

'Crimestoppers passed on any info yet?'

'Not so far,' he said.

They would, Ella was sure.

'Get your purse,' she said. 'First stop Damien Millerton's.'

On the way to Cherrybrook she told him about Callum. 'I thought after we see Millerton, we'd drop in on the Pieterses and you can meet them for yourself. Tamara'd be happy to see another face.'

'Yeah, I saw her on the news last week,' he said. 'But I don't know about this memory stuff. How many times have they listened to little kids and charged adults with weird sex crimes then realised it was all crap?'

'This is different,' she said. 'He wasn't struggling with some horrific episode in his past —'

'His cousin was murdered.'

'You know what I mean,' she said. 'The barbecue was before that.'

'It's all part of the same thing. He's recalling the barbecue in the light of the murder, plus you're suspicious of John and he's no doubt picking up on that. Why would he ask if Tamara blamed him if you hadn't put that idea into his head?'

'It's his family,' Ella said. 'He wants to understand what happened more than anyone.'

'Nevertheless,' Murray said. 'You should proceed with extreme caution. What actual evidence do you have? Twenty-year-old vague half-memories from somebody who was eleven at the time aren't going to stand up in court.'

'I'm building a picture, that's all.'

'Picture schmikshure,' he said. 'Hey, that's hard to say.'

'Don't say it then,' she snapped. He was bursting her balloon with a memories-are-so-unreliable, proceed-with-caution lecture. He hadn't been there listening to Callum. She knew what she knew.

Damien Millerton's house was a pink cement-rendered two-storey McMansion. One of the two garage doors was open and inside a man sat writing at an old schooldesk, surrounded by boxes. He got up and met them on the driveway.

'Damien Millerton?'

He nodded. His black hair was cut short at the sides, exposing the first few greys. He wore jeans and a plain grey T-shirt and brown sandals. 'Come in.'

Murray looked around. 'This is your office?'

'Yep. My wife and I sell Candy's Candles.' He pulled a brochure from the desk drawer and gave it to Ella. 'Biggest candle franchisers in the country. You might have heard of us?'

'Nope.' She handed the brochure straight to Murray. 'Tell me about Tim Pieters.'

'I don't know anything more than what I told the detectives

at the time, and again six years ago.'

'Nevertheless,' Ella said.

'Starting with what? When we met in kindergarten?'

Pissed because I dissed his candles. 'Tell us about when he told you he might be gay.'

'He didn't say that,' Damien said. 'He asked if *I* thought he was gay. I said no. He said that something had happened with a man, and he came, and he was worried what that meant. Then we met some friends who came past in their car and we never talked about it again.'

'None of his family or other friends knew anything about that,' Murray said.

'I know. I'm just telling you what he told me.'

'Did you believe him?'

'Why wouldn't I believe him? He was almost crying.'

'That night when you were in the pub,' Ella said. 'What did he say about the family argument?'

'Just that there'd been one. He didn't say what it was about and I didn't ask.'

'And you last saw him when?' Murray asked.

'About half past eleven. We realised about midnight that we couldn't find him. We looked for him in the toilets and outside, then I said to the others that he probably took a taxi home, so we went back into the pub.' He rubbed his forehead. 'I don't regret much in my life but I regret that.'

'That's why you were reluctant to see us?' Ella said.

He nodded. 'When I saw his mum on the news I knew you'd be coming around again and it made me feel sick. I wish I'd gone out and found him, and then none of this shit would've happened, and I wouldn't feel so awful every time it comes up.'

'It can't be easy,' Murray said.

'It's not.'

Enough with the pity party. 'Damien, with the benefit of adulthood and hindsight, do you have any new insights into Tim and what was going on in his life?'

'None whatsoever.'

'No further thoughts on what was going on at home?'

He shook his head. 'I wish I could help you. I wish it was solved and whoever did it was locked up, and then I could never think about it again.'

'And focus on your candles instead,' Ella said.

'Well, yes. Is there anything wrong with wanting that?'

'Not at all,' Murray said quickly. 'Thanks for your time.'

In the car, heading to Pennant Hills, Ella said, 'Do you think they'll all be so helpful?'

'What can you realistically expect when it's been almost twenty years? What could you remember after so long?'

'More than that,' she said darkly. 'How'd you go with the other ones? Did the stoner remember you were waiting for him?'

'I gave up and called Chris Patrick. He works in the CBD and said anytime today would be fine. When I tried Steven Franklin's number again he beat the flatmate to the phone and said he'd be home today.'

'Good.'

They could get them out of the way quickly and concentrate on what might be coming in from Crimestoppers about the newspaper pictures. Ella turned off Pennant Hills Road and headed for the dump site.

When she parked, Murray got out and stood at the edge of the scrubby brush.

'Right there.' Ella pointed.

He looked at the roadway, the streetlights, and the closest houses.

'It's all pretty much the same, except that there were more low shrubs so it was even harder to see from the houses.'

'It'd be a quiet place late at night.'

'That's for sure.'

At the Pieterses' house she knocked and waited. No answer. She knocked again, wondering if Tamara was home alone, staring at a blank wall in the granny flat.

'We'll see them another day.' Murray started back across the lawn.

Ella wanted them all to meet. Tamara might be more open with another detective, and Murray might see something in John that he currently thought was all in her mind. She knocked again, harder.

'Come on,' Murray said from the car. 'Places to go, people to see.'

She turned reluctantly away. *I'll be back.*

Georgie struggled to wake up. She could hear the knocking but felt drugged and half-paralysed. She fell out of bed and lurched across the room. 'Coming!'

She staggered up the hall to the door, part of her mind waking up enough to say that she should've stayed in bed asleep, she should've put in the earplugs; yes, it was quiet way up here but she should've thought about people knocking on the door. The pre-nightshift sleep was precious beyond words. Once that was stuffed, so were you.

She slid the chain back and opened the door. A young man smiled and held out a massive bunch of flowers.

'Whassat?'

'Flowers,' he said. She could make out the emblem of some florist on his shirt. 'For you. If your name's Georgie.'

'Oh.' She blinked. 'Thanks.'

She took the bouquet, almost dropped it, then closed the door. *Oh Matt!* They smelled fantastic, a colourful mix of who knew what. She wasn't good with her flowers; if they weren't easily identifiable, like roses or banksias, she was pretty much done for. 'It doesn't matter what you are,' she said, and took them into the kitchen to see if Chris kept such a thing as a whopping great vase. *Oh Matty . . .*

There was no vase. She got a bucket from the laundry, half-filled it with water, cut the plastic from around the stems and sat them in it. Then she pulled the envelope from the top, opened it and took out the card.

You fucking bitch.

She dropped it and backed away.

The flowers were silent in their bucket. The card lay face down on the floor.

That couldn't be right. She was half-asleep still. She'd misread.

She crouched down and looked at the blank back of the card. There was no clue there, no hint of what was written on the other side. No raised lines where the writer had pressed down hard.

She got a fork from the drawer and lifted the card by one corner, flipping it over.

You fucking bitch.

'Matt Riley, Finance.'

'It's me.' Her voice shook.

'What's wrong?'

'Somebody sent me flowers,' she said, her voice starting to crack. 'The card says "You fucking bitch".'

'Call that detective,' he said. 'Hang up and call her. No, stay on the line, call from your mobile. Stay on the line with me.'

'She's on Tim's case.'

'Call her.'

'Okay.' She put the handset down and turned the volume up. 'Can you hear me?'

'I can.' His voice was tinny and small. 'Is the door locked?'

'Yes.'

'Who brought them? How did he get into the building?'

'Some florist guy. I guess somebody held the door open.' She scrolled through the call register on her mobile. 'Hang on, I'm calling her now.'

'Marconi.'

'Hi, it's Georgie Riley.' Her voice was tight and she took a big breath. 'I'm sorry about this –'

'Don't apologise,' Matt called.

'– but I just got an abusive card attached to some flowers.'

'From?'

'I'm guessing the people who sent the letter,' Georgie said. 'I told you they hate me.'

Ella was silent for a moment.

'I don't know what I should do,' Georgie said.

'Ask her to come over,' Matt called.

'I mean,' Georgie said, 'should I –'

'Ask her,' Matt shouted.

'Sit tight,' Ella said. 'You're in the city?'

'North Sydney. Milsons Point, I mean. Upper Pitt Street.'

'I'm on my way.'

'Thanks,' Georgie said. When Ella was gone she picked up the handset and said to Matt, 'She's coming.'

'So am I.'

'It's okay.'

'It's not,' he said. 'I'll get a cab and I'll see you soon. And listen, you have to tell her the rest too.'

No.

'It's for the best.'

She shook her head though he couldn't see it.

'You know I'm right,' he said. 'I'll see you soon.'

She hung up and sat on the end of the bed with tears starting down her face. She didn't understand why her life had to be so hard, with Ross and his bullying reaching her even here, and Freya and her manipulative speeches and behaviour at work. She'd told Matt about it last night and his advice was to work hard, try to forget it and just get through the next six weeks. She would try, she'd said, but oh God, she just didn't know if she could.

And now she might have to talk about the rest too.

'She's not exactly part of the investigation,' Murray said.

'Following up on it might lead us to whoever sent the letter and made the call.'

'But you don't know it was the same people.'

'This will help us find out,' Ella said. 'It's not going to take long. You go and talk to Steven Franklin and I'll meet you in the city afterwards to talk to Chris Patrick.'

'I'll be done with Franklin before you even hit the bridge.'

'Go see that aunt from yesterday as well then,' she said.

'Where that boy with the Commodore was supposedly eating pizza.'

'Yes, boss.'

Georgie watched Ella pull on gloves and pick up the card from the kitchen floor. She slipped it into an evidence bag and turned it over to read the front, then collected the envelope and put that into a bag too.

'Thanks so much for coming over,' Matt said, his arm tight around Georgie.

'No problem,' Ella said. 'What did the delivery guy look like?'

Georgie tried to recall. 'Young, maybe twenty. Short, brown hair. Big smile. He wore a green shirt with the florist's emblem thing on the chest. I don't know what florist it was though.'

'It's okay, I've got it.' Ella held up the bagged envelope. 'What time was it, roughly?'

'Forty minutes ago, I guess. I was trying to sleep before nightshift tonight so I'm not really certain.'

Ella inspected the bouquet itself.

'You're going to get those guys now, I hope,' Matt said. Georgie could hear the anger in his voice and feel the tension in his body.

'First step is to work out where this came from,' Ella said. 'I'll talk to the florist, see if we can get any prints, that sort of thing.'

'It has to be them.'

'One step at a time,' she said.

'Because that's not all that's happened,' Matt said.

Georgie's heart sank. She dug her fingers into Matt's side. *Not now. Not yet.*

He looked at her. 'You tell her or I will.'

'What's been going on?' Ella said.

Georgie felt weak. 'We'd better sit down.'

In the lounge room she sat close to Matt while Ella took the centre of the other lounge.

Georgie resisted the urge to cover her face with her hands. 'I told you about the death of that man on the road, and what his family and my boss did.'

Ella nodded.

'I thought I saw his brother in the city last week,' Georgie said.

'More than once,' Matt put in.

'I thought he was following me. The most recent time was a couple of days ago when I was walking home across the bridge.'

Ella said, 'Why didn't you tell me before?'

Georgie looked at the coffee table between them.

Matt took her hands in his. 'After the road accident, Georgie was involved in another bad case. There was a flood and a girl was swept away. Georgie was part of the rescue attempt but the waters were too strong and the girl couldn't be saved.'

'I almost had her,' Georgie said. 'If I had held on for longer she would have lived.'

Matt squeezed her hands tight. 'You don't know that.'

Georgie's vision blurred with tears.

'It all combined to have a big effect,' Matt went on softly. 'She thought she saw the dead girl following her.'

After a moment's silence Georgie glanced up at Ella. The detective was nodding, and didn't look surprised, or shocked, or horrified. 'That's tough,' she said.

'It was.' Georgie wiped her eyes. 'I had psych treatment. I was on medication and spent time in hospital. I'm better now. Thing is though, the guy who died in the road accident and his brother Barnaby look just the same.'

'So you weren't sure what you were seeing, and didn't want to call in case.'

'Exactly,' Georgie said. 'We know you talked to the sergeant out there, and Matt's brother is a cop there too, and he checked for us, and we know that Barnaby was in town on some particular days, but that there was still time enough for him to be coming and going.'

Matt put his hand on her back. 'But the way I see it is that it doesn't matter who she saw on the streets and the bridge. These flowers and that shitty little note are something else entirely. They're concrete. Somebody sent them and for that they need to be pulled into line.'

'Absolutely,' Ella said. 'Couldn't agree more. That's why I came over.'

Georgie felt something loosen inside her chest. She didn't feel like a nut, like Ella saw only a crazy person when she looked at her. She was still frightened, but she was being taken seriously and that mattered so much. 'Thank you.'

'You're more than welcome,' Ella said. 'Listen, it might be an idea not to tell anyone about this, okay? And call me again whenever you need to.'

Georgie nodded, and tried to appear braver and calmer than she felt.

Freya lay wide awake in bed. James and the kids had gone to school an hour ago, and she couldn't even doze. She'd hardly slept overnight and now nightshift was coming up and everything was crap.

Her mobile rang.

'Look at the paper.' Dion's voice was high and tight.

'Why?'

'Just look.'

She got out of bed. James had left their home-delivered copy of the *Herald* in a mess on the kitchen bench. 'What page?'

'Six.'

She flipped through.

'See it?'

She couldn't breathe. There were two photos – one of Tim in his school uniform, the other a CCTV still of a dark-haired woman who, according to the accompanying story, had contacted police with information about the discovery of the body.

'Do you know her?'

'Why would I know her?' she said, trying to keep her voice

firm. 'She's part of the thing against Georgie. They're making it up.'

'How can we be sure?'

'Because nobody could know anything,' she said.

'But what if there was somebody?'

'Who? Where?'

'I don't know!'

'It's just those people,' she said. 'It's nothing. It won't lead the cops anywhere near us.' In the background she heard an announcement. 'Sounds like you're at the airport.'

'I've got meetings in Melbourne all day,' he said. 'Uh . . .'

'What?'

'Nosebleed.'

'You still get those?'

'Not for years,' he said. 'Listen, I have to go.'

'Remember,' she said, 'it's nothing.'

'Okay.' But he sounded about as certain as Freya felt.

She hung up, grabbed the paper and shoved it into the bin. The cops would get calls about this woman, she'd turn out to be some pal of Ross Oakes's, she'd get a kick in the arse for making nuisance calls and that would be that.

Because nobody could know anything.

She went back to bed and pulled the covers over her head.

Callum pushed open the door to his father's surgery. The waiting room was mostly empty. An old couple sat on one side, the man gaunt and nodding off – cancer patient, on morphine. Opposite them was a younger woman, alone, flipping through a magazine without seeing any of it.

His mother, Genevieve, smiled at him from behind the desk. 'Cuppa?'

'Thanks.' He followed her into the staffroom.

'You look tired.'

'Busy day. I've become the poster boy for cold cases.' All morning his electoral office had been full of sad people clutching photos, yellowing newspaper articles and copies of their police statements, wanting him to do for them what he'd been able to do for Tim. 'It's really hard hearing their stories.'

'Can you help them?'

'I write down the details and promise them I'll speak to the Minister for Police, but whether it'll go on from there, I don't know.' He rubbed his face. 'I know so well what they're feeling, and I feel terrible that their cases might not get looked at again.'

'You're doing what you can.' She handed him a mug of tea. 'That's all anybody can ask.'

He sipped and put the mug down. 'It's still –'

'Barry!' The cry came from the waiting room. 'Doctor!'

Genevieve slammed down her cup and rushed out. Callum trod on her heel following. The old man was unconscious and deathly pale, slipping sideways off his chair, and his wife and the other woman were trying to hold him up.

'Let me,' Callum said.

He grasped the man under the arms and heaved him onto the floor. He was skin and bone but heavy still, an awkward dead weight. Callum was careful to lower him gently onto the tiles without bumping his head. There he pressed his fingers to the man's carotid. Alistair was suddenly by his side and he heard Genevieve calling an ambulance. 'Arrest,' he said.

Alistair locked his elbows and his fingers and started compressions. 'The Laerdal bag's in my office.'

Callum scrambled to his feet. In his father's office a man sat on the examination bed, his shirt off.

'He might be a while,' Callum said.

'Can my wife come in?'

Genevieve was already bringing the lone woman through.

Callum grabbed Alistair's doctor's bag as well as the Laerdal bag. He hadn't worked an arrest for more than a year. Drug doses and joules per shock rushed through his mind, but he knew his father didn't have a defibrillator here and wasn't sure about his drug stocks.

Back in the waiting room, he dropped to his knees at the old man's head as Genevieve helped the weeping wife into the staff-room. The man's eyes were open, their surfaces drying already. Callum eased them closed as he fitted the mask to his emaciated face.

Alistair pumped up and down. Callum counted. Alistair paused after the fifth.

'The rates have changed,' Callum said in a low voice. 'Thirty compressions to two breaths.'

Alistair grunted and started compressions again.

'We should be going faster too.' *And by 'we' I mean 'you'*.

Alistair increased his pace a little. His stethoscope swung back and forth. Callum watched it and counted in his head. All his life he'd seen a stethoscope around his father's neck. It was as much a part of him as the smell of antiseptic soap on his hands. When Callum had become a doctor too he'd realised the appeal of wearing the stethoscope, understood how for his father it was a badge of knowledge and learning and dedication. He shied away from it himself, however, because others saw it as a symbol of the same thing, something that set him – all doctors – apart, and he didn't want to be that way.

'Thirty,' he said, and Alistair paused for a second to let him inflate the old man's lungs. Genevieve's calm murmur to the wife crept under the staffroom door.

Down Alistair went again.

'A little faster,' Callum said.

'Rate's ridiculous.'

'What drugs have you got?'

'I don't know.'

Callum said, 'Thirty', gave the man another two breaths, then pulled Alistair's bag close. There were vials of morphine loose in the bottom.

'Jesus, Dad, this is Schedule 8 stuff. You should have this locked up.'

Alistair wiped sweat from his chin onto his shirt.

Callum scratched around in the bag, finding Valium and more morphine. 'Where's your adrenaline?'

'Probably expired,' Alistair puffed. 'Probably tossed it.'

'And never replaced it?'

Alistair didn't answer. Sweat dripped from his forehead onto the old man's shirt. The man's eyelids crept back up. They never stayed shut for long.

'Swap,' Callum said.

Alistair straightened and put his hands to his lower back. Callum gave the man two breaths and scrambled to his side, grasped his left wrist with his right hand and started compressions. The man's ribs and cartilage were stiff. He imagined the brittle old bones, made more so because of the cancer and its treatment. He lightened up a fraction.

He couldn't hear a siren. Apart from the murmur of his mother reassuring the patient's wife, the atmosphere was strangely quiet and calm. Alistair pressed the mask to the man's face and the stethoscope swung across his chest. His long fingers were wrapped around the Laerdal bag, ready to squeeze air into the dead lungs, and Callum felt a rush of affection for him, a desire to be close, to share.

'Dad,' he said, 'that detective asked me if I thought Tamara blamed John for Tim's death.'

Alistair squeezed the bag twice. The seal was bad and air leaked out.

'Better do another one, just in case,' Callum said.

This one was little better. Alistair's knuckles were white with the effort and he didn't speak.

Callum focused on the man's chest under his hands. 'What if he did it?'

'Do you think he's even capable of such a thing?' Alistair said.

'I don't know,' Callum said. 'Thirty.'

Alistair squeezed the bag twice. 'What are you basing these imaginings on?'

'Memories mostly.'

'Of what?'

'Of them arguing.'

Alistair looked at him. 'Do you remember how often we argued?'

'I know it sounds ridiculous but I can't shake it,' Callum said. 'Thirty.'

Alistair gave the man two leaky breaths. 'He's his father, for God's sake. Your uncle. Think about what you're saying.'

'It's just a feeling.'

'This is our family.' Alistair's hands were trembling. 'This is a man you've known all your life.'

'But how well can we really know anyone?' Callum said. 'Thirty. You see it all the time as a GP – how people show only what they want to, how they can hide so much and don't tell you unless they absolutely have to.'

Alistair shook his head. 'No.'

'I'm not saying it's true,' Callum said. 'But it is possible. He can't say where he was that night, and he was so angry. The police still suspect him.'

Drops of sweat were falling onto the old man's face. Callum had the sudden thought that his dad might be having chest pain. 'Dad?'

Alistair turned his head and Callum saw that it wasn't sweat at all. His father was crying.

'You make me feel like everything's falling apart,' he said.

'Dad –'

'This is our family. Our life.'

'It's okay.'

There was a siren in the distance. *Thank God.*

'I'm a good doctor.'

'When did I say you weren't?'

'I'm a GP, I do palliative care.'

'I know you do, Dad.'

Alistair bent over the dead man's face. 'So I don't have all the fancy gear. I don't have a defibrillator. You know how much they cost? A lot. A *lot.*'

'Thirty,' Callum said. Alistair fumbled for the bag. 'Dad, you're doing fine.'

'I don't have the drugs, but they wouldn't have saved Barry anyway. You know that as well as I do. Yet you criticise me, you tell me how to do my job, you think these things about your own uncle. You have no right to any of it.'

Callum wanted to stop compressions to hug him. 'I'm sorry.' At least the siren was close.

Alistair shook his head. 'I'm old and I need to retire,' he croaked through his tears. 'But this job is my life.'

'Don't think about it now,' Callum said. 'Thirty.'

Alistair clutched at the bag and managed a weak squeeze, weeping. 'This job is my life.'

The siren was closer.

'Mum!'

Genevieve opened the staffroom door.

'Help Dad,' he said. 'Put him behind the desk.'

Alistair didn't want to go, kneeling with his hands on the sides of the man's face and sobbing. Genevieve pulled on his arm, and Callum grabbed the bag and gave the man a breath from the side, and Alistair finally got up.

The siren stopped outside. Callum kept on with compressions. The man was dead. His blood was pooling, his nose turning stark white, his ears and the back of his neck going darker purple. His skin was cool and clammy. His open eyes were dry. Callum looked into them and apologised for not letting him go peacefully. *But at least this way your wife knows that everything possible was done.*

The paramedics came in with their gear and started attaching the monitor and hooking oxygen up to the Laerdal bag. 'What's the history?'

'Collapsed while waiting to see my father,' Callum said.

Genevieve came forward with a folder. 'He has CA with metastases in the brain and liver.'

The paramedics looked at each other. 'Is his doctor here?'

'I'm here.' Alistair stood up, wiping his eyes. 'You can stop. I'll certify.'

'You're sure?'

He nodded.

Callum got to his feet. Alistair came around the desk and put his hand on his shoulder, then turned to go into the staffroom where the dead man's wife waited. He closed the door behind him and a second later a wrenching wail broke out.

'Thanks,' Callum said to the paramedics.

They nodded and picked up their gear and left.

Genevieve got a sheet and draped it over the body, then closed and locked the front door and pulled the verticals across. Callum went into his father's office and found the first patient still there. He'd put his shirt on but had stayed sitting on the examination bed. His wife stood beside him, holding his hand. They looked at Callum in shocked silence.

He led them to the back door. 'May we reschedule you for another time?'

They didn't reply.

'Genevieve will call you later,' he said as they walked slowly away.

He washed his hands. In the mirror over the small sink he could see his father's framed degree on the wall. He tore a paper towel from the roll and turned away.

The florist was in the CBD just off King Street. Ella smiled at the pink-haired woman behind the counter and showed her badge. 'I'd like some information about a delivery made this morning to a Georgie Riley in Milsons Point.'

The woman nodded. The name embroidered on her green shirt said Poppy. 'Mixed bouquet of gerberas, freesias, lilies and carnations. I made it up myself. I hope it was okay?'

'Could you tell me who ordered them, and when?'

She typed something into the computer. 'The order was made yesterday afternoon. Steve took it. Hang on.' She went out the back and returned with a young man who blinked owlishly at Ella from behind round glasses. Poppy pointed at the monitor. 'Do you remember who placed that?'

He looked closer. 'I do. Odd, skinny man. Edgy. Looked like a labourer.'

'Height?' Ella said. 'Hair and eye colour?'

'He was wearing reflective sunnies,' Steve said. 'Didn't take them off. Rude, I thought. Brown hair with a bit of grey through it. About my height. I'm one seventy.'

'Don't suppose he paid with a credit card?' Ella said.

'Cash,' Steve said.

Of course.

'Did you see him write the card?'

'I was typing the order details,' Steve said. 'I mean, I knew he was doing it but I didn't watch him or anything. Although I noticed he dropped it on the floor at one point, then picked it up and kinda brushed it off on his shirt like it had got dusty.'

'I bet he held it by the edges,' Ella said.

Steve nodded. 'He did, come to think of it.'

Of cooourse.

'Would you recognise the man again if I brought in a photo?'

'I'll give it a try.'

'Might see you again then,' she said. 'Thanks.'

In the car, she texted Murray. *Finished?*

As soon as she pressed send, the phone rang.

'Hi, Mum.'

'Hello, Ella, darling,' she said. 'That Wayne is lovely. Just lovely.'

'Thanks.'

'When are you bringing him over again?'

'We're both pretty busy with work.'

'You have to have a life.'

Jeez, that sounded familiar.

'Ask her,' her father called in the background.

'I will in a minute,' she said to him. 'Ella, would you like me to copy out the eggplant recipe so you can make it for him at home?'

'That's fine.'

'He really seemed to like it.'

'We can save it to enjoy at your place,' she said.

Murray, for God's sake, hurry up and text me back!

'Ask her now!' Franco called.

'All right! Ella, your father wants to know if Wayne would like some cuttings from our Cecile Brunner?'

'Your what?'

'It's a rose,' she said.

'I don't know. I'll ask him.'

'I think he will, they're very popular. Lovely fragrance.'

'Mum, I have to go.'

'How about dinner tomorrow? The two of you? Will you ring him now and ask?'

'I'll let you know,' Ella said. 'Bye.'

She hung up. She wouldn't ring him now. She might not even ring him later. Last night had been lovely: it was flattering to have somebody tell you they loved you, and by God the man was good in bed! But she worried about what the whole love thing might mean. The way she saw it, the saying 'if you love something, set it free' wouldn't have been invented if people didn't need to be told.

The phone beeped with an incoming text.

Done. Meet you at Ruby's Café on Market Street. Patrick's the cook.

Ella took a booth in the café and ordered a coffee. Murray came in just as it arrived. 'Get me one?' he asked.

'Nope.'

'Aw.'

He went to the counter and spoke to the waiter, who went back into the kitchen. After a couple of minutes a tall, thin man brought Murray's coffee and sat down.

'I'm Chris Patrick.'

Murray introduced himself and Ella. Chris Patrick shook their hands and looked from one to the other. 'So this is about Tim?'

Ella nodded. 'Does that bother you?'

'Not at all,' he said. 'He was a good mate. I'd love to help find who killed him.'

'Tell us about the night he died.'

Ella watched him closely as he recounted the evening. It was the same story she'd read in their statements, over and over. He was direct and clear and looked them in the eye.

'What about the gay rumour?' she asked.

'I only heard about that after he died,' he said. 'I can't see it being true.'

'Why is that?'

'He was always going on about these girls he got with when his family went on holidays,' he said. 'I know that's just bragging, it doesn't mean anything, but there was that other girl too.'

Ella's ears pricked up. 'What other girl?'

'The girl I saw him with one afternoon after school.'

She felt a shiver of excitement. 'Go on.'

'It was four months or so before he died,' he said. 'They were in a record shop and I was walking past with my mum. I saw him standing there next to this girl. They weren't in uniform but she looked a bit familiar, I thought she went to our school. They were looking through the records, not really close together, almost like they *weren't* together, but then I saw him put his hand on her waist. She didn't push it away but didn't reach down and, you know, caress it, or put her hand on his. After a moment she moved and his hand dropped off her, and then my mum was at me to catch up and I had to go. The next day at school I said something to him, poking fun, "Timmy's got a girlfriend", that sort of thing, but he flatly denied it. He said I was wrong, said he'd been in the shop but not with any girl. He was so insistent that I thought maybe I had made a mistake.'

'Really?' Ella said.

Patrick raised his eyebrows. 'Don't you know about this? I told it to the detectives back then.'

'It's not in your statement.'

'I told them later, maybe a week or so. They didn't seem to think it was much, especially when I couldn't say who she was or even for certain that she went to our school, and I guess also because I still wasn't sure if I'd actually seen anything, do you know what I mean? That it actually meant anything. They never came back and asked me about it again, anyway.'

'Not even six years ago?'

He shook his head. Ella and Murray looked at each other. It happened.

'Do you still have doubts?'

'The more life I live, the more teenagers in love I feed in this place, the more certain I am that those two were in some kind of relationship.'

Ella said, 'Do you remember seeing her around after Tim died? Did you notice any girls who were particularly upset, who looked like the girl you saw?'

He frowned. 'Come to think of it, I don't recall seeing her again actually.' He paused. 'I guess that sounds strange, that on the one hand I can't say who she was, then on the other I think she wasn't at school any more.'

'Yes,' Murray said.

'No,' Ella said. 'Not at all.'

Murray said, 'Did you never look at the girls there and try to pick her out?'

'Of course I did, but it's not like they stood in a line and I was able to go along and say, not you, not you, hmm she's not here. In a big school like that kids are milling around constantly. I thought I'd know her if I saw her, and I didn't see her.'

'It's okay,' Ella said. 'Do you think you could identify her if we got some school photos?'

'All I can do is try.'

Outside the café Ella turned to Murray. 'Let's go to the school and check their records, see if any students left after Tim died.'

'But he doesn't know if she went there,' he said. 'He doesn't even really know what he saw.'

'It's enough for me. Where are you parked?'

He sighed. 'I'll meet you there.'

TWELVE

The Macquarie Secondary College office was in a blond-brick building by the main gate. Ella sat in her car for five minutes watching students in grey and gold uniforms go in and out before Murray pulled up beside her.

Inside the office a squat woman in her late fifties smiled up at them from a low desk. 'May I help you?'

'Detectives Marconi and Shakespeare, New South Wales Police.' Ella flashed her badge. 'Is the principal in?'

'I'm afraid he's in Melbourne for the day,' she said. 'Can anyone else help? The deputy perhaps? And may I ask what it's regarding?'

'The deputy would be fine,' Ella said. 'It's about a homicide. We need to look at your student records from 1990.'

The woman went away and brought back a smooth-haired young woman with a broad smile. She put out her hand. 'Detectives, how lovely to meet you. I'm Penny Flatt, the deputy head. Is this about Tim Pieters?'

'It is.' Murray stepped forwards. 'We're looking into the movements of students in the weeks following his death.'

Amazing, Ella thought. *He doesn't think this idea is worth much, but put a pretty woman in front of him and he's suddenly all go.*

'We're happy to help in any way we can,' Penny said. 'Come on through to Admin and we'll see what Mary can dig up for us.'

They followed her down a corridor. Ella saw Murray watching her legs and elbowed him. He smiled sheepishly but kept watching.

In an office full of filing drawers Penny introduced them to a woman in bright red glasses behind a computer. 'This is Mary.'

'What specifically are you after?' Mary asked.

Ella said, 'Let's start with female students who left the school in the month after Tim's death. That was the twenty-first of October in 1990.'

Mary typed quickly then looked at the monitor. 'Okay. There's a bunch of them, but most actually graduated. Let me take the Year Twelves out of contention and see what else we have.' She typed again. 'Hmm. Just one. Freya Marie Gregory. She was in Year Nine and left the school that week. It says here she moved to Orange and enrolled in Oaktree College.'

Ella looked at Penny. 'Any chance we could see a photo of her, please?'

'It'll be in the files.' Mary pulled open one of the huge drawers and ran her finger along the dividers.

Ella nudged Murray. 'Ring Chris Patrick and see if he has a fax.'

He took his mobile into the corridor as Mary lifted out a folder and flicked through pages.

'All I have is a class photo, but there's a name list so I can tell you that Gregory is . . .' she brought it over and placed a long red nail on a girl, '. . . this one here.'

Freya Gregory had long brown hair and brown eyes and a nice smile. She stood in the back row of the group so was obviously one of the tallest in the class. She looked like any of a million teenaged girls out there, Ella thought.

Murray came back. 'He's got one, but he said you could also scan and email it to him.'

'Brilliant,' Ella said. 'Do you have facilities for that here?'

'Absolutely,' Mary said. She cut a hole in a piece of paper and laid it over the photo so that only Gregory's picture was visible, then put the lot in the scanner. 'What's his email address?'

Murray held out his notebook and she copied it down, typed a message, attached the file and hit send.

Murray's phone rang a moment later. 'Chris, hi,' he said. 'Oh. Okay. No worries. Thanks anyway.' He hung up. 'He doesn't know.'

Dammit.

Mary handed Ella a colour copy of the photo and a page with Gregory's enrolment details.

Penny said, 'Would you like us to look further? The school year ended not long after that, but we could see who didn't return the next term if you like?'

Murray nodded and gave Penny his card. 'That'd be great. I'll be in touch soon.'

Penny shook their hands. 'Anything we can do to help.'

In the car park Ella said to Murray, 'You men are so obvious.' He smiled.

'Listen,' she said, 'where have we heard the name Freya recently?'

'I don't think we have.'

'I'm sure of it,' she said. 'But where?'

He shrugged. 'Beats me. Think about it on the drive back.'

'Yeah,' she said, distracted. 'See you there.'

At the office, Murray went to the computer while Ella took the bagged florist's card and envelope into Galea's office and brought him up to speed.

Galea nodded. 'Send it off and see what comes back. Be interesting to know just what's going on with all that.'

'Much come in from Crimestoppers about the newspaper piece?'

'A few,' he said. 'The faxes are on your desk. I think Jackie had a bit of spare time and went through some for you.'

Murray looked up from his monitor when she reached her desk. 'I found a Freya Marie Craig, same DOB, living in Homebush.'

'Good,' she said. 'Any record?'

'Only as a witness. She's a paramedic.'

She punched him in the shoulder. 'I knew I'd heard her name.'

'Ow.'

'At The Rocks station yesterday when we went to talk to Georgie, she asked her partner to bring in another chair and I'm certain she called her Freya. Don't you remember?'

He was still rubbing his shoulder. 'Are you sure?'

'Absolutely,' she said. 'The age looked right too. I bet it's her.'

'Hmm.' He frowned.

'Exactly. Why didn't she mention that she'd been a student there too?'

'I'm thinking more that Georgie should've let us know.'

Ella tapped a nail on the desk. 'Let's go see Freya at home.'

'She might be at work,' he said.

'Georgie's on nights tonight, she told me. Freya would be working the same. She'll be home asleep.' *Perfect.*

But he was frowning again.

'What now?'

'I think we'd be better off getting stuck into the Crimestoppers reports.'

'Galea said Jackie had started.'

He held up two pages in one hand. 'This is what she did.' He picked up a thick wad in the other. 'This is what remains to be done.'

'Okay,' she said. 'You stay and do that while I talk to this Freya.'

'What are you going to say? You have no evidence of anything at all. It could be complete coincidence that she left. You don't even know if she knew Tim, let alone was the girl Chris Patrick saw with him in the record shop.'

'She's still worth talking to.'

'It's such a long shot it's ridiculous.'

She shrugged. 'Time will tell.'

Freya kicked the doona off. She should get up, she was way too wired to sleep, but what then? There was housework to do – oh God, there was always housework to do – or she could cook dinner and put it in the fridge for James to reheat tonight. Neither idea appealed, and she suspected that if she did get up all she'd do was pace the house. *May as well stay in bed and toss and turn.* At least she was lying down.

She turned the pillow over. She couldn't get comfortable. Her head and stomach hurt. She felt guilty and worried and, oddly for her, almost teary. But lack of sleep could do that to you. It meant nothing more.

There was a knock at the door. She pulled the pillow over her head and lay there listening. Jehovah's Witnesses, she bet. They were always coming around. They'd try once more then go away.

Another knock, a little louder. She used to get up and tell them no, but they didn't listen, and she got so wound up saying, 'No means no, don't you get that?' that she could never get back to sleep afterwards. Now she just avoided the issue altogether.

Another knock, and another. Bloody hell. Freya pressed the pillow against her ears and shut her eyes. *Can't you tell I'm sleeping?*

'Freya Craig? It's Detective Marconi. I need to speak with you.'

That. Fucking. Georgie.

The cop was practically hammering. 'Freya Craig, please open the door.'

If I had nothing to hide, I'd answer.

She threw on jeans and a T-shirt and went nervously

downstairs. A big deep breath and she opened the door. 'Hi, can I help you?'

The woman half-smiled and flashed her badge. 'I'm Detective Ella Marconi. I saw you briefly at the ambulance station yesterday.' She put her hand on the door. 'Mind if I come in?'

'Certainly.'

You have nothing to hide, you are pleasant and cooperative. You lead her into the lounge room and offer her a seat like a normal person. You sit yourself down, relaxed, perhaps a little on edge, curious, but not, not, guilty.

'What's this about?'

'Do you know the name Tim Pieters?'

'He's the murdered boy you've been talking to Georgie about. He went to our school. Or I went to his school.' *Chuckle. Nice touch.* 'However you'd like to put it.'

'How well did you know him?'

'He was two years ahead of us,' she said. 'I'd seen him around. When I heard he was dead I knew who they were talking about. But that's about it.'

Ella stared at her. 'Really?'

'Yes.'

'We've recently learnt that Tim may have been in a relationship. Do you know anything about that?'

Fuc-king Georgie. 'No, I don't.'

'You don't know of any girl he might have been seeing?'

'Nope,' she said. 'Like I said, I hardly knew him.'

'Big co-ed school like that, you'd often see couples wandering around together, wouldn't you?'

'You may do.' Freya shrugged. 'But as you say, big school. Kids everywhere. You didn't see everyone all the time.'

'Hmm.' Ella's gaze was even. 'You know, it strikes me as odd that you knew we were talking to Georgie about Tim and you never volunteered the fact that you were at school with him too.'

'I had no idea you would be interested,' Freya said. 'I assumed you were talking to her as the girl who found the body, not as one of his thousand fellow students. *Are* you talking to everyone?'

'Just to those students who left abruptly after his death, or who've been brought to our attention for some other reason.'

'Regarding the leaving, you can blame my mother,' Freya said. 'The murder sent her into a complete spin and she decided all of a sudden we had to get out of the city. I didn't want to go, but I was sixteen, so what say did I have?'

She felt beads of sweat running down her ribs. She hoped her face looked dry and open and honest. *Brought to their attention for some other reason – Georgie, you bitch.*

Ella took out a notebook and wrote something down. Freya brushed fluff from her sleeve and glanced out the window. *Please leave*, she thought. *Please, please leave.*

Ella's phone beeped. She kept writing. Freya tried to look uninterested, feeling the silence drag out, feeling like Ella was testing her to see how long before she spoke. She bit her tongue harder and harder, and kept her mouth shut.

Finally Ella clicked her pen away and stood up. 'Well, I guess I'll let you be. Hope you have a quiet nightshift tonight.'

Trying to breathe, Freya shut the door, waited till she heard her car drive off, then ran to get her mobile. Dion's number was still in the received calls list. She almost dialled it then thought of call tracing, phone logs, line taps. *Oh God.*

No. That was paranoid. If they knew anything Ella wouldn't have just left like that.

Would she?

Freya peered around the edge of the curtain. She couldn't think. Better safe than sorry. With a shaking thumb she deleted all calls received, and tried to tell herself again that nobody could know anything.

She just wished she still believed it.

The water heater in the office kitchen was working again, and Murray was making a coffee when Ella came in. 'How'd you go?' he asked.

'She said she knew nothing about it.'

'Told you.'

She reached around him for a cup. 'I don't know if I believe her.'

'Based on, let me guess, a hunch?'

'Laugh if you want.'

'Oh, I am,' he said. 'Did you talk to Georgie as well? Ask her why she never mentioned Freya was at school then too?'

'I don't consider that a problem. She answered the questions we put to her and we didn't ask for her thoughts on anything else.'

'But surely if you have a concern about one you should have a concern about the other.'

'Whatever.' She stirred her coffee and tossed the spoon into the sink.

'Whatever? What are you, fifteen?'

'That's not what they say,' Ella said.

'What do they say then?'

'I don't know, but it's not that.'

She walked from the kitchen. Chris Patrick couldn't say if it was Freya, and the only people who knew for sure were Tim, now of course dead, and the girl herself. Maybe it was Freya, maybe it wasn't, but for now she could just sit glowering in the back of Ella's mind. It was time to get on with other stuff.

Her phone beeped and she remembered the earlier one indicating the arrival of a message. She opened and read it. *Hello, how's your day going?*

She didn't recognise the number.

The second message was from the same person. *It's rude to ignore your mother lol.*

She dialled it.

'Hello, Ella.'

'Mum . . . ?'

Netta started laughing. 'You got our messages!'

'Of course I got them,' Ella said. 'When did you get a mobile?'

'Just now. Those were my first thingies. Texts. Not bad, huh?'

'Great,' Ella said.

'Lol.' Netta laughed. 'I love that. Lol. Lol!'

Ella heard male voices in the background. 'Is that . . . Who is that? Is Wayne there?'

'He brought the phone and showed us how to use it,' Netta said.

Ella's head was spinning. 'Why? How?'

'He rang to thank us for the dinner and I told him about the Cecile Brunner and he came straight over. Then when we were in the garden we talked about you and I said how sometimes it's hard to get hold of you and he went out and got us this lovely little phone.'

'I can't believe this,' Ella said.

'I know, isn't it wonderful? Now we can keep in touch all the time,' Netta said. 'I can let you know where we are and what we're doing, and you can do the same!'

Ella closed her eyes. 'Could you put Wayne on, please?'

'Hang on. Lol.' She went away giggling.

'Hey, honey.'

'What're you doing?'

'Helping out.'

'I don't think that's what it's called.'

'It's good for them to have a mobile,' he said. 'They want to keep in touch with you more.'

'It's not necessary.'

He lowered his voice. 'Are you forgetting that we almost lost you last year?'

'So now you need to know where I am every second of the day? And what's with the "we"?'

'We're all concerned,' he said.

'Lunch is ready,' Netta called.

'Don't you have work to do?' Ella said.

'It's good to have a break,' Wayne said. 'Why don't you come over?'

'I have to go.' She hung up and sagged in her chair.

'Sounds like trouble,' Murray said.

'Not. Another. Word.'

He held up his hands.

Focus on work. Forget them. Focus. Focus.

She took a deep breath and looked up. 'How'd it go with the Commodore aunt and Steve Franklin?'

'Nothing useful from either of them,' Murray said. 'But the DNA report on the blood spots on the leaves came in.'

'Tavris?'

Murray shook his head sadly. 'They even compared it to Tim's blood, to see if it was from a relative.'

Ella sat up straight. 'And?'

'No match, so there goes your idea that it might've been his father.'

'It only means the blood isn't his, not that he didn't do it,' Ella said. 'There could've been somebody else there helping. A body is a dead weight.'

'Ha ha,' Murray said. 'Want some Crimestoppers reports? I haven't looked at these ones yet.'

Each page was a record of a separate call to the Crime-stoppers hotline, and the calltaker had entered what the caller said and whether they'd given their name. Ella knew sometimes people rang hoping to cause somebody a bit of hassle by having the cops turn up on their doorstep. The first two reports she read were anonymous so were possibly mischief calls. The next two had given lots of detail, both about themselves and the woman they thought they recognised.

The first of those callers, Anton Simic, had said the woman was named Carolyn Pearce. She lived in Bronte and worked as an interior designer. When asked by the calltaker why he thought she might have called the police about the murder, he'd said, 'She told me once that she knew things.'

'What things?' the calltaker asked.

'She wouldn't say. She was very mysterious. And I swear that picture is of her.'

Ella typed the names into the system. Neither had a record. Pearce still lived in Bronte, while Simic lived in Randwick.

'How do you know this woman?' the calltaker had asked.

'We used to go out.'

Ella made a note about that. The potential for it to be a mischief call was high.

The second detailed report came from a Julia Palmer who rang about a woman who was often in the shop where she worked. 'Her first name's Dani,' she'd said. 'She's about forty, forty-five. I don't know her last name but I think it might start with K because she's got those personalised plates on her red Mini: DK something something something.' The shop was a corner supermarket in Asquith. Palmer lived nearby.

Ella entered the details. Julia Palmer had no record. A search for a red Mini with plates starting with DK produced one result, in the name of Danielle Kingsley, forty-three years old. A check of her criminal record showed that in 1988 she'd been charged with possession of stolen property and given a fine and suspended sentence.

Interesting.

Ella wrote down Kingsley's address, then typed in the details from the two anonymous sheets. The first alleged that the woman in the photo was Suzette Dearbridge. The computer showed her to be nineteen and living in Wollongong, and while pictures could sometimes lie, Ella would've put money on the CCTV woman being at least thirty-five. The second report said that the woman was Josephine Smith, and a check of the computer gave three results for the name: one eighty-three years old, one sixty and one thirty-nine. Ella checked the record of the younger one and found only a seven-year-old drink-driving charge. She lived in Katoomba. Ella scribbled down her details just in case.

She ran her eye quickly over the list of names and addresses of Commodore owners but nothing matched.

She took another report from Murray's pile. An anonymous caller, a male, gave the name Christine Harrington and said, 'I know she killed that guy because she's a fucking bitch.' Ella liked how the calltakers transcribed every detail. She typed in the name and found her, twenty years old, so too young to have actually killed Tim. Somebody was angry at her, so angry he couldn't read.

Her phone beeped.

wyn is tchn me txt tlk. lolol!!

Oh for God's sake.

Her phone rang. 'What!'

'Is this a bad time?' Callum said.

'Sorry. No, it's fine. How are you?'

'Good,' he said. 'I just thought I'd let you know – I mean, you might know already – but Tim's sister, Haydee, is up from Adelaide for a couple of days and staying in the house. I thought you might want to talk to her.'

'Thanks,' she said. 'We didn't know. Thanks very much.'

She hung up and said to Murray, 'Fancy a trip to the Pieterses'?'

He didn't lift his eyes from the report. 'Now?'

'Tim's sister's in town.'

'You go.'

'I think you should meet them.'

Now he looked up. 'So I can see the father's horns and pointy tail?'

'Exactly,' she said. 'And while we're in the area we can check out one of these Crimestoppers reportees and the Hornsby PQW Commodore as well.'

'Efficiency, thy middle name is Ella,' he said.

'Shut up and come on.'

Josh opened the door and leapt into Ella's arms. 'Hello!'

'Hi, Josh. This is Murray.'

Josh hugged him too. 'Did you catch the bad man?'

'Not yet,' Murray said.

John came to the door. 'Come in, come in.' He shook Murray's hand. 'It's a pleasure to meet you.'

'You too,' Murray said.

'You're just in time for afternoon tea.' John led them into the kitchen where Alistair McLennan was cutting slices from an iced cake. 'Coffee?'

'Not for me,' Ella said.

'I'd love one, thanks,' Murray said. He nodded at Alistair. 'Detective Murray Shakespeare.'

Alistair wiped his hands on a tea towel then shook Murray's hand. 'Dr Alistair McLennan. Tim's uncle.'

'Ella, come see!' Josh was in the backyard, waving through the kitchen window. 'Haydee found a spider!'

A woman in her late thirties with cropped blonde hair stood in the garden holding a stick. Ella went out.

'This is the police lady,' Josh said to the woman.

'I'm Haydee.' She tossed the stick in the garden and put out her hand. 'Nice to meet you.'

'You too. May we talk?'

'Sure.' She looked at Josh who was crouched over a hole in the grass. 'Don't put your finger in there.'

'I won't.'

Ella said, 'I know this isn't easy. It must feel like things settle down and then along we come and stir it all up again.'

Haydee shook her head. 'It's always there. Anything I can do to help I absolutely will do.'

'Were you and Tim close?'

'Once I would have said yes,' she said. 'That last year or so, though, he'd really changed.'

'In what way?'

'He'd turned nasty. He'd pick fights with me and Joshy and was terrible to Mum and Dad. I know they say you shouldn't speak badly of the dead, but truly he'd become a bit of an arsehole.'

'Any ideas why?'

'Because he was a teenage boy?' She shrugged. 'When I heard afterwards about the drinking I thought that probably had something to do with it as well.'

'You didn't know about that?'

'No,' she said. 'I feel like I should've known, but I didn't.'

'What about girls?'

'I think there was one earlier that year,' she said. 'I never met her or anything, and he certainly never mentioned her, but I had the impression for a while that he was meeting somebody now and then.'

'Why was that?'

'Just a feeling,' she said. 'He sometimes had this look on his face. He looked happy. Like he was in love. But then it was almost like he realised he was showing it and would lock that face away. I don't know why. But that whole experience might've had something to do with his nastiness as well. When it stopped, you know. Might've broken his heart.'

'But you don't know for sure?'

'No.'

'Do you think it could've been a boy rather than a girl?'

'The gay thing,' she said. 'I heard about that later. I couldn't say really. I couldn't see it then, but kids can hide stuff pretty well when they want to.'

Ella nodded. 'Do you remember anything unusual happening in the time leading up to his death?'

'Just the fight on the night he died.' She looked down at Josh who was trailing a golden ribbon through the grass. 'Tim was being a complete turd, arguing with Mum and Dad, being mean to Callum, rude to Uncle Alistair and Aunty Gen, and then when Dad said he couldn't go out that night he lost it. Started shouting at them, saying they never listened, they didn't let him talk, just told him to shut up and get on with whatever they told him to do, all they ever did was boss him around. Blah blah.'

'Did you agree with his assessment?'

Haydee shook her head. 'Our life wasn't like that. We were just expected to help out a bit, clean up after ourselves. That's all.'

Ella wondered if they were her true feelings at the time. Through the prism of adulthood such requirements might look more reasonable than they felt then. 'Then what?'

'He and I argued as well. I told him he was being a little shit and to pull his head in. He told me to fuck off and he walked away. Later we realised he wasn't there any more.' She wiped her eyes with the heels of her hands. 'Dad was furious but I thought good riddance. The party was better without him hanging around being shitty. I didn't know I'd never speak to him again.'

Ella could imagine.

'I went to bed about ten so I didn't know Dad went out looking till the next morning,' she said. Mum went up to his room and he wasn't there. She called his friends to ask where they'd been the night before, I guess they were hedging because I remember she started yelling at them, then Dad got on and was all serious and angry. They said they'd been at the pub and Tim had left, nobody knew when or where he went but they'd just assumed he came home. I went to his room and his stuff wasn't there, no wallet or anything, and his bed was made like he usually made it, just kind of dragged up to the pillow, and it was eerie, seeing that. His room still smelled like his deodorant as well.' She wept.

Ella lowered her gaze. Josh was kneeling at their feet and drawing the golden ribbon across Haydee's bare toes. 'Better?' he said.

'I'm all right, Joshy.' She wiped her face on her forearm. 'I'm okay. It just hits me sometimes. He should still be here, you know?'

Ella nodded.

'Do you think you'll catch whoever did it?'

'I hope so,' Ella said. 'I wish I could give you more than that.'

Tamara called from inside. 'Haydee, phone.'

'Need anything more?'

'I'll catch you later if I do,' Ella said. 'Thanks very much.'

When Haydee had gone inside Ella crouched beside Josh. 'Where's the spider?'

He pointed to the hole. 'Don't put your finger in.' He dangled the ribbon in the air. 'Do you like my ribbon?'

'It's lovely. Where did you get it?'

'It's Tim's. He told me I couldn't play with it but Callum said it's okay now.' He laid it flat on the grass. 'Haydee was crying because you were talking about Tim.'

'Yes, she was.'

'I sometimes cry when I think about Tim.'

Ella nodded. 'Do you think about him a lot?'

'We used to play Star Wars and now I don't have anybody to play it with.'

'That'd be tough.'

'I want you to catch the bad man who hurt him.'

'So do I,' she said.

'Then the bad man can't hurt me.'

She looked at him. 'Are you worried about the bad man hurting you?'

'A bit,' he said. 'Tim was big and strong and he couldn't stop him.'

'Josh.' She put her hand on his arm, the blood suddenly buzzing in her head. 'Do you know who the bad man is?'

He shook his head. 'Is he like a monster who comes when it's dark?'

'No,' she said, blood subsiding a little, 'and he's nothing for you to worry about. We won't let him hurt you, I promise.'

In the car Murray said, 'They all seemed lovely.'

She sighed and tried to clear her mind. 'Did you talk to Tamara?'

'She's the nicest of the lot! While you were playing Steve Irwin in the yard, we had a good chat.'

'Really,' Ella said. 'What about?'

'About stress, how it affects relationships, how it's been tough for her and John.'

'What'd you think of John?'

'He's a bereaved father but a nice guy,' Murray said. 'Alistair's decent too. We had a chat as well.'

'You've been quite the conversationalist.'

Her phone beeped. She looked at the screen. *hlo, hw r u? im eatng aple, dad eatng pch. lol!* Delete.

'It's always interesting talking to doctors,' he said. 'We discussed my cruciate ligament problem. He had some thoughtful opinions on the various physical therapies.'

'I bet he did.' She indicated and turned left. 'Who doesn't love talking shop on their day off?'

'It wasn't like that. He was really into it. Told me about different cruciate ligament injuries he'd seen and everything.'

'You like saying cruciate ligament, don't you?'

He waved a hand at her. 'He's concerned about Josh too. He was watching when you were talking out the back and saying how he's put on weight lately, how he hoped all this wasn't stressing him too much. Asked Tamara to take him in for a check-up.'

'Stressed is the last word I'd use to describe Josh.'

'Still, he's worried,' Murray said. 'And you know what? I don't think any of them have horns.'

Danielle Kingsley's house was a little green weatherboard in a quiet street in Asquith. Ella rattled the old cowbell fixed to the front door.

The door opened. 'Yes?' The woman was in her early twenties with long blonde hair and a blue-eyed toddler on her hip.

Ella showed her badge. 'Is Danielle Kingsley here?'

'She's out.'

'At work?' Murray said.

The girl shook her head. 'Shopping, I think. I don't know when she'll be back. Sometimes she's gone for friggin' hours.'

'And you are?'

'Her daughter, Kelly.'

Ella smiled at the toddler who dribbled rusk. 'Do you have a photo of her that we could see, please?'

'Can I ask why?'

'To confirm something.'

The girl frowned but fetched one. She unlocked the screen and held it out. Ella studied it and Murray looked over her shoulder. It looked similar to the woman in the CCTV, but it was hard to say for certain.

'Is this recent?' Ella asked.

'A year, maybe.' The young woman hoisted the toddler higher. 'She's lost a bit of weight.'

That could be it. They'd have to see her in person. 'She still got the Mini?'

'Yes.'

'You live here with her?'

She nodded.

'Do you have a car?'

'The yellow Datsun on the street there.'

'Anyone else live here, and have a car?'

'Dad. He has a black Ford Falcon. That's it.'

'His name?'

'Paul Kingsley.'

Ella gave the woman one of her cards. 'Have your mother call us when she gets in, please.'

'What about?'

'We just need to talk to her,' Ella said. 'Straighten some things out.' She smiled at the toddler. 'Thanks.'

The corner supermarket where Julia Palmer worked was three blocks down. Ella parked at the back and they walked around.

'Morning.' The woman behind the counter had her light brown dreadlocks tied up in a pink scarf. Her name tag said Julia. 'Can I help you with anything?'

'Are you Julia Palmer?'

'Ye-ess.'

Ella got out her badge. 'Can we talk for a moment?'

'Wow, that was quick!' Julia said. 'So is it her?'

Ella glanced around. There was nobody else in the shop. 'We haven't spoken to her yet. We just met her daughter.'

Julia was nodding. 'Yeah, her daughter, that's right. She's got a little girl herself.'

'How often do you see Danielle?' Murray asked.

'Every week, sometimes twice a week. Usually for milk and stuff like that, stuff you run out of quick. Although sometimes her husband comes in instead. Hey, you want to know how long it took me to work out that it was her? How I was so certain that I rang you guys up?'

'Well —' Murray said.

'I knew it was her because she has this manner,' Julia said confidingly. 'I study people, see? I watch them all the time. I saw that photo in the paper and I just *knew*. I could almost see her in action, walking. Just like I was watching her on the screen myself.' She squared the air with her hands.

'Thanks,' Ella said. 'We'll be in touch.'

Outside in the car Murray said, 'What do you think?'

'She seems loopy rather than deliberately misleading.'

'I agree,' he said. 'At least we can check out that Hornsby PQW Commodore while we're up this way.'

Edgeworth David Avenue was long. Ella drove them past the girls high school and down the hill, through the dogleg at the shops and further. The house was set back on an overgrown block with the garden spilling across the lawn. It made Ella wonder if her roses were dead yet.

The patio was pebblecrete with a low cast-iron railing. Murray knocked on the white door. The man who answered was in his forties. He was on crutches with a cast on his right leg, and his salt-and-pepper hair was trimmed around a fresh line of sutures above his right temple.

Murray showed his badge. 'Is Lisa Peterson home?'

'She's at work,' he said. 'I'm her husband, Ashley. Is everything okay?'

Ella said, 'Does she still have the Commodore with the plate PQW 199?'

'Has there been an accident?'

'No, it's fine,' Ella said. 'Is the car here?'

'In the garage. You want to have a look?'

'Thanks.'

He pulled a bunch of keys from the back of the door and hobbled out. 'I'm sure there's been no accident with it. She would have told me.'

They followed him along the pebblecrete path to the garage

door. He unlocked it and awkwardly started heaving it up before Murray took over. The cream Commodore was parked nose in. Ella squeezed along next to it, looked inside, checked out the pristine front panels and the bonnet.

'Has somebody complained or something?'

She squeezed back out. 'Was Lisa driving this on Sunday night?'

'I don't know,' he said. 'I was in hospital. Motorbike spill. I only got home yesterday.'

'Do you know where she was that evening?' Murray said. 'Was she visiting you?'

'She wasn't with me,' he said. 'She's not good with hospitals. You'll have to ask her if she went out anywhere but she doesn't usually.'

'Does anyone ever borrow this car?'

He shook his head. 'What's it supposed to have done?'

'Can we see a photo of Lisa, please?'

'Well, sure. If you want.'

He hobbled out of the way as Murray pulled the door down then he locked it again. He went back into the house and came out with a wedding photo.

'How recent is this?' Ella asked.

'Six months,' he said.

Lisa was short and round. Her hair was short and spiked and dyed bright blonde. She grinned at the camera, as did Ashley beside her.

'Nice photo,' Murray said. 'Congratulations.'

He smiled. 'Thanks.'

Ella handed it back. 'Thanks for your time.'

'What should I tell her?'

'It doesn't really matter,' Murray said.

'I could say you just needed to check a couple of things.'

'That's fine.'

'She'll want to know why, though.'

'It's just part of a case,' Ella said. 'Thanks again.'

He was still leaning on his crutches on the patio, the frame in his hand, when she started the car. 'They always want to know every last little detail,' she said.

'Drives me nuts,' Murray said. 'Anyway, another bust. Home, James.'

Georgie held Matt's hand as they walked across the bridge. She considered herself lucky: after the fight they'd had about whether she should go to work tonight or not, she hadn't expected he would walk her in, let alone touch.

They passed the southern pylon. He slowed a little. 'Dayshift would be different.'

She kept walking.

'I bet Freya would love to get off nightshift for a few weeks. Why don't you ask if you can both go on a day-only roster for a while?'

'No such thing.'

'You have a legitimate reason to ask them to create one.'

'But somebody will have to cover the extra nights and that's not fair on them.'

'I don't care about them.'

She was practically dragging him along. 'I'm going to be late.'

'Listen to me,' he said.

'Nothing's going to happen.'

'Why even take the chance?' He pulled on her hand and made her stop. 'If we explain the danger to your bosses I'm sure they'll understand.'

'But it's just another thing, you know? One more reason why I'm a pain, why they should just wash their hands of me. I can't risk that.'

'The job's no good to you if you're dead.'

'I'm not going to die.'

He stood there looking at her.

'Come on,' she said. 'Or I'll really be late.'

He didn't move. Tourists pushed past. Somebody in the

traffic blew their horn and the lowering sun made their shadows long against the fence.

She put her free hand on her hip. 'What do you want me to say?'

'That you won't go to work tonight.'

'I can't.'

'Call in sick.'

'I'm on assessment. I need a certificate for even one shift.'

'So get one,' he said. 'There are doctors everywhere.'

'I'm not sick.'

'So lie.'

'Matt.'

He let go of her hand. She stared at him until he frowned at the Opera House instead.

'I can't do this now,' she said. 'I have to go.'

'So go.'

'Not like this.'

'Like what?'

She eyed him angrily. This passive front drove her nuts. 'Walk with me and we can keep talking.'

'What's the point? You're not going to change your mind.'

'If that's the only reason you want to talk to me then you're right, there is no point.'

He turned away.

'Oh, so you're going? That's it?'

'Have a good night,' he said over his shoulder.

The muscles in her neck and back were locked up tight. She wanted to scream and punch something. She wanted to chase him down and push him over and make him talk to her, make him see that this wasn't about safety, it was about keeping her job. But the clock was ticking and, just like she couldn't afford to go sick, she couldn't afford to be late either. She took one last glance at his receding back and turned south.

Further along she looked back. She could just spot him, still getting smaller. She watched but he didn't turn around. She bottled her anger up tight and started down the steps to the road below.

She made it to the station with a minute to spare. The day-shift paramedics were getting their bags out of the truck. One nodded to the back. 'Freya's in there already.' He dropped his voice to a whisper. 'Good luck.'

'With what?'

He raised his eyebrows and didn't answer.

Georgie went to the open rear door. 'Hi.'

Freya slammed the drug drawer shut. 'Hello.'

Feeling ill, Georgie went to get her bag from her locker. The phone rang and one of the dayshift guys answered, then handed her a slip of paper with an address as she came back out. 'Query stroke in Potts Point.'

At the ambulance she tossed in her bag and climbed up after it. 'CVA.'

Freya hurled the Oxy-Viva into its compartment. 'So day-shift couldn't be bothered.'

'It's right on six.'

Freya slammed the back door so hard Georgie felt her ears pop with the air pressure. Freya threw herself behind the wheel.

'Potts Point,' Georgie said.

Freya didn't answer. She cranked the key and roared out of the station.

Georgie got out the street directory and tried to focus on the map. This bad start didn't mean the whole night was bug-gered. They would do the job and do it well; a CVA was no big deal, and through it they would find their equilibrium. Freya would get over whatever was up her nose at the same time as Georgie got over the argument with Matt, and the night would be okay.

'It's in Macleay Street,' she said.

'Paddo's job.'

'Must be busy.'

Freya shot her an *oh really?* look.

Georgie frowned at the map. 'Next left.'

Freya went straight ahead. 'I know where it is.'

Georgie closed the book and stuck it down the side of her seat. *CVA*, she thought. *Posture, oxygen, get the history, check blood pressure and blood sugar.* She didn't need to run through the list really; she'd done so many she could do them in her sleep. It was just a way to block out the angry woman hunched behind the wheel. It was as if Georgie had done something really bad to piss her off, but she knew she'd done nothing. It was probably domestic, like the thorn in Georgie's own side. Best thing to do was leave her alone.

Freya ripped through the evening traffic, scowling and muttering. In Macleay Street a woman stood in the centre of the road and waved frantically at them. She kept waving even though Freya was driving straight at her, then started pointing at an apartment block on the left and almost got herself hit by a car as she tried to get traffic to move aside.

'Jesus,' Freya said. 'Don't we have enough to do?' She flicked off the lights and siren and double-parked next to a BMW.

The waver hammered on Georgie's window, mascara and tears running down her face. 'Please hurry!'

Georgie called on scene to Control then got out and grabbed the Viva from the back. Freya could bring the rest.

'What's happened?' she asked the woman.

'My sister's collapsed, I don't know what it is. She couldn't talk and then just collapsed.'

'Was she still conscious when you came downstairs?'

'I think so. She was moaning.'

They hurried into the lift. The woman attacked the button but Georgie put her foot against the door. Freya stalked across the lobby and into the lift with the monitor and drug box, and Georgie let the door close.

'What's her medical history?' she asked.

'She's got none.' The woman kept pushing the button as if that would make them rise faster. 'Oh, except she had an operation done on her knee a couple of days ago. But that's all.'

'Has she been up and about much since then?'

The woman shook her head. 'She was told to rest it. That's why I was over today, to help with the kids.'

'Is she on the pill?'

'I think so.'

The doors slid open and the woman leapt out and rushed down a short corridor to an apartment door held open by a phone book. She shoved it back and Georgie heard wailing.

In the living room, a man and a woman struggled on the floor, the man trying to restrain the woman's thrashing limbs. Georgie smelled vomit and saw it was all over both of them. Three small children stood pressed against an armchair, the littlest with his head hard into the cushion, the other two sobbing with their hands to their faces.

Georgie put the Viva down. 'They don't need to see this.'

The sister gathered them up and took them into another room as Georgie touched the man's shoulder. 'What's her name?'

'Susie,' he panted. 'I'm Darren. I can't hold her much longer.'

'Ease off a bit,' Freya said.

'She just thrashes.'

'It's okay,' Freya said.

Georgie was on her knees by Susie's head. Her long blonde hair was stuck to her face with vomit. She wore denim shorts and a pink T-shirt and had a brace strapped around her left knee. She tossed her head from side to side and grunted and moaned.

'Susie!' Georgie said.

The woman didn't respond.

'Has she talked to you at all?'

'She came out of the bedroom and said she had a funny headache then fell over. That was it.'

'She was fine before then?'

He nodded.

With one gloved hand Georgie cleared the wet hair from across Susie's face and shone a torch into her pupils. 'Sluggish but equal and reacting.'

Freya said nothing. She reached around Darren's hands to

attach the monitor's leads then turned the machine on. Georgie put an oxygen mask on Susie and cranked the flow rate to fourteen litres per minute. She wrapped the sphygmo cuff around Susie's upper arm and inflated it while Freya looked at the monitor screen and ran off a strip and stuffed it in her pocket.

'Well?' Georgie said.

'Normal sinus of one hundred.'

Georgie stuck the earpieces of her stethoscope into place and listened to Susie's blood pressure. 'One fifty on eighty-five.'

Again no answer from Freya as she got the blood sugar kit and grabbed one of Susie's waving hands.

Georgie leaned into Susie's face. 'Susie!' Still no response. She was moving all her limbs and didn't appear to have any facial droop. She cried out and struggled against her husband's grip. Georgie checked her pupils again. No change.

Freya read the glucometer screen then started packing the machine away.

Georgie felt heat rise in her throat. 'Well?'

'Four point two.'

Anger filled Georgie's vision with red spots. Freya was going to force her to ask for every little thing and it made her want to spit. But she should've known the blood sugar was fine, really – surely not even Freya in this foulest of moods would allow something like a hypo to go untreated.

She tried to breathe and concentrate. They would need help to carry her into the lift and outside.

'Got the portable?' she said to Freya as she clipped a tourniquet around Susie's arm.

'Nup.' Freya got up and left the room.

Georgie gritted her teeth. Her hands shook as she palpated Susie's arm for a vein then swabbed the skin inside her elbow. 'Keep her arm as still as you can, please,' she said to Darren.

He looked around just as she slid the cannula under Susie's skin, and went instantly white. 'Oh God.'

Oh no. 'Look away,' she said sharply. 'Don't think about it.'

'Oh God,' he said again, his head already starting to loll.

His grip loosened and Susie's flailing pulled her arm away from Georgie. She couldn't control her and hold the cannula properly in place at the same time, and as Darren slumped in a dead faint across his wife the tip of the cannula came out of the vein and the blood immediately started to spread under Susie's skin and pour out of the hole as well. Georgie pressed her hand against it but the blood leaked like hot oil between her gloved fingers and onto her knee and the carpet.

'Freya!'

Freya came back in with a wet tea towel. 'What are you doing?'

'Just throw me a pad and get him off.'

Freya did as she was asked, to Georgie's relief. Georgie pushed the pad hard against Susie's arm with one hand and stuck the cannula into the sharps container. Susie heaved in her grip and the oxygen mask twisted off her face as she vomited again. It splattered hotly on Georgie's arms. She could feel the cannula site developing a haematoma and increased her pressure. *What a nightmare.*

Freya dragged Darren aside and put him on his back on the floor with his feet up on the lounge. He groaned as he started to come round.

The sister came out of the bedroom and pulled the door closed behind her. 'What's happening?'

Georgie said, 'Can you phone triple 0 again, please, and tell them that we need another crew to help us load?'

The sister went into the kitchen and Georgie heard her dialling. 'I could've used you,' she hissed at Freya.

'She needs cleaning up.' Freya picked up the tea towel and wiped vomit off Susie's cheeks.

Georgie glared at her. 'That's a low priority and you know it.'

Darren moaned and put his hands to his face.

'Let's try and be a little professional here, shall we?' Freya shot back at her.

'Let's,' Georgie said. 'Beginning with you.'

Freya huffed. 'Like you didn't start it.'

The sister came back in. 'He said to tell you they're on their way.'

'Thank you,' Georgie said. 'May I have a bandage, please, Freya?'

Freya passed one over. 'We're fine here for the moment,' she said to the sister. 'Best if you stay with the kids.'

'Do you know what's wrong with her?'

'It might be a blood clot in her brain,' Georgie said. 'It might have been caused by the surgery and the bed rest she's had since then. Being on the pill increases her risk too. Once the other crew gets here, we'll get her straight to hospital and they'll be able to find out there.'

The sister stared at Susie, who was throwing her head from side to side. 'Will she be okay?'

'It's difficult to say,' Georgie said. 'We're doing all we can right here, and, like I said, we'll get on our way as soon as we can.'

'How about Darren?'

'He just fainted,' Freya said. 'He'll be okay in a minute.'

The sister looked unsure but went back into the bedroom. The instant the door closed Georgie said, 'How did I start it? I never did a thing.'

'You told that detective.'

Georgie stopped bandaging and stared at her.

Darren groaned and struggled to sit up, clinging to the edge of the coffee table. 'What happened?'

'You fainted,' Freya said. 'Stay on the floor.'

He put his hand to his forehead. 'Is she okay?'

'We're doing all we can for her,' Georgie managed to say. Through the cloud of red dots she taped the end of the bandage down snug over the haematoma on Susie's arm and clipped the tourniquet around her other arm. She had to clear her mind, just long enough to get this line in. 'Look the other way.'

His eyes widened and he lay down on his face.

Freya grasped Susie's arm to hold it still as Georgie reached for a swab. Their heads were close together and Georgie muttered, 'I said nothing.'

'Don't lie.'

Georgie gritted her teeth as she tore open the cannula packet. 'It's true.'

'Bullshit.'

'Think what you want.' Georgie pushed the tip of the cannula through Susie's skin. 'I didn't say anything.'

'Again, I say bullshit.'

Georgie saw the flash of blood in the chamber and advanced the cannula into the vein. 'If I told her, why would I deny it?'

'Because –' Freya stopped.

Georgie released the tourniquet. 'Say it.'

Freya held Susie's arm in silence while Georgie taped the cannula in then strapped on the armlock splint to prevent Susie's elbow flexing and blocking off the line.

'Say it,' Georgie said again.

Darren said into the floor, 'Finished?'

'Not yet,' Freya said.

'Say it.' Georgie fixed her with a cold stare.

Freya adjusted the mask on Susie's face. 'Because maybe you aren't thinking right.'

'Because I'm nuts?'

'Is that what I said?'

'That's what you meant,' Georgie snapped.

'Is everything okay?' Darren said, his voice muffled by the carpet.

'She's doing well,' Freya said to him. 'The other crew will be here soon and then we'll get her off to hospital.'

'It sounded like there's a problem.'

'No problem.' Georgie glared at Freya.

Freya lowered her voice. 'Just admit you told her.'

'I didn't say a word.'

'She came to see me today and she was pretty blunt.'

'I didn't,' Georgie said.

Freya shook her head. 'A bit of courage,' she said, 'a bit of decency to admit –'

'I didn't tell her.'

There were footsteps in the corridor and Georgie heard the crackle of an ambulance portable. She leaned close. 'I didn't.'

'Get away from me,' Freya said.

THIRTEEN

Georgie's heart wouldn't settle and her back itched with nervous sweat. Freya hadn't spoken a word to her since the back-up crew had arrived on scene to help carry Susie downstairs and load her into the ambulance. At St Vincent's Hospital they'd unloaded her, and Georgie had given the handover to the triage nurse then filled in paperwork while Freya cleaned up the back in total silence. Now Freya sat behind the wheel, arms folded, fury coming off her in waves. If Georgie couldn't persuade her she was wrong, she could kiss her assessment goodbye.

She put the folder on the dash and got into the passenger seat. 'I swear to you I didn't tell her anything.'

Not even a blink.

'I swear.'

Freya spoke without turning her head. 'You saw her today.'

'What? No.'

'She knew I was working nightshift tonight. You saw her today and told her that. That's how she knew to come to my house.' Now she looked at her, her brown eyes cold. 'Admit that much.'

'Okay,' Georgie said. 'Yes, I saw her, but it was about something else.'

'What?'

'I can't say.'

Freya snorted and faced front.

'She asked me not to tell anyone.'

'Sure.'

'She's a detective. If she says that, who am I to go against her?'

'What's so important you have to keep it secret even in a situation like this?'

'She asked me to,' Georgie said.

Freya started the engine.

Georgie sighed, and picked up the microphone. 'Thirty-three is clear.'

'Thanks,' Control said. 'I'll get you to head over to Hunter Street, cross is Phillip, for a cancer patient unwell on the footpath.'

'Thirty-three's on the case.'

Georgie hung up the mike and rubbed her forehead. She wanted to cry. She'd texted Matt while writing the case sheet, hadn't apologised but thumbed a friendly *hey, how's it going*, just to start smoothing things over, but he hadn't replied so she didn't even have that to cling to. *What a shit night.* Her scalp was so tight she could feel it pulling up against her skull.

Hunter Street wasn't far, and Freya left the siren off. Georgie yanked on gloves and felt a headache start to pulse against her temples.

Freya flicked the high beams on when she turned into Hunter Street, and a man waved down the block. When they got close Freya put the hazards on to double-park. A driver some-where behind them blew his horn. In her head Georgie told him to fuck off. Freya turned the engine off and got out without a backwards glance.

'This poor woman's very ill,' the waver said to Georgie when she opened her door. 'You might want to hurry.'

'Really? Thanks.'

Georgie pulled out the Oxy-Viva and thought how many times she'd heard similar stories, usually when people were suffering something terrible like the flu. Funny that the closer people actually were to dying, the less the bystanders came up to tell you about it.

She followed the man to where two women sat on the steps leading down into Chifley Place. Freya was ahead of her and suddenly stopped dead, then turned and walked straight back past Georgie without speaking.

Georgie kept on to find Hilary weeping loudly against the neck of a well-dressed woman.

'Hi, Hilary.'

Hilary mopped her tears on the sleeve of her grimy shirt. 'Hello, lovey.'

Back on the street, the ambulance door slammed.

Georgie said, 'What's the matter today?'

'She has cancer and is feeling poorly,' the woman said in a dignified voice.

She was the wife of the waver, Georgie guessed. They looked like they'd been on their way to a nice night out. She felt sorry for the woman, now with Hilary-stink all over her.

'She has nowhere to go,' the woman went on.

'Cancer,' Georgie said.

Hilary stuck a hand in her dirty knotted hair and held out four loose strands. 'It's cancer, I just know it. I seen those little baldy kids on the telly.'

'Your hair falls out from the treatment, not from the cancer itself,' Georgie said.

'Well, somethin's wrong,' Hilary said. 'I feel terrible.'

Georgie looked at the man. 'Thanks for calling. You can go on your way now if you like.'

'You don't need us?'

'No. Thanks anyway.'

He helped his wife up. Hilary grasped the woman's hand. 'Thank you so much, my love.' She kissed her hand then pulled her down to hug her. The woman hugged her back then Hilary went for the kiss on the lips. The woman twigged at the last second and turned away so it landed on her chin. 'Thank you, my darling.' Hilary wouldn't let her go. 'My lovely. Oh thank you.'

'Hilary,' Georgie said. 'Let the lady go and talk to me.'

Hilary released her grip. The woman staggered back against her husband, both of them looking nauseated. Georgie thought that was probably the end of their nice night, pictured them returning to the parking station and getting back into the Beemer with its safe smell of leather and wealth, so different from the smell of unwashed body and bad teeth they'd just encountered extremely close up.

They walked slowly away and Georgie sat down at the far end of the step, making sure she could leap up pdq if Hilary made a move. 'So what's new with you?'

'Oh lovey, I am so sick.'

'Really.'

'If you knew how sick I am, you'd be getting your friend to bring the wheely bed over and lifting me onto it. You'd be taking me to hospital and making me a cup of tea.'

'I don't think so.'

'Soo sick.'

Sitting there was a waste of time, and she could hear at least two sirens going elsewhere in the city and knew everyone else was working flat out, but she didn't want to get back into that four-wheeled hell.

'Seen any good movies lately?' she said.

'Sooooo sick.'

Georgie sighed. 'You want to go to hospital?'

Hilary stopped moaning. 'Which one?'

'Vinnie's.'

'Who's on?'

'Keelie was doing triage when we were there just now.'

'That cow.' Hilary shook her head. 'Take me to RPA. They sometimes have cake.'

'Too far,' Georgie said. 'It's Vinnie's or nothing.'

'You're a fucking bitch.'

'I know,' Georgie said. 'And life sucks, and then you die.' She got to her feet. 'Vinnie's, yes or no.'

Hilary spat on the ground. 'Piss off.'

'Good night to you too.'

Georgie picked up the Oxy-Viva and went back to the ambulance. She threw it in the back then got in the passenger seat.

'Whores,' Hilary screamed as Freya U-turned past her.

'At least we know her lungs are fine,' Georgie said.

Freya didn't answer.

It was 5 am before they pulled back into the station. Georgie stomped inside and slammed the door. Freya stayed in the ambulance, arms folded on the wheel, watching the sky lighten with the coming day. She felt sick of herself, sick of everything. The night had been hellish. If it wasn't already bad enough being around Georgie, the lying cow, who insisted endlessly that she hadn't told the detective, they'd faced a stream of shitty cases, including a drunk at 1 am who'd smeared vomit all over himself and kept trying to grab her, and a domestic at three where she'd had to duck to avoid getting the snot smacked out of her by an ice user who was pissed because the cops were trying to protect her husband and children. Just now they'd been to an old man who'd slipped on the way to the toilet and been too feeble to get up again, and after they'd lifted him up, stripped him of his wet pyjamas, dried him and dressed him, listening all the while to his even feebler wife promise and promise that they could manage, don't take him, he'll die if you put him into a home, they'd helped him back to bed, and on the way Freya had become aware of things crawling on her legs. As soon as they'd sat him down on the yellowed sheet, she'd pulled up her trouser legs and found a bunch of fleas. She'd managed to catch them all but even now the thought made her reach down and scratch.

How had her life turned so bad so quickly? This time last week she'd been looking forward to meeting her assessee, planning how she'd ask her questions to test her knowledge, intending to do a thorough and proper job, and pass her if she was good enough or help her see what she needed to fix if she wasn't.

But now here she was, having threatened and then been betrayed by that same assessee, on the brink of being investigated by homicide detectives, with the entire fabric of her life at risk of unravelling if somebody got hold of just one thread.

1990

It was quiet and dim inside the hall. The rest of the drama group had gone home, Georgie included. Freya had walked out with her then turned back, saying that she was thinking of entering the eisteddfod and wanted to discuss monologues with Mr Entemann.

Now she locked the door then walked up behind him. He dropped the prop hats he'd been packing away, looking first nervous then shocked as she slid her hands around his waist.

'This isn't . . .' he said. 'I mean . . .'

She moved her hands down across his hips then turned him to face her. He was breathing fast.

'I can't –'

'Yes.' She pulled him close and kissed him, and felt his hands skim her back.

'Really?' he said.

'Yes.'

He was different from Tim. She clung to him, her back pressed against the wall, his thighs so strong beneath her, his knowledge clear in his eyes and his hands. She had to fight not to bite his shoulder.

Later, she sat on his lap, comfortable in the silence between them while his fingers stroked her back through her uniform. Crickets started up in the gloom outside.

'I should go,' she said.

He nodded. 'I don't know what to say.'

'Say I'll see you again next week,' she said. 'Or sooner.'

He smiled.

He unlocked the door and they went out together, close but not touching.

'Slut.'

She spun around. Tim stood by the shrubbery, stiff with rage, a broken cricket stump in his raised hand.

'Don't be an idiot.' Dion wrenched the stump out of his hand and threw it away.

'We were talking about the eisteddfod,' Freya said.

'For all that time? Yeah right.'

Freya shrugged and went to walk past but Tim blocked her way. 'I know what you were doing.' His voice was shaking.

He couldn't know: there were no windows and the door had been locked. 'We were *talking* about the *eisteddfod*.'

Indecision crossed Tim's face.

Dion put a hand on his shoulder. 'Let's just all go home, eh? You need a lift?'

Tim jerked free. 'Get your hand off me.'

'Calm down,' Dion said.

'You're my girl,' Tim said to Freya.

'I'm not yours, I'm not anybody's,' she said. 'Just go home.'

'I'll tell,' Tim said.

'Tell what? We were talking about –'

'I'll tell!' His voice rose shrilly in the gloom, then he turned and ran away across the grass.

Dion stood close to her. Close but not touching. 'You okay?'

'Yeah,' she said. 'I better make sure I go in that eisteddfod now.'

Tim hadn't told. He followed her around the school at a distance over the next few weeks and lurked outside the hall when drama group was on, and eventually Freya and Dion took to meeting late at night.

Dion's daughter, Chelsea, had bad reflux and he would put her in the car and go for a drive so his wife, Andrea, could sleep. He would come past and Freya would sneak out of the house and, with Chelsea oblivious in her capsule in the back of the Volvo, they'd go park somewhere. Dion made her feel good, made her laugh, and sometimes had to put his hand over her mouth to keep her quiet.

Her parents never suspected a thing. She'd felt a little guilty about that sometimes, but really, what she was doing seemed no big deal.

Until that night.

After that, she'd been relieved when her mum had freaked out and insisted they move. More than relieved: she'd been downright glad.

The phone rang. Another job. It was twenty to six. Seagulls were already aloft in the pink and blue sky and Freya stared up at them through the windscreen as Georgie stamped back across the plant room.

Oh God, she was so tired. So sick and so very tired. She needed . . . She didn't know what she needed. To talk? She thought briefly about ringing Dion when the shift was over, then remembered she'd deleted his number from her received calls log yesterday.

It didn't matter anyway. There was nothing to say.

Callum was already running late when he detoured to West Pennant Hills, but what Anna didn't know wouldn't hurt her. He'd say it was traffic, and that somebody should do something about the state of the roads in this place, and she'd laugh and let him be.

He pushed open the door to his father's surgery to find the waiting room empty. His mother looked out of the staffroom. 'Tea?' she asked.

'I'm fine.'

He went in there. Tamara sat at the small table and clutched a mug with both hands. Her eyes were red. Genevieve rested a sisterly hand on her arm.

'Your father's examining Josh,' she said to Callum.

'Is he okay?' Callum asked.

Tamara welled up. 'I brought him in for a check-up, but your dad just told us Josh said he's been having dizzy turns. I didn't know anything about them.'

Callum walked through the waiting room and knocked on the office door. 'Dad?'

'Come in.'

Josh lay on the examination bed with his shirt off, patting his belly. 'Hello, Cal!'

'Lookin good, Joshy.'

'See the octopus on me?'

He was hooked up to the ECG machine, the leads connected to the six tags stuck across his chest and one on each of his arms and legs.

'Nice.'

Alistair frowned at the ECG printout on his desk. Callum looked over his shoulder.

'This look okay to you?' Alistair said.

'Yes.'

'Josh told me he's had some little dizzy episodes and I thought there might've been something here to explain it.'

'Maybe a twenty-four-hour monitor might be the go.'

'I have already thought of that.'

Callum heard the edge and softened his voice. 'I wasn't telling you what to do.'

Alistair didn't reply.

On the bed Josh slapped a rhythm on his stomach. Callum turned to him. 'When do you get dizzy?'

'What?'

'There's no pattern,' Alistair said. 'It's not even every day.'

'When was the last time?' Callum asked Josh.

Josh frowned at his handfuls of white belly.

Alistair lowered his voice. 'He's embarrassed. He won't tell you anything about it. But at least he's admitted it to me, and now I can help him.'

'I'm okay,' Josh said.

'It's all right, buddy,' Callum said to him before turning to

Alistair. 'What are you going to do?'

'I'm thinking about antihypertensives.'

'He could lose some weight.'

'You know how hard that would be for him. He could arrest before then.'

'But –'

'He's got the heart murmur, his weight, hypertension, and he's having dizzy spells. Plus Tamara's lost one son already.'

'Okay, okay,' Callum said. 'You're his doctor.'

'That I am.' Alistair pulled a prescription pad out of a drawer and started writing.

Callum watched him for a moment. 'Quiet in the waiting room today.'

'Economics,' Alistair said without looking up. 'People want bulk billing and I can't afford to do it.'

'So they're not coming any more?'

Alistair shrugged.

It seemed odd to Callum. People loved his dad, had loved his granddad too, and kept coming because they wanted the whole family tradition thing. There'd been considerable pressure for him to join the practice too and keep it all going. People liked continuity of care, and why wouldn't they?

'That's the only reason?' he asked.

'Why else?' Alistair signed the script, tore it from the pad and folded it in half.

'Speaking of drugs,' Callum said, 'I came to tell you that I talked to a friend of mine, a rep for a drug company. He's sending out some adrenaline and so on to restock you.'

'No, thanks.'

'Dad, you need this stuff. He's sending it for free.'

'Do I get a lollipop?' Josh said.

'I'll see if I can find one,' Alistair answered, then said to Callum, 'What are the odds of it happening again?'

'It doesn't matter. You're a doctor and this is a surgery. You need to have it on hand.'

'No.' He fossicked in the desk drawer.

Callum stared at the top of his father's head. His hair was thinning out. His father was old, he realised.

'Look, I can run you through it. I'll write you out a drug chart, what to give when. It'll be simple.'

'I'm not stupid.'

'It's not easy to remember all that stuff when you hardly ever use it, that's all,' Callum said. 'In hospital we have the information stuck on the wall, plus there're always other people to ask. Here you're on your own.'

'I don't need your help.' Alistair produced a misshapen yellow lollipop in wrinkled plastic. 'Put your shirt on, Josh. We're all done.'

Josh buttoned up his shirt then accepted the lollipop. 'Thank you.'

Callum sat back in the chair. He would have his friend send the drugs regardless. If by some shocking chance he was here when somebody else arrested, at least he'd be able to do a bit more than the average first-aider.

Josh jumped down. 'Am I good?'

'You're a doozy,' Alistair said. 'Let's go see your mum.'

'Bye, Cal.'

'Bye.'

Callum was left sitting alone in the office, thinking about his father, and the future, and the past.

'Coffee,' Ella said. 'I need coffee.'

Murray didn't look up from his reading. 'Plenty of hot water in the kitchen.'

'Gee, thanks.' She slumped into her chair. 'A proper partner would run and make me one.'

'If you're tired because you've been up all night shagging it's no concern of mine.'

'Ha,' she said.

Shagging was the complete opposite of what had happened. Wayne had called round, knocking at the front door until she'd heard him over the shower and grabbed a towel and gone to let him in. He'd tugged at the towel but she'd kept it firmly in place and it pretty much all kicked on from there. No, he couldn't see a problem with giving her parents a mobile. Wasn't it great to keep in touch? Why was she so angry? There was no need to shout! Blah blah. Slamming doors. Crappy sleep, thinking, *I am right, aren't I?*

'Earth to Ella.'

'I'm here,' she said irritably.

'Penny Flatt from Macquarie College emailed some more photos of Freya Gregory.' Murray clicked the mouse through three pictures of girls playing soccer. 'This is the best one.' It was a side view of teenaged Freya with her hair tied up in a golden ribbon, watching something intently. 'I've emailed it to Chris Patrick but not heard back yet.'

Ella nodded.

'And I've just put the Kingsleys into the computer.' He turned his monitor so she could see.

'Interesting. Has she rung?'

'Not yet,' he said. 'But somebody else rang Crimestoppers and said it was her on the CCTV.'

He handed her the report. This caller was a librarian and knew Danielle Kingsley as a regular borrower, and was one hundred per cent certain it was her in the picture.

'Let's go,' Ella said.

At the Kingsleys' house Murray rattled the cowbell and Ella stood with her hands on her hips. The woman who answered was in her early forties and had short, dark hair and Ella recognised her immediately from the CCTV tape.

'Danielle Kingsley,' Murray said. 'You never rang us back.'

She flushed.

'Mind if we come in to talk?'

'There's really nothing to talk about,' Danielle said. 'I have no clue about any of it.'

'Let's sit down and chat, shall we?' Ella moved closer to the door and put her hand on it.

'Kelly said something about a car? I only have my red Mini.'

'How about we sit there?' Ella pointed past her to a lounge. One end was piled high with folded washing. She could hear the toddler laughing somewhere in the house. 'Let's just have a little chat.'

This time when she moved closer, Danielle gave way.

When they were inside, she shut the door and picked up the washing and put it in a basket. 'I don't know anything about anything.'

'Where's Paul today?' Murray said.

'Out.' She sat at the table and held the basket on her lap. *Nice defensive wall*, Ella thought.

'Where were you on Sunday night?'

'Here.'

'Alone?' Murray said.

She looked at the floor. 'Yes.'

'Where were Paul and Kelly?'

'She and Marcie stayed at her boyfriend's. Paul went to a mate's place for a barbecue. He got back about eleven.'

Plenty of time for her to have gone to Miranda and back. 'Did Paul steal the car for you?'

'What car?'

'The car you drove to Miranda.'

She shook her head. 'I don't know what you're talking about.'

'You're going red again,' Ella said. 'It's not as easy to lie as it used to be, is it?'

Danielle dug her hands into the washing. 'I really don't know what you're talking about.'

'In 1988, when you and Paul got busted for burglary,' Ella said. 'He went to jail and you got a suspended. Because Kelly was just a few months old, right?'

'I wasn't really involved.'

'Involved enough,' Ella said. 'But you either stayed clean or under the radar for the next ten years, didn't you? While Paul got picked up for burglary three more times.'

Danielle smoothed a toddler-sized shirt over the top of the basket.

'Did he steal the car you drove to Miranda?'

'I truly honestly don't know what you're talking about.'

'Danielle, look at me,' Ella said. 'Saying that is not going to save you. You know something and you need to tell us what it is.'

Danielle couldn't hold her gaze. 'I need a drink.'

'Stay where you are,' Ella said. 'Tell us.'

Danielle shook her head, and pressed the toddler's shirt to her face. Ella took the moment to glance around the room, looking for something, anything, to help her out. On the shelves above the TV were an array of photographs and she got up to see. There were the usual pictures of kids on Santa's knee, grinning family groups at weddings, a man she guessed was Paul leaning against a shiny black Falcon. She looked closer at one of the weddings, then grabbed the frame and thrust it under Murray's nose.

'Ashley's bike crash give you a fright?' she said.

Danielle looked up sharply. 'What?'

'Scary things, motorbikes.' Murray held up the frame. 'I'd be pretty concerned about my sister's new husband riding one.'

Danielle's face fell.

'Did Lisa know where you were going when you borrowed the car?'

'I told her a friend had had a baby and the Mini was playing up,' she said softly. 'She didn't know a thing.'

Ella sat down. 'Tell us.'

Danielle wiped her eyes. 'It was because of Marcie.'

'How do you mean?'

'When Marcie was born I thought of that boy's grandparents.'

'By the boy you mean Tim Pieters.'

'Yes. And when I saw his mother on the news, I knew I couldn't keep quiet any longer.'

A shiver ran up Ella's spine. 'Tell us what's so important about the girl who found the body.'

'I need immunity.'

'What did you do?'

'It's for Paul,' she said. 'He didn't hurt her, I swear. He went there and it happened and he left, he didn't touch a hair on her head. He even called for help. That counts, doesn't it?'

'Who are we talking about?'

'The old lady.'

A light went on in Ella's head. 'Lucille Oldham.'

'I don't know her name,' Danielle said. 'He thought there was nobody home.'

The dots started to connect. 'Paul was doing a burglary.'

'He found the door unlocked. He went in and she was up, God knows why, and she collapsed. He said he knew just looking at her that she was gone. Freaked him and he got out of there.'

'Why didn't he ring triple 0, let somebody know?'

'He did,' she said. 'Muffled his voice through his shirt, folded up over a payphone.'

'Maybe muffled too well,' Ella said. 'Nobody went there. The police found her the next morning when they were door-knocking about Tim.'

Murray said, 'Why didn't he call triple 0 from her house and just leave it off the hook? They would've come to check straightaway.'

Danielle started to cry. 'How was he to know that? He was worried they'd say he killed her and put him away for years. He honestly didn't touch her. He didn't even take anything.'

Ella held up her hand. 'What about the girl and Tim Pieters?'

'It was when he left,' she said. 'He was running down the street to his car when another car pulled up over the road.'

Ella leaned forward. 'Did he see the plates?'

'It was dark.'

Ella narrowed her eyes. Dark? Georgie found Tim at six. Early, but definitely light.

'He had to hide behind some shrubs. He saw the girl get

275

out. She was laughing, somebody was shushing her. She went into the bushes then made this noise, and Paul said it sounded like she fell over. The man got out of the driver's seat and rushed round there, and then a minute later he came stumbling back to the car holding his hand up to his face, like, I don't know, Paul said sort of like he was going to be sick, a bit like that, and he bent like he was falling or something, and by then the girl was already in the other side and he got in and they took off.'

Ella frowned at Murray, who looked as confused as she felt.

'So this isn't Georgie at all?' he said.

'Paul was about to run on down to his car when another car came down,' Danielle said. 'Slow, this time. Creeping past. Like looking out for who might be around. Paul stayed down behind the shrubs and the car went past and turned around then drove real slow to the same spot.'

Ella imagined the crunch of tyres turning slowly on the gravel.

'Nobody got out at first. Then this guy climbed out, looking around, then went over into the grass there. Paul said he was back real quick, carrying something in his hand. He couldn't see what, but the guy got in the car and –'

The front door opened. Ella looked around and recognised Paul from the photo of him leaning against his car. He shot them a glare that left her in no doubt that he knew who they were.

'I had to,' Danielle said.

'No, you didn't.'

'You may as well tell us the rest,' Ella said.

'It's hearsay. You've got no proof I did anything.'

'We just want to know about the girl who found the body,' Murray said.

'That's what you say now,' he said.

'They didn't find her till the next day, Paulie. That poor old lady.'

'That's not my fault,' he said. 'I rang. I told them. System's fucked if they can't listen any better than that.'

'For God's sake, just tell them,' Danielle said. 'Think of the parents.'

Murray said, 'If you tell us what you know it can help you once we look at the break-in.'

'Can, he says,' Paul said. 'It wasn't a break-in, neither.'

'I'll tell them if you don't,' Danielle said.

'Shut it.'

Danielle was on her feet. 'Don't you remember when Marcie was born and you held her and you cried and you said then we should say what we knew, we should help that family out?'

'I was half-pissed.'

'Paul,' Murray said. 'Sit down.'

He paced instead.

'Here's what we know,' Ella said. 'We know you tried to get the old lady some help.'

'I left the door open too, I thought the neighbours would see.'

'We know you saw a girl and a man find the body and clear off. Then another car came along and you saw that man get out, go to near the body and pick something up,' Ella said. 'We need the rest. What kind of cars were they, what did the people look like? Did you get the plates?'

Paul swallowed hard.

'You can help that family.'

He lifted a small pair of trousers out of the washing and flat-tened them on the table. 'He was crying.'

'Who?'

'The second man. I could hear him. He went over and picked up whatever it was and came back, and I could hear him doing this terrible quiet crying. Weird. If he killed the kid, he's a pretty bad man, right, but then he's crying.'

'This thing he picked up – what do you think it was? How big was it?'

'Not big. It was in one hand. It was kind of . . . long, maybe like a bit of cloth or something. I couldn't really say any more than that.'

'Like a tie?'

He frowned. 'Maybe.'

'Can you describe him?'

'White guy, tall, dark hair cut short.'

'Clothes?'

'Not sure. Trousers and a shirt.' He shrugged.

'Car?'

'Falcon. Darkish. Maybe grey. Not black, not that dark.'

'What about the other two?'

'They were in a Volvo station wagon, light-coloured, maybe white,' he said. 'She was slight, looked young. Like in her teens. He was bigger and older, maybe twenties. I think he was in jeans. They were playing around at first. Before they came rushing out of the grass, I mean. Then when they did, he almost tripped and fell.'

'You didn't catch any names?'

'Nope, couldn't make out any words at all. They were whispering.'

Ella exchanged a puzzled glance with Murray, trying to fit the pieces together in her head.

'That's why I told you to talk to the girl who found the body,' Danielle said. 'She might've seen what the other guy picked up.'

'I get that.'

It wasn't worth the bother to go into the subject of which girl found the body.

'So now that we've helped, you're not going to charge Paul, are you?' Danielle said.

'You'll have to come in and make a formal statement, and we'll see.'

Paul swore under his breath.

Murray drove away from the house frowning while Ella dug in her bag for Panadol.

'So some other girl found Tim, but didn't report it.'

'Right,' she said.

'Because . . . why?'

'The million dollar question.'

Ella threw back the tablets. Her phone beeped. *mthr hre, hlo! nce day :) lol! pls cme for dnr?* Delete.

Murray wound his window down. 'Do you believe what he saw?'

'I can't imagine he would make stuff like that up.'

'Same here,' he said. 'But how the hell do we find them?'

His phone rang.

'Shakespeare. Hang on, I'm driving. I'll put you on loud-speaker.' He handed the phone to Ella who pressed the button. 'Okay, Chris, go ahead.'

'I got those photos of the girls playing soccer,' Chris Patrick said. 'But I still can't say if it's her. They all wore those golden ribbons and it's just impossible to say. Sorry.'

'It's fine,' Murray said. 'Thanks for letting us know.'

Ella pressed the button to hang up. 'Golden ribbon,' she said.

'Yeah, Freya had one in her hair in the photos.'

'I know,' she said. 'It's just made me think of something.'

'What?'

'Drive to the Pieterses' house and I'll tell you on the way.'

Georgie fell into bed with a sigh. The codeine she'd taken for her headache was starting to kick in, and between that and her exhaustion she was slipping pleasantly under when the phone rang. *Dammit.* She'd left her mobile off, but after the patch-up call to Matt at his office she'd forgotten to take the landline off the hook.

She pulled the quilt over her head but could still hear it ringing, and finally got up to answer.

'It's me,' Adam said.

'Hi.' She put her face on the kitchen bench, her eyes closed. 'I'm between nights.'

'Shit, sorry. I just wanted to let you know about Barnaby.'

She opened her eyes. 'Is he dead?'

'No such luck,' he said. 'There was a burglary the other day and the prints came back to him. We went out to get him this morning and he's gone. Faye and everyone swear up, down and sideways that they don't know when he went and they don't know where.'

Georgie was wide awake. 'You have no clue?'

'Not a one,' he said. 'The good thing is there's a warrant on him, so if you do spot him you can call and he'll be arrested.'

Yeah, Georgie thought, *but the bad thing is that he could be on the loose here in the city*.

Adam said, 'He'll probably come home in a few days. We'll be keeping an eye out, and when he does turn up I'll let you know.'

'Thanks.'

'Okay,' he said. 'Sleep tight.'

Georgie put the phone down slowly. If she rang Matt he would want to come home, but then he'd want to talk, or get in bed with her, and she needed silence and solitude to sleep. There was really nothing he could do. She was safe up here. She wouldn't answer the door, and the chances of somebody leaving the building right when he wanted to come in, like had happened with the flower guy, were slim.

She couldn't think straight. She needed to sleep. She rubbed her face and went back to bed and pulled the quilt up high. The codeine slowed but didn't stop her thoughts, and she rolled onto her side and stared at the wall and worried.

Josh was lying on his bed when John showed them upstairs.

'Hi, Ella,' he said.

'Feeling a bit off, buddy?'

'I went to see Uncle Alistair and he said I have to take it easy for a while.' He was winding the ribbon between his fingers.

'He has a heart condition, and Alistair started him on some new medication and said it might take a while for his body to adjust,' John said.

Ella nodded. Murray was looking at the Luke Skywalker poster on the wall.

'Isn't he cool?' Josh said.

Murray smiled. 'I bet you've seen all the movies.'

'I have!' Josh sat up then blinked. 'Whoah.'

'Lie down,' John said. 'Lie still.'

Josh sagged back on the pillow. 'Feel funny.'

'Remember what Uncle Alistair said, that it's only for the first couple of days,' John said. 'You just have to take it easy.'

Ella crouched by the bed. 'Josh, your dad said it was all right for me to ask you some questions but I want to make sure that's okay with you too.'

'Yep.' He smoothed the ribbon over the back of his hand.

She touched the end. 'This is lovely. Where did you find it?'

'In Tim's cupboard. He said I couldn't play with it but Callum said it was okay.'

'Why wouldn't Tim let you play with it?'

'He said it was too special. You want to hold it?'

'Thanks.' She pulled it gently from his hands. 'Did he say why it was special?'

'Because it belonged to the beautiful fairy princess.'

'Did you ever meet the princess?'

He shook his head. 'Nobody meets the fairy princess, and after a while even Tim couldn't see her because the evil wizard stole her away and put a spell on her so she wouldn't talk to him any more.'

Ella's scalp prickled. 'Was Tim sad about that?'

'He said he wasn't, but I could tell that he was.'

Ella leaned close and dropped her voice to a whisper. 'Did Tim tell you the princess's name?'

Josh lowered his voice to match. 'Fairy princess.'

'That was all?' Murray said, frowning.

'Yep,' Josh said. 'Can I have the ribbon back?'

'Say please,' said John.

'Please.'

Ella let it drop into his hand. 'Thanks so much for your help.'

'That's okay.' He smiled. 'Did you catch the bad man yet?'

'Not quite yet,' she said. 'But I'll let you know when we do.'

In the car Ella said, 'Did you hear that?'

'Fairytales have a lot to answer for.' Murray shook his head as he turned the key. 'Princesses, wizards . . . I'm surprised he didn't bring Skywalker into it as well.'

'Think for a moment, idiot,' she said. 'This was Tim telling Josh what was going on in his life, both in a way that he could understand and that didn't give away too much if he let it slip to anyone else.'

'I don't think so.'

'That ribbon belonged to our girl.'

'What?'

'The fairy princess is Freya.'

'Now you're really –'

'The evil wizard who took her means Freya started seeing someone else.'

'No way.'

'Yes way,' Ella said. 'She meant a lot to Tim. What if there was trouble, jealousy, he couldn't let her go, and this new boyfriend killed him?'

Murray blinked in confusion. 'I don't know what to say.'

'Say oh my God, Ella, you're a genius.'

Her phone rang. 'Marconi.'

'It's Georgie Riley.' She sounded tense.

'Are you okay?'

'Not really.' Ella heard her take a deep breath. 'That Barnaby McCrow, the one who I thought was following me, is missing from Woolford. My brother-in-law's a cop there and they went to get him for a burglary and he was gone.'

'Have you seen him? Has he made any contact?'

'No, I haven't been out of the flat since I heard,' she said. 'But I have to go to work again tonight.'

'Might be an idea not to.'

'But I'm on this assessment with Freya,' she said. 'It's tricky to take time off.'

'Even so.'

Georgie was silent.

'Well, look,' Ella said. 'We don't know for sure that he's in the city, and we have no real proof that he's even actually done anything. The print results for the card and envelope that came with the flowers aren't back, and even then I doubt we'll find anything. It sounds like he was careful.'

'I know,' Georgie said.

'On the other hand, you think you've seen him watching you.'

'What would you do if you were me?'

'I can't answer that,' Ella said. 'You're the only one who knows how you feel. It has to be totally your call.'

'I guess so.' She went quiet again. 'Okay. Thanks.'

'Hang on.' Ella took a deep breath. 'Give me your side of things on Tim Pieters and Freya.'

Silence. Ella raised her eyebrows at Murray. 'Georgie?'

'I'm glad she told you,' Georgie said. 'I only learned about it on Saturday and it's been on my mind ever since.'

'I can imagine.' Ella pulled out her notebook and pen. 'She didn't tell me exactly how you found out.'

'Her husband, James, was over and saw the photo of Tim in the paper, and said Freya told him she'd lost her virginity to him but never said he was murdered.'

Ella scrawled madly. 'Uh-huh.'

'I brought it up the next time we worked but she denied it. I didn't really believe her – I mean, it seems a weird thing to make up. So I'm not surprised now to know that it's true.'

'Yes,' Ella said.

'It makes me feel strange, though,' she said. 'I was her best friend at school and I never had any idea.'

'Even after he died? Wasn't she upset?'

'No,' Georgie said. 'She was supportive of me, and just her normal self.'

'Maybe it was over by then.'

'Maybe,' Georgie said.

'Did you ever see her with any other boy?'

'No, never,' Georgie said. 'And then she left the school, and I didn't see her again until I got teamed up to work with her last week.'

'Has she still been denying it?'

'We don't even speak at the moment. She thinks you found out about her and Tim from me, when you came over about the flowers, and when we worked last night she was so furious she couldn't even look at me.'

Ella scribbled a star and circled it. When someone got angry over a possible talk to the cops it was for just one reason: because they had something to hide.

FOURTEEN

Freya squeezed her knees to her chest. She ached, she felt sick, she wanted to vomit, but when she got to the bathroom nothing came up and then she invariably almost fainted on the way back.

James sat behind her on the side of the bed. 'Your back is all tight.' He'd taken the day off work, worried about her. He gave her a final rub. 'I'll leave you be so you can sleep.'

'Don't go.' Usually she wanted to be alone when she was sick. With this behaviour he would think she was at death's door. 'Will you snuggle me?'

He lay down behind her and fitted his body to hers. She liked the feel of him there, his elbow bent on her shoulder, his fingers stroking the back of her neck.

He felt her forehead, smoothed her hair. 'Do you want me to get the doctor?'

She couldn't tell him it wasn't that sort of sickness.

There was a knock at the front door. James sighed in her hair. 'Somebody selling something?'

'Hopefully.' She pulled his arm tight around her.

Another knock. A call: 'Freya.'

Oh God.

'It's Detective Marconi. We need to talk.'

'It's who?' James said.

'I think I'm going to be sick.'

Freya launched herself out of the bed. In the bathroom she curled over the toilet.

'You all right there for the moment?' James asked.

She nodded, eyes closed, stomach in her throat. She heard him go downstairs and open the door, then the murmur of conversation.

She retched but nothing would come up.

Oh God.

James knelt beside her. 'There's two of them. I told them you were sick but they said it's important.'

Freya slid to the floor and rested her cheek on the cold tiles.

'Frey?' He bent to look into her face. 'Oh, honey. I'll send them away. You're too sick for anything, no matter how important. And then I'm calling the ambulance. You need to be in hospital.' His voice was shaky with emotion.

'No, I'm okay.' She forced herself to sit up. 'It's okay. I'll talk to them.'

'No,' he said. 'You're in no state.'

'James.' She grabbed his wrist. 'It's time.'

'For what?'

'For me to come clean.'

He frowned. 'About what?'

'Help me up.'

Once on her feet she found she was a little better, a little stronger. Was this what telling the truth could do?

James brought her dressing gown and helped her put it on.

'About what?' he said again.

'Hold my hand.'

They went downstairs together.

'Lean on me,' he whispered.

'I will.'

'I mean now, while we're walking.'

She squeezed his hand.

In the lounge room, Ella stood with one hand on her hip and the other tapping a notebook on her thigh. The male detective who'd come to the station to see Georgie had his hands in his pockets and a cold look on his face.

'Detective Murray Shakespeare,' he said.

'I want to say straight up that I don't think this is right,' James said. 'My wife is very ill.'

Freya squeezed his hand again. 'It's okay, really. I can do this.' She sat down and he sat next to her.

'Actually,' Ella said, 'we'd prefer to speak to your wife alone.'

Freya nudged him. 'Go upstairs. I'll be okay.'

He didn't look like he believed her.

She kissed his cheek. 'I'll explain everything later.'

He kissed her in return, then went.

Freya felt hot and sick and frightened, but somewhere inside herself found a small, still place on which to stand. *It is time.*

Ella stared at the pale woman. 'Tell us about Tim.'

'Okay.'

What?

But she was already talking, about after the soccer match, about the movies, the bus shelters and the classrooms and the bushland, and about Tim's house.

Can it be this easy?

'When did it end?' Ella asked.

'A couple of months before he died.'

'Was killed, you mean,' Ella said.

Freya nodded.

'Who ended it?'

'I did,' she said. 'I mean it was nothing official anyway, but I started seeing somebody else.'

'How did Tim respond?'

'Not well.'

'What did he do?'

'Called me names, followed me around.'

'Were there any fights?'

She shook her head.

'Any threats?'

Freya looked at the floor.

'Protecting a murderer makes you an accessory,' Murray said.

She looked up. 'I'm not protecting a murderer.'

'Who, then?' Ella asked.

Freya rubbed her face.

'Freya,' Ella said.

'I see him in my dreams.'

'Tim?'

'And not only there. I saw him after it happened. I saw him at school. In the corridors. Looking at me.' She stared at the floor. 'I was pleased when Mum freaked out and said we had to move, and I went to that boarding school in the country. But I still saw him, even there.'

Ella shot Murray a look. 'And you still say you're not protecting a murderer?'

'We didn't kill him.'

Maybe she was going to say it was self-defence.

'So what did happen?'

Freya started to cry.

'You've come this far,' Ella said. 'Take it step by step. Tell us one thing at a time.'

'I went into the bushes cos I was busting.'

'Say that again?' Murray said.

'I walked into the long grass laughing and stepped on his leg and almost died on the spot.'

Ella was astonished. 'Wait a minute. You stepped on . . . Tim?'

Freya nodded.

Ella stared at Murray, who looked as stunned as she felt. She fumbled for words. 'And then what?'

'I must've made some noise because then, um, he got out of the car and came around. He was more freaked than I was, but I made him touch him, to see if he was warm or cold. He hated that. And I hate myself for not having had the courage to do anything.'

'He who?'

Freya went on. 'He said he was dead and we had to go. We rushed back to the car. He almost fell over, he was trying to get out of there so fast. He ... he ... In the car we argued about what we should do. We decided we couldn't do anything. Tim was dead. It didn't matter if we called or not.'

Murray said, 'So you were the girl who found the body.'

'Yes. Though we didn't tell anyone. We couldn't.'

'Why?'

'Because it would've ruined our lives.' Freya wept. 'He was married and I was sixteen, for God's sake. He had a baby. She was asleep in the car at the time! What do you think would've happened?'

Ella said, 'There's nothing to be gained in hiding the truth now.'

'I can't.'

'You can.'

'No.'

'You have to,' Ella said, then was struck by a thought. 'He was bleeding, wasn't he?'

Freya looked startled.

'We have his DNA, and we can start going back through your life,' Ella said. 'We can go to the papers. It doesn't have to be a big thing, but we can steer it that way if we have to.'

'That's not fair,' Freya said.

'Tell that to a family whose seventeen-year-old son never came home from a night out.'

Freya curled up into a ball and put her head on her knees. 'What will happen to him if I give you his name?'

'You were sixteen. That's over the age of consent.'

'But.'

'But what?'

'He was a teacher.'

'Then that's different,' Murray said. 'He could get eight years.'

'But I honestly don't think he knows any more about it than

289

I do. What if we do all this and tell the truth and you get nothing out of it?'

'That's the risk you have to take,' Ella said. 'Look, we don't know what he knows till we talk to him. Somebody who saw you two said that another car came soon after, and a man got out and picked something up. We think this might have been the killer, and he'd left something behind and had to come back to get it.'

'Like what?'

'That's what we need to find out.'

'But I didn't see anything,' Freya said. 'Just grass and sticks and leaves. I don't think D– he saw anything either.'

D. 'We need to ask him ourselves,' Ella said. 'And we can show both of you scene photos and you might realise then that something is missing.'

'I don't want to see them.'

'It might be necessary.'

Tears ran down Freya's face. 'Oh God.'

'Tell me.'

She closed her eyes.

'Tell me, Freya.'

She whispered, 'Dion Entemann.'

Ella knew the name, and in a moment had placed him. 'The principal of Macquarie Secondary College?'

Freya nodded.

'What was his position when you were there?'

'He wasn't with the school then, he taught an after-school drama group. He didn't push me into anything. I persuaded him.' She pressed her hands onto her knees. 'What will happen now?'

'We'll go and speak to him,' Ella said. 'Our top priority is the murder. The rest we'll discuss later.'

'Even if we don't know anything, we still helped, right? That still counts?'

'Here's my card. We'll be in touch. If you need me before then, just call.'

Freya accepted the card. 'I'm sorry. Tell them I'm sorry.'

Ella and Murray headed out of the room. In the hallway she saw movement from the corner of her eye. James stood there, his face pale. She turned to the door and followed Murray out, and before she closed it heard James say, 'Freya, honey, it's okay.'

Ella kept the car at a high idle while Murray fetched the scene photos from the Unsolved office, then dropped it into gear the second he was back in the passenger seat.

'White Volvo was registered to Andrea Entemann in 1990.' He clipped in his belt. 'Galea said good luck.'

'Don't need luck with our skills.'

He looked through the photos. 'How did Paul Kingsley describe the thing the guy went back for?'

'Long, like a bit of cloth, maybe like a tie.' Ella gripped the wheel. *This could work, this could really work. If the item wasn't too generic. But if it was, why'd he go back to get it?*

'This is what I like,' he said, putting the photos back in the manila envelope. 'Talking to witnesses, getting decent clues. Not that fairytale hoo-ha.'

'Don't dismiss it yet,' she said. 'If this goes nowhere, I'll be back onto that like stink on a monkey.'

Her phone beeped. *wayn cmin to dnr tnyt, u2?* She blinked at the screen. What the hell was happening? How was it that he was going and they didn't even know if she could go too? She narrowed her eyes at the plans they might be cooking up together, all no doubt to the soundtrack of wedding bells in her mother's head. Well, whatever. She couldn't deal with it now. Delete.

'Here we go, here we go,' Murray said.

'Yes, we do.'

They grinned at each other.

Penny Flatt was carrying a pile of folders through the college's office when they walked in. 'Detectives! How nice to see you again.'

'We need to speak to Dion Entemann,' Ella said.

'Certainly. Follow me.' Over her shoulder, she said, 'Were those photos of any use?'

'They were good,' Murray said. 'Thanks.'

She smiled and tapped on a closed door with a brass plate saying 'Principal'. A long bench ran along the wall and at the far end a teenaged boy slumped against the armrest.

'Come in.'

Penny opened the door. 'Detectives here to see you.'

'Certainly, certainly.' Dion was on his feet. 'Come in. Pleased to meet you.'

He wore a grey suit with a white shirt and a grey and gold striped tie. He shook their hands. Ella kept hold for a fraction longer and looked into his eyes. He looked away.

This was going to be good.

'Coffee for anyone?' Penny asked.

'We're fine,' Ella said.

'I'll see you later then.' She went out and closed the door.

Dion sat behind his wide desk and laced his fingers. 'I'm sorry I wasn't here to help you yesterday, but what can I do for you today?'

'We've just been talking to your ex-student Freya Craig,' Murray said.

He blinked. 'I'm sorry – who?'

'Also known as Freya Gregory.'

'Hmm.' He looked perplexed. 'I'm not sure. We have so many students through these doors, it's difficult to remember them all.'

For a one-time acting teacher he couldn't lie for shit.

'She told us everything,' Ella said.

'I don't –'

Ella held up her hand. He stopped talking. She let him stew in his own juice for a moment. 'Everything.'

He seemed to consider this, trying to decide how to respond.

'A piece of advice,' Murray said. 'Tell us what you know and we'll do what we can when it comes to charging you.'

His ears went pink. 'With what?'

'Sexual intercourse with a child between the ages of sixteen and eighteen under special care, that is, when you're the teacher and she's the student,' Ella said. 'How many years do you get for that again, Murray?'

'Eight.'

'Eight years,' Ella said. 'You feeling okay there, Principal?'

Dion had gone grey. He unlaced his fingers and shakily straightened papers.

Ella had no sympathy. There were things she needed to know, and it was about time this guy faced what he'd done nineteen years ago and learned to deal with it. She slapped the manila envelope of scene photos down on his desk. 'Tell us what you remember about the night that Tim Pieters died.'

'Who?'

'Cut the bullshit or we'll arrest you, call the media, and walk you out the front gate right on home time.'

'But I remember nothing. Really.'

'Tell us.'

'But what's to tell? What do you want to know?'

'Every last thing you remember, whether you think it's relevant or not.'

'I used to pick her up from home.' He was almost whispering. 'She climbed out the window, she said her parents never had a clue. She'd meet me down the street. Our daughter was a bad sleeper and Andrea was always desperate for sleep, so I'd volunteer to take Chelsea for a drive because that always did the trick. We'd park somewhere, Freya and I, and Chelsea would sleep through everything in the back.' He shook his head. 'I can't believe it myself. The risks that we took . . . We were stupid.'

No, Ella thought. *You were stupid. You should've known better.*

'That night was the same,' he went on softly. 'She had a fit of the giggles because she thought her dad had woken up and realised what she was doing. Next thing she said she was busting and I had to pull over *now*. She got out and went into the bushes, then I heard her make this noise and got out to see what was wrong. And I saw that boy there.

'Freya was freaking out. She made me touch him. I didn't want

293

to. She made me.' He was rubbing his fingers and thumb together. 'I can still feel his skin.' He looked up. 'Does that go away?'

Probably not for you.

'He was still a bit warm, but he was dead. I just knew he was dead.'

He put his fingers to his nose then looked at them. Ella saw blood.

'I had a nosebleed then too,' he said. 'I used to get them a lot. The doctors said it was stress.' He took a folded handkerchief from a drawer. 'I've had a few again lately.'

Ella wasn't surprised and neither did she care.

'The person who saw you and Freya at the scene, and described the white Volvo which was then registered in your wife's name, saw another car pull up after you left,' she told him. 'We think it was the killer. He'd left something behind and came back to get it. We need to know what you saw there.'

'The body,' he said. 'That's all.'

'Think for a moment.'

'I've thought about it for nineteen fucking years.' He lifted the handkerchief away but he was still bleeding.

She opened the envelope and thrust the photos in his face. 'See if anything is missing.'

He turned his head away.

She stood and leaned across the desk so he had no choice but to see. 'Open your eyes. Look. *Look.*'

This time he did so. Tears welled in his eyes.

'What's different?' Murray said.

'Nothing.'

Ella put her free hand on her hip.

'I swear,' he said. 'I would tell you. I swear.'

Murray said, 'What happened after Freya made you touch him?'

'I said we had to get out of there. She was crying. She stumbled back to the car and I ran around the front. I tripped and almost fell over.'

'In the grass?' Ella said.

'Actually I got my foot caught. I had to reach down and yank this thing off. It was a bit of black plastic, rubbery tubing type thing. My nose was bleeding and I grabbed up some of the leaves I'd bled on and threw them in the rubbish when I got home.'

There had been nothing collected from the scene that was black plastic or rubber or tube-like. 'Show me where it was,' she said.

Dion studied the photos and put his finger on a patch of grass. 'Probably about there.'

Ella stared at the grass in the shot. Nothing like that was evident.

Dion tentatively cleared his throat. 'What happens now?'

'Get yourself a solicitor and wait to hear from us,' Murray said.

'And tell your wife,' Ella said, her mind still on the missing item. *Where do we go from here?*

Georgie slid her epaulettes onto her shirt. In the mirror she could see Matt frowning on the end of the bed behind her. They'd been over it and over it, and there was nothing left to say.

The phone rang and Matt got up. He brought the handset in. 'It's Control.'

'Hey,' the controller said. 'Just calling to let you know your partner's off sick tonight, and you'll be working out of Wahroonga. Pick up a truck and head off when you get in. Hopefully I won't need to use you on the way.' Phones were ringing in the background. 'Call me when you're mobile.'

Georgie ended the call. 'Freya's off sick and I'm headed to the burbs tonight. Make you any happier?'

'Not really.' But he smiled.

Half an hour later she was pulling out of The Rocks station. She drove north checking her mirrors, on the lookout for any car that kept appearing, that seemed to be tagging along. Traffic was heavy. Going through St Leonards she noticed a white Camry change lanes to slip into a spot three cars back. She watched it in the mirror for a while then chided herself. Cars were changing lanes all over the place, every driver wanting to move one spot ahead in their eagerness to get home.

She heard her mobile beep while waiting at a red light in Killara.

Sorry for everything. Freya.

She smiled, and texted back. *It's all good. Talk tomorrow.*

The lights changed and the traffic crawled on. There looked to be three white Camrys in the crowd behind her now. She shook her head. *Enough of the paranoia.*

At the Wahroonga station her shift partner was leaning against the doorway, drinking a cup of coffee. He smiled and nodded at the darkening sky. 'Beautiful, isn't it?'

The phone rang before she could answer. He went to get it, and she hauled her bag out of her ambulance and slung it into the one parked on the drive.

He came out with a Post-It stuck to one finger. 'Male with Downs, collapsed in Pennant Hills.'

They roared down Pennant Hills Road with the traffic parting before them like the Red Sea.

'I'm Jim, by the way.' He put out his hand and they shook.

'Georgie.'

'Nice to have you aboard.'

It was nice to be there. The air was tension-free. Jim didn't yell at dithering drivers or stare daggers at her. She glanced in her side mirror and saw nothing suspicious, no white Camrys, and started to relax.

The house in Pennant Hills was not far from her childhood home and it seemed familiar. All the lights were on and the front door stood open. A woman called out from a window upstairs, and Georgie grabbed the Oxy-Viva and headed in while Jim was close behind with the drug box and monitor.

In the hall she saw a family photo on the wall and it hit her.

Tim Pieters's house. His family still lived here. She felt suddenly young and bewildered again, the sight of Tim smiling out of the portrait taking her back twenty years in an instant.

'Up here!'

Jim said, 'You okay?'

She took a big breath. 'Fine.'

Upstairs she found the woman who she guessed was Tim's mother in a bedroom. A heavy-set man in his thirties lay on the bed holding her hand.

'Hi, I'm Georgie and this is Jim. What's happened?'

'Josh has a heart murmur and his GP just started him on some medication.' Mrs Pieters held out a packet. Georgie didn't recognise the name.

Jim took it and frowned. 'Must be new.'

'Tonight he came upstairs after dinner and fainted at the top there,' Mrs Pieters went on. 'He was lucky he didn't fall all the way to the bottom.'

'It was scary,' Josh said.

'I bet it was.' Georgie knelt by the bed and felt his pulse. 'Did you hurt yourself?'

'No.' Josh smiled. 'Your hands are nice and warm.'

'When he'd recovered a little I helped him in here,' Mrs Pieters said. 'I called my brother-in-law, who's his GP, but he's tied up with one of his palliative patients. Then I called his son, who's also a doctor, and he's on his way but said to call you in the meantime.'

'You did absolutely the right thing,' Georgie said. 'How do you feel now, Josh? Are you back to normal?'

'I feel okay.'

His skin colour was good, and he wasn't sweaty or cold to the touch.

'Jim's going to put three sticky dots on your chest so we can see what your heart's doing, and I'm going to take your blood pressure on this arm here.'

He held it out for her. She wrapped the cuff around his stocky upper arm and inflated it. 'One forty on ninety.'

Jim was looking at the monitor screen. 'Normal sinus of eighty-eight.'

'So far so good, Josh,' Georgie said.

A car door slammed outside. Mrs Pieters looked out the window. 'It's my nephew.'

Doctors on scene could be good or bad, helpful or obstructive. Georgie prepared herself.

'Little stab in your finger here, mate,' Jim said to Josh. 'Just checking there's enough sugar in your blood.'

Georgie patted Josh's other arm to get his attention. 'So have you fainted like that before?'

Josh stared at his hand where Jim squeezed a drop of blood out of his third finger. 'What?'

'Have you felt like that before?'

He shook his head.

'He told my brother-in-law that he'd been having dizzy spells, though he never told us,' Mrs Pieters said. 'That's why Alistair put him on this medication.'

'Do you ever have any pain when it happens?' Georgie asked him. 'Pain in your chest or anything else? Or is it hard to breathe?'

'My finger hurts,' he said, still watching Jim, then he turned his head and looked behind Georgie as a man entered the room. 'Hi, Cal.'

'Hey, buddy.' The man crouched beside Georgie. He had a friendly manner and an easy smile. 'I'm Callum. Thanks so much for coming. How's he look?'

'All stable so far.'

'BSL's four point three,' Jim said across the bed.

'I nearly fell down the stairs,' Josh said to Callum.

Mrs Pieters smoothed his hair. 'He was right out of it for a couple of minutes. There were no warning signs or anything, he just climbed the stairs and fell over.'

Georgie felt his pulse again. Steady and strong. 'How are you feeling, Josh?'

'Fine.' He sat up. 'Good.'

'Would you like to come to hospital and see the doctors there?'

'I want to watch TV.'

Georgie looked at Callum and Mrs Pieters. 'What's your preference?'

'He seems good,' Callum said.

Mrs Pieters nodded. 'Alistair said it would take a couple of days for his body to adjust to the medication and that this might happen.'

Georgie checked his blood pressure again. One thirty-five on ninety.

'I think we're fine to keep him home,' Callum said.

Georgie nodded. 'You can always call us back.'

'I can't wait till Dad gets home and I can tell him what happened,' Josh said.

'I'll just need you to sign our paperwork,' Georgie said to Callum.

'No worries.'

'I'll bring the folder up,' Jim said, disconnecting the monitor leads and taking the machine with him.

Georgie packed away the BP cuff and zipped up the Oxy-Viva. She picked up the medication and read the box. 'Haven't heard of this one.'

Callum looked too. 'Neither have I. Though I must admit I'm a bit out of the loop.'

Georgie put the Viva and drug box at the door. Callum helped Josh up.

'Want to play Star Wars?' Josh asked.

'How about you take it easy for a while instead?' Mrs Pieters said.

Georgie looked into the hall. Jim should've been back by now. She saw another framed family photo on the wall, and wondered whether she should say anything. She couldn't think of a decent reason to do so, however. What would the knowledge bring them? Nothing. She was there to do a job, that was all. And she'd done it well. She smiled at Josh and he smiled back, and out of nowhere she felt all her lost confidence return in a rush, all her doubts since the accident weaken and die, all her worries about whether she'd pass or fail just fade away. *I am good at this job!* Despite Freya's promising text, if things remained bad and she failed her, Georgie would fight it with everything she had. She would take them to court, make them give her another assessor. It wasn't her fault that Freya had problems. She was going to do this, and get back to Woolford, and show them she was made of seriously tough stuff.

She looked down the hall again. Where the hell was Jim?

There was a noise outside and Mrs Pieters glanced out the window. 'Oh my God! Your ambulance is on fire.'

Georgie flew down the stairs. The back doors of the ambulance were open and the fire was inside. Flames licked the edge of the roof and spewed acrid smoke into the twilight. Jim lay motionless on the roadway and she ran to him.

The brightness of the fire showed the dark blood from the laceration on his head. She put her hand to his neck and felt his pulse, then felt his chest to check his breathing. It wasn't safe there for either of them. She couldn't see beyond the light of the fire and didn't know who was out there watching. But he was unconscious and could have a spinal injury. The heat from the fire was making her skin hot already, the smoke was black and choking, full of fumes from the melting plastic, and there were oxygen cylinders and a full fuel tank to worry about as well.

'I've rung the fire brigade,' Callum called as he hurried out of the house.

Before she could answer she was knocked flat. A man was on top of her, grasping for her throat. She fought him and he banged her head against the road. 'Fucking bitch.'

She saw stars. He seized her belt with one hand and the back of her neck with the other and started dragging her.

Georgie struggled to clear her head and regain her wits and her strength. The fire was hot and bright somewhere close by. Callum was shouting, 'Hey! Hey!' A car raced up close, then somebody else grabbed hold of her leg.

They're taking me away.

Nothing good could come of that.

She twisted her head and saw Barnaby's face above hers in the glow from the fire, saw that Ross Oakes had hold of her leg. Callum grabbed Ross's arm. Ross flung his elbow back, hard and sharp, and Callum dropped.

Georgie scratched at Barnaby's face, catching the corner of his eye with her nail.

He turned his head away but didn't let go. 'Bitch!'

'Let her go!' Mrs Pieters screamed. 'I've called the police!'

Georgie punched at Barnaby's stomach and groin. She kicked out at Ross, still holding her other leg, managed to plant her boot in his chest and made him stagger, then slammed one into his face. She felt her heel sink into his cheekbone and heard him yowl. He dropped her leg and, now on the ground, she rammed her fist into Barnaby's groin. He doubled over. Something exploded inside the ambulance.

Barnaby staggered towards the car. Georgie struggled to her feet, her head spinning, and kicked him in the side of the thigh with the toe of her boot. He lurched but didn't go down. Ross fell into the car, one hand to his face, blood trickling between his fingers. 'Barn!' he yelled.

Georgie tried to focus her double vision on Barnaby. He was almost at the car, a white Camry. She was furious, vengeful, wanting to hurt him. Mrs Pieters ran up behind him and hit him with a broom, and as he wrenched it out of her hands Georgie lashed out again with her boot, catching him in the side of the knee, and he screeched and dropped like a stone.

Suddenly Callum was there, tackling Barnaby flat to the road. Georgie got a glimpse of other people approaching in a group, safety in numbers. Somebody else was yelling about having called the cops, and Ross hit the accelerator and almost sideswiped the burning ambulance as he took off.

'I've got him,' Callum panted, his forearm across the moaning Barnaby's ear. Somebody else jumped on his feet.

Georgie stumbled to Jim. Mrs Pieters knelt beside her,

trying to shield him from the heat of the fire. Sirens wailed in the distance.

'All of you,' Georgie pointed to the watchers, 'kneel here, please. We have to move him.'

Her head was still spinning. The evening was the strangest mixture of bright orange light and darkness. The smoke and stink of burning plastics added to the nightmarish quality. She ached and sweated and felt sick. *Focus!*

'Help me roll him onto his back. On one, two, three.' She supported his head and neck. 'Slide your hands under him. We'll lift as one. Everybody take some weight. We're going to the lawn there. Ready?'

People nodded. Something else exploded in the ambulance.

'One, two, three.' They stood slowly, and walked.

The lawn was cool under her hands when they put him down.

'Now gently, gently, on his side.' She kept his head in alignment. 'You three,' she made eye contact with them, 'stay and keep him on his side, please.'

They nodded. Flashing lights bounced off the house. Josh waved from the step.

On her knees, she sagged close to Jim. *Be okay, please be okay.* She touched her head to his. *Please.*

Sometime later a hand squeezed her shoulder. 'Georgie? You okay?'

She looked up into Ella's face.

'Let me help you.' Ella's hands slid under her own. 'I've got him.'

'Keep his neck straight.'

'I will.'

Somebody tried to help Georgie up but she shook them off. She had to stay and look after Jim. She rested her face on the grass for just a moment.

'Georgie?' A different female voice. Two paramedics were looking after Jim now, and he was coming around. The woman supported her as she tried to sit up. 'Where are you hurt?'

'I'm okay,' she croaked. 'It was Ross.'

The woman was nodding. 'He drove into a tree around the corner. The cops have him.'

Georgie saw the supervisor's epaulettes in the firelight and the name Lilian on her paramedic badge. 'I'm sorry.'

'For what?' Lilian laughed, a throaty sound. 'You did good.'

'Jim got hurt and the ambulance is melted onto the road.'

'You did good,' she said again. 'Everything's going to be okay.'

Ella sat on the step next to Josh and watched the news crews filming the fire officers as they hosed down the smouldering mess on the street. She hadn't had a chance to talk to Georgie, but had seen her helped away to a supervisor's car, so knew she wasn't too bad. Her mate had been moving and talking at least by the time the ambulance took him away, and the bad guys had been cuffed and taken in another one.

'Smells,' Josh said.

She nodded. The chemical-smelling smoke lingered in the air. She could even see it in the glow of the lights down the street.

Callum sat on the other side of Josh, a bag of frozen peas wrapped in a checked tea towel against his jaw. She'd heard him telling the paramedics he'd just been stunned by the blow, not knocked out, and nothing was broken. As she looked across he gingerly worked his jaw from side to side, then saw her watching and smiled.

Tamara stood drinking coffee inside the doorway. Ella had heard what she'd done to help Georgie, and told her how brave she'd been to do it. She'd seemed shy, soft, and didn't seem to mind for once that Ella was there.

'I fainted,' Josh told her. 'The ambulance lady looked after me.'

'I'm glad you're okay.'

He smiled. 'You look nice.'

'Thanks.'

She'd been at dinner at her parents' when the duty officer in Comms rang to tell her there was an attempted abduction and a fire at the Pieterses' house. She'd leapt up from the table and invited Wayne along, but he'd shaken his head and pointed at her open-mouthed mother and father. 'Bye then,' she'd said, and run.

There'd be fallout of course, but driving over here, worrying about who was involved and why, things all of a sudden got clear, like they had after she'd been shot. She knew again for certain what was important. *The case.*

'Did you find the bad guy yet?'

'No,' she said, 'but we found the fairy princess.'

'Really?'

She nodded. 'I think she misses Tim a lot.'

'So do I.' His eyes were wide and dark in the gloom. 'He looked after me.'

'How did he look after you?'

'He said he was like Superman,' Josh said. 'He said he'd save me from the bad man no matter what.'

She thought for a moment. 'Has anybody ever hurt you?'

'Kids at school used to tease me,' he said.

'Anyone else?'

'Nope. Everybody looks after me. There's Mum and Dad, Haydee, Callum, Uncle Alistair, Aunty Gen, and Tim used to too. He always told me that, that he would look after me.'

'What else did he say?'

'That he loved me,' Josh said. 'And I am his little brother.'

'Did he talk to you a lot about the bad man?'

'Sometimes. He just kept saying that he would save me.'

'That was all?'

'Yep.'

'Did he know who the bad man was?'

'Yep.'

Ella heard Tamara gasp. She said, 'Did he tell you that?'

'Yep,' Josh said. 'I asked him the bad man's name and he said I didn't need to know and that he knew and he would tell people and stop him so he didn't hurt me.'

Ella looked out at the fire trucks, trying to think.

'They were bad men, those ones,' Josh said helpfully. 'Those ones who hurt the nice ambulance lady.'

'They were,' Ella said. 'Lucky we caught them.'

He patted her hand. 'Don't worry, you'll catch this one too.'

The stink of the burnt ambulance was hard to get out of her hair, Ella found later in the shower. She washed it three times, then used a leave-in conditioner and walked through the house wrapped in a towel. She pressed the message button on her answering machine.

'Hi, it's Pam from Gladesville Physiotherapy. You missed your appointment this afternoon. If you need to reschedule could you call me back, please? Thanks.'

Oops.

'Hi, it's me.' Wayne sounded flat. 'You're obviously not home yet. I'll try your mobile.'

There'd been five missed calls on her mobile from him, none with messages.

She cleared the machine and sat on her bed to call Murray.

'I heard already,' he said.

'What you didn't hear about is the conversation I just had with Josh.'

'More fairies?'

'Quite the opposite.' She told him what Josh had said.

'Still,' he said.

'Still what? Tim told Josh he knew who the bad man was and would stop him so he couldn't hurt Josh.'

'He might've been talking about anything! Last story we heard involved an evil wizard –'

'Which was Dion, when Freya started seeing him instead of Tim.'

'Nevertheless,' Murray said, 'this really could be anything, and unlike when we could talk to Freya, now we have nobody to check the story with.'

'I don't know,' she said. 'I still think there's something there.'

'Tomorrow,' he said.

When he'd hung up, Ella got comfortable on her bed and thought about bad men, black plastic tubing, and how to get the truth from somebody who didn't even know he held it.

FIFTEEN

The next morning on her way to work, Ella put her mobile on loudspeaker and called Callum. 'How was Josh? Did he say anything more after I left?'

'Not really. Just about the fire.' He sounded distracted.

'Is this a bad time?'

'I'm about to head to the surgery,' he said. 'Dad started Josh on some new medication, and I checked with a drug rep friend and it's contraindicated for people with heart murmurs like Josh's.'

'What?'

'I just called Aunty Tar to say don't give Josh any more and take him to hospital as a precaution, then I rang Dad and he was really upset so I'm going across to make sure he's okay.'

'That's why Josh fainted?'

'We're lucky that's all he did,' Callum said. 'It could easily have killed him.'

'Why would your father have prescribed it then?'

'I guess he's getting old and forgetful, and probably didn't look up the details.'

Ella thought back to when she'd met Alistair McLennan at the surgery. He'd walked in tall and strong, stethoscope swinging, and his hand had gripped hers firmly. She couldn't imagine him doing something so clumsy and dangerous because he forgot to look up a drug, especially not when it came to his own family.

Unless . . .

. . . he hadn't forgotten.

She screeched to a halt on the side of the road. 'How did your dad respond when you told him?'

'He asked about the details of the collapse last night, what Josh's pulse and blood pressure were and what the paramedics did,' Callum said. 'He'd seen the fire on the news, and asked why you were there, and I told him how it seemed like maybe Josh has an idea who the bad man is and hopefully the case would be solved soon. Then he said he had to go. He didn't sound good, which is why I'm heading over there.'

'What was the medication for?'

'I don't really have time –'

'Just quickly.'

'Josh was apparently having dizzy spells.'

'Apparently?'

'Dad said Josh confided in him about them. Nobody else knew.'

'No one ever saw it happening? Not you, not your aunt?'

'No,' he said. 'Ella, I really have to go.'

Ella dialled Murray's mobile with trembling fingers.

'Shakespeare.'

'Where are you?'

'Just reached the office.'

'Look up what car Alistair McLennan had in 1990.'

The click of the keyboard. 'Grey Ford Falcon.'

'Isn't that what Paul Kingsley saw at the scene?' she said. 'What was McLennan's alibi again?'

Murray shuffled papers. 'Kingsley described a darkish Falcon, maybe grey. McLennan said that he was with a dying patient in Berowra.'

'Close to Hornsby where Tim went missing.'

'The patient's husband stated he was there from eleven twenty pm until one am, and the woman died at midnight.'

'Why would he stay for an hour after a death?' Ella said. Her heart was pounding.

'Beats me.'

'Reckon that guy is still alive?'

The click of keys again. 'Computer says yes. Aged eighty-three and living in a retirement home in Westmead.'

'Do me a favour and go have a word?'

'Tell me why we're suspecting Alistair first.'

She told him about the medication. 'You met him – he hardly seems the forgetful type.'

'You think it was deliberate?'

'I think Josh knows more than he realises and Alistair is afraid of that getting out,' she said.

'I don't follow.'

'What if the episode Tim told Damien about, which we all interpreted as some kind of gay experimentation, was actually abuse?'

'By Alistair?'

'What if Tim thought Josh was going to be targeted next? And decided he had to tell? Remember the stories from the barbecue, that Tim had wanted to talk to his father? What if Alistair realised that?

Murray was silent.

'What if he saw him later, drunk on the street in Hornsby, and picked him up?' Ella said. 'And what if the thing Paul Kingsley saw him come back to get was a stethoscope with his name engraved on it like the one he wears now?'

'Hmm,' Murray said.

'If Alistair is an abuser, he wouldn't have done it just once,' she said. 'We need to check his patient records, talk to his young patients.' She thought of the boy he'd mentioned who he 'just knew' was gay. Then she thought of Callum. 'Oh man.'

'What?'

'Callum.'

'You're going to ask if his father ever abused him?'

'He told me once that he and Tim looked very much alike as teenagers,' she said.

'Listen,' Murray said, 'let me talk to this old man first. Let's see where we stand with that.'

They hung up. Her skin tingling, Ella checked for traffic and did a speedy U-turn. Callum was going to see his father – she would just happen to drop by too.

At the surgery, she parked in the driveway. The door was locked, the vertical blinds drawn. It was after nine.

'Hi.'

She turned to see Callum come from around the back of the building.

'Is he here?' she asked.

'I can't get an answer, and the back's all locked up too.' The bruise on his jaw stood out, dark purple. 'Usually he's here till nine thirty doing paperwork, then heads out on his house calls.'

'Where's your mother?'

'Morning off. She'd be shopping.'

Ella tried to see through a gap in the blinds.

'His car's still round there. Maybe he's gone for a walk.' Callum took out his mobile.

Ella heard a faint ringing. 'You hear that?'

Callum pressed his ear to the glass. 'It's inside.' He ended his call and the noise stopped. 'Why would –' He suddenly pounded on the glass with his fist. 'Dad!'

No response.

Callum leapt into the garden bed and seized a rock. He hurled it through the sliding door. The glass shattered into little cubes and he pushed his way through the blinds, Ella close behind.

Alistair lay on his office floor, his sleeve pulled up high and a needle and syringe by his side. He was unconscious and purple.

'Oh shit, Dad. Dad!'

'Tell me what I can do,' Ella said.

'Call an ambulance. Tell them it's a cardiac arrest. No, wait.'

He had his fingers pressed hard to Alistair's throat. 'He's brady-cardic. Close to arrest.'

Ella got on the phone and repeated the information to the ambulance calltaker.

'Morphine overdose,' Callum said.

She relayed that too, and the address, then got on her knees next to Alistair. 'Tell me.'

'Grab that box on the wall with the bag thing in it. And that unopened box on his desk labelled drugs.'

Also on the desk was a folded handwritten note. She brought it back too and put it on the floor.

'Press the mask onto his face and breathe for him.'

She tilted his head back like they'd learnt in CPR class and squeezed the bag with her other hand. 'Like this?'

'Good.'

Callum did a few compressions, then ripped into the box of drugs. Ella could see the slow pulse in Alistair's throat. His colour had improved already.

Callum stuck a needle in Alistair's arm and injected something. She squeezed the bag again then unfolded the note.

'Read it out,' he said.

'Are you sure?'

'Do it.'

'*I am sorry,*' she read aloud as she squeezed the bag. '*I'm too old for this now. My patients know I can't look after them like I used to, and finally I have realised it too. The last straw was the medication for Josh. The dose was wrong, I realise that now, and the thought that I almost killed my nephew weighs so heavily on my mind.*'

She stopped. This wasn't the note she'd expected.

'That's it?'

'No.' She gathered her thoughts and squeezed the bag and read on. '*I can't live without this work. I am sorry.*' She looked up. 'That's all.'

Callum blinked back tears as he injected something else. 'That's a stupid reason to want to kill yourself.'

Ella focused on Alistair's throat. His pulse was faster. His colour was less purple and more pink. He took a breath by himself. He might not have confessed but she felt sure. *Come on back, you bastard.*

'I knew he was starting to lose it,' Callum said. 'I tried to help him but he can be so stubborn. I should've tried harder. I should've seen this coming.'

'It truly isn't your fault,' Ella said.

Alistair was breathing better and better. Callum watched for a minute. 'Okay, you can take the mask off. Keep it handy though, in case we need it again.'

Ella stayed on her knees looking down into Alistair's face. *Open your eyes, weasel.*

'Where's the ambulance?' Callum rubbed his knuckles down his father's sternum. 'Dad!'

Alistair groaned.

That's right, Ella thought. *Welcome back to the land of the living. The land of justice, no matter how cold.*

'Dad! Open your eyes!' Callum rubbed his father's sternum again and Alistair's eyes shot open.

Ella smiled into them. 'Hello.'

He started to retch.

'Quick, help me roll him on his side.' Callum grabbed Alistair's shoulder and hip and heaved him over.

Ella stayed close by, getting down low so she could look into Alistair's eyes. 'Lucky we came by when we did.'

Alistair turned his face into the floor.

'It's okay, Dad.' Callum rubbed his arm. 'It's all going to be okay.'

She watched Callum look after his dad until the ambulance arrived. Alistair was still groggy – or pretending to be – and didn't look her way once, moaning and groaning in Callum's arms. The paramedics treated him then loaded him into the ambulance, and she stood with Callum on the steps to watch them drive off.

'So he'll be okay?' she asked.

'Should be,' he said. 'I'd better ring Mum.'

While he made his call she made one of her own. 'Alistair just tried to kill himself.'

'You're kidding,' Murray said.

'Callum saved him,' she said. 'He'd written a note moaning about work and how he'd made a mistake with Josh and how bad he felt, but didn't look at all happy to see me. How's it going there?'

'Young Robert is fit and well and remembers the night perfectly. Says he was given something to help him calm down and he was asleep when the good doctor left.'

'So he doesn't know when it was.'

'Exactly,' Murray said. 'He told me that when the detectives spoke to him, on the Monday, he was so deep in his grief he could hardly talk let alone think straight. They said they'd come back later but never did.'

Ella nodded. It happened, like with Chris Patrick. Things, facts, people fell through the tiny cracks, and it was only later you realised their significance.

'I'm about to take a formal statement then I'll research more about abuser profiles. Have you found out anything from Callum?'

'Not yet.' She heard Callum crunching towards her over the glass and said to Murray, 'I'll see you back at the office.'

When she'd hung up, Callum said, 'I never asked you why you are here. Did you find out something new?'

She felt sympathy stir in her stomach. There was no way around this, though. 'Let's go inside and sit down.'

She started as gently as she could, talking about Josh's fairy princess and how that led them to Freya and then Dion, and what Kingsley had said, until Callum put up his hand.

'What are you trying to say?'

She blew air between her teeth. 'I suspect your father.'

'No.'

'Yes.'

'You're wrong. He was working that night, looking after a dying patient.'

'The timing of that is in doubt.'

'It can't be.'

'Murray is interviewing the husband right now.'

'He's old, surely. He couldn't possibly remember.'

'He does,' she said. 'Look, it's not just that.'

'I don't want to hear.'

'Callum, let me explain.'

'No. I want you out of here. I can't believe I trusted you to do a decent job and now you accuse him. He wouldn't hurt a soul.'

'There's Josh's medication –'

'Out.' He pointed to the door.

'We need to talk to him.' She laid one of her cards on the reception desk. 'Bring him when he's out of hospital. If I'm wrong, then show me.'

Callum said nothing.

She walked across the shattered glass and looked back at him from the doorway. His eyes were wet and the bruise on his jaw was dark against the pallor of his face. She felt bad and wanted to say she was sorry, but instead said again, 'Bring him in.'

SIXTEEN

At three that afternoon, Ella finished reading another article on the psychological profile of sexual abusers and slapped it back on the pile.

'Did Callum call?' Murray said.

She shook her head. She'd rung his mobile four times. 'I guess they're not coming in today.'

He stretched in his chair. 'Want coffee?'

'Thanks.'

Though she'd known she couldn't expect Callum to bring Alistair in this afternoon, and had to admit there was a strong chance they'd take legal advice and not come in at all, she'd been so fired up. She and Murray had talked with Galea, reviewed the evidence and planned interview strategies. She'd managed not to think too much about how Callum must be feeling and worked hard to ignore the realisation that she'd come to see him almost as a friend.

Tomorrow, she told herself. *Tomorrow*. She would just have to not think about Callum. If she could.

She put her elbows on her desk and her face in her hands.

Murray brought in the coffee then the lift dinged. He elbowed her. 'They're here.'

KATHERINE HOWELL

Ella jumped to her feet, her heart thumping.

Down the corridor they came. Callum met her gaze with a hard stare as he and Genevieve helped along a pale and weepy Alistair who looked to have aged fifteen years since that morning. Tamara glared with the old anger. Behind them came John, red-faced and indignant, and a tall woman in a pink pantsuit carrying a black leather briefcase.

Callum said, 'This is our solicitor, Julia Armstrong.'

'Officer.' Armstrong put out her hand, fingers glinting with gold rings.

'Detective, actually.'

Murray stepped forward to shake her hand as well.

'I have one condition regarding this interview,' Armstrong said. 'Since Dr McLennan has come in voluntarily, and so soon after a serious health crisis, I require that his son remain in the interview room as medical support.'

Murray started to shake his head but Ella saw a simultaneously bright and dark avenue open up before them. 'That will be fine.'

While Murray showed the rest of the family where they could wait, Ella took Callum and Alistair and the solicitor into an interview room. 'How's Josh?'

'They've admitted him for twenty-four hours but he should be fine.' Callum didn't look at her as he helped his father shuffle around the table.

'I'm glad.' She watched Alistair sink down onto the chair, the very image of a doddering old man. His eyes were red and wet and his hands shook as he folded them in his lap. In the bright fluorescent light his almost-white hair looked thin, the scalp underneath fragile.

Armstrong sat on the left and laid a new legal notepad and pen on the table. Callum repositioned his chair to sit closely on the right, as if worried his father might slump into a faint at any second.

Ella took the chair directly opposite Alistair and went over her questions in her mind. She scanned the ways she could

316

exploit Callum's presence, pushed away the shiver of regret at using him, and made herself calm.

Murray started the tape recorder and listed the names of those present. He asked Alistair to state his name, date of birth and address. Alistair croaked out the words like they were the last ones he'd ever be able to say.

Ella said, 'How are you feeling?'

Alistair didn't speak. His head drooped a little lower.

'Can we get you a cup of tea or coffee?' Ella said. 'Dr McLennan?'

'That name belongs only to my son now.' The voice was even weaker than before.

Callum rested his hand on his father's arm. 'That's not true.'

Julia Armstrong leaned back in her chair to speak to Callum over Alistair's shoulders. 'May I remind you that we are under no obligation here. If you're worried about him we can get up and walk out right now.'

'It's just a few questions to clear things up,' Ella lied. She could see how badly Callum wanted her to know she was wrong. She was counting on that to keep them there for now.

'Dad, are you okay?' he asked in a soft voice.

Alistair sighed and nodded slowly.

Callum said, 'I think it'll be good to sort things out now, then we can go home and the police will get on with what they should be doing.' He shot Ella a cold look. She kept her face open, empty.

'All right,' Alistair whispered.

Julia Armstrong jotted something on her pad that Ella couldn't decipher then sat back and folded her arms.

Alistair sagged a little more in his chair.

Ella drew a deep breath. They didn't have enough evidence to charge him, let alone get a conviction, and so they needed a confession. The statistics showed that killers and abusers who confessed felt the interviewing police were sympathetic to them, cared about them as people, wanted to help them. It was a tricky path to walk, though, because when you didn't honestly feel that way your expression and speech patterns could betray you. Ella fixed a mental mirror on herself and began. 'Dr McLennan, I'm sorry about everything you've been through lately.'

Callum glanced up but Alistair didn't move.

'I remember when I first spoke to you in your office about our investigation, you told me you were worried about the emotions that would be brought to the surface for everyone in your family. I can see now what a lot of heartache you've all been through and I'm sorry about that.'

Callum frowned. Julia Armstrong made another indecipherable note and put down her pen. The room was silent, Alistair said nothing, and Ella's hopeful heart rose.

'And what you must have felt this morning, to make you attempt suicide, is something none of us could imagine.' She made her voice soft and warm. 'To feel responsible for your nephew's life the way you do must be hellish.'

'We take it that you are talking about Josh,' Armstrong said.

'Of course,' Ella lied. 'I read your note, Dr McLennan, and I feel for you.'

Alistair raised his head. Julia Armstrong frowned at him then across his back at Callum. Callum was focused on his father and didn't notice.

'Callum told me that work hasn't been going so well for you lately,' Ella went on.

Alistair said in a low voice, 'It hasn't.'

'What happened, do you think?'

He gave the slightest shrug. 'I'm getting old.'

'You don't strike me as old,' she said. 'When we met in your surgery I thought you were full of energy and wisdom.'

He looked down. 'Hardly.'

'I'm serious,' she said. 'Murray felt the same, didn't you?'

'Yep,' Murray said.

Ella could feel Callum's eyes on her. It was essential that he believe she meant all this, because if he didn't, and took his father by the arm and said they should go, it would be all over. Julia

Armstrong had no doubt already advised them against coming here unless Alistair was actually arrested, but the fact that she'd been overruled was promising.

Ella smiled at Callum. He looked like he didn't know how to respond.

'I'm really pleased that Josh is all right,' she said to Alistair. 'It must've been a terrible moment when Callum told you about the dangers of that medication.'

Alistair nodded.

'Was it then that you decided to kill yourself?'

'Yes,' he whispered.

'Even though the mistake had been caught in time, and Josh was more than likely going to be okay?'

He wiped his eyes with the back of his hand. 'It was the thought of what had almost happened.'

'Were you also worried about facing your family?'

'Yes.'

Ella nodded sympathetically. 'I don't know if you remember, but I was at the surgery with Callum when he found you.'

'He told me how you helped,' Alistair said. 'Thank you.'

'I was glad that I was there,' Ella said. 'I got into this job to help people, the same reason why you and Callum got into yours.

'Callum was so upset,' she went on. 'I imagine so were the rest of the family when they saw you at the hospital.'

Alistair nodded.

'Were they angry, as you'd feared?'

'They didn't seem to be,' he said softly.

'They were just worried about you?'

'Yes.'

She leant towards Alistair. 'Isn't it funny how something you can feel so worried about – in your case worried enough that you'd rather die than face it – can work out to be not so bad after all?'

His red eyes slid off her and he nodded, just barely.

'And did you feel better for having it all out in the open?'

He rubbed his eyebrows with the tips of his fingers.

'Doctor?'

'Yes.'

'Guilt's a terrible thing,' she said. 'I can't tell you the number of times I've sat in this very room and listened as people told me their deepest secrets, and I couldn't describe to you the relief on their faces when it was over. Although I'm sure I don't have to, because being a doctor you've witnessed your own share of unburdenings, right?'

'Right,' he croaked.

Julia Armstrong cleared her throat. 'If you are feeling unwell, Dr McLennan, I suggest that we leave.'

Ella prayed for Alistair not to move. He sighed a little but didn't get up. Armstrong raised her eyebrows at Callum but again he was watching his father.

'Guilt,' Ella said again. 'Terrible thing.'

'Yes,' Alistair whispered. 'Yes.'

The room was still, then Ella felt something change. Alistair looked to be holding his breath. His eyes closed in what she thought – hoped – was resignation. Murray pressed his foot hard against hers under the table and she willed him to calm down. They still had a long stretch of tightrope to walk.

She said, 'And the longer one holds onto it, the heavier the weight becomes.'

Alistair swallowed and glanced up. She saw something in his eyes. Remorse? *Please, oh please.*

'So heavy,' she went on, 'that the lifting of it can far outweigh any other ramifications. It might not look like it on the outside, but on the inside, the soul feels washed clean, at long, long last.'

Armstrong put her hand on Alistair's arm. 'We need to stop right there.' She looked at Callum. 'I cannot say this more strongly: we should leave now.'

Alistair pulled his arm out of her grip and Ella's heart soared.

'Dad?'

Armstrong said, 'You are paying me to advise you.'

'I don't want to listen to you any more,' Alistair said. 'I've had enough.'

'Let's go then.' She stood up.

'I mean I've had enough of lying,' he said.

Callum gripped his arm. 'Dad, do you feel faint?'

'I want you both to leave,' he said.

Armstrong said, 'I must tell you that –'

'Out!'

Armstrong stalked away. Callum stumbled to his feet with tears in his eyes. Murray said for the tape, 'Callum McLennan and Julia Armstrong are leaving the interview room.'

Ella closed the door behind them then sat down, her chest tight with anticipation. Alistair put his elbows on the table and his head on his hands.

'Dr McLennan,' she said gently. 'You do not have to say or do anything if you do not want to. We will record what you say or do. We can use this recording in court. Do you understand?'

'Yes.' He laid his hands flat on the table.

They waited. He stared into the space between them and Ella wondered what he was seeing.

'I can't believe what I did.' Tears ran down his cheeks. 'I didn't mean any of it.'

'It's okay,' Ella said.

'Take your time,' Murray said.

But he shook his head. 'I can't.'

'You can,' Ella said. 'Start at the start.'

'I really can't.' He bowed his head. The sobs tore out of him.

Swallowing her revulsion, she said, 'We'll do it together.'

He nodded.

'You remember Robert Edwin?'

'Yes.'

'He told us that soon after you arrived, at eleven twenty on that Saturday night, you gave him an injection to calm him down,' Ella said. 'He asked for it because he was distraught over his wife's impending death. He said he fell asleep.'

'Yes.' Alistair wept.

'And he didn't know when you left,' Ella said. 'You rang him the next morning to check whether the funeral home had come to collect Mrs Edwin's body, and you told him then that you had left at one am.'

'Yes.'

'You actually left earlier than that, didn't you?'

'Yes, about twenty past twelve.'

'Tell us what happened.'

Alistair turned his head to the side and stared across the room. 'I saw Tim on the street in Hornsby.' His voice was full of tears. 'He was staggering, drunk. I pulled over. He wasn't safe: he could've been hit by a car or anything. I was just going to drive him home.'

'In your grey Ford Falcon?'

'Yes.'

Ella glanced across to make sure the interview was still being recorded. 'What did he do when he saw you?'

'He started swearing at me.' Alistair closed his eyes. 'I told him I would take him home. He wouldn't get in the car.'

'Did anyone see this?'

'A couple of cars drove past but didn't slow down.'

'What happened then?'

'I got back in my car and drove off.' He paused. 'I couldn't stop thinking about him and I went back, maybe five minutes later. He was slumped in the gutter, semiconscious. He was too drunk to put up a fight this time and I got him in the car, talking to him, saying I would take him home. And that's what I was going to do, honestly.'

Ella held back a shiver.

'We were almost there when he started to wake up,' Alistair said in a low voice. 'He was crying, in and out of consciousness, saying he was going to tell everyone, that he needed to make sure Josh would be okay. I tried to tell him he didn't need to say anything to anyone and that Josh was fine. But he wouldn't listen.'

'What did you do?'

'I just wanted him to be quiet.' Alistair's face filled with pain and tears crept from his tightly closed eyes. 'I put my hands over his mouth. He was too drunk to fight me off. He passed out.'

Goosebumps crept up Ella's spine.

'I kept my hands there. I was just trying to keep him quiet, there in the car. I wasn't really thinking about anything else.' He wept.

'But he was already silent,' Murray said.

'Yes.' Alistair covered his face with his hands. 'I kept my hands there.'

'Did you know what would happen?'

'Yes,' he said. 'I knew that he would die. I knew it and I didn't know it. Does that make sense? I knew it, and I didn't want it to happen, but I still kept my hands there.'

Ella checked the recording again. 'What did you do then?'

'I cried,' he said. 'I held him. He was gone.'

'You didn't try to save him?'

He shook his head.

'Please speak for the tape.'

'No, I didn't.'

'You didn't call an ambulance?'

'No.'

'What did you do?'

'I started driving,' he said. 'I ended up near Pennant Hills Park. Tim was just lying there on the passenger seat. I felt this panic rising up.' He touched his chest. 'I pulled over and took his wallet, then got him out of the car and left him there.'

'And then?' Ella said.

'I drove partway home then realised my stethoscope was missing. It'd been on the front seat. It must've got caught and dragged out.'

Ella clenched her hands under the table. 'And it had your name on it?'

Alistair nodded. 'I went back to get it.'

'You were crying.'

'Yes.'

'What did you do with his wallet?'

'I threw it down a drain on Pennant Hills Road,' he said. 'I don't know why. I think I thought that if it took a while to identify him, then . . . I don't know.' He wept. 'None of it makes any sense, and I'm so sorry.'

Ella could feel her heart beating in her chest and the skin tingling all down her arms. *We've done it.* 'So just to clarify,' she said, 'Tim was going to tell about how you abused him.'

'Yes.'

'You had abused him and he was angry and hurt and worried that you would do the same to Josh.'

He hung his head. 'Yes.'

'How many times did it happen?'

He didn't answer.

'Did you ever actually touch Josh?'

'No.' He wiped his eyes.

'What about other boys? Patients you saw?'

He pressed his hands to his face.

Ella leant forward. 'What about Callum?'

'No!' he said. 'No. Never.'

'But other boys?' Murray asked.

'I never meant to do any of it,' Alistair said. 'The stress of my work, of looking after palliative patients, getting to know them and their families and then seeing them die: that takes a toll. And then, in contrast, there was the life in the boys.' He held out his hands as if in supplication. 'The sheer *life*.'

Ella clenched her fists under the table. It was so typical of abusers to think they could rationalise their behaviour.

'How many boys?' Murray asked.

'I can't talk about this now.' Alistair sagged onto the table. 'I don't feel well. I need to lie down.'

Ella and Murray exchanged glances. They had the confession to the murder and that was enough for now. The rest would come out later today, or tomorrow, or maybe after that. At least the main part was done.

'I'll fetch Callum,' she said.

'Wait,' Alistair said.

She stopped, her hand on the door.

'How can I tell them?'

There was no answer to that.

'Will you tell them?' he asked her.

'If you're sure that you want me to.'

He nodded.

Ella stepped out and closed the door as Murray told the tape recorder she was leaving.

She drew a deep breath. She felt sick for Callum, almost teary. She stood for a moment in the empty corridor, thinking about the poisonous secret she was about to release and the effect it would have on his family.

Callum . . .

But there was nothing she could do. She let out her held breath and walked on.

Alistair's family were in the meeting room and as she turned the corner Callum straightened in the open doorway. A second later Tamara, John and Genevieve crowded out. There was no sign of the lawyer.

'Is Dad okay?' Callum asked.

'He's not feeling too great, and I'll take you to him in a moment,' she said.

'Now would be best.' His tone was sharp.

'I understand your concern but I need to speak to all of you first.' She shepherded them back into the room and asked them to sit. Callum stayed on his feet by the door but the others sat down, pale and tired-looking, anxiety coming off them like smoke from low fires.

Ella said, 'I'm very sorry to have to tell you that Alistair has confessed to Tim's murder.'

Tamara gasped. John looked stunned. Genevieve shook her head, back and forth, back and forth. Callum grasped the door-frame with a white hand, his mouth open in shock.

'I'm sorry,' Ella said.

Tamara burst into great wrenching sobs. Genevieve wailed, 'No! No!' John seemed paralysed.

'You made him say it.' Callum's eyes blazed at Ella. 'If the solicitor had stayed this wouldn't have happened.'

'You were there; you heard your father ask her to leave.'

'You orchestrated all of it.' But his voice wavered.

She shook her head. 'Come and see him.'

John and Tamara were holding each other and crying, and Genevieve sobbed into her hands.

Ella touched Callum's arm. 'Come and talk to him.'

In the corridor she pulled the door quietly closed. Callum's hands hung empty by his sides and he stared inwards. She laid her hand on his shoulder and was about to ask if he was okay but the question was stupid and pointless.

'Did he really do it?'

'Yes.'

'Why?'

'He was abusing Tim and Tim was going to tell.'

Callum put a hand over his eyes.

'I need to ask,' she said. 'Did he ever touch you?'

'No.'

'You're sure?'

He looked at her.

'I'm sorry.'

He turned down the corridor, then faced her again. 'He really did it?'

She knew it was rhetorical and that he was asking in order to grasp the fact.

'He really did it,' he said and started to cry.

She slid her hand down his arm and inside the crook of his elbow, and they stood like that for a minute, then walked together down the corridor to the interview room.

SEVENTEEN

The next morning Matt swung Georgie's hand as they walked across the bridge in the early sunlight. 'You are one tough cookie,' he said.

'There's nothing to fear any more,' she replied. 'And what's a few bruises?'

'Reckon Freya will be there?'

'I don't know. She might still be sick.'

He kissed her at the top of the steps. 'Sure you don't want me to walk you down?'

'I'm fine. You get going or you'll be late.' She grabbed him and kissed him hard, then let him go. 'See you tonight.'

The station roller doors were up and she walked in to find Freya leaning against Thirty-three.

'Hi,' Georgie said.

'Hi.' Freya smiled. 'I just got off the phone to Stronach. I told her everything. And I mean everything.'

'Oh. Thanks.'

'She's coming over to see you, but she said in the meantime you can stand down if you want. If you don't want to work with me any more, I mean.'

'Oh.'

'It sounds like your assessment's going to be scratched. Now that Oakes has proved himself a complete and total loony.'

'Great,' Georgie said. 'And what's happening with you?'

Freya looked out the doorway. 'I have to make a formal statement about how we found Tim's body.'

'What?'

'Didn't the detective tell you?'

'No,' Georgie said. 'I thought you just slept with him.'

Freya told her what had happened.

'Oh my God,' Georgie said. 'I can't believe you did that and then hid it for all these years.'

Freya flushed. 'I was young and stupid, and then as time went by it felt harder and harder to admit. I know how silly that sounds now, and I know I'm going to have to pay. James got online and thinks I could be charged. He's finding a lawyer.'

The station phone rang and she went to answer it while Georgie tried to absorb the information. She'd been shocked to see on the news that morning that Tim's uncle was his killer, and it made her head spin now to learn that Freya had both been so close to Tim and found his body, and had known all about it when she'd hugged Georgie that next day at school.

She pressed her hands against the ambulance. The fibreglass was cool and smooth, the truck reassuring in its solidity. She let her eyes follow the striping along the side and started to understand why Freya had cut off communication when she left, why she'd looked at her with dismay that first day here.

Freya came out of the office rolling her eyes. 'Hilary's pissed herself but is claiming she's in labour with waters broken.'

Georgie took a deep breath then let it out. 'Let's go.'

'You don't want to stand down? You still want to work with me?'

'Why not?' Georgie said. 'All you really did was make a mistake, right?'

Freya smiled and handed her the keys. 'Your turn to drive, I believe.'

They got in the ambulance and Freya picked up the mike. 'Thirty-three is on the case, both officers on board.'

'Thanks, Thirty-three, and good morning.'

Georgie smiled across at her friend then drove out of the station into the sunlight.

It was all over the papers. The opposition was practically dancing in the streets about new MP Callum McLennan's father being a murderer. Ella read the articles twice over and sighed.

Her mobile rang. She looked at the screen and let it go to voicemail like she'd done when Wayne had rung the first time, and when her parents had called. They were no doubt ringing to congratulate her but she didn't feel like hearing their pride or their questions about why she hadn't told them at dinner last night.

Murray came in. 'High five!'

She smiled but didn't hold her hand up, and he dropped into his chair.

'I just heard Galea talking on the radio about the success of the unit, how we dedicated officers hate to let the unsolved cases lie, how the –'

'Past haunts the present,' Ella finished. 'I heard him too.'

'We dealt out the justice.' Murray clenched his fists in glee. 'Are we shit-hot or what?'

Ella looked at the grainy newspaper photograph of Callum pushing through a mob of journalists outside Parliament House, and thought how haunted he appeared.

'Do you ever feel like sometimes even though we win, we lose?' she said.

'Huh?'

She shook her head. 'Never mind.'

extracts reading groups
competitions books new
discounts extracts extracts
competitions events
books extracts discounts
new events
events books reading groups
new extracts
books
new titles reading groups
interviews extracts new
events extracts events reading groups
books extracts interviews new books
discounts new books
new books events events books extracts
events new interviews new extracts
discounts extracts discounts books
www.panmacmillan.com
extracts events reading groups books
competitions books extracts new